A WOMAN ALONE

A WOMAN ALONE

PAMELA OLDFIELD

G.K. Hall & Co. • Chivers Press
Thorndike, Maine USA Bath, England

This Large Print edition is published by G.K. Hall & Co., USA
and by Chivers Press, England.

Published in 2001 in the U.S. by arrangement with
Piatkus Books, Ltd.

Published in 2001 in the U.K. by arrangement with
Judy Piatkus (Publishers) Ltd.

U.S. Hardcover 0-7838-9364-7 (Romance Series Edition)
U.K. Hardcover 0-7540-1569-6 (Windsor Large Print)
U.K. Softcover 0-7540-2431-8 (Paragon Large Print)

The text of this Large Print edition is unabridged.
Other aspects of the book may vary from the original edition.

Set in 16 pt. Plantin by Rick Gundberg.

Printed in the United States on permanent paper.

British Library Cataloguing in Publication Data available

Library of Congress Cataloging-in-Publication Data

Oldfield, Pamela.
   A woman alone / Pamela Oldfield.
     p. cm.
   ISBN 0-7838-9364-7 (lg. print : hc : alk. paper)
   1. Cornwall (England : Country) — Fiction. 2. Inheritance and
succession — Fiction. 3. Mothers and daughters — Fiction.
4. Women educators — Fiction. 5. Single women — Fiction.
6. Large type books. I. Title.
PR6065.L38 W66 2001
823′.914—dc21   00-051243

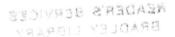

For Pat and Richard at the
Tye Rock Hotel

Prologue

Porthleven, Cornwall. Summer 1882
Something woke the child from her afternoon nap and she opened her eyes, reaching instinctively for Bruin.

She sat up and stared anxiously around. The nursery was empty.

'Dodie?' she murmured.

She peered round the large room. She was never alone. Someone was always with her. Either Mama or Dodie. Sometimes Papa.

Alone. She breathed a little faster, pressed the teddy bear to her chest and then bent her head to hide her face in the soft brown fur. He smelled familiar and briefly she was reassured.

Then, from downstairs a door slammed and she heard her father shouting and someone was screaming and it sounded like Mama, but she never screamed and Papa never shouted.

She said again, 'Dodie?'

There were footsteps and then more shouting and a crash. The nursery door was open. Should she go outside on to the landing?

Her father's voice: 'Get out of my house. You disgust me.'

Her mother's voice: 'For pity's sake, George!

Don't do this to me.'

'It's what you wanted, isn't it? Well, it's what you're going to get.'

'Not like this, George. Not without —'

The child closed her eyes, aware of a strange bumping feeling inside her chest. Something very bad was happening. She knew it.

Her father said, 'I trusted you, you . . . you cheap little whore —'

'George, *please* listen to me. Don't you see? Rose must —'

'What I see is an ungrateful wife, and I want you out of my house. Out of my life — for ever!'

'*George!*' Her mother's voice was different. 'Oh God! You're breaking my heart!'

'And how do you think *I* feel? Put yourself in my position for a change. See what you've done to me — or is that impossible for you? I suppose it is. You are utterly selfish, you always have been. I should have known what to expect.'

The child's mouth trembled. She knew about God and Jesus. She said her prayers every night with Mama. She tried to remember one now but the words wouldn't come. Everything was different and she didn't like it. She would go and find Dodie, she decided, and slid from the bed. Still clutching Bruin, she crossed to the door and stepped fearfully on to the shadowed landing.

While she hesitated, she heard carriage wheels and a horse's hooves on the gravelled drive outside the nursery window. Running across to the window, she looked down on to the head of Mr

8

Breek as he sat waiting in the gig. She could see the horse's broad back and heard the faint jingle of the harness. As she watched she saw her nanny run out and speak to Mr Breek. She was shaking her head and suddenly she lifted her apron and wiped her eyes.

'Dodie?'

Was Dodie *crying*?

The child turned from the window and stared at the nursery door. She wanted to go downstairs to her mother, but didn't dare. She stayed where she was, frozen into immobility by a nameless fear.

Her mother's voice again. 'Give me another chance, George. I beg you.'

'I've told you — no! You're not the person I thought you were. Leave my house. You no longer belong here.'

'Leave my house'?

The child blinked as she picked up the teddy and hugged it tightly.

Her mother: 'I've admitted I was wrong. All I want is to be forgiven, George. Please let me stay.'

Her father: 'Maud! Help Mrs Vivian with her boxes. She's leaving immediately.'

There was another scream and then sobbing.

Dodie's voice: 'Oh please, sir! You can't send her away —'

'If you want to keep your job, Maud, you will mind your own damned business and do as I say.'

Her father stepped back and disappeared from view. Moments later she heard his footsteps on the stairs and turned in alarm. When he came into the room she hardly recognized him. His face was white, his expression was grim and there were tears in his eyes.

'Papa —' she began, but the rest of her question died on her lips.

He said, 'Come away from that window at once!'

As she obeyed, he slammed the bedroom door and locked it. Then he leaned back against it. She waited but he was silent, breathing heavily. Suddenly he covered his face with his hands as though he were playing peekaboo, thought the child. 'Oh my God, Catherine! My *sweet* Catherine! How *could* you?'

His voice sounded strange. He crossed to the window in long fierce strides and stared down. The child edged her way towards the bed and climbed on to it, still clutching the teddy bear.

He heard the creak of the bedsprings and turned his head briefly.

'Good girl. Stay right where you are. There's no need for you to see this.'

So she waited fearfully in the middle of the bed and listened as the wheels rolled again and the horse's hooves clattered and the gig carried her mother out of her life.

CHAPTER ONE

April 24th, 1908

Rose glanced up from her stitching. 'What is it, Maud?'

'Ma'am! It's the *police*. It's Sergeant Wylie.' She stared at Rose, wide-eyed, her arthritic fingers fiddling with a stray lock of grey hair.

Rose pulled her needle through the silk before answering. 'The Headmaster is out walking — with Mr Tremayne. They may be half an hour or so. Ask the sergeant if he can wait?' She reached for the scissors and carefully cut the thread, avoiding Maud's eyes, hoping that the small tremor in her voice would not betray her. She envied her father nothing except his walks with the young history master.

'The sergeant asked for *you*, ma'am.'

'For me?' She didn't bother to hide her surprise. 'Nobody asks for me, Maud,' she added, and smiled to soften the words.

'He said "I have to speak with Miss Vivian." '

'How very strange. Then I'd better see him.'

She stood up and glanced round the spacious drawing room. It was tidy, and smelled of lavender polish. Through the large windows the bitter winds blew dead leaves across the lawn. A small

11

fire burned in the grate, but Rose was grateful for the shawl which she had thrown around her shoulders. 'You can show him in here,' she told Maud.

Maud hesitated. 'He looks sort of — sort of *gloomy*, ma'am.'

'Gloomy?'

'Sort of *doomy*.'

Rose laughed. 'Then I'm glad my conscience is clear.'

As she watched Maud hurry out of the room her mouth twisted ruefully. Yes, sadly her conscience was clear. Her sheltered life at Tye Rock House offered her no opportunity for anything but a blameless life. And if it did, her father would certainly frown on even the mildest attempt to 'kick over the traces'. For a moment she pressed her lips together. At least he couldn't control her mind, she thought rebelliously.

Standing up, she smoothed her dress and tidied her soft brown hair. She wondered idly what Sergeant Wylie could possibly want, unless it was a donation — or a request to use the ground for the local Sunday School's annual picnic. Sergeant Wylie, a strong churchman, acted as their spokesman. Last year the children's treat had been held in Penrose, near Helston. The year before Dane House School had lent its grounds. Perhaps this year they would ask Tye Rock House School again. Set high on the clifftop amid three acres of grassland, the school grounds were ideal for such events, although Rose doubted whether her father would give permission. He had refused them many times already, but presumably they lived in hope of a change of heart. Or was the sergeant hoping that by appealing through the daughter he might achieve the miracle? If so he would be disappointed, for she had no influence with her father.

'Sergeant Wylie, ma'am.'

Turning towards him, Rose's welcoming smile faltered as she saw his expression. She said, 'Good evening, Sergeant.'

Sergeant Wylie was a bear-like man with a weather-beaten face and kindly brown eyes. He had removed his helmet. Behind him, Maud hovered in the doorway until she caught Rose's eye and withdrew, closing the door behind her. Probably spying through the keyhole, thought Rose, with resignation.

She said, 'What is it, Sergeant?' and suddenly she understood the maid's reaction. The sergeant *did* look ill at ease. He did not meet her gaze and was twisting his helmet in his hands.

'I'm very sorry, Miss Vivian, but —' He stopped.

'Is something wrong, Sergeant?'

'Do please sit down, Miss Vivian.'

'Sit down?' she echoed. Something in his tone chilled her and she obeyed, her legs suddenly weak. 'Tell me, please.'

He took a deep breath. 'There's been an accident, I'm afraid. Your father slipped and fell —'

13

'Papa's fallen? Oh dear! Is he hurt?'

When the sergeant hesitated she went on, 'He was walking with Mr Tremayne.' Even now she couldn't resist using his name. 'They weren't going far.'

The sergeant raised his eyes to meet hers and she recognised compassion. 'Your father's dead, Miss Vivian. Killed in the fall.'

For a moment nothing registered. Her father had had a fall . . .

He said, 'I'm so sorry to be the bearer of such terrible news.'

She gazed up at him, still finding it hard to comprehend. He had said 'killed in the fall'. Surely that meant that her father was dead. But how was that possible? Her father was a strong person, a strict disciplinarian, a man who liked to be in control. George Vivian was not at all the type of man to die accidentally while out walking.

'Papa is dead?' she repeated.

'I'm afraid so. A most terrible thing. I'm so sorry.'

Frowning, Rose stared into the fire. Just like that, she thought dully. A few words from the sergeant and her father was *dead*.

The sergeant shook his head. 'It appears they were walking along the cliff path and he tried to climb down and lost his footing.'

The word 'they' jogged her memory and she said dazedly, 'Mr Tremayne is our history master. They often walk together.' Mark Tremayne's appointment had proved a happy one. He and her father enjoyed an immediate and unexpected rapport; they shared a love of walking and they played chess together on occasions.

'Is Mr Tremayne hurt?'

'He's in Helston. Your own doctor was not to be found, so he was taken to Doctor Ellis in Helston. They've put him to bed there and will keep him a day or so until he's well enough to come back here.' He consulted his notebook. 'Dazed and badly shocked. Might have slight concussion. And one ankle possibly sprained.'

'Good heavens! Poor man. They might *both* have been killed.'

'He got off lightly, though, considering. Had a narrow escape, poor young man. I've had a few words with him and —'

'When did this happen? Oh God! Poor Papa!' As the full extent of the calamity dawned on her she began to tremble and kept her voice steady only with an effort. Papa was dead. She was alone. 'I can't believe it!' she whispered.

Sergeant Wylie tried again. 'It seems that Mr Vivian was trying to climb down and slipped. He managed to catch hold of a small bush — a shrub of some sort — about half-way down. Mr Tremayne tried to reach him but he was too late. Either your father lost his grip, or the bush pulled loose; Mr Tremayne didn't see what happened because he was climbing down himself. The tide was almost full and your father fell into the sea. It must have been instantaneous. Maybe knocked unconscious on one of the rocks. Couldn't swim, I daresay. Not that that would have saved him. A fall on to a rock from that height . . .'

Rose hardly heard him as the reality crowded in. Papa was gone. In her mind's eye she saw his fingers desperately scrabbling at the loose soil, frantic for a fingerhold. She could imagine his relief when he found the bush — and his despair when it failed him. But to fall from the cliffs around Tye Rock? Her father knew the area around the school so well. It wasn't at all like him to do something carelessly or rashly; it simply wasn't in his nature. Could he swim? She hadn't the faintest idea, and the realisation startled her. How much *did* she know about her father? However little it was, it was more than she knew about her absent mother. The familiar bitterness washed over her. She drew in a shaky breath and put a trembling hand to her face.

The sergeant said, 'Now don't take on, Miss Vivian. I'm here to offer my condolences and to ask if there's anything we can do to help. It's a bad business, no doubt about it.'

Rose didn't reply. She was trying to imagine her father slithering down the cliff-face and falling into the sea. But why? What on earth had inspired him to decide to climb down? He was hardly the most adventurous man.

There was a knock and the art master put his head round the door. Seeing the policeman he hesitated. Then he said to Rose, 'I was hoping

16

for a word with the Headmaster, but he's not in his room.'

Rose said, 'Oh . . . I'm afraid . . .' then looked helplessly at the sergeant.

Sergeant Wylie said, 'This is not a very convenient moment.'

Startled by his manner, Mr Rivers looked from Rose to the sergeant.

Rose shrank from explanations. She said, 'Would you come back later, Mr Rivers? Perhaps in fifteen minutes.'

He nodded, appeared about to add something but changed his mind and closed the door quietly.

She supposed she would have to tell everybody, and quailed at the thought. But one thing at a time. Drawing a long breath, willing herself to stay calm, she turned her attention to the sergeant. 'My father always walked the cliff paths. He loved them. He's very — I mean, he *was* very experienced.' Another thought occurred. 'Have you recovered his body?'

'Yes, we have. Mr Tremayne pulled him from the water and left him on the beach while he hurried as fast as he could to raise the alarm. He was in a bit of a state himself, but that's understandable. I took Constable Dean with me, and we were able to bring your father up before the tide turned and took him out.' He shook his head. 'A sad day for you.'

Rose became aware that he was looking at her rather strangely. For a moment she was puzzled, but suddenly it came to her. She had shed no tears. A father had died and the dutiful daughter had shown no emotion — apart from shock. Guiltily she put her hands over her eyes, pretending to struggle with tears.

'There, there!' he said, averting his eyes.

Praying that I won't break down and cry, thought Rose. Men are no good with tears. Not that she knew many men, but certainly her father had no time for such weaknesses. She wanted to think of him kindly, but it wasn't easy. George Vivian had lived a humourless life, interested only in the school. He had had no time for affection; no sense of family. Since his wife's desertion, he had never applied for a divorce; had never shown any interest in remarrying. Rose sighed. It was her view that his poor opinion of women had crystallised over the years into a deep dislike. Ironic, then, that Tye Rock House School was home to fourteen young women aged from thirteen to seventeen. Sad, too, that his only child was a daughter. Rose had always been aware that she was a disappointment to him and had wondered if a son would have changed him. Over the last two years, of course, Mark Tremayne had brightened his life; but school teachers came and went. As she considered the young man's eventual departure, Rose was aware of a small panic. Mark Tremayne was the one bright spark in her own life. Feeling horribly wicked, she offered up a silent prayer of thanks that Mark Tremayne had suffered nothing worse than a mild concussion.

'Poor Papa!' It had a hollow ring to it and she wished she could be more convincing.

'Gathered into God's heaven,' said the sergeant. 'A sad day, Miss Vivian. A very sad day.'

'Indeed. I hardly know what to say or do. It's been so sudden. If it had been a long illness . . .' She shrugged.

'Of course. An illness *prepares* you, doesn't it?' He nodded. 'Gives you time to expect the worst. An accident — now that's different altogether.' He cleared his throat. 'I'm afraid, Miss Vivian, that someone will have to identify the body.'

Rose swallowed hard, beginning to panic. She would have to identify a body because from this moment forward there was no one else to shoulder the responsibilities. She was alone. *Alone!* How would she manage, and what would become of the school? So many decisions had to be made on a daily basis. Her father had made them all, rarely if ever involving her — never asking her for an opinion and rarely needing her help.

She said, 'I can't — I mean the school . . .'

As the sergeant shook his head and murmured something non-committal, Rose felt anxiety grow within her, deadening her senses. She seemed to be surrounded by a wall of blackness and she could hear nothing. The disaster overwhelmed her.

'The school!' she repeated. There was no way she could run Tye Rock House now that her father was dead, and yet it was her home — the only home she had ever known. Where would she go and what would she do? Her mouth felt dry and her heart beat uncomfortably.

The sergeant said, 'There's the matter of identification . . . of the body.'

She stammered, 'The body. Oh yes. I . . . I'm sorry, sergeant. Would tomorrow do? At the moment I don't feel I could . . .'

'Tomorrow will be fine. You take your time. A nip of brandy might help. Many people find it soothing.'

'Should we both have a — a nip?' Perhaps she should have offered him something. A sherry or a cup of tea? Her father would have known exactly what to do in the circumstances. All Rose had had to do was teach singing to those girls whose parents paid extra for the optional tuition.

'Not while I'm on duty, Miss Vivian.' He sounded reluctant. 'Well, I ought to be off. Forms to fill in, and the doctor will be calling in. Death certificate and so on.' He held out his hand and she stood up and shook it. What was he waiting for, she wondered. Then it came to her. Of course. She rang for Maud, who came in a little too soon.

'Please show Sergeant Wylie out, Maud, and then . . .' And then what? She thought frantically. 'And then come back to me.' She sat down heavily.

As they left the room she whispered, 'I'm sorry, Papa. I truly am,' and wished she could shed some tears. It was so unnatural to be sitting in the drawing room as though nothing had changed. But she *was* sorry. Sorry for her father and sorry for herself. It had been bad enough that her mother had deserted them. Now her father was gone, too. Rose moved closer to the fire, shivering. She felt insubstantial and strangely unattached, like a leaf blowing in the wind.

Chrissie's eyes strayed to the window and her pencil faltered and was still. Her thoughts were on a certain young groom who lived not a mile away and the words he had whispered to her the night before. His lips had brushed hers for the first time in their short relationship and his fingers had traced a tantalising path along her thigh. Forbidden territory. Her face flushed with excitement at the memory.

Mr Rivers appeared beside her and she could smell the old-fashioned patchouli oil he plastered on his thinning hair.

'Miss Morgan, I will ask you one more time. Please pay attention to your drawing. You have talent and a nice light touch, but you are so lazy.'

Chrissie sniffed. 'I can't concentrate. I'm tired. I didn't sleep well last night. I was tossing and turning. In the end I had to throw back all the covers.' She heard one or two shocked gasps. 'I was so hot. Maybe I had a fever.' Let him imagine *that,* she thought. He surely would. She was by far the prettiest girl in the school with her chestnut hair and large brown eyes. At seventeen, she was already a beauty and knew it; she saw it in men's eyes wherever she went. Now it was the art master's turn for a little fantasy. He would imagine her stretched on the bed with her hair tumbling loose across the pillow, her body pale in the moonlight.

But he was apparently giving his full attention to the sketch she had been working on. 'You need shading here — and a little here to suggest the shape. The stem of that glass looks like a flat tape at the moment. It is actually round. Shading will —'

'It's so *boring!*' She adopted the little-girl voice her father had loved. 'Boring old bottle, boring old glass and boring, *boring* old apples!'

She heard a ripple of laughter from the other girls and resisted a smile. It was always fun to bait Rivers. He dare not complain to 'Georgie-Porgie' too often or it would make him look incompetent. 'Why can't we draw flowers — or people? We could pose for each other.' She lowered her voice. 'In something flimsy, perhaps!' She gave him a sideways glance from beneath her eyelashes. 'You'd like that, wouldn't you, Mr Rivers?'

His lips tightened with annoyance, but by way of answer he moved on to Lucy Unwin. Poor man's probably terrified, thought Chrissie. With that scraggy dried-up wife of his, the temptation at Tye Rock House must be enormous. And one day he might succumb! Artists were notoriously eccentric. Except poor old Rivers; he was dull as ditchwater. Still, he could paint. Her gaze moved to one of several pictures which adorned the classroom wall. One of them was his. The Headmaster had commissioned him to paint Tye Rock House and, even in her present mood of disenchantment, Chrissie couldn't pretend that he had failed to do it justice. A late Victorian manor house, Tye Rock House was a large, symmetrical building, built of cold grey stone under a slate roof. The only splashes of bright colour came from a pot of scarlet geraniums on the front step. Outlined against the sky, the house stood on the cliff-top, facing out across the grey water of Mounts Bay. With greys and soft purple, his clouds threw deep, haunting shadows across the house and the granite cliffs behind and below it. Chrissie had to admit that Arnold Rivers had caught the mood exactly.

Losing interest, she returned to her own sketch. Rivers insisted that she had considerable artistic talent, but that gave him the chance to say she was lazy. She knew that she had talent but didn't care. Smiling, she felt that being beautiful and desirable and exciting was enough, and her parents already had a suitably rich suitor in mind for her. With a sigh, she pressed the point of her pencil into the paper so hard that it snapped off. Now she could waste a few more precious moments of the lesson sharpening it. Her sketch was only half finished — she had achieved less in the past hour than any other girl in the class. But that had been her aim. Art bored her. School bored her. If it hadn't been for the men, life itself would have bored her. Still, she was leaving at the end of the summer, thank the Lord. Only a few months to go. If she could get through April and May it would be time for the tennis — the only thing she enjoyed. She was longing to be seen in the new tennis dress her mother had sent from India. A lightweight lace over a slip with short sleeves and a deep neckline, it was short enough to show a couple of inches of ankle and that ought to make the men sit up and take notice. That was really all she required of young men — that they admired and adored her. She missed her father quite desperately when she allowed herself to dwell on their relationship. Everything she had ever said or done had filled him with wonder, much to her mother's annoyance. Chrissie knew she would never find a man like her father, but she would accept as her husband whoever he recommended. Papa would always have her best interests at heart; she would be safe with his choice.

But that was several years away, and in the meantime she would have as much fun as possible.

She blew into the pencil sharpener and returned it to the cupboard, glancing up at the clock as she did so. Ten minutes to go. She sat down again and stared at the still life. Rivers was leaning over Mary Trease. Poor old Mary, with her fat face and lacklustre hair. What a thrill for Rivers. If he fancied 'Mary Quite Contrary' he was in serious trouble. Could be fatal. Chrissie giggled.

Next to her Lucy sat back, considering her own handiwork with a critical eye. 'It's not *too* bad,' she murmured, pleased. 'The glass looks a bit solid but the apples are rather good. What do you think, Chrissie?'

Chrissie shrugged. 'Not bad,' she agreed. Lucy had no flair for art but she tried hard. Rivers' little pet. He always gave her a good mark at the end of the term: 'A' for effort.

Leaning across to her friend, Chrissie whispered, 'I wonder if it's true about his wife.'

Lucy said, 'Oh, it *is*. Definitely. The baby's due in August. Bit of a shock, I should think, at her age. She's got four already.' She rubbed out the rim of the glass and redrew it, her face screwed up with concentration.

Chrissie sighed. Children were the problem. She knew a little about sex. A very little. Mostly the veiled hints about 'duty' that she had gleaned from the various women's magazines which were smuggled into the school from time to time. She knew nothing about babies or child-birth, and what she didn't know frightened her. She had decided not to have a family. Her current plans were to enjoy life while she was young, then marry the rich suitor who was a widower with a grown-up son. He, of course, would adore her. Chrissie could then enjoy the grandchildren without any of the unpleasantness which seemed to accompany giving birth.

She sighed, thinking about Mark Tremayne. He was the only eligible man who refused to fall under her spell, and she was at a loss to understand why. She had made enquiries and there was no sign of a lady friend — at least, not locally in Porthleven. He might, of course, have a fiancée tucked away in some other part of the country, but Polly the maid had insisted that he rarely received letters. Tremayne was young and good-looking and although she didn't want to marry him a fling would be fun. A declaration of undying love from him would be even better. So far her efforts to interest him had mostly failed, although she had worked very hard at history since the day he joined the school. She always earned high marks for her work but that was hardly romantic. She had sent him a Valentine and he had winked at her across the dining room, so presumably he had recognised the handwriting, but he had said not a word on the subject. She was intrigued by her lack of success. Didn't he *like* women?

She could just imagine the Head's face if Tremayne fell in love with her. Anything that disconcerted 'Georgie-Porgie' would please her after the way he had spoken to her on the many occasions when she had been sent to his room. George Vivian definitely disliked women; she could tell by his eyes and the tone of his voice. Why he ran a school for young ladies was a mystery. And how his daughter put up with his autocratic ways was another.

A bell pealed suddenly along the corridor and there was an excited flurry in the classroom.

Mr Rivers said, 'Do try to be quiet, girls!' and gave an exaggerated sigh. Ignoring him, the girls scrambled to put away easels, hand him their drawings and collect their belongings. There was an unladylike rush for the door. It was twelve o'clock and dinner-time was upon them.

Chrissie followed them out without enthusiasm. She was hungry, but Friday was always fish which she hated — unless it was salmon, which it never was. Steamed cod was considered suitable for growing girls, being light on the digestion and bland on the palate. The school food was fresh and nourishing but unadventurous. As usual Chrissie would give her cod to Lucy in exchange for her mashed potatoes.

By the time she reached the dining-room it was full. Voices were low, cutlery clattered, the smell of steamed fish was overpowering. Still, history was the second lesson on Friday afternoon. She looked for Mark Tremayne across the tables but he wasn't there and the entire lunch passed without a glimpse of him. Curious, she thought.

An hour after the sergeant's departure, Rose sat alone in her father's study. *In the Head's room.* In his familiar chair. The one that swivelled, which had so fascinated her as a child. Worn black leather, with one stud missing. In a rare fit of childish temper she had pulled it off and, as a punishment, had been sent to bed early without tea or supper. Now, tightening her arms across her chest, she shivered. She was dazed but, try as she would, her tears would not flow. She felt sure she would be better able to face up to her loss once she had cried. In the meantime, deeply shocked, she was paralysed with indecision. What should she do first? And *then* what? The problems crowded in, tumbling in their eagerness to confront and confound her.

Was she actually in charge now that her father was dead? The staff would have to know and so would the girls — and, of course, the parents of the girls . . . They would need a mathematics teacher now that her father was gone — *if* the school was to continue.

'How *could* you?' she whispered to her absent father.

Staring round the room, she noticed the timetable and gave it her full attention. The squares were coloured for ease of comprehension. History was blue, English was red, Art was green . . . Needlework orange . . . She frowned, remembering that Mr Rivers had wanted to talk to her father. What had he wanted, she wondered? She had little idea of the problems experienced by the staff, for they were her father's responsibility. He had overseen the running of the school, the day-to-day business, the relationship with the parents. Rose dealt with the domestic staff, arranged the occasional outings and seasonal festivities and supervised the matron.

Shaking her head in a vain attempt to clear her mind, she looked at the rest of the room as though seeing it for the first time. If she took over from her father this would be *her* study, she thought, incredulous. She would preside at this large mahogany desk and would keep her papers and documents in the matching mahogany bureau. Perhaps she should advertise for a deputy head — someone with experience and authority. She herself would never be able to manage; it was out of the question. If only she had someone to turn to — but there was no one. At least, there was no family.

The small fire caught her eye and she moved across to add a few coals. Then, feeling in need of warmth and comfort, she added a few more. Guilt filled her. Her father would have been appalled. He had never advocated what he called self-indulgence.

'But I need warmth, Papa,' she told him firmly. Briefly she was filled with a new sense of power. There was no one now to deny her requests, to correct her manners or to disapprove her actions. She didn't know whether she was pleased or unnerved by the notion of so much freedom. With an effort, she brought her mind back to more pressing problems.

The desk in front of her was neat and ordered. Correspondence waited in a tidy pile, and somehow she would have to answer the letters. She recognised a file of end-of-term reports awaiting her father's signature. There was a new set of poetry books to be stamped with the name of the school. For want of something practical to do, she poured herself a glass of water from her father's carafe and was still sipping it when there was a knock at the door.

'Come in!'

Arnold Rivers entered the room, his face creased with anxiety. 'I wanted to see your father,' he said. 'Something rather disturbing. It might be nothing but . . .' He shrugged.

For the first time she really looked at him. He was almost middle-aged, married with a family, thin as a rake and losing his hair. But he was a good artist and made a reasonable living from his watercolours, mainly landscapes. She assumed that he was a good teacher — or at least an *adequate* teacher. Her father had never complained about him. She knew only that he lived in Porthleven and came in twice a week.

Rose struggled with a sudden longing to tell him what had happened, but somehow she held back. After a moment's hesitation she said, 'Something disturbing, Mr Rivers? What has happened, exactly?'

In any other circumstances, his look of surprise would have been almost amusing. The staff had never been encouraged to confide their problems to anyone but the Headmaster. George Vivian had always insisted that Rose was not 'to be troubled' — his way of keeping the reins very firmly in his hands. Normally Rose would have asked Mr Rivers to return when her father was available, yet here she was asking for further details.

Later he would understand why, but at the moment she felt unable to speak of the tragedy. Also, intuitively, she felt that it would be unwise to do so. If she *did* tell him, it was probable that the rest of the staff would feel he had been favoured by the early confidence and they might be resentful. Also, she would have lost the chance to tell it in her own way in her own time. Silently she congratulated herself on her discretion. She was learning already, she thought, astonished.

Mr Rivers held out a piece of paper. It was half a sheet from an exercise book. The single sentence written on it said, *Ask Chrissie Morgan where she was last night.*

She looked at him with raised eyebrows.

He explained, 'I found it in my desk about twenty minutes ago.'

'It must have been one of the girls.'

'Obviously.'

So where *had* Chrissie been — if anywhere? Rose wondered what her father would have done in the circumstances.

He said, 'I thought Mr Vivian should see it.'

'Yes, of course.' Except that he would never see it; would never deal with it in that incisive way of his. A second or two to decide, and then into action. Rose smothered a sigh.

'So you'll show it to your father?'

Another tricky moment; somehow she must

avoid a direct lie. She said, 'Leave it with me, Mr Rivers,' and smiled dismissively.

When he had gone she thought about Christina Morgan. A pretty girl, foolishly indulged by her absent parents who gave her more pocket money than was good for her. Still, she was leaving at the end of the school year. Rose frowned, turning the note thoughtfully between her fingers. What exactly did it mean? Had Chrissie simply left her dormitory or had she left the school building? The other girls would know, no doubt, but would they tell? Chrissie was a popular girl. It occurred to her that there might be a man involved — but if so, then who was it? There was the gardener-cum-groom . . .

'Hardly likely,' she muttered.

Arnold Rivers would never attract a girl like Chrissie — which left Mark Tremayne.

'Oh, Lord!'

Thinking of him reminded her of the accident and Rose cursed her stupidity. Mark Tremayne, injured, was in the care of the doctor at Helston. He had tried to save her father's life and, wrapped up in her own problems, she had forgotten all about him. Her spirits rose dramatically and she drew in her breath sharply.

'I can visit him!'

A smile brightened her face. Surely it would appear callous and uncaring if she did *not* show concern. Abruptly the smile vanished.

'His lessons!' Who would take them? Hurriedly she consulted the timetable and saw that he was due to take a class at quarter past two. Her confidence ebbed once more.

'Now what do I do?'

No doubt her father would have stepped in and given a lesson on *something*. He was rarely at a loss.

'No, I can't,' she told herself.

But she *could* set them some work and ask one of the other teachers to sit in with them. She would send for the pony-trap and get the gardener to drive her the few miles to the doctor's. She nodded slowly, cheered by the prospect of seeing Mr Tremayne. As well as giving her a breathing space she could also consult with him, because he already knew of her father's death and might even be anticipating her problems. Yes, she could talk to him; in the circumstances it would seem a natural thing to do.

On her return she would call the staff together after lessons and tell them what had happened. The girls would be told when they assembled in the dining room for high tea. Rose covered her face with her hands and drew a long, slow breath. Was that the way to do it , or had she forgotten anything?

From outside on the gravelled drive she heard the clatter of hooves and the swish of wheels and, hurrying to the window, she was surprised to see James Edgcombe alighting from their dog-cart. An appointment with her father, no doubt. A quick search in his diary produced the correct date but no mention of the solicitor. Odd.

'Think, Rose!' she muttered. Was she going to tell him what had happened? Presumably she would have to. The Edgcombes would have to know sooner or later that the man in charge of Tye Rock House was dead.

Another knock.

Maud said, 'It's Mr Edgcombe, ma'am. The young one. He says he doesn't have an appointment but hopes you'll see him.'

'Show him in, Maud, please.'

Rose tidied her hair and smoothed her skirt, wishing that she had put on the new green serge. James Edgcombe had once paid her the only compliment she could remember receiving, and as a young girl she had been very smitten.

He came into the room with both hands outstretched, and she could tell by the expression on his round face that he knew what had happened. As she stood up he reached across the desk and took her hands in his.

'My dear Miss Vivian, I'm so very sorry. I came as fast as I could.'

Again Rose regretted that her eyes showed no signs of the passionate weeping which might be expected from a daughter whose father has just died.

'Thank you, Mr Edgcombe,' she said. 'But how on earth did you know? The accident happened less than two hours ago —'

She indicated a chair and they both sat down.

'I happened to pass the doctor on my way to visit a client,' he told her. 'He told me what had happened. For one dreadful moment I thought it was you, that *you* were dead.' He regarded her earnestly. 'I was so relieved . . . Oh! I don't mean that I wasn't upset. Your father is — was — a very good man, Miss Vivian, and it's a terrible tragedy, but I had thought it was you, you see. I don't mind admitting that my heart was in my boots.'

Taken aback, Rose could think of nothing to say. Had he just paid her another compliment? Surely he was suggesting that *her* death would cause him considerable grief. Disconcerted, she stared into his eyes. They were a sandy brown colour which exactly matched his hair. With his round face and ingenuous smile he was the image of his father, Harold Edgcombe, who had been their solicitor for as long as she could remember.

She said, 'You're very kind.'

As a child she had developed a schoolgirl crush on young James who had, at her insistence, been invited to her seventh birthday party. James, then aged thirteen, had failed to appear, much to Rose's dismay, but her grandmother had explained that he was 'much too old'. Now, with only the vaguest memories of the old lady, Rose found herself thinking about her. When Catherine left, George Vivian had persuaded his mother to move into Tye Rock House to act as housekeeper and to supervise his daughter. The strain must have told, for her grandmother died prematurely when Rose was seven.

James leaned forward. 'I want you to look on me as a friend, Miss Vivian. A trusted friend and adviser. Better still, someone to confide in.' Before she could answer he rushed on, 'It will be such a responsibility for you, so much to think about. I'd like to think my experience will be of value and you have only to ask, Miss Vivian. Just say the word and I will drop everything and come to Tye Rock House.'

'As you have done now, Mr Edgcombe.'

'Indeed.'

Silence fell. Rose, astonished, was aware that he assumed she would be carrying on where her father had left off. What made him think she would *want* to take on such a responsibility? And did he really think she could do it? She herself had simply wondered how she could get through the next twenty-four hours. Bewildering thoughts flooded her mind.

At last she said, 'I'll have to tell them tonight. All of them. Unless . . .' Dare she leave it until the morning?

'A very wise move, if I may say so.' He smiled encouragement. 'No point in delays. The sooner they know, the sooner they'll get used to the idea. Get in first before the rumours start to fly.' He put a finger inside his collar and eased it.

Rose said, 'Are you too hot? I'm afraid I banked up the fire. I was so cold.'

'It's the shock. Perfectly natural in the circumstances.' He smiled again. He was a cheerful man, comfortably built. Rose had a sudden vision of him as a plumpish thirteen-year-old boy with spectacles and a mop of reddish hair.

He said, 'You are smiling.'

'Smiling?' She shook her head. 'At a time like this!'

'Life goes on.'

She hesitated. 'I was remembering when I sent you an invitation to my party.'

He laughed. 'I was terribly impressed. Deckle-edged card with squirly writing. I couldn't accept, of course, although I was longing to. Much too grown-up to go to a children's tea party!'

'But you sent me a birthday card. I've still got it.'

The sandy-brown eyes widened. 'You *kept* my card?'

'I keep *all* my cards, Mr Edgcombe.'

His face fell briefly, then brightened. 'You had a Shetland pony, I recall. You were riding it one day when I called at Tye Rock House with my father. While he was busy with your father you were showing me how well you could ride.'

'And did I ride well?'

'No. You fell off into some stinging nettles and were extremely mortified.'

Her laugh was spontaneous. 'Good heavens! I'd forgotten.' For a moment she allowed her mind to wander into the past. Then, with an effort, she brought her thoughts back to the present. Glancing at the clock she said, 'But I mustn't waste time delving into the past. I have to see to the history class in ten minutes.' Ignoring his obvious disappointment she went on, 'Then I'm going to visit poor Mr Tremayne. I want to know exactly what happened. I just cannot imagine my father attempting to climb down from the path. Unless . . .' She frowned. 'Unless he was after a rare plant. He was a keen botanist.'

'That might be it.' He nodded. 'A moment's carelessness is all it takes sometimes. I was assured by the doctor that Mr Tremayne is not seriously hurt.' Suddenly his face brightened. 'But of course! If you will allow me, I will drive you into Helston myself. I can wait until you have spoken to your pupils. We can talk as we go. There will be the matter of the will, naturally, but that can wait. And the funeral arrangements . . .'

'The funeral! Oh dear!' And there was the business with Chrissie Morgan and all the correspondence to be answered. Rose shook her head. 'Thank you for your kind offer, but I have no idea when I shall be ready to go into Helston and I cannot expect you to waste your day. Robb will drive me down and back. I will call in at the office as soon as I can about other matters.'

'And you will allow me to help and advise you?'

'Of course.'

'I mean *personally*.'

She smiled. 'Yes, Mr Edgcombe. I shall feel honoured to have a personal adviser.'

Whilst she watched from the window as he

left, Rose's problems crowded in once more and she sat down, aware of a growing exhaustion. How wonderful it would be to faint clean away and be put to bed with smelling salts and drawn curtains. 'Beset by devils' was the phase that entered her mind, and she thought it summed up her situation very neatly. Her once dull but secure existence had been snatched away by a cruel and pointless accident, and Rose had the uneasy feeling that she would never know that kind of life again. She also suspected that worse was yet to come, so why didn't she feel totally crushed, she wondered. Allowing herself just a few moments to examine her feelings, she realised that, behind the shock and grief, there was an unmistakable glimmer of excitement.

Tye Rock House, a small, private boarding-school for young ladies, was divided into the upper and lower school by age. Girls entered the school at thirteen years of age and went into the 'lower school'. At fifteen they moved into the 'upper school' and could stay there until they reached eighteen. Most, however, left at seventeen, and many went on to a finishing school in London or Switzerland. At present there were seven girls in the upper school and they were allowed to stay up until nine o'clock — an hour later than the others. Girls over sixteen were allowed to wear their own clothes at weekends, but the school uniform was *de rigeur* for the rest of them except on Sundays.

Rose found herself facing seven young ladies dressed in high-necked white blouses and ankle-length navy serge skirts. All eyes turned to her in surprise and the chatter faded.

She drew in her breath and tried to remember her speech. 'I'm sorry to tell you that Mr Tremayne will not be taking your lesson this afternoon,' she began.

Chrissie murmured, 'Shame!' and giggled. Lucy Unwin mimed applause.

Ignoring the interruption, Rose went on, 'He has been unavoidably delayed but —'

Chrissie said, 'Unavoidably delayed?'

'Yes, but he'll be back at Tye Rock later. In the meantime Miss Hock will supervise you.'

There were loud groans. A strict disciplinarian, the mannish English teacher was without a shred of humour and was universally feared.

Rose said, 'Now, Lucy, please tell me what you did last with Mr Tremayne.'

In a loud whisper, Chrissie said, 'Yes, Lucy. What *did* you do with Mr Tremayne?'

The girls tittered dutifully and Rose longed to slap her.

Lucy stood up. 'We were talking about the abolition of the slave trade.'

'I see.' Rose hesitated. 'What were you expecting to do today?'

'Mr Tremayne didn't say. Miss Vivian, is he ill?'

'No. At least — not ill but indisposed. Nothing to worry about, thank goodness.' The slave trade, she thought desperately. So what should

40

they do now? Inspiration struck. 'Today, then, I want you to imagine that you are writing an article for a daily newspaper, let's say *The Times*, in favour of the abolition of slavery. Write at least two pages, setting out the reasons in favour of abolition.'

Someone said 'Two pages!' and there were muffled grumbles.

'In favour *and* against,' she amended.

Lucy said, 'An *article?*' and rolled her eyes.

Chrissie asked, 'Do we have to give it in?' Which meant: Do we have to bother with it?

'Yes, Chrissie, you do.'

Rose remembered the anonymous note that the art master had given to her. So where *were* you last night, Chrissie, she wondered. Later on she would have to talk to the girl, but this was not the moment.

'Chrissie, I would like you to collect up the work at the end of the lesson and hand it to Miss Hock, who will bring it to me — or take it to Mr Tremayne,' she added, recognizing the error.

Kate Lairde's hand shot up. A nice child, just turned fifteen. Her father was in Burma. Something to do with the railways, Rose thought vaguely.

'Yes, Kate?'

'Mr Tremayne wasn't at dinner,' she said eagerly. 'We all wondered where he was. We thought he *must* be ill because he hates to miss a meal. He said he enjoys food and that a good appetite is a sign of a clear conscience.'

41

'Does he?' She smiled. 'How interesting.'

Lucy said, 'Last summer he was going to take some of us on a picnic to Loe Pool, but Mr Vivian wouldn't allow it. He said it was unsuitable.' She gave Rose a challenging look.

Chrissie repeated, 'Unsuitable!' Her tone was scathing.

Rose, vaguely recalling the incident, felt obliged to support her father. She said, 'Mr Vivian was quite right. The Loe Pool has a rather sad history. Local people insist that every seven years someone dies in its waters.'

Lucy said, 'You mean *drowns* in it?'

She had caught their interest, thought Rose. 'It has happened,' she told them. 'I expect my father —'

'We were only going to picnic, not swim.'

'Please don't interrupt me, Chrissie.' She tried to sound authoritative but obviously failed because Kate spoke up.

'We walked to the Loe Pool once with Mr Rivers — to get inspiration!' She laughed. 'It wasn't terribly inspiring, but there was someone rowing a boat on it. The water was very still and it was so quiet there. All you could hear was the ripple of oars.'

Lucy said hesitantly, 'It was almost too still. Quite scary really.'

Chrissie snorted. 'You'd find your own shadow scary!'

Kate said, 'It looked perfectly safe.'

Chrissie said scornfully, 'Of course it's safe.'

Rose said, 'That's enough!' Ignoring their surprise she continued, 'Get out your books and pens and start work.'

Mouths tightened, there were sullen whispers and one or two desk lids banged but fortunately, at that moment, Miss Hock appeared in the doorway. Tall and bulky, of indeterminate age, she carried a pile of books under one arm and a bulging raffia bag under the other. At her entrance the class fell immediately silent.

'Taken poorly, is he?' Miss Hock enquired in a tone which suggested she was not surprised at this sign of weakness. Her breath smelled, as always, of violets.

'I'm afraid so.' Rose lowered her voice slightly. 'I've set the girls some work. Chrissie will collect it at the end of the lesson.'

Miss Hock dumped the books on the desk and put her bag on the chair. She stared round the class and demanded, 'Haven't you started yet? You've been told what to do. Get on with it.'

In a subdued silence books were opened, pens found, brows were furrowed with apparent concentration on the task. Rose thought how easy it looked.

She said, 'Well, I'll leave you to it, Miss Hock — and thank you for giving up your free period.'

'Needs must!' said Miss Hock and slipped a violet cachou into her mouth.

CHAPTER TWO

When Rose returned to the Head's room she found the cook waiting for her. So Maud *had* been eavesdropping! Before Cook could speak, Rose smiled.

'Come in,' she said and led the way. Once inside, she drew a deep breath and searched for a way to impart the bad news.

The cook, a matronly woman by the name of Cripps, found her words first. 'Is it true, Miss Vivian? About your father? Being killed. If Maud's having us on I'll have something to say to —'

Rose said, 'I'm afraid it is true, Mrs Cripps.'

'Oh my gawd!' She blanched visibly.

'Sit down, please. It's a terrible thing, a dreadful shock. Maud had no right to listen to our conversation but, in fact, I assume that what she has told you is correct.'

Mrs Cripps was dragging a handkerchief from her apron pocket. She dabbed at her forehead, breathing heavily. 'The master *dead!* It doesn't seem possible. Oh, Miss Vivian. Losing your father like that! So sudden. We're all so sorry.'

Rose could imagine the consternation that the

news had caused in the kitchen.

She said, 'Well, since you already know, I'd best come back with you and tell the staff in person.' To make sure Maud had got all her facts right. 'Then I'll trust you all to say nothing until I've had time to assemble the teaching staff — and the girls will have to know some time, of course.'

'How did it happen, ma'am? It doesn't sound like the master to go taking silly chances like that. Not that I mean he was *silly* — never! But climbing down a cliff?'

'I thought the same thing,' Rose confessed. 'But I suppose we all make mistakes. A moment's rashness. It was just bad luck.' She regarded the cook anxiously. Apparently, Mrs Cripps was prone to 'funny turns', and now her face was colouring and there was perspiration on her face. Maud had hinted that it was 'that time of life' and nothing to worry about.

Rose hoped so. She stood up. The sooner the staff were told the truth, the better for everyone. 'I'll come downstairs with you,' she said.

Mrs Cripps was wiping away a few tears and Rose waited hopefully for some of her own. Stubbornly her eyes remained dry.

'Shall we go?' she asked at last.

Wordlessly, still sniffling, Mrs Cripps heaved herself from the chair and lumbered after her.

In the kitchen, Maud listened to Rose Vivian in silence, longing for her to be gone. As the door finally closed behind her, she could contain herself no longer.

'So?' she cried triumphantly. 'Didn't I tell you? Now who's making it all up?' She placed her hands firmly on her hips and glared at Mrs Cripps.

It was a particularly satisfying moment for her. Maud, frail and elderly, was the longest-serving member of the Tye Rock staff, having moved in as nanny to little Rose. Later she had acted as housekeeper. When George Vivian considered her too frail to continue the responsibility of full-time work, he had engaged Mrs Cripps as cook-housekeeper and Maud's authority had suffered in consequence. She felt the loss keenly, and fought at all times to maintain a position of seniority.

Today Mrs Cripps, annoyed, refrained from answering and instead snapped at Polly, 'Your cap's crooked! Straighten it.'

Polly said, '*Dead?* I can't hardly believe it,' and fiddled obediently with the white cap, pinning it securely on her blonde curls. She winked at Robb, the gardener, and began half-heartedly to peel another potato.

Robb said, 'The master dead? Well, there's a turn-up!'

The kitchen was quiet for a moment or two as the staff absorbed confirmation of the bad news. Maud smirked openly. Mrs Cripps fingered the rolling pin but made no attempt to roll out the pastry which sat on the board in front of her.

Robb, tall and gangling, with rough good looks, added a third spoonful of sugar to his mug of tea and stirred it slowly.

Maud said again, 'I *told* you! You wouldn't none of you believe me. Fell down a cliff and killed hisself — that's what I said, and that's how 'twas.' Pointedly, she moved the sugar bowl out of Robb's reach.

Mrs Cripps said, 'You shouldn't ought to have told us nothing because you shouldn't have been listening at the door!' She mopped her face.

Maud tossed her head. 'I was passing the door and I couldn't *help* hearing. Any rate, there's no harm down. I wasn't spreading gossip. It was the truth, but you as good as called me a liar!'

Polly said, 'Well, he's gone, and I'm not going to pretend I care.' She looked at the cook. 'What you looking at me like that for? I'm not going to cry for *him!* I never liked him and neither did any of you.'

Maud wagged a finger at her. 'I didn't *like* him, but I *understood* him. There's plenty you don't know and I'm not saying.'

Mrs Cripps said, 'You'll cry if you lose your job, Polly.'

This remark went over Polly's head as she elaborated. 'He was a mean old devil,' she insisted, 'and everyone knows it, and that's the truth. When my ma was took bad with her heart, he wouldn't let me go home. Wicked, that was. Said we was too busy and I couldn't be spared.'

'Well, you couldn't!' Mrs Cripps protested.

'We was bottling and we needed every pair of hands. How was he to know she was going to die? None of us knew she was that bad.'

Robb put down his mug. 'Lose our jobs? Why should we? What we done? Not our fault master's snuffed it —'

Mrs Cripps said, 'That'll do from you, Robb, thank you very much! Snuffed it, indeed! It'll have proper respect for the master in this kitchen. And that goes for all of you. Show a bit of respect for the dead. It'll be your turn one of these days.'

Robb frowned and his heavy face crumpled. 'But I ain't *done* nothing.'

Polly said, 'No one said you have, Robb.'

She softened the words with a smile and Maud groaned inwardly. The silly girl had her eye on Robb, unless she was very much mistaken. He would be no match for a girl like her, but maybe she could liven him up a bit.

Robb scowled. 'I never listened at the door. 'Twas Maud done that.'

Maud rolled her eyes. 'For Lord's sake, Robb!' He wasn't exactly dim, but he certainly was slow on the uptake. 'I mean, we could *all* lose our jobs if the school closes. How can Miss Vivian run Tye Rock House, poor lass, with her pa dead? Can you see her as Headmistress?'

The stark question silenced them. Their differences forgotten, they exchanged worried glances.

Polly said, 'Well, I don't care. If one of them had to fall and die I'd rather it was old Mr Vivian and not young Mr Tremayne.' She wriggled her shoulders suggestively. 'I really fancy him.' She glanced at Robb. 'He's just up my street, he is!'

Mrs Cripps shuddered. 'What a terrible way to die — falling off a cliff.'

Maud said, 'Tell me a *nice* way to die!'

'In your sleep. That'd be nice. Just drift off to sleep, have a lovely dream and then not wake up.'

Robb frowned at Polly. 'So Tremayne's up your street, is he? Told him that, have you?'

Polly said, 'I just might, so there! Would you be jealous, Robb?'

She looked at him hopefully and Maud tutted. Don't be so *obvious*, girl, she remonstrated silently. The problem was that Robb didn't need a wife. His mother cooked for him and darned his socks. All he asked was a pint of ale at the end of a long day.

Aloud, Maud said, 'We was talking about our *jobs*, Polly, if you don't mind. Mr Tremayne's got nothing to do with it.'

'I only said —'

'Well, don't.'

Robb said, 'He's too old for you, Tremayne is. Must be thirty if he's a day.'

Polly said, 'So? That's true — and you're only a few years older'n me. You think you're about right, I suppose.'

Smiling, she pushed the sugar bowl back within his reach. Thoughtfully, he added another spoonful of sugar to what remained of his tea and took a large mouthful. Maud wanted to shake the pair of them.

Mrs Cripps intervened quickly. 'I reckon we should carry on like always and give Miss Vivian all the help we can. Be on our best behaviour. Maybe she'll decide she *can* keep it on, and then we'll be safe.'

'Best behaviour?' Polly frowned. 'Like what?'

'Like not moaning when we get extra work to do. There'll be the funeral to think about and —'

Polly said, 'The funeral? Oh Lord! I haven't got anything black to wear!'

Mrs Cripps tutted. 'Who says we'll be invited to the funeral? I was thinking more about the food. Lord only knows how many we'll have to feed.'

Polly shook her head. 'That poor girl. Miss Vivian, I mean. First her ma and now her pa.'

Robb asked, 'What did her ma die of?'

Maud hesitated. She knew more about the family than any of the others, but had never dared pass on what she knew. She said carefully, 'If you must know, she isn't dead. At least not that we know of. She just left — years ago.'

This had the desired effect. Robb stared at her and Polly's mouth fell open.

Mrs Cripps stammered, 'Left? *Left?* You sly piece, Maud! All these years you've let us all think she was dead and —'

Maud relished the moment. 'You thought what you was meant to think! Don't talk about it, the master said. So I didn't.' One up to me,

50

she thought. That had wiped the smile from Cook's face. Thought she was so clever, with her son who was a clerk on the railway and her precious reference from Lady 'whatever-her-name-was'.

Polly said, '*Left?* How d'you mean? Walked out?'

Maud could remember it clearly. She had been devoted to Catherine Vivian and her little daughter, and the young mother's departure had been a disaster. Maud had lived with the memories for years but now, with George Vivian dead, she was suddenly tempted to talk about it.

'Poor soul was thrown out, more like it! She went off suddenly in floods of tears. Don't ask me why 'cos he never told us. No explanation. Nothing.' This was a slight distortion of the truth but Maud felt there were limits to what she could tell, even now. Catherine Vivian had been 'up to something', Maud was sure, but she had never known exactly what it was. Afterwards, the few questions she had dared to put to the master had received short shrift.

'We all thought she must be coming back,' she told them, 'but she never did. Poor Rose was only a tot, poor little mite.' She sighed heavily. ' "When's Mama coming back, Dodie?" she used to ask when she was old enough to be knowing. She called me Dodie. Mrs Vivian used to call me Nanny Maudie but little Rose could never get her tongue round the word. Catherine — that was Mrs Vivian's name. Whatever she

51

done she paid for it, poor soul.' She stole a quick look at Cook and was pleased to see that the revelations had had the desired effect. Like a pricked balloon, thought Maud.

Robb, losing interest, looked at Polly. 'How old are you then, Poll? You can't be no more'n sixteen if you're a day!'

Polly, jolted momentarily from Maud's fascinating revelations, gave him a withering look. 'Sixteen? I was eighteen last month, for your information, Robb. I'm not very tall, that's all. Take after my ma. My pa calls her "Tiddler" and she hates it.'

Maud swore under her breath. Trust Robb to spoil her moment of glory. 'Who cares how tall you are, you silly girl? We've got more important things to talk about — like our *livelihoods* . . . and *death!*' She sometimes despaired of the younger generation.

Mrs Cripps sprinkled flour over the pastry, then gave it a half-hearted roll. The look she gave Maud was challenging. 'Mothers don't just go off and leave their children.'

Gratefully, Maud regained centre stage. 'Well, she *did!* I'm telling you. We were forbidden to ask about it and you know what he's like . . .' She hesitated. '*Was* like, I should say. Dismissed with no reference — that's what he said if any of us gossiped.' In her mind's eye she saw the old gardener loading Catherine's belongings into the gig. ' "Help your mistress," he told me. "She's leaving." Just like that. But she was cry-

52

ing her eyes out, poor thing. It was heartbreaking. I never forgave him for that. I tried to speak up for her, but got my head snapped off for my trouble. Mind your own business, he told me, or you'll be dismissed!'

Polly was finally paying attention again. 'And Miss Vivian?'

'She was only a baby, bless her. Too young to understand. She must have wondered what was happening, poor little mite, with her ma suddenly disappeared and her pa like a bear with a sore head! We hardly dared say a word to him for fear of getting our heads snapped off.'

There was a long silence.

Mrs Cripps lowered her voice. 'Some men beat their wives. You don't think —'

'No, I don't. Someone would have seen — bruises and that.'

Mrs Cripps said, '*You'd* have *heard,* with your ear stuck to the doors!'

Maud ignored the jibe, which was too close to the truth. 'We'd have known, living in the same house and everything.'

Polly giggled. 'Perhaps he had a fancy woman and his wife found out and demanded that he give her up, and he refused and she gave him an ultimatum so —'

Robb said, 'Ultimatum?'

'Never mind!' She giggled again.

Robb shook his head. 'Who'd fancy the master?'

Polly said, 'I wouldn't, for a start.'

Maud gave her a withering look. 'Ultimatum, indeed! You read too much romantic twaddle, Polly. That's your trouble.' She blamed the magazines. Turning the young girls' heads. Rouge your cheeks and splash yourself with perfume. How to interest a man. She shook her head. 'He had his good points. No one's all bad.'

Robb drained his mug with a loud slurp. 'Eighteen, Poll? I'd never have guessed.'

Polly grinned provocatively. 'Well, now you know, don't you? I'll be courting and getting wed before you can say "wink"!'

Maud said, 'And you'll have half a dozen kids before you can say "knife"!'

'I don't mind. I *like* kids!'

Maud, a spinster, decided to drop the subject. She had assisted at Rose Vivian's birth and it hadn't inspired her. A spinster by force of circumstances, she had finally convinced herself that motherhood left a lot to be desired.

Mrs Cripps asked, 'Who's going to pay our wages, then, come Friday?'

Maud was flattered that, instinctively, they all turned towards her. With more confidence than she felt, she said, 'Why, it'll be Miss Vivian. She's family. We'll get paid, don't you worry.'

But worry they did.

Outside the staff room Rose smoothed her dress and tidied her hair. The teachers, she was sure, would be supportive. It was in their own interests to help her through the difficult time

54

ahead. They would no doubt talk about her behind her back, that was only natural, and they might well consider her unsuitable and less than competent; but they would keep these uncharitable thoughts to themselves.

When Rose entered the staff room she became aware, for the first time, just how shabby the furniture was. She rarely used the room, believing that the staff would feel inhibited by her presence. The leather on the Chesterfield was showing signs of wear, and the covers on the upholstered chairs had faded. But it was comfortable and roomy, and each member of staff had a small private cupboard. There was a table for the cups and saucers in readiness for the two large pots of tea which were sent up from the kitchen at regular times throughout the day. The fire had been built up and blazed cheerfully, but the room was otherwise unheated and today the teachers were clustered around the fire.

They had left a chair for her, she noted, and moved forward self-consciously to take her place. Miss Hock had one of the armchairs to herself. Adèle Dubois, known as 'Mam'selle', shared the Chesterfield with Jane Anders, the Matron, who was approaching retirement age. Mr Rivers occupied another armchair. The other two members of staff, Mark Tremayne and her father, were of course absent.

Aware of their curiosity, Rose sat down and without preamble said, 'I'm afraid I have some bad news.'

Five pairs of eyes fastened on her instantly.

Miss Hock said, 'Shouldn't we wait for the Headmaster?'

Matron added, 'Mr Tremayne's not here either, and he didn't come in to dinner.'

'Thank you. I was aware of that.' Rose knew that if she hoped to maintain any kind of control over the staff in the future she must impress them now. Any sign of weakness would be exploited; it was human nature. She went on firmly. 'There has been an accident, a *fatal* accident.' The expressions changed. 'My father has been killed in a fall while out walking.'

Rose could see by their expressions that her words had not immediately registered and quickly explained what had happened.

Mam'selle muttered something. Closing her eyes, she crossed herself.

Miss Hock said, 'Killed? You mean the Headmaster's *dead*?' Her voice, louder than normal, made it sound like an accusation.

'Yes, Miss Hock. That's exactly what I mean.'

Mr Rivers said, 'Good God!'

'And poor Mr Tremayne?' Matron asked. She was a widow with a son about the same age, Rose recalled.

'He's only slightly hurt, thank goodness. He did his best to save my father, but he was unsuccessful. He's in Helston, under the supervision of a doctor, but will be back at Tye Rock as soon as possible. I'm sure you will understand that this has been a terrible shock, and that I shall be

56

relying on your help and cooperation in the next week or two until I decide how to proceed.'

She glanced down at her hands which were folded in her lap, unwilling to see their reactions. Her father had never been popular, although he had been well respected.

Mr Rivers, visibly shaken, spoke at last. 'Well, this *is* a bit unexpected. A sad blow.'

Matron said, 'Poor Mr Vivian. What a terrible thing to happen! So very sad. I'm sure we — that is, we all offer our condolences. How very dreadful for you.' She leaned forward and rested her hand briefly on Rose's knee.

Murmurs of regret now mingled with expressions of incredulity. After an awkward silence, Arnold Rivers asked the question uppermost in all their minds. 'But who will run the school?'

'I will.'

They exchanged startled glances, and Miss Hock said, *'You?'*

'At least for the time being.'

'Do you think that's wise?'

Startled by her directness, Rose hesitated. Miss Hock looked at the others for support but, embarrassed by her remark, no one spoke.

She said quickly, 'I mean — I didn't mean to imply that you aren't capable but . . . we have felt for some time that your father should have appointed a deputy. We wondered what would happen if he ever fell ill.'

Matron said, 'Naturally, we weren't expecting anything like this.'

Rose said, 'I understand, Miss Hock. I admit I haven't been very active in school affairs but that — that was my father's choice. He didn't wish to involve me.'

Miss Hock, unwilling to back down, said, 'It's no reflection on you as a person, Miss Vivian, but your father was a strong hand at the tiller. The school needs another forceful personality.' She gave Rose a challenging look.

There was another silence. Obviously Miss Hock considered herself the ideal candidate for the job, thought Rose.

Matron said, 'I'm sure that Miss Vivian will do her best.'

Mr Rivers smiled. 'You certainly have my support, Miss Vivian.'

Mam'selle nodded. 'There's really no one else, is there? I mean, Mr Rivers is part-time and Mr Tremayne is too young.'

Rose clasped her hands to keep them from trembling. Trust Miss Hock to make things awkward, she thought. Aloud she said, 'I shall of course take advice from the solicitors — I have already spoken with James Edgcombe. And I shall discuss the financial situation with the bank manager. Then there is the matter of my father's will. I cannot make any kind of commitment at this stage until I fully understand the situation. I realise that from your point of view this will be a very trying time, but I trust you will be patient.'

Was the worst over, she wondered. They would all consider her hopelessly unfit to step into her father's shoes, but no one had laughed outright at the idea of her running the school. She was thankful for small mercies.

Miss Hock said, 'And in the long term? What I mean is . . . we all have to earn a living, and if Tye Rock House is to close we shall have to look elsewhere.'

'I appreciate that, Miss Hock, and as soon as I decide what is to be done I will let you know.'

'But do you *want* to run the school?' Again her tone suggested that this might not be a good idea.

Rose hesitated. 'There's a lot to consider,' she said, 'and at present I'm feeling very confused and unhappy. Taking responsibility for Tye Rock House is the last thing I want to do, but when I think about it more carefully it might seem a shame to close the school. We have a good reputation.'

Miss Hock said, 'Hmm! You might sell it, of course.'

'Sell Tye Rock House?' Mr Rivers blinked.

Rose could see that she was losing control. 'There are a number of options open to me,' she told them, 'but for the moment I want to get through the next week and see my father respectfully laid to rest. Then I will think about the school, and I will consult with you on any major issues.'

Even Miss Hock appeared mollified by this concession.

Mr Rivers asked, 'In the meantime, who will

take your father's classes? None of us is qualified in geography or mathematics.'

Rose hadn't considered that problem and thought quickly for an answer. 'I will try to find someone locally who can fill in while I advertise the post,' she said, trying to sound more confident than she actually felt. Unspoken, but obvious, was the teachers' lack of confidence in the Headmaster's daughter. And no wonder, thought Rose. She had not been encouraged by her father to take any part in the management of the school. She had her own small sphere and was never expected to take an interest in the overall running of Tye Rock House; had never known anything about the financial situation. Engaging the teaching staff had been her father's province, as had the preparation of the termly timetables and the requisition of equipment and stationery.

Miss Hock said suddenly, 'I could take over the school assemblies, if you wish.'

Rose hesitated, inwardly shuddering at the picture this provoked. 'I'll bear that in mind,' she hedged. 'Thank you very much. I appreciate the offer.'

To forestall any other offers which might prove difficult to refuse without giving offence, she hastily changed the subject. 'I shall tell the girls at assembly tomorrow morning. Oh — one other matter. Mr Rivers found this note in his desk.' She read out the note referring to Chrissie Morgan's nocturnal wanderings. 'Does anyone have any ideas about this? Have you heard any rumours? Or can anybody suggest who might have written it?'

Mam'selle said, 'It does not surprise me. That girl is a precocious little minx!'

Miss Hock agreed. 'Needs a firm hand. She's been spoilt.'

Matron nodded. 'She certainly is. "Darling Papa", as she calls him, writes to her every week from India.'

'Every *week?*' Miss Hock snorted.

'Oh yes, Miss Hock. She told me as much. All the girls read his letters. She's very proud of her father.'

'A military man?' Rose asked.

Matron said, 'Yes. A colonel, I believe. Or is it a major? Something high up, anyway. Mind you, she does have a sweet side to her. Chrissie, I mean. Once when I had one of my sick headaches she brought me a lavender sachet she had made herself and a handful of butterscotch. She said they wouldn't cure me but they'd make feeling ill a little better. I thought it very kind. None of the others bothered at all.'

Miss Hock gave her a scornful look. 'Trying to curry favour, I expect.'

'Oh no! She was genuinely concerned. Chrissie Morgan's not all bad.'

Rose said, 'That's nice to hear. So her father dotes on her —' She felt immediately envious. The girl had everything. Money, good looks and a devoted father. 'What about her mother?'

'Always ailing, from what I gather.' It was Ma-

61

tron who answered. 'Some kind of trouble with Chrissie's birth which has left her mother very fragile. Apparently mother and daughter aren't close at all.'

Disregarding these details, Miss Hock ploughed on. '*And* the wretched girl has too much pocket money. I brought the matter up at the last staff meeting, but Mr Vivian did nothing about it.'

Rose ignored the implied criticism. 'But where does she go? Where *could* she go?' She looked at Matron, who seemed to know most.

'We did have a girl once who stole from the larder,' Matron admitted. 'They were having secret feasts in the dormitory. It was all very nasty because the kitchen staff were under suspicion for a time. Most unpleasant. The Head expelled her instantly. He is — *was* — always very firm in these matters. Joan Tate, her name was. A very silly girl.'

Rose vaguely remembered the incident. 'No other ideas, then?' she asked.

There was much shaking of heads.

Mr Rivers said, 'I'll ask around in Porthleven. if you like. Discreetly, of course. Not that she has necessarily been to the village, but there's nowhere else to go.'

Rose said, 'Has she got a . . . a gentleman friend, does anyone know? Could you all make a few enquiries? Be as tactful as you can, naturally.'

Mr Rivers said, 'Let's hope not. Papa wouldn't like his darling daughter to do anything like that.'

Rose said, '*I* wouldn't like her to! It's our responsibility to see that none of the girls get up to anything . . .' She searched for a polite way to express her fears. 'Well, anything of that nature.'

Matron said, 'It might be nothing — the note, I mean. Just a little malice on the part of one of the girls. So-called young ladies can be very spiteful.'

'Let's hope it's nothing.' Rose stood up. 'Forgive me if I hurry away, but I have to visit poor Mr Tremayne. I'll give him your best wishes, shall I?'

On this more positive note she made her exit. Outside the staff room she stood still, both hands over her face. Her first staff meeting. How had she managed, she wondered. She had an overwhelming desire to follow Maud's example and listen at the keyhole but, smiling faintly, she resisted the urge and made her way upstairs. She must fetch her coat and ring for Robb. When he brought the gig round to the front door she would set off for Helston. The thought of seeing Mark Tremayne brought a faint smile to her face. The thought of seeing him *in bed* made her blush.

The history master was sitting up, propped against numerous pillows. He was very pale and his smooth fair hair was almost completely hidden by bandages. As Rose approached the bed she saw a large purple graze down the left side of his face which still oozed blood. The doctor's wife was bending over him and for a moment he didn't see Rose. His face wore an expression of concern and his fingers picked nervously at the blanket.

'Best not to think about it,' the woman was saying. 'You did all you could. Just put it out of your mind and concentrate on getting better.' She straightened up and Mr Tremayne caught sight of his visitor.

'Miss Vivian!'

His face lit up with obvious delight and Rose felt a rush of pleasure at the unexpected reaction.

She said, 'Hullo, Mr Tremayne,' and to the woman, 'Mrs Ellis?'

The doctor's wife nodded. 'And you're George Vivian's daughter? Oh dear. What can I say? Such a sad loss.'

'Yes. Thank you. I felt I should see how Mr Tremayne is faring. I know he tried to save my father, and I'm so grateful.'

'Of course you are, my dear. But I was just telling Mr Tremayne that he mustn't blame himself. He did what he could. Put his own life at risk, even.'

'Certainly not!' Rose looked at him. 'I'm so glad you were together when it happened. If my father had been alone it would have been so much worse. I mean, we might never have known — if his body had been carried away by the tide . . . At least we *know*.'

There was a chair beside the bed but Rose hesitated.

Mrs Ellis said, 'Do sit down, Miss Vivian.' She glanced down at her patient and patted his hand, and Rose found herself envying the small intimacies that could exist between a patient and a nurse.

'Now remember, Mr Tremayne,' the doctor's wife went on, 'you mustn't go tiring yourself out now. You've had a nasty experience and shock can be delayed, you know.'

To Rose she added, 'Just a few moments and then he must rest. Body and mind need time to heal. And please do make sure he looks after himself when he comes back to Tye Rock House.'

She gave him a motherly smile and hurried away, leaving Rose acutely aware of how the doctor's wife saw the history master. A good-looking young man with charming manners. It occurred to her that she knew very little else about him herself.

They both watched her go and then Rose sat down. 'Your head,' she said. 'How bad is it?' If only *she* could pat his hand.

He managed a smile. 'Slight concussion, that's all, as far as they can tell, although it aches like the devil. I feel a bit of a fraud actually, but better than when they brought me in, bruised and battered. I thought my ankle was broken — it's very painful, but the doctor thinks it's only a sprain.' His fine eyes darkened. 'Miss Vivian, I can't tell you how badly I feel about your father. I did all I could, believe me, but by the time I reached him he'd gone. He must have hit his head on the way down, or else struck a rock when he landed in the water. I dragged him to the shore but I — I think I already knew there was no hope. I was torn between staying with him — to reassure him if he regained consciousness — or to go for help. I decided that he needed a doctor more than he needed me.'

Rose looked into the grey eyes and pitied him. He was pale and drawn and looked years older than when she had last seen him at the morning assembly. That moment, so reassuringly normal, seemed such a long time ago.

'He was fond of you, Mr Tremayne,' she told him. 'He looked forward to the walks and the chess. He always wanted a son but it was not to be.' She shrugged. 'We had so little in common. He tried to teach me chess, but my progress was too slow and he lost interest. But I can't thank you enough for all you did.' Then she frowned. 'What I *can't* understand is what my father was *doing*. It's so unlike him.'

'Yes, it is. And yet again it wasn't. He spotted what he said was a something or other — I'm afraid it didn't mean anything to me. Botany's not my strong point and my Latin's very rusty.'

'A plant, you mean?'

'No, it was a butterfly. He was leaning over to see it better and I warned him that the edge was crumbly. We've had so much rain lately. Then he knelt down and had another look and said, "It *is!* How wonderful! So early in the year, too." He was so excited. Then he said, "Look, I'm just going down a little further," and began to slide down. He went slowly at first and I wasn't particularly worried — surprised but not worried. The next thing I knew he'd slithered out of sight. He gave a sort of cry and then —' He closed his eyes.

Rose felt cold as she imagined the scene. Poor Papa! He must have been terrified.

Mark Tremayne opened his eyes. 'I started to go down after him, shouting to him to hang on. He said, "It's giving! Oh, God help me!" ' He looked up at Rose. 'I think he was holding on to something — a root, or a small bush. Then there was another cry, rather muffled, and . . . and a splash. Then silence.' He said desperately, 'I can't get it out of my mind. I go over and over it to see what else I could have done. I'll never forget it. Never!'

'How ghastly for you. I'm so sorry.' The words sounded so inadequate.

'I climbed back up and ran on to where the old steps go down, and I was in such a panic that I didn't look what I was doing. I slipped and rolled most of the way. That's how I got this.' He pointed to his head.

Before Rose could answer the doctor's wife reappeared. 'Two more minutes!'

Rose opened her mouth to protest but hastily closed it. The patient's welfare was what mattered most. The fact that, for the first time in her life, she was sitting close to an attractive young

67

man was of no importance. Two minutes.

Rose asked, 'Would you like me to notify your family? If you give me your address —'

'No!'

She was startled.

'That is . . . no thank you. I — I don't have any family. My parents are both dead.' He shrugged. 'My mother a long time ago, my father quite recently.'

Rose cried, 'Oh, how awful! Nobody? No brothers or sisters? Oh, Mr Tremayne, that's so sad.'

Now she felt guilty. This young man was quite alone in the world, and neither she nor her father had known or cared. Unless her father *did* know. Presumably on their walks the two men had chatted about their lives. Or rather, Mr Tremayne would have chatted. Her father would no doubt stride out in silence, prepared to offer an occasional comment but not to initiate conversation, He had always been inward-looking, apparently content with the workings of his own mind. He had rarely showed the slightest interest in Rose's feelings; had never encouraged an exchange of confidences.

This Rose had accepted over the years. She would like to have asked about her mother, whom she could not remember, but her timid questions on that subject were always rebuffed. Catherine Vivian had left them years ago, but that was the sum of Rose's knowledge. Why she had left them and under what circumstances she would probably never know.

Mr Tremayne was looking at her enquiringly and she realised that he had been speaking to her.

'I'm sorry?' she said.

'I said we're two of a pair now.'

She looked at him blankly. Two of a pair?

'Our parents,' he explained. 'They've all gone.'

Rose wanted to say, 'Oh but I've got a mother somewhere', but for some reason she let it pass, unwilling to tell him that her mother had deserted them. Rose had always considered it a matter for shame. What sort of child had she been if her own mother could abandon her so lightly?

Mark Tremayne was regarding her closely, a strange expression on his face. He said, 'What's the matter? Have I said something wrong?'

'No. Not at all. I — It's just that . . .' If only she could confide in him! There was something about him; an intangible quality that drew her to him. Intuitively she felt that he would understand her and the shared secret would be a bond between them. If he were alone in the world then there could be no wife or fiancée lurking in the background. Which meant that there was no reason why the two of them shouldn't become much closer. Dare she trust him, she wondered, in an agony of indecision. She swallowed, but her throat was dry as she searched for the right words. 'Mr Tremayne, there's something . . .' If only she could call him Mark. She already loved the name and it would be so easy to love the man.

He asked gently, 'What is it, Miss Vivian? If I can help in any way . . .'

Rose made up her mind. 'The truth is —' she began, but at that moment the doctor's wife returned, glancing pointedly at the mantelpiece clock.

Rose bit her lip and fell silent. In a way she felt relieved that the interruption had prevented her revelation. Mark Tremayne was really little more than a stranger to her — a member of her teaching staff. The rest existed only in her imagination and she had no right to burden him with her troubles. She would have made a fool of herself; she would almost certainly have wept, and that would have embarrassed him. She stood up quickly, saying, 'I have to go, but I'll try to call in tomorrow — unless, of course, you are allowed home.'

Home, she wondered. Was Tye Rock House the only home he had?

'Goodbye then, Mr Tremayne.'

To her surprise he reached out and took hold of her hand. 'We have a lot in common, don't we? I do feel we could be very good friends, Miss Vivian.'

The touch of his hand was wonderfully exciting. 'Good friends? Why yes, I hope so.' Her heart was pounding.

From the doorway of the room she glanced back. He was watching her go, she thought, and was intrigued by the look in his eyes. Impulsively she raised her hand in farewell, and he waved back. If only she knew him a little better. Perhaps they could invite him to stay on for a nightcap one evening, after a game of chess? She sighed. Her father would never agree to . . . She clapped a hand to her mouth, shocked. For a few moments she had actually *forgotten*. She had *forgotten* that her father was dead; that she could never ask him anything again. Unbidden came the thought that he could never refuse her anything again. Appalled, she thrust the uncharitable idea from her. Stop this, Rose, she told herself fiercely. What sort of daughter are you if you cannot grieve properly for your own father? Please forgive me, she begged silently.

She had a sudden vision of him standing beside her in church, singing in his strong, tuneful voice. He had always enjoyed singing and had loved the Sunday service and now, in death, that simple pleasure was taken from him along with everything else he had ever loved. A picture of his still, silent body rose uninvited and she thrust the thought from her in horror. She wished now that, when he had left for that last fateful walk, she had run out after him and flung her arms around him. However, he would have found such a display of affection rather unnecessary. Instead she had called a careless, 'See you later, Papa.' She would never see him now, except in his coffin, and she shuddered at that prospect.

Rose was beginning to realise that death was a

very permanent condition. She had been very young when her grandmother died and, cushioned by those around her, the full significance of the event had eluded her. Today, years later, the worst of the shock was behind her but slowly she was becoming aware of her loss. Her father's death was leaving a gap in her life which could never be filled. As she moved out of the room her joy at speaking with Mark Tremayne abruptly faded, giving way to an overwhelming sense of apprehension.

The doctor's wife came into the hall to meet her and led her back to the front door. As they stood together on the doorstep she lowered her voice. 'Poor Mr Tremayne. I felt so sorry for him. Sergeant Wylie was *so* persistent when he came. He must have made the poor young man feel almost guilty.'

'Guilty?' Rose looked at her in surprise. 'Of what, exactly?'

'Goodness only knows. Five minutes, I told him, but after ten minutes he still wasn't done with his questions. Not that I was listening, don't think that, Miss Vivian. But I was in the hall. "Where exactly this?" and "How exactly that?" It was like the Spanish Inquisition in there. In the end I couldn't bear it. I went back in and I said, "Time's up, Sergeant. Mr Tremayne's had a terrible experience. He needs to rest now." '

Rose frowned. 'I wonder why? I mean, all those questions.'

Mrs Ellis shrugged. 'Police procedure, I expect. They have to stick to the rules, don't they? But an accident's an accident. What does it matter exactly where or how? Your poor father's dead, God rest his soul, and mercifully young Mr Tremayne was spared.'

Rose nodded. 'At least all that's over now,' she said. 'Mr Tremayne will be able to get some rest.'

She said, 'Goodbye' and went back to the waiting gig. She was very quiet on the way back to Porthleven, but it was not the police inquiry which occupied her mind. That had slipped from her mind completely. It was her own feelings for Mark Tremayne that filled her thoughts. Those and his feelings for her.

Later the same night Rose climbed wearily out of bed and, shivering, pulled on her dressing gown. The fire in the small grate was almost out, and she made it up with the last of the coals. She longed for a hot drink, but the thought of the long trek to the kitchen on the far side of the house deterred her. Crossing to the window, she pulled back the curtain and stared out across the wide lawn to the trees that bordered the curving drive. Her thoughts turned unwillingly to Chrissie Morgan. Did she leave the house? Was she secretly meeting someone? If so, it would be a man. The idea of one of their pupils behaving with such reckless abandon was appalling. The school accepted responsibility for the welfare of the girls and Chrissie's parents would be rightly incensed if they ever learned of such a flagrant breach of the school rules.

'Bother you, Chrissie!' Rose muttered.

She had enough to worry about without a disruptive pupil, she told herself. But somewhere, half-hidden in her thoughts, was a touch of jealousy. If it were true then, albeit unwillingly, Rose envied the girl her romance. At twenty-seven, Rose had never had an admirer, and she was beginning to fear that she never would.

On a sudden impulse she crossed the room and let herself out into the darkened corridor, lit only by the moonlight filtering thinly through the landing window. She made her way down the stairs and along the main first-floor corridor to the western wing of the house where the girls slept. The younger ones slept in a large dormitory which adjoined Matron's room, but the older girls shared smaller rooms — some three to a room, some four.

Outside in the corridor she waited, hugging herself to keep warm. All the doors were closed and there was no sound from any of them. She had never visited this area except in minor emergencies, and had never realised that the girls' names were printed on each door. It was easy to find the room shared by Chrissie Morgan and Lucy Unwin. Rose hesitated. If Matron suddenly appeared she would no doubt assume that Rose didn't trust her to do her job and would take offence. But what if Chrissie *was* out somewhere? In that case Matron *was* neglecting her duties. What would her father have done, she wondered, but she already knew the answer. He would not be worrying about the matron's reaction; he would be doing what he felt necessary.

'So do it, Rose!' she told herself.

Stepping up to the door she grasped the handle and slowly turned it, praying that it wouldn't squeak. If Lucy was alone, she was hopefully asleep and Rose didn't want to alarm her. Nor did she want the girl to alert Chrissie Morgan to the fact that Rose was checking up on her.

The handle made no sound and Rose stepped quietly into the room. It took her eyes a few seconds to become accustomed to the darkness, but then her heart began to pound. Lucy slept in one bed, her head just visible above the bed-clothes which she had pulled close around her neck. The other bed was empty and had obviously not been slept in. Rose drew in her breath sharply. In spite of her suspicions the proof had come as a shock. She withdrew as quietly as she had entered and closed the door behind her. What now? She considered waking the matron, but on reflection decided against it. Whatever needed to be done did not require more than one person.

'How did you get out, you little wretch?' she muttered. The bedroom window had been firmly closed but was on the first floor — hardly likely that Chrissie had risked her neck to climb down the ivy. So it had to be somewhere downstairs. Rose retraced her steps and went down to the ground floor. She then began a systematic inspection of the doors and windows. After five minutes she found what she was looking for — a large sash window in the dining room which was open a few inches at the bottom. Rose opened it further and peered out. Below the window was a flower bed. It would be comparatively easy to jump down and climb back in again later.

Rose came to a decision; she would sit and wait. She lowered the window a little so that it looked undisturbed. Then she drew up a chair and sat well back in the shadows. Chrissie Morgan would have quite a shock when she returned from her little jaunt.

Chrissie, still warm with excitement, was smiling as she turned back from the gate and began to retrace her steps along the drive. Jerry was such a darling. She made a small crooning sound in her throat as she thought of the forbidden words he had whispered as he unfastened her blouse. She had been powerless to stop him; unwilling to do so. The feelings he inspired deep within her were so strange, and she wanted to know more. Longed for them to go further, and yet she was afraid to discover whatever else there might be.

'Oh Jerry! My love!'

'Beautiful breasts.' That's what he had said and, choked with elation, Chrissie had been unable to reply. Rarely at a loss for words, she was often silent when he was near her, his body warm and vibrant in the reassuring darkness of the stable loft. If only the other girls could see her and *know*. It was all so — so *worldly*. So wonderfully far removed from the schoolroom and stupid lessons and bossy Miss Hock and dreary old Rivers. She pitied the other girls who knew nothing of such sensual pleasures and had never known such a thrill. They never could, of course, because none of them had the nerve to do what she did. They were such children, she thought disparagingly. So immature. She, Chrissie, was learning about love while they were learning only history and maths.

Her smile widened. Next time perhaps she would learn a little more about *his* body. So far she had experienced little more than the smell of him in the darkness and had felt the hairs on his chest when he thrust her hand inside his shirt. Chrissie knew nothing about men. She had no brothers and no male cousins. She had never seen a man naked, although she had seen a picture of a male statue. When she mentioned this to Jerry he had laughed aloud and said, 'All in good time, Miss Morgan!' She loved the way he called her 'Miss Morgan'.

She drew a long sigh of contentment. She was young and pretty and she had a lover. In a few years' time she would be married and all this would be over. Surely life could never be so sweet again.

The moon had been hidden by a cloud and

Tye Rock House loomed up darkly as she drew nearer and turned right towards the dining room. In any other circumstances she would have felt nervous, but recent memories kept other emotions at bay. She pushed up the window with practised ease, hoisted up her skirts and clambered up on to the window sill. Within seconds she was inside and turning to close the window. As she reached up to refasten it there was a sound behind her.

Someone said, 'And what do you think you're doing?'

Shock and fright made her stumble backwards and she clutched at the nearest table to steady herself.

'Who . . .' she stammered. It was a woman, but not Matron. 'Who is it?' she asked, suddenly icy cold.

'It's Miss Vivian.'

Of course. Now she recognised the voice.

The voice continued, 'But you haven't answered my question, Chrissie. Where have you been? It is nearly midnight and you should be in bed.'

Chrissie let out a sigh of relief. Thank heavens it was only 'Rosadora'. It might have been Miss Hock. Gathering her wits together, she decided to brazen it out.

'I couldn't sleep,' she said. 'I went for a walk in the grounds.'

'You're lying.'

Chrissie was startled. As her eyes became accustomed to the gloom she saw Miss Vivian sitting less than a yard away. Chrissie could clearly see the expression on her accuser's face, and she didn't like what she saw. Nor did she like the steely note in the voice. Almost certainly she would be sent to 'Georgie-Porgie' in the morning.

She thought quickly. 'I was hot. Really hot, Miss Vivian. And perspiring. I think I may have a temperature. I wanted to cool down. I thought the night air —'

'If you thought you were ill, you should have woken Matron. That would have been the sensible thing to do.'

'I didn't want to disturb her.'

'You're lying again. You must think me a fool. This isn't the first time you've sneaked out of the house.'

That *did* startle her and she began to feel less confident. Could she *know* or was she guessing? Had Lucy finally betrayed her? If so, she would live to regret it.

She would bluff it out. 'Are you calling me a liar, Miss Vivian?'

'Yes, Chrissie, I am. I think you went out to meet someone.'

'I didn't. I swear to you.' Her heart was racing and even to herself her voice sounded unconvincing. Had anyone seen them walking together from the stables? If so, she must never reveal Jerry's name. In desperation she said, 'I couldn't sleep and I thought I heard someone skulking around the stables. I went down to take a look. I — I was afraid for the horses . . . that someone might be stealing them. Clipper is such a darling and —'

'Nonsense! You are adding insult to injury, Chrissie, if you think I will believe such a ridiculous story. First you say you are ill, and now it's concern for the horses. You are lying and I intend to discover the truth. But not now. I have wasted too much of my time on you and your silly antics. I intend to get back to my bed as quickly as possible.' She stood up. 'Tomorrow morning you will not leave your bed until Matron has been along to examine you. You will *not* go down to breakfast; you will wait for a message from me. When you get it you will come straight to my father's — to *my* — to the Head's room.'

'But, Miss Vivian —' she began. Saturday breakfast was a social occasion to which all the girls looked forward. There was no reason to hurry and the usual plain breakfast was replaced by something a little more adventurous. Dare she protest? She was in so much trouble that it could hardly make things worse. Recklessly, she said, 'I don't think my father would approve of me missing breakfast, Miss Vivian. He has paid for all my meals and he —'

'I doubt if he would approve of you sneaking out at night and doing God knows what! I'm sure he would be most upset. Presumably he trusts you? It will be a great disappointment for him to hear of this escapade.'

'He doesn't have to know, does he?' The words came out before she could stop them.

'I may feel it necessary to tell him, Chrissie.'

Chrissie swallowed. 'You're going to tell the Headmaster, then?' Her bravado was deserting her.

'I — perhaps not . . . that is . . .'

Miss Vivian sounded strangely flustered, thought Chrissie, intrigued. Perhaps she would *not* be reported to the Head? She felt her hopes rise marginally.

'We shall see. A lot will depend on how you behave in the morning.'

Chrissie groaned inwardly. Hadn't the miserable cow ever been young? No, probably not. Poor Rosadora. No men in *her* life. She was on the shelf. Who'd want to unbutton *her* blouse? But she was also a threat. If she told 'Georgie-Porgie', he would definitely tell her parents and would probably expel her. Chrissie knew that her parents would be terribly distressed if that happened and dearest Papa would be devastated. Another thought occurred. If he thought she couldn't be trusted, he might even change his mind about letting her go to finishing school in Paris. Oh damn! Why did this have to happen tonight? She had been so lucky on previous occasions. That had probably been her undoing, she thought. She had become too confident.

Miss Vivian turned to go. 'You do understand, I hope, how serious this is? You are to stay in your room until I send for you.'

'Yes, Miss Vivian.' No, Miss Vivian! Be damned to you, Miss Vivian.

'Then go straight back to your room, get into bed and stay there.'

Chrissie waited just long enough to register her disgust and then turned away. She muttered, 'Stupid old trout!'

'What was that?' The voice was sharp with anger.

'I didn't say anything,' Chrissie protested.

For a long moment Chrissie wondered if she had gone too far but, as nothing further was said, she took her chance and half ran out of the room. Still seething with anger and dismay, she made her way upstairs and along the corridor.

'Miserable old spinster!'

Once in her room, however, she was careful not to wake Lucy. Best friend she might be, but Lucy had warned her against her clandestine meetings with Jerry and she would be sure to crow. As she slipped between the sheets Chrissie's thoughts were murderous. She had been so happy and excited and Jerry had been such a wonderful lover. Now Miss Vivian had spoiled it all.

CHAPTER THREE

The following morning at half-past seven, the smell of frying bacon greeted James Edgcombe as he hurried downstairs to the kitchen where his mother and father waited. The eggs would not go into the frying pan until they were all present. It was one of his mother's few rules.

His mother said, 'Ah, there you are!'

James kissed her briefly, smiled at his father and said, 'Morning, both!'

From behind his paper, his father said, 'Mm?'

James smiled. Reading *The Times* before breakfast was a ritual without which his father could never face the day.

His mother, Elspeth, glanced at James as she splashed hot fat on to the egg yolks. 'You're looking pleased with yourself,' she told him. 'Cat got the cream?'

'Not especially,' he answered, settling himself at the table and reaching for a slice of bread.

His father said, 'The miners have come out in Indianapolis. Still, it was on the cards.' He tutted irritably.

James winked at his mother and said, 'That's miners for you. Troublemakers, the world over!'

The paper was lowered a few inches. 'They

might have a legitimate grievance.'

'When do they *not* have a grievance? Eh?'

Elspeth said, 'Now don't start, you two. You know I can't abide this political stuff. Let's just enjoy our breakfast.'

James said, 'I shall need the trap this morning. Is that inconvenient for anyone?'

'Not for me, dear,' she said. 'Where are you off to, then?'

'Falmouth. I said I'd take Miss Vivian to the hospital to identify her father's body. It's in the mortuary there.'

'Oh, that poor girl!' Elspeth placed a plateful of food in front of each of them — eggs, bacon, sausage, fried bread and grilled tomato. She sat down. 'What she must be going through.'

James said, 'Wonderful!' the way he always did and gave his mother an appreciative smile. His mother believed that an army marches on its stomach and liked nothing better than to feed her little family. For that reason her cook began work at nine o'clock each morning. She relished the fact that neither her son or husband could be described as skinny and took it as a compliment to her cooking.

As James cut the bacon into manageable pieces he asked casually, 'What *did* happen to George Vivian's wife all those years ago?'

His mother said, 'Eat it while it's hot, will you.'

Harold folded the newspaper carefully and put it to one side. He buttered a slice of bread, cut it in half, folded one half and dipped it into the egg. His wife rolled her eyes but said nothing.

Turning to her son, she said, 'Catherine Vivian? No one really knows for sure. That man was involved — the fellow from the bank. I forget his name. It all sounded very unlikely to me, but these things happen all the time.'

James frowned. 'You mean she was in love with someone else?'

His mother shrugged. 'You can't choose the one you love. It just happens. Falling in love is one of life's mysteries. And if she *did* love him you couldn't blame her. George Vivian was much older than her, and by all accounts a dry old stick.'

Harold looked up. 'Elspeth! Dry or not, George Vivian was her husband. She had no call to go gallivanting off with *anybody*. She had a good home. Whatever his faults, George Vivian was a good provider.'

She said mildly, 'What about love, dear? Shouldn't that come into it?'

'Love? Of course it should, but if she didn't love George Vivian she shouldn't have married him.' He attacked his sausage and asked, 'Where's the mustard?'

Elspeth muttered an apology and fetched it from the dresser cupboard. 'A man like that could have killed off any love she felt for him. Think how he carried on when the child was a daughter and not a son. Wouldn't look at either of them for days if you believe all you hear.'

Harold said, 'That's natural enough. All men want a son.'

James asked, 'Suppose I'd been a girl? Would you have made all that fuss?'

A shrug was his only answer. His mother cut more bread and they ate in silence until the plates were empty. James started on the toast and marmalade, still thinking about Rose Vivian. The truth was that he wanted to know more about her background, but he didn't want to arouse his mother's suspicions. She had been nagging him to find a wife for the past ten years and James had always hoped it would be George Vivian's daughter. He had tentatively suggested as much to Rose's father four years ago, but had been quickly and firmly rebuffed. Rose, George Vivian had informed him, was not the marrying kind. She knew her duty, he told James. In other words, she would remain at her father's side. Firmly rejected as a suitor, James had said nothing to Rose, glad that he had refrained from alerting his parents to his hopes. Even now he would remain quiet on the subject until he had something positive to report. If Rose herself rejected him they need never know.

Elspeth shook her head slowly. 'Mind you, I never did understand how she could have left that poor child. Desertion. There's no other word for it in my opinion. Imagine, James, if I'd walked out on you.'

He couldn't imagine such a thing. The

86

Edgcombes were a very affectionate and close-knit family.

He said, 'I wonder what she'll do now, poor girl.'

'Find herself a husband if she's got any sense,' said Harold.

'Another cup of tea, anyone?' His mother re-filled the cups. 'Marriage? Yes, why not? She's very personable.'

'Personable? She's more than personable,' James protested.

His mother raised her eyebrows. 'Is she now?'

He grinned. 'Well, I think so.'

He was thinking about the five pounds he had won on the Grand National a few days earlier, when Rubio had obligingly romped home first. He had been planning to buy a couple of leather-bound books for his expanding collection but now, with George Vivian's death, he wondered if he might spend it on Rose instead. A gift might be too direct but perhaps, after the funeral, he could take her out for the day — to cheer her up. To Bath, perhaps. She might enjoy the train ride. He longed to make her laugh; to see her being happy and carefree. She had been the dutiful daughter for so long that she had probably no idea how to relax.

It was time someone brought a little excitement into her life and if it had taken this tragic accident to make it possible — so be it. The Lord moves in a mysterious way, he told himself.

Elspeth said, 'If her mother left her husband

and child, she must have had a very good reason. Despite what they said about her, she could be very sweet.'

James gave her a quick glance. 'What *did* they say about her?'

Elspeth gave a little shrug. 'She came from rather Bohemian parents. Father was a traveller of some kind — always away. Feckless is probably the right word. Mother was an artist with rather modern ideas. They were in and out of debt, from what you hear. I daresay Catherine *was* a little wild, but you can see why. And, of course, she was a real beauty and rather — well, let's say "passionate". Some women are made that way.'

Her husband raised his eyebrows. 'Passionate, eh?' He grinned at his son. 'A passionate woman! Now there's a thought.'

Elspeth said, 'You know what I mean, Harold, so take that look off your face. Let's just say that Catherine Vivian was hardly the docile kind, and leave it at that.'

James frowned. 'Then why on earth did she choose a dry old stick like Vivian?'

His mother shrugged. 'Maybe she needed security. She couldn't play the field for ever, and poor old George had been a most persistent admirer. He had prospects, too.' She replenished the cups from the large brown teapot. 'Speak as you find. That's my motto. All I know is that when my mother died Catherine was the first person to write offering condolences and help. I liked Catherine Vivian.'

And I like her daughter, thought James. No, I *love* her daughter, and I've loved her for as long as I can remember.

His father swallowed the last of his tea and refused his wife's offer of a third cup. 'I'll have to dig out Vivian's will,' he remarked. 'There's no other family, so it should all go to the daughter.'

Elspeth said, 'But what about Catherine?'

'Good Lord, Elspeth, he won't have left *her* anything.' Harold frowned. 'The runaway wife doesn't really deserve anything, does she? Not that anyone quite knows what became of her.'

James said thoughtfully, 'I daresay she could be traced. There must be ways. We have letters, don't we?'

'Do we? Blowed if I remember, but you may be right. If she *has* been left something we'll advertise in the usual way.'

Elspeth began to clear the table. 'Surely she should get something. She did give him a child — even if it *was* a daughter.'

Harold stood up, patting his stomach. 'A nice bit of bacon, that, dear. Not too salt. Now I must get myself down to Sam's for a haircut and then over to Helston. See how Jack's getting on with that suit. Second fitting if all goes well. I might look into the office later. Still some work to finish.'

Elspeth said, 'Oh Harold! Not another Saturday spent in the office! Why can't you ever catch up on this wretched work? You're not getting any younger. I thought you were going to take on another pair of hands.'

He sighed. 'We wanted to, but where the devil do we put him? In the broom cupboard? I've told you before, but you don't listen. The premises are too small. That's the truth of it. If we're going to expand — and James thinks we should — we'll have to find larger office space in Helston or else open a small branch in Falmouth.'

As Harold left the room, his wife turned to her son. 'Do you really need to expand? It's such a risk. All that extra rent.'

James shrugged. 'I think we do, Mother. The trouble is that the outlay and expenses would be doubled, and we'd need to find a great many more clients.' He waved his hands in a helpless gesture. 'It's taking the plunge. Father's a bit reluctant. You know how it is. Knowing it's sensible is one thing. Actually *doing* it is another.'

'But then you'd need another partner, wouldn't you?'

'I could run the Falmouth office with a junior.'

He thought, but didn't say, that if new premises *were* to be leased in Falmouth then he, James, had plans for the accommodation above the office.

His mother looked unconvinced. 'But is there any point, dear? Your father is nearly sixty and he'll retire when he's sixty-five. At least I hope he will. He's wearing himself out at the moment. Then it will be yours and it will be big enough, won't it?'

James hesitated, longing to confide in her but afraid that she would raise some objections. She was very aware of what she called people's 'station in life'. Before the accident, Rose would have been a suitable choice, but if she now inherited Tye Rock House that would make her a wealthy woman. People might think he was marrying her for her money, and his mother would hate that.

He sighed. Patience was not one of his strong points. As far as he knew Rose had no other suitors and their friendship was obviously important to her — and she *had* agreed to his becoming her 'personal adviser'. He pressed his lips together at the prospect of explaining that to his father. Harold Edgcombe had always made such decisions, but James had blurted out the idea to Rose without prior discussion.

Elspeth, sharp-eyed as ever, said, 'Penny for them, James!'

Instead of answering, he glanced at the clock.

'Good Lord! I must get down to the stables. If I don't keep an eye on Garret he won't polish the trap properly. He's a lazy blighter. Father ought to get rid of him.'

Elspeth smiled. 'You know your father. As soft-hearted as they come.' She held up a hand. 'And you're so like him. A chip off the old block. Now off you go, James.' Her mouth twitched. 'Won't do to keep Rose Vivian waiting!'

He tried to look both surprised and amused. 'Mother!'

Her smile broadened. 'You don't fool me, James. I'm your mother, remember?' As he spluttered a denial she laughed. 'For heaven's sake, dear, why ever not? I'm on your side. About time you settled down, and Rose is a sweet girl. Of course, she's not good enough for you — but then no girl is, in my book. Mothers are like that. But if she were to become my daughter-in-law, I'd be very happy.'

'In spite of her rather unconventional background?'

After the smallest hesitation, she said, 'Rose shows no sign of inheriting her mother's wild streak. She has always behaved well. I suppose we should give full credit for that to her father.'

'I doubt if George Vivian ever gave her the chance to be anything else. I would think her life so far has been entirely uneventful, not to say *dull.*'

'Maybe so, James, but bringing up a little girl without a mother couldn't have been easy. He's probably been overprotective because of her mother's wild streak.'

'He could have remarried.'

'But Catherine isn't dead, James.' She carried the kettle to the sink and poured hot water on to the dishes, which now awaited the arrival of the daily help. James watched her, wondering whether to say more.

At last she could wait no longer. 'So are you going to court her, James? She's a pretty girl and she won't be short of suitors now that her father's gone. She's always had a soft spot for you, James . . .'

'Do you think so?'

'Oh yes, dear. Certain of it.'

James resisted the temptation to cheer.

'And you've scarcely looked at anyone else. But the years are passing you both by, and if you want a family . . .'

'A family? Good heavens!' The idea *had* occurred to him more than once, but he was still cautious. 'Don't hustle me, Mother! Anyone would think you wanted to get rid of me!' Suddenly he realised that he was grinning, surprised to find that in fact he didn't mind her knowing and was delighted that she approved. 'I will ask her — in my own good time. I don't think I have any rivals at the moment. The thing is, Mother, that things have changed,' he said. 'Rose will inherit. She'll be a rich woman. Independent. She might decide to sell Tye Rock House and travel in Europe.'

Elspeth refilled the kettle and returned it to the hob. 'A woman alone? I doubt it, dear.'

'She could afford a travelling companion.' The idea was a new one and it filled him with dread. He wanted to marry Rose, and he wanted to do so as quickly as was decent.

Elspeth crossed the kitchen to rest a hand lightly on her son's shoulder. 'She may be rich, James, but she'll also be confused and lonely. More than anything she'll be needing someone to love. Don't leave it too long, dear, or you might find you've missed the boat.'

The sun shone as the trap bowled along the lanes towards the town, but Rose was unable to enjoy the beauty of the fields which lay, bleak and damp, on either side. She said little and was thankful that her companion seemed to understand her need for silence. The rattle of the wheels and the rhythmic clopping of the horse's hooves had a soothing quality to them and Rose was content to sit back, warmly ensconced in a tartan rug, and let the miles slip by.

At last James Edgcombe turned to her. 'Soon be over the worst, Miss Vivian. Nobody expects to find identifying a —' He stopped short of the word 'body' but it hung in the air nonetheless. 'Well, I mean, it's hardly a happy prospect.'

She nodded by way of agreement. 'I can hardly believe that I shall see him — lifeless. Although I know he's dead, I shan't believe it until I see it with my own eyes. Poor Papa. He's had such a . . .' She was going to say 'dull' life but it seemed unkind. Instead she said, 'Such an unexciting life. I never remember him *happy*. Isn't that awful? Unless he was in his own way. Maybe his walks and his chess . . .' Her voice trailed off. Walks and chess. What sort of life was that?

'He probably took great satisfaction from the school,' James suggested. 'My father enjoys his work as a solicitor. Men do.'

Rose thought about it. 'Perhaps. It always seems to be fraught with problems.'

He grinned. 'That's part of the satisfaction. I'm looking forward to the time when my father retires and it's my turn to make all the decisions.'

For a moment Rose was silent, lost in thought. Then she sighed. 'If only I'd been a boy. He longed for a son. He enjoyed Mr Tremayne's company these last months. I could see that.' She felt the usual frisson of excitement as she spoke of the young teacher. 'Mr Tremayne went out of his way to make friends with him, which couldn't have been easy, Papa being the sort of man he was. Reserved, I mean. I'm so pleased he wasn't seriously hurt.'

James raised his whip in greeting as they passed someone he recognised. He said, 'I'm sure your father loved you even though you weren't the son he'd wanted. If he hadn't, he wouldn't have insisted on keeping you when your mother left.'

He was trying to make her feel better, thought Rose, and was touched by his kindness, but what he'd said about her mother brought deeper thoughts to the surface. Why *had* her mother left her behind? Had she done so willingly? Rose had always assumed so but now she wondered afresh. Was it possible her father had prevented her from going? Not for the first time she wondered *where* her mother had gone. When she was little she had asked her grandmother the forbidden question. She had answered, 'Miles away, no doubt, and a good riddance!'

95

When they reached the hospital James offered to go in with her. Rose accepted gratefully and they went in together. They walked along a white tiled corridor that echoed to their footsteps, and then down a flight of stone steps which led to the basement.

An attendant, a small man in a white coat, looked up from his desk with a harassed expression on his face. 'Name of the deceased?' he asked without preamble.

Taken aback, Rose said, 'George Vivian from —'

He wrote something in a small ledger.

Rose felt her lips tremble. No 'Good morning'. No polite condolences. No hint of respect for the next of kin.

'From?' He didn't bother to raise his head.

'From Porthleven. He died yesterday.' Rose was astonished. Had it really been less than twenty-four hours since the accident? So much had happened that it was hard to believe she had been alone for such a short time.

'Date of death?'

Rose swallowed as, somewhat unnerved by his unsympathetic manner, she tried to remember the date. She felt James's hand on her arm in a gesture of reassurance.

Annoyed on her behalf, James snapped, 'Miss Vivian has just told you that her father died yesterday.'

The man ignored him and looked at Rose. All she really wanted was for the ordeal to be over, but James was trying to help her and she decided she must not give in to the man's bullying approach.

She said, 'You can work it out for yourself, I'm sure.'

He looked up, his lips tightening, but he said nothing as with obvious reluctance he made another note in the ledger. Then he closed the book with more force than was necessary and said, 'Follow me.'

No 'Please', thought Rose. Half-way along another corridor he threw open a door and crossed the room. They followed him inside and Rose shivered in the cold air. They watched in silence as the white sheet was lifted from a still figure which occupied one of the trolleys. Rose was seized with a sudden panic and cried out, 'Oh no! I can't!'

She turned abruptly away from the sad sight and found herself in James Edgcombe's steadying arms. Briefly they tightened around her.

'You can, Rose,' he whispered and released her. 'Just a quick glance. He is still your father.'

Rose was trembling from head to foot and her mind was filled with an unreasoning dread. Her father, dead, frightened her. The thought of his thin body, stark and vulnerable, made her feel ill.

The attendant coughed and, without looking at him, she could sense his impatience. She looked at James Edgcombe and his eyes were so full of compassion that tears sprang into her own eyes.

He said softly, 'No one should die without a kiss from a loved one.'

For some reason that she couldn't understand his words made it possible. She turned back to her father's body and, through tear-filled eyes, saw the familiar face. It looked so normal. She bent her head and kissed the cold forehead.

'Goodbye, Father,' she whispered.

As the attendant re-covered the body, Rose straightened up.

James said, 'Well done. That wasn't so bad, was it?'

Rose shook her head. With this last glimpse of her father, a vaguely realised idea had begun to take shape in her mind and now it was crystal clear. She was aware of a growing sense of urgency as she looked at James.

He said, 'What is it?'

She stared at him.

'Miss Vivian? Is anything wrong?'

Rose shook her head, but her smile was a little shaky.

'I'm going to find my mother!' she told him.

Side by side in the pony trap, they rode in silence for a moment or two and then James said, 'What an ill-mannered wretch! That attendant, I mean. I've a good mind to report him. They should employ someone with more tact and compassion.'

Rose dragged her thoughts back to the present. 'Maybe it's hard to find anyone for that job.

But don't worry on my account, Mr Edgcombe. I have already put it out of my mind.' She smiled. 'I've more important things to think about.'

'Still thinking about tracing your mother?'

'Yes, I am. And I won't give up until I find her.' She gave him a sideways glance and saw that he was unhappy with her answer. 'You don't approve?'

'Let's just say that it worries me a little, but if it's what you want . . .' He smiled.

'Wouldn't you want it — in my shoes?'

'I daresay I would.'

'So you'll help me?'

'I'll be your most loyal accomplice!' He laughed. 'The things men do for love!'

For *love?* Rose allowed the word to pass unchallenged.

She sat up a little straighter. 'There's no time like the present. Don't take me straight back to Tye Rock House, Mr Edgcombe, but stop off in Helston. I would like to speak to your father.'

He made no attempt to hide his disappointment. 'I'm sure I can give you any help you need,' he protested. 'It would be easier if you dealt with just one of us. Less confusing, don't you think? And I thought we had an understanding . . .'

'Certainly we do,' she told him, 'but the things I want to ask your father go back many years. I need to know about my mother's departure. I'm afraid you were only a young boy at the time,

99

whereas your father was acting as our solicitor. He must know something. He must have papers or letters — anything that might help me.'

He urged the horse on, then looked at her unhappily. 'Do you really think that's wise, Miss Vivian? I don't mean to dampen your enthusiasm but —'

'But you will!' She had sharpened her tone unintentionally but she needed to resist any pressures brought to bear upon her. It seemed to her at that moment that she had spent her life giving in to other people's wishes and now she must learn new ways.

She said, 'I'm sorry, but a moment ago you were promising to help.'

He leaned across her to tuck in the lap rug which showed no sign of slipping from her knees.

'Thank you,' she said. The closeness of his body was surprisingly disconcerting. She also found the back of his neck very vulnerable, and imagined running her fingers through the short cropped curls. She came to her senses abruptly, angry with herself for the lapse. Closing her eyes, she forced herself to think instead about Mark Tremayne.

He sighed. 'Believe me, I only speak with your best interests at heart. We do have a little experience in these matters and sometimes the missing relative, once discovered, is a great disappointment. Perhaps even a problem.'

'I can't believe that my mother . . .'

'There was a case a few years ago when a

middle-aged woman traced her twin sister. She was appalled to find her living in a state of great poverty with a man who proceeded to scrounge money from her and generally to make a nuisance of himself.'

'*Thank* you, Mr Edgcombe!' Rose interrupted, hastily pushing aside unwelcome images. 'I doubt if my mother is likely to be found in such sorry circumstances, but I take your point.'

He shrugged and the small gesture spoke volumes. Rose resisted the impulse to be even more forthright. He meant well, she reminded herself, and of course he might well be right. But if her mother were in straitened circumstances, there was even more reason to find her and to offer help. Even, dare she consider the idea, to offer her a home at Tye Rock House? The truth was that, in her present mood, Rose was determined to pursue this particular dream at whatever cost to herself.

She said, 'I do realise that it may not work out, but it's a risk I have to take. You can have no idea how it has been all these years, longing for a mother and frightened even to ask about her. I have never seen a photograph of her, you know. There was one taken of the three of us when I was born, but my mother has been cut out of the photograph. Can you imagine a grown man doing such a thing?' Before he could answer she went on, her voice rising slightly. 'When I went to school in the village I felt so different from the other children. I almost hated any girl who had a mother. I had a fight with one girl. She said her mother was a pig — for reasons I forget now — and I flew at her. I couldn't understand how she could speak that way about a mother. Didn't she know how disloyal she was being? To me *any* mother was better than none. I pulled out a handful of the poor girl's hair and was sent home in disgrace with a note. My father was horrified, but naturally I couldn't explain to him how I felt. He was furious because I'd "let him down." He gave me two strokes on the hand with a ruler, and then I hated him too!' She gave James Edgcombe a quick look to see if she was making any sense, but his attention appeared to be fixed firmly on the horses.

'You're not even *listening!*' So much for the loyal accomplice. Rose stared crossly ahead.

He said slowly, 'I'm so sorry that he hit you.'

'It was the only time.'

'But to strike you? He should have understood how you felt.'

'Perhaps he did,' she murmured with sudden insight. 'Perhaps he couldn't bear to be re-minded of what he had done to me — separating me from my mother, I mean. I don't know . . . Or maybe after my mother left I was a reminder of what he had lost. My grandmother said that I looked just like her.'

'There's no excuse for him,' he said angrily.

She looked at him, surprised by his vehe-mence. 'You didn't like him, did you?'

102

'To be honest, no, I didn't. But I had my reasons.'

His reasons? Curious, but reluctant to probe further, Rose remained silent. Eventually she sighed. 'What do any of us know about another person? How could you ever understand our problems? You have a mother and a father and a happy family situation. You're one of the lucky ones, Mr Edgcombe.'

'I'd like to say that I understand but I doubt if I do.' He turned towards her. 'I only want to save you heartache.' He hesitated. 'That's all I ever wanted, Miss Vivian. Your happiness.'

She stared at him. 'My happiness? I don't quite understand.'

He gave her a sideways glance, then concentrated on the horses. 'Forget I said that,' he suggested. 'This isn't the time.'

'The time for what?' The time to talk about her happiness? She gave an exaggerated sigh. 'Everyone keeps things from me. Even you. I don't —'

She broke off as abruptly he reined in the horses and shouted a warning to a small boy who had run into the road. They both watched as the mother snatched up the child and mouthed an apology. They drove on and James Edgcombe finally turned to her.

'I asked your father once if I could court you. He said "No" very emphatically and —'

'You wanted to *court* me? You mean that you wanted . . .'

He stared ahead. 'I wanted to marry you, but your father rejected the idea. He also forbade me to speak to you on the subject. If I wrote to you, he said, he would intercept the letter.'

Rose tried to remember whether her father had given her any idea that James Edgcombe was in love with her. 'You wanted to *marry* me and I didn't even *know it?* I can't believe it.'

He shrugged. 'I was devastated, as you can imagine. There seemed no good reason. I have to admit I've been prejudiced against him ever since.'

Rose stammered, 'He should have told me.' She would have said 'Yes' with all her heart. Now, of course, it was too late.

'I daren't tell my parents. My mother wanted me to find a wife and settle down. If she'd known about my summary rejection she might well have taken him to task! My mother thinks I'm the most wonderful man in the world — next to my father, of course.' He smiled mirthlessly. 'So there you are. My luck ran out.'

Startled by the intensity of his expression, she glanced away. 'That was a — a great compliment,' she whispered. 'I'm sorry. I mean, I'm sorry that I didn't know.'

'I have loved you for years. I always will —'

'Don't say that!' she cried. Why was Fate so unkind, she wondered. For years there had been no man in her life and now, suddenly there were two.

He said, 'I know this isn't the time to talk

about my feelings. Or to ask about yours. Later, perhaps, when you have recovered from the shock of your father's death.'

'Of course, but I should say . . .' Letting the sentence die, she considered what she *could* say. That she wanted to marry Mr Tremayne, perhaps. But did Mr Tremayne want to marry *her*, or was he simply interested in a friendship?

Fortunately he solved the dilemma by saying, 'No. Please, Miss Vivian. This really isn't the right time.' He gave her a wry smile and added, 'I'm not going anywhere and I doubt that you are. We'll talk later.'

She looked directly into the brown eyes, trying to imagine how different her life might have been. She might have had a husband and children . . . He had said that he would always love her, so was that why he had never married?

Rose put a hand to her chest, aware that she was breathing too fast. She could clearly picture the younger James Edgcombe, thinner but with the same mop of brown curls. He hadn't worn spectacles then, but basically he was still the same man. Gentle, thoughtful and desperately sincere. A very *vulnerable* man. Her father had been so cruel to deny him a chance of happiness. James Edgcombe. One of life's gentlemen. So why didn't her heart leap at the thought that he might one day propose again? Somehow she would have to tell him that she couldn't love him; that there was someone else. Or rather, that she *hoped* there might be.

He said, 'But to get back to your search. My father will be out most of the morning, but I can dip into the files for you. If there's anything that will help, I'll find it.'

With an effort Rose dragged her thoughts back to the present. This was *her* chance and she mustn't let it slip away.

'Let's go then.'

Ten minutes later they had collected the key to the Edgcombes' premises. Soon they were inside the office, standing beside a large cupboard which overflowed with files of all shapes and sizes. Dusty ledgers and boxes and bundles of letters suggested that, unless they were very lucky, their search would take hours rather than minutes. Rose, undaunted by the prospect, had now pushed all other thoughts from her mind. The search was all-important.

James pursed his lips thoughtfully. 'They *should* be in alphabetical order if the filing system works, but I'm not too confident. Let's see now . . .'

Hardly able to contain her impatience, Rose watched as files and bundles were examined and rejected. At last, greatly to her relief, he found the one he was looking for. They drew up chairs beside the large mahogany desk and settled to their task.

The documents went back a long way. There were deeds of Tye Rock House when it was still a private dwelling, and a faded map showing the further purchase of land.

'That's where our tennis courts are!' Rose exclaimed. 'Strange to imagine how it was before I was born. Or rather, before I can remember it.'

A bundle of duplicate certificates surfaced. Birth certificates for both parents. A marriage certificate. A rolled document tied with red ribbon to which James Edgcombe referred briefly as 'The will!' Also a birth certificate for Rose May Vivian. Rose picked up the latter.

'Poor Papa,' she murmured. 'Grandmother told me once that they didn't even have a name ready for me. Victor George were the names they had chosen; Victor after my father's father.' She handed it back. 'I could have been a Victoria, I suppose.'

'Rose is much nicer.' He smiled. 'Aha! This looks promising.' He held up a folded paper. 'A letter from your mother.'

He handed it to Rose, who opened it with nervous fingers. The writing was unfamiliar, the message short but poignant.

Dear Mr Edgcombe,
This is to let you know that we are residing at the above address for a short period until we are able to make further plans. You can contact me here until further notice.
                          Yours truly,
                          Catherine Vivian.

The address was in Falmouth. Rose tried to imagine her mother's feelings as she wrote the letter. Without a word she handed it back.

'*We?*' she queried, when he had read it. 'What does that mean? Who was with her?'

'I don't know,' he admitted. 'I'll ask my father. Here's a later one,' he told her.

The second letter was sent from another address in Devon — a small village that Rose had never heard of. The date was seven months after the first:

Dear Mr Edgcombe,

I am now at the above address. Financially I am in great difficulty, and wonder if you would ask my husband to offer something in the way of help. I know it is unlikely, but matters are somewhat desperate. I owe a month's rent and am unable to find employment. Just a few pounds would see me through, and I will repay every penny once I find a residential position. I have one interview in ten days' time and will inform you of the outcome.

The letter surprised her. It was well written in a clear hand, suggesting an educated woman. The tone indicated a proud woman to whom begging for help would be anathema. She had even offered to repay the money.

'And did he send her any money?' she asked aloud.

'I don't know that either,' he confessed.

Rose looked at him, puzzled. 'Doesn't it seem

strange that a woman would desert her family and then write asking for help? Surely if she was planning to abandon her husband and child, she would at least have made some kind of provision for her upkeep before leaving? Did she find a residential position, I wonder.' She regarded James Edgcombe through eyes brimming with tears. 'It's so frustrating. Nothing but glimpses. All I know is that she left here with someone and was alone before the year was out. Poor Mama.' Her lips quivered and the tears ran in earnest.

James Edgcombe handed her a handkerchief and patted her arm consolingly. 'Please don't distress yourself,' he begged. 'Remember that whatever agonies she suffered they are all in the past. It was a long time ago. She might be wonderfully happy now.'

'And she might not!' Rose blew her nose and stowed the handkerchief in her coat pocket. 'I'm sorry. That was foolish.' She gave him a watery smile. 'Is there anything else?'

'Not in this file, but I'll talk to my father when he gets back. There may be another file. Probably is. I'll find out whatever I can and bring you any new information.' He smiled. 'Any excuse to visit you again!'

Rose, engrossed in her own thoughts, smiled dutifully in return as she stood up. 'I must be getting back. I have a difficult task waiting for me. I have to reprimand one of the girls, and I'm dreading it.'

He rolled his eyes. 'A *reprimand?* What did she do?'

Rose decided not to advertise the girl's escapade. The fact that she had succeeded in her nocturnal ramblings was hardly good publicity for the school. 'The usual with girls of that age,' she hedged. 'Flouting discipline.'

As they rode back to Tye Rock House he suggested, 'I could collect your Mr Tremayne from the hospital if you like. I'm not busy today, and I like to make myself useful.'

Rose found the idea disconcerting. 'You're very kind, but there's no need. I shall send Robb. He loves driving the trap. Second only to his vegetables is Clipper, his favourite horse. I sometimes suspect that the animal gets more than his rightful share of the carrots we grow — not to mention the time he spends grooming him.'

'Robb is the gardener?'

'Gardener-cum-handyman-cum-groom!' She laughed. 'He's very strong and he works like a horse. He's been with us for six or seven years. Slow but sure, that's Robb, and he has a way with plants. Strange, because his father and brother were fishermen in days gone by, but the family seem to have gone downhill. The father took to drink, the boat had to be sold and the brother sells fish on the beach.'

'Robb sounds like a useful man to have around.'

They turned off the lane and drove up to the front door. James Edgcombe jumped down from

110

the trap and hurried round to help Rose.

She said, 'Thank you for all your help.'

'I'd do anything for you.'

Christina Morgan was still in her room and had had no breakfast. Serve her right, but Rose wasn't intending to starve her into submission. With a hurried wave she watched the young solicitor drive away and then reluctantly made her way indoors.

'Sit down, Chrissie.'

One look at the girl's face was enough. If Rose had expected contrition she would be disappointed. That was not Chrissie's overwhelming emotion. Suppressed anger seemed the most likely, thought Rose, with a sinking heart.

'Miss Vivian, I'm *starving!*'

So, Chrissie had decided that attack was the best form of defence. Perhaps she could learn from the girl. Rose certainly envied her confidence.

'That's part of your punishment,' she said crisply and heard, with horror, an echo of her father. 'That *hurt*, Papa!' she had exclaimed when the ruler bit into her palm. His reply had been engraved on her heart: 'It was meant to hurt. It's part of the punishment.' Looking back, she thought that her humiliation had been the major part. With an effort she returned to the present.

'I want to know where you went, Chrissie, what you did — and whether or not you met anyone last night. I shall be making enquiries and if you lie to me —'

'I told you. I walked in the grounds for some air.' The girl's voice was sulky.

'Around midnight in this weather? You can't expect me to believe that.'

Chrissie shrugged.

Rose counted to ten and tried again. 'You don't seem to understand the gravity of what you did. While you are a pupil at this school we are responsible for your welfare, Chrissie. You might have come to some *harm*.'

'Well, I didn't, so what's all the fuss about?'

'You broke the school rule.'

Chrissie tossed her head. 'The rules are stupid. They ought to be different for the older girls. We ought to be able to have friends outside school whom we can meet.'

'So you were *not* alone? You were meeting a friend.' Rose knew she would have to ask but she dreaded the girl's answer. If it had been a man friend, then *anything* might have happened. She drew a deep breath. If only her father were still alive. He would have known exactly what to do. She was beginning to appreciate just how good a headmaster he had been. Never once had he complained about his onerous duties or resented the time he spent on school matters. In fact he had had very little spare time. His walks and his chess had sufficed. He had never worried her with problems relating to the school, and she had been grateful for that. It had left her with

112

time for her reading and the embroidery she enjoyed so much. Now, she tried to imagine how he would have dealt with Chrissie Morgan. He would have remained calm and unruffled, she decided, but he would have been very strict. He wouldn't have shirked unpleasant measures.

She said, 'So you went out to meet a friend. Was this friend a man?'

Chrissie tossed her head, lips pressed close.

'Was it?'

Still no answer.

'Was it?'

Rose's heart was racing. Chrissie wasn't denying her accusation, so she *had* met a man. How on earth could Rose deal with this? She said, 'You left the school buildings in order to meet a gentleman friend.'

'What if I did?' Chrissie allowed herself a smile of triumph.

Rose knew exactly what the smile meant — that Chrissie had succeeded where Rose had failed. It was meant to be a slap in the face, and it felt exactly that. Rose struggled to retain her composure. Slapping Chrissie's smug face in return would solve nothing.

'I shall need to know his name,' she said.

'I shall never tell you.' The sulky expression returned. 'You can starve me to death, but I won't tell you anything about him.'

Rose said, 'This man was trespassing. I might find it necessary to inform the police.'

'He wasn't trespassing. I invited him. That's not trespass.' Her words were defiant, but Rose thought she detected a small tremor in the voice.

She said, 'That will be for the police to decide. It really depends on what else happened, if anything.'

Suppose Chrissie denied anything more than conversation? Should the matter then be allowed to drop? But suppose the girl was lying? Rose felt sick with worry.

'Chrissie, we are responsible for you. Can't you see the position I'm in? Why can't you —'

'We didn't do anything — anything serious. Is that what you want to hear?' There was a faint flush to her cheeks now. 'Just a kiss or two.'

'And his name?'

'I'm not telling you or anyone else.'

'I'm afraid you may have to. I shall probably have a talk with Sergeant Wylie.'

The colour fled from Chrissie's face but she refused to give an inch. 'My lips are sealed,' she said with an attempt at melodrama.

'Oh, don't be ridiculous!'

But Rose knew when she was beaten. She stood up. 'You can go now, Chrissie,' she said, keeping her voice steady with an effort. 'I shall discuss what's best to be done with Matron, but in the meantime you can go in to lunch and you may resume your lessons. But first you must promise never to do such a thing again.'

'I shan't!' Chrissie jumped to her feet. 'He's in love with me if you must know, and I love him!'

Her face was furious. 'You're just jealous! Well, I won't promise anything and you can't stop me seeing him!'

Rose, humiliated by the suggestion that she was jealous, thought bitterly that two whacks on the hand with a ruler might have brought Chrissie Morgan to her senses, but she didn't seriously consider that an option. The vague suspicion that perhaps she *did* envy the girl was an uncomfortable one. On the other hand Chrissie was very headstrong, but she had been placed in the care of Tye Rock House School. Rose *was* responsible for her well-being, and in spite of their recent clash she was beginning to feel a glimmer of sympathy. Chrissie Morgan was almost a woman and the attentions of a young man must be exciting.

She said, 'For your own sake, you must be stopped, Chrissie.' She thought frantically. 'If you refuse to be reasonable, we may decide to lock you in your room after "lights out". I shall also write to your parents today informing them of your outrageous behaviour.' Suddenly all her good intentions deserted her and she longed to be rid of the girl. She heard herself say, 'And I shall also write to your grandmother in Hertfordshire, to ask her to take you home temporarily. A — a suspension while I decide what to do and discuss your case with the rest of the staff.' She drew a deep breath and added, 'You may be expelled. Have I made myself clear?'

Chrissie was very pale. 'I don't care if I am expelled!' she told Rose with a toss of her head. 'I don't want to stay in this awful place a moment longer than I have to!'

Without waiting to be dismissed she turned, rushed out of the room and slammed the door violently behind her. Rose, shaken, sat down heavily and put her head in her hands. She had *not* handled the girl at all well, she decided, and cursed her lack of experience. Perhaps, in view of what had happened, it would have been better if her father *had* allowed her more involvement in the running of the school. But that was only obvious with hindsight, since his early death could not have been anticipated. She sat back in the chair and let out a long breath. She had failed the first test, she thought, discouraged. How many more mistakes would she make? The prospect terrified her, and for the first time it occurred to her that she might sell the school.

'And to the first bidder!' she muttered and managed only a thin smile.

Later that afternoon Rose sent Robb in to Helston to bring back Mark Tremayne. Then she settled to her next task — writing a letter to Daneside School. This private school, on the far side of Helston, was for younger children, but they sent a few girls to Tye Rock House each year. Rose knew that her father had been in touch with them on a number of occasions, and found a note in his diary which included the address and the name of the headmistress.

Dear Miss Playden,

You have probably heard by now of the untimely death of my father, George Vivian, in an accident. We are all deeply shocked, but I am endeavouring to manage in his absence. Naturally my long-term plans for Tye Rock House will have to be considered once the funeral is over and the final position is clear. In the short term I am without a teacher for mathematics and geography, and am writing to you in the hope that you can help.

I shall be advertising the vacant post in the educational press for a summer term appointment. Meanwhile, I wondered if your own teacher in these subjects might be free to give us a few hours each week on a part-time basis. This would only be with your approval, naturally. If this seems a possibility we could meet to discuss the matter. If not, I will try elsewhere.

I would appreciate an early reply as the situation here is difficult and I myself am somewhat unskilled in the matter of school management. I should be grateful for any help or advice you can give me.

Yours truly . . .

Rose reread it, made a few minor changes, wrote a fair copy and signed it. She kept the original for reference later if the help from Daneside did not materialise.

She slipped it into an envelope and added a stamp. Sitting back, she felt rather pleased with herself. After her unsuccessful confrontation with Chrissie Morgan it was a relief to feel that she had done something right. A part-time teacher would solve one of her problems.

Five minutes later she had written a second letter enclosing brief but succinct copy, advertising the post as permanent. When that, too, was ready for posting she drew a long breath. Glancing at the clock she realised that Robb would be at the hospital. Before long he and Mark Tremayne would be back. His return to Tye Rock House, however welcome, would present her with another problem. As the only permanent male member of staff she was tempted to ask for his support, but he had been at the school for a shorter time than any of the others. He was also younger. He might well be able to assist her, but the move could well be misconstrued, even resented, by the rest of the staff. It might solve one problem only to create another.

From his perch in the gig, Robb watched with a sour expression as the wounded hero made his farewells to the doctor's wife. Tremayne (Robb wouldn't grant him the 'Mr') was making the most of it, he thought, and his frown deepened. His left ankle was bandaged, Robb noticed, and a few scratches and bruises decorated his face. As he crossed the forecourt to the waiting vehicle

118

he was limping. Putting it on, most likely, Robb told himself. Tremayne reached the gig, smiled at Robb and waited for some assistance. Robb averted his eyes and waited in silence as his passenger clambered awkwardly aboard.

'All set then?' he asked and, without waiting for a reply, cracked his whip over the horse which tossed its head and broke into a leisurely trot.

After a few miles Tremayne felt obliged to break the silence.

'Very pleasant woman — the doctor's wife. Very kind.'

'You reckon?'

'Yes.'

Typical. Thinks about nothing but women. Robb marked him down again. And he'd best keep away from Polly . . .

'A very kindly soul.'

Robb said, 'Fell down the cliff, then, the pair of you?' Silly buggers, he thought scornfully. Should have looked where they were going.

'Yes, we did. Nasty business. Very sad.' After a pause he added, 'Poor Mr Vivian.'

'I was telling my brother.'

'Oh yes?'

' 'Cos he knows you.'

Tremayne glanced sideways at him. 'Your brother knows me? Does he?'

'And you know him. You and Mr Vivian that was.'

Robb failed to see what a girl like Polly saw in a man like Tremayne. In Robb's eyes, a real man

119

— a *manly* man — was rather like Robb himself, with a strong body, broad shoulders and a mop of dark hair. Tremayne was a very different kettle of fish. Fine pale hair that flopped over his grey eyes, a face like a girl and a weedy body. He wasn't even very tall. When he smiled he reminded Robb of a puppy waiting to be petted.

'I don't think so, Robb.'

He wasn't smiling now. He was thinking, probably remembering what had happened. Robb knew that he had suffered and tried to feel kindly towards him, but it was difficult now that he knew Polly fancied him.

'You do know him. You bid him a "Good evening" more'n once. On the beach. Selling fish — that'd be him.'

Tremayne turned to him. 'That chap is your brother?' He looked surprised.

'Aye, that's my brother Tom. Fisherman all his life.'

There was another silence, broken when Robb shouted, 'Come up, you lazy animal!' and cracked his whip again. He meant nothing by it, though. The whip-cracking was intending to impress Tremayne. Clipper, the horse, was getting on in years and moved at his own stolid pace. Robb, who loved the horse, would never dream of trying to hurry him. He liked horses better than people. Not like Poll. She was scared of them. She had funny ideas, that girl. Scared of horses and fancied Tremayne. He shook his head. Women! He never had understood them

120

— not that he'd ever tried.

He glanced at the man next to him. Tremayne had crossed his arms across his chest to keep himself warm but Robb didn't offer the rug. Not up to him to mollycoddle the man.

Tremayne asked, 'So how's Tye Rock House? Still standing, I hope?'

'Was when I left it.'

'Hasn't burned down then!' He smiled.

If the man thought that was funny, Robb didn't. He said, 'Not that I've noticed.'

Pansy. The word suddenly came to him. That was the word for Tremayne, he decided. What Cook called 'a ladies' man'. The whole trouble was that it wasn't only doctors' wives who found him irresistible. Polly had taken a shine to him as well. He tried to remember exactly what she had said about him . . .

'Right up her street!' he said aloud. Yes, that was her exact words. Or something like that.

Tremayne said, 'What's that you say?'

'Nothing!' In fact Robb wanted to say quite a lot, but he didn't dare. Miss Vivian also seemed to like the man, and Robb didn't want to lose his job. 'Right up her street.'

And she'd said she *fancied* him! Huh! Fancied this pansy fellow who was sitting next to him, all shivery, hugging himself to keep warm. Poor devil couldn't stand a bit of fresh air. He sighed. He could just imagine the fuss they'd all make of him at the school, with his bandage and his limp. He glanced at his companion and saw that he had closed his eyes. Suddenly the glimmer of an idea crept into his head. As it grew, he smiled to himself. Then, without warning, he brought his whip down across the horse's back. Startled, poor Clipper leaped forward and broke into a resentful canter. Beside Robb, Tremayne was thrown backwards off the seat and fell into the well of the trap. His anguished cry was music to Robb's ears.

CHAPTER FOUR

Two days later, on Monday morning, Chrissie Morgan made her way down to breakfast. As she approached the dining room she heard the noise grow and knew that she must be one of the last to arrive. The realisation pleased her. Since her brush with Miss Vivian she had done her utmost to show, in small ways, her utter disregard for the school and its rules. She pushed open the door and went in. She held her head high, aware of the many glances from other girls, all of whom seemed to have heard of her escapade and no doubt admired and envied her. The worst that could happen was expulsion and that would be a relief, she told herself. Her grandmother wasn't fit enough to care for a grandaughter full time, so Chrissie would have to travel out to India to join her parents. She would write to dearest Papa and give her own version of the story and he would forgive her. She had another letter from him in the pocket of her skirt and she patted it for reassurance.

Chrissie surveyed the familiar scene. A large panelled room arranged with long tables for the girls and a smaller round table for the staff. The air throbbed as usual with dozens of voices and the clatter of cutlery. Maud and Polly scurried from table to table, clearing plates and replenishing where necessary. It was eight o'clock and barely light outside, so all the gaslights were lit, casting a soft light over the proceedings. Maud disappeared with a trolley loaded with crockery. Polly hurried past her with a jug in either hand.

Chrissie settled herself in her seat next to Lucy and glanced towards the staff table. Miss Hock was pouring tea. Mam'selle was getting up to leave, folding her napkin and easing it back into its ring. There was no sign of Miss Vivian, Chrissie was pleased to note. She waited for Polly to bring a plate of porridge. When it came it was almost cold, but Chrissie knew that was her own fault for being so late.

Lucy said, 'Where were you?'

Chrissie heaped her porridge with sugar but found the milk jug empty. Opposite her Sarah said, 'We thought you weren't coming, so we used it all.'

'Thanks very much!' Chrissie waved her hand and, catching Polly's eye, mouthed 'milk' and sat back to wait.

Lucy asked again, 'Where did you get to?'

Down the middle of the table plates of bread and racks of toast were rapidly being emptied by hungry scholars. Jam and marmalade were also available. While she was waiting for more milk, Chrissie buttered a slice of toast and spread marmalade. After a couple of mouthfuls she leaned closer to Lucy.

124

'I was arranging for a letter to go to Jerry!'

Lucy gasped. 'You did *what?* Chrissie, are you mad?'

As Polly arrived with a smaller jug of milk, Chrissie busied herself with the porridge.

Lucy gave her arm a pinch. '*Chrissie!* Tell me!'

Chrissie smiled. Deliberately aggravating her friend, she finished her porridge before answering. At last she whispered, 'I bribed Robb to take my note.'

Lucy clapped a hand to her mouth. 'Robb? You *didn't!* Oh, Chrissie! Suppose he tells?'

'Why should he? I gave him a sixpence and promised him another if he brings me a reply.'

'But he'll be dismissed if he's caught!'

Chrissie shrugged. 'That's not for me to worry about. If he's stupid enough to get caught . . .' She reached for more toast.

'But you know what he's like,' Lucy protested. 'Not a deep thinker. And what about you? If he's caught he'll tell on you for sure. Not out of malice but because they'll drag it out of him.'

'I can't be in more trouble than I am already. If stupid Rosadora wants to expel me I'll say, "Thank you very much, Miss!" I don't want to stay at Tye Rock House a moment longer than I have to.'

Lucy sighed, then she grinned. 'What did it say — the note?'

'That's my business, Lucy Unwin. Don't be so nosy!'

'Chrissie! You beast!'

Both girls collapsed into loud giggles, bringing a warning look from Miss Hock.

'Silly old fool!' muttered Chrissie. She leaned a little closer. 'Actually I've told him I'm being kept in and if he wants to see me he'll have to come out here. I've told him which is my room —'

'You mean *our* room!'

'I daren't use the dining room again, so when he throws a pebble up to the window I'll go down the fire escape and —'

'Chrissie Morgan! You *mustn't!*'

'Well, if I don't go down to him, he'll have to come up to me.'

Lucy frowned and bit her lip. 'What are you going to allow?' she whispered. 'You know what might happen. He might make you have a . . .' She lowered her voice further. 'A *baby.*'

Chrissie felt a shiver of apprehension. 'Of course I won't allow *that.*'

'But how will you know if he's — if he's *done* it — whatever it is? You might not notice it happening until it's too late and then . . .'

Her kind face was pinched with worry and Chrissie suddenly wanted to hug her. She was such a good friend. Lots of the girls, jealous of her popularity, would secretly welcome the excitement if something went wrong for her, but Lucy truly cared.

'If the worst happens I'll just jump off a table. That's what my aunt's maid did.' They had discussed these measures many times, among other similar mysteries, but although Chrissie spoke with confidence, she wasn't too sure that it would work in every case and hoped quite desperately that she would never have to try it. She and Lucy had laid elaborate plans for the future. In one of their many forbidden talks after 'lights out' they had agreed between them that Lucy would have a large family and Chrissie would be the elegant, childless godmother who would arrive at the family home from time to time, dispensing expensive presents and worldly advice in equal amounts.

'Please, Chrissie!' Lucy begged. 'Don't do it. Any of it. You'll get into the most dreadful row, and I'll be dragged into it. Miss Vivian will question me — do I know anything about it? You know what a hopeless liar I am. And if my parents —'

'Oh, you baby!' Chrissie laughed. 'What a scaredy cat! Well then, I won't drag you into it but I shall do it. Being with Jerry is so wonderful. He makes me feel like a woman and not a schoolgirl.'

'But you *are* a schoolgirl,' Lucy protested. 'We all are.'

'I may be a schoolgirl in Rosadora's eyes, but Jerry sees me differently.' She lowered her voice theatrically. 'He finds me *desirable*.'

Lucy jumped to her feet. 'Stop it. I don't want to hear any more.'

'Of course you do!'

'No, I *don't!* You're going too far, Chrissie.

You really are, and I don't want to know any of it.'

Chrissie watched her run out of the dining room and fought back her disappointment. Half the fun was sharing it all with Lucy, but now she was backing out. She stood up slowly, screwed up her table napkin and stuffed it into her ring. As she left the room she walked straight-backed and threw Miss Hock a defiant look as she passed the staff table. Chrissie, however, was not quite as reckless as she appeared and desperately needed her friend's approval. Lucy's words had rattled her more than she would admit.

Sergeant Wylie presented himself at the hospital at nine o'clock precisely and made his way reluctantly to the mortuary in the basement. This was a part of his job that he hated. A murder — rare enough thank goodness — was terrible, but even an accident was a grim business. He stood outside the door with his hand raised, delaying his entry by a few more seconds while he arranged his features into an expression of disinterest. It was partly the cold, partly the smell of disinfectant, plus the sight of all those surgical instruments. Knives, saws, metal clips and worse. He had only rarely attended a post mortem and at the first, being young and inexperienced, he had fainted at the first incision. The second time he had stood beside a corpse in this particular mortuary, he had been sick.

He tapped on the door.

'Come in!'

No escape, he thought regretfully, and opened the door.

The pathologist looked up and smiled. 'Morning, Sergeant!'

Ian Hardy was a Scot in his late fifties, thin and wiry and invariably cheerful. His white coat was newly laundered but suspicious-looking traces still remained. Blood, no doubt, the sergeant thought, and hastily averted his glance.

The familiar scene had not improved. A small, barred window was set high in one wall and, facing north, let in a minimum of daylight. A single strong light-bulb under a large shade hung from the middle of the ceiling, casting its unsympathetic light on the room and the trolley beneath it. Shelves revealed bottles and jars containing unrecognisable specimens; cupboards hid unimaginable horrors. A table held trays of instruments. A body, which he presumed was that of George Vivian, lay on the trolley beneath a white cloth, and Sergeant Wylie hoped it would stay that way.

He asked, 'All done? Straightforward, would you say?' He took out his notebook. He was going to have to tread carefully. 'Anything out of the ordinary?' He avoided the other man's eyes.

The pathologist nodded. 'Nothing exciting. Apart from the head there's very little real damage.'

Thank the Lord for small mercies. He took out

a pencil and licked the point. 'Just the bare facts,' he suggested. 'No need to —'

Too late. Hardy whipped back the white sheet and the sergeant stepped back a pace. George Vivian, naked as the day he was born, was revealed, stark and lifeless. The incisions had been roughly stitched with dark thread.

The sergeant tutted. 'Poor fellow. What a way to die,' he murmured.

'Better than a lingering illness, though.'

'I daresay.' He didn't care to dwell on the various possibilities. Heaven might be a beautiful place, as his wife constantly reassured him, but the sergeant was in no hurry to find out for himself.

The pathologist opened a notebook which lay on the small table and thumbed through it. 'It's coming to all of us, I suppose.' He smiled cheerfully.

Sergeant Wylie hoped not. He reminded himself never to walk along the cliffs and, if he did, *never* to lean down after a rare butterfly.

Hardy looked up and, as though reading his thoughts, said, 'Cause of death — butterfly.' He laughed uproariously. 'That'll sound good at the inquest!'

Sergeant Wylie registered silent disapproval. He would remember to crack jokes when Hardy lay on the slab.

Seeing his expression, Hardy said, 'Don't take it too seriously, Sergeant.'

'Let's just get on with it, shall we?'

The pathologist grinned. 'Right then, where

are we? Ah yes! Severe damage to the back of the head. Considerable damage, but then if you fall down a cliff on to a rock you can expect nothing less.'

The sergeant scribbled in his notebook. 'So — he definitely fell?'

The pathologist was no fool. Catching something in the sergeant's voice, he looked up sharply. 'Isn't that what happened?'

'Of course — but I have to be sure. He couldn't have jumped, then?'

'I couldn't tell that from what I've got here. *Jumped?* You mean *suicide?* Are you serious, Sergeant?'

Sergeant Wylie cursed inwardly. Obviously he hadn't been subtle enough. He shrugged. 'Just checking out the possibilities.'

The pathologist was staring at him. 'But *why?* Have you any reason to think so?'

'No, no. At least, none that I know of.' He pursed his lips. Mustn't say too much. 'I've been down to the beach to where it happened. Couldn't quite see it the way it was described.'

'You mean, if he jumped the young man is trying to spare the daughter's feelings?'

'Maybe.'

'What was wrong exactly? I mean, how was it different from what you'd heard?'

The sergeant took a chance. 'This is just between you and me. That clear?'

Hardy looked offended. 'I *am* a professional man, Sergeant!'

131

'Of course. Sorry.' He drew in a long breath. 'The body was a long way out. If he'd simply slithered down the cliff-face, he'd have been nearer the bottom of it. And Tremayne says he moved him *nearer to the cliff* — to avoid the tide taking him out — while he ran for help.'

'Did he now? Hmm.'

'And I saw no marks on the cliff-face. No sign of scrabbling fingers; no sign that a small bush had been pulled from its roots. Nothing much, really, but it doesn't *smell* right.'

They were both silent, thinking.

The pathologist looked helplessly at the corpse as though it might yet reveal something else. 'I don't think I've missed anything,' he said at last. Suddenly his expression changed. 'Could it have been a different kind of accident? Suppose the young chap tripped and *knocked* Vivian over? Then he'd be to blame for the death. Might be facing manslaughter.' Hardy was warming to his theme. 'Tremayne panics and concocts this other story about the butterfly. Once he'd lied, he'd have to stick to his story. Poor chap.'

'Manslaughter? I doubt that would stick. More like "accidental death" . . . But you're right. Some folks would blame him. The daughter, perhaps . . . Hmm.'

Sergeant Wylie narrowed his eyes thoughtfully, wishing he had thought of this himself. It was very feasible. 'It's worth thinking about,' he admitted. 'I must admit that George Vivian would be the last man I'd expect to kill himself.' He made a few more notes, then looked up. 'Well, thanks, anyway. Better get on with it, I suppose.'

Hardy's disappointment showed but he rallied. 'Now where were we, Sergeant?'

'Severe damage to the back of the head.'

'Ah yes . . . How's that wife of yours, Sergeant? Leg still bothering her?'

' 'Fraid so. Still, she's not one to complain. Takes it in her stride.' He smiled. 'No pun intended.'

'Not like some people, then. My sister-in-law loves nothing better than a good moan.' He leaned lower over the corpse. 'Laceration wounds typical of a blow on the head with a blunt instrument. Could have been bludgeoned, but probably wasn't. Depressed wound with ragged edges consistent with a fall on to something hard like a rock . . .' He whistled tunelessly under his breath. 'See that?'

Sergeant Wylie cursed silently but stepped forward. The head wound looked uninspiring — a dark red mass speckled with something unmentionable. The face was grey, skin taut over the bone structure. With a muttered 'Oh yes!' he quickly withdrew.

'Skin, tissue and bone splinters embedded in the brain. Massive blow or blows, but any blood would have been washed away by the sea.' He smiled. 'Lucky he wasn't alone or the tide would have taken him. If there's one thing I hate it's a "floater".' He flipped the page.

Sergeant Wylie hesitated. 'So did he drown, or what?'

'He didn't have a chance to drown. Dead as soon as he entered the water, if not before. Might have been simultaneous. Either he killed himself on the way down or the moment he landed. Can't be more definite. Entered the water and immediately struck his head on a rock. Killed instantly, so no time to suck in salt water. Lucky in a way. I wouldn't choose to drown. Panic, choking, waterlogged lungs.' He shook his head. 'Takes too long, you see. And you *know*. This way you keep hoping you'll somehow survive the fall and you don't, but at least it's *quick*.'

The pathologist resumed his whistling, and this time the sergeant thought he recognised 'Lily of Laguna'.

'Time of death?' he asked.

The pathologist shrugged. 'Not normally so easy when a body's been immersed in freezing sea water — distorts the body temperature — but fortunately we have Mr Tremayne's account. Call it between ten-thirty and eleven-fifteen A.M. Of course, sudden immersion into cold water *might* bring on what we call reflex cardiac arrest, but this was not so in this case. Poor Mr Vivian.' He patted the dead man's shoulder as though to comfort him. 'Amazing, isn't it. The young history master has a couple of free lessons on Friday mornings, the Headmaster feels like a brisk walk to blow away the cobwebs, and what happens? The latter ends up under my

134

knife with the back of his head smashed in!' He covered up the body. 'Do you believe in Fate, Sergeant Wylie?'

'Never thought about it. Wife does, though. It was meant, she told me when her mother fell down the stairs. Her time had come. Lot of nonsense.' He sighed heavily, finished writing and put away notebook and pencil.

Hardy shrugged. 'I try to believe, Sergeant. Makes it all that much easier, you see. No point in struggling against Fate. Might as well enjoy yourself. Throw caution to the wind. When your time's up — that sort of thing.' He laid down his instruments and re-covered George Vivian's head. 'Any more questions? No? Then off you go. I'm expecting my next customer any minute now.' He nodded to the other trolley on which two feet were the only clue to the mound beneath the sheet. 'Mrs Penrose. Son thinks she's been poisoned. What a world!'

'Poisoned? First I've heard about it.'

'You won't. Absolutely no case. Son's a bit . . .' He tapped his head.

'Thank goodness for that.'

As Sergeant Wylie closed the door behind him he snorted. Fate, indeed! The pathologist might throw caution to the winds if he wished, but *he* would continue to hold it close. If he had *his* way, the sergeant would live for ever.

That evening, Rose rang the bell for Maud.
'Yes, ma'am?'

135

Rose shook her head. 'I've asked you to call me Rose, Maud.'

Maud regarded her uncertainly. 'Very well then, ma'am. I'll try to —'

'*Maud!*'

'Oh!'

They both laughed.

'Maud, please tell Mr Tremayne that I'd like to see him. *If* he feels well enough, that is. If not, I could visit him briefly in his room if he is not in bed.'

Maud departed. Rose began to worry about the proprieties of the latter suggestion, but she needed to speak to him. She had to know, for instance, when he would be able to resume his teaching duties.

While she waited, she turned to the timetables on the wall behind her. Tomorrow, Tuesday, the first lesson for the younger girls was mathematics. Since no teacher was free, she herself would have to fill in. The idea terrified her, but perhaps she could give them a test. Somewhere there must be a book with mental arithmetic in it. They could spend half the time doing the tests and the rest marking them. She frowned. Yes, that was an idea. They could swap papers with their neighbours and mark each other's work. That way there would be no cheating. Feeling quite pleased with herself she studied the rest of the day. The older girls had geography last lesson in the afternoon.

'A geography test?' she wondered. What is the

capital of India? Name three countries which lie on the equator. Which ocean separates Great Britain and North America? Hardly. It would take too long to prepare and too short a time to perform. She could also imagine the protests from the girls: 'But, Miss Vivian, we haven't done India.' Perhaps she could bring forward Wednesday's singing lesson? By tomorrow she might be able to think of something geographical which would keep them busy — an essay, perhaps . . . 'If you could live anywhere in the world . . .' That was suitably vague. Instead of marking them all, she could let one or two of the girls read their efforts aloud. Or she could simply cancel it and give the girls free time.

She was still pondering the problem when a knock at the door interrupted her.

'Come in.'

It was Mark Tremayne, looking slightly less frail than when she had last seen him in the hospital.

'Please sit down,' she urged him. 'I hope you don't mind, but I need to talk to someone.'

He leaned forward. 'Miss Vivian, I was going to ask to see *you* if you hadn't sent Maud along to my room. I wanted to offer any help I can. My ankle's a bit painful but I can move around — and my brain still functions! The sudden burden on *you* must be enormous. Quite terrifying, I should imagine.'

His grin was infectious and Rose smiled back at him. 'You're very kind,' she told him. Was he the only member of staff to fully appreciate the difficulties she laboured under, she wondered? 'I have to admit that I am feeling rather lost — with all this.' She waved a hand around the study. 'I wish very much that my father had allowed me to help him more than he did. I know so little of the day-to-day running of the school. There are the assemblies, for a start.'

'Ah! I was wondering about that while I was laid up in Helston.'

Rose was astonished. He had been through a terrible ordeal but had found time to consider *her* problems. Was that because he felt a kind of kinship because of his friendship with her father, or something else? Did it mean he cared for *her*? As a person?

He said, 'Unless you wanted to take the assemblies yourself I was going to suggest that the staff — that is, the permanent staff — take it in turns. I don't see why they should object, and it would mean that no one person held full responsibility. I'm quite prepared to take assembly for a week. Then there's Miss Hock, and probably Mam'selle. Not too heavy a load, really, and they might quite enjoy it.'

Rose nodded. Why hadn't *she* thought of that? It was so simple.

'That's a wonderful idea,' she said. 'Really, I'm impressed.'

She could imagine him standing on the dais, hands together, eyes closed or singing a hymn. If only her father had made him deputy head —

but he was very young.

'But I think *you* should suggest it, Miss Vivian. Don't mention that it was my idea. We don't want anyone taking umbrage.'

'Oh, but is that fair on you, Mr Tremayne?'

'Of course it is. I simply want to help in any way I can. I was a great admirer of your father and, if I may say so, I feel the same about his daughter.'

Rose, her heart thumping, said, 'Thank you' and hoped she wasn't blushing. To help her through her confusion, she gave his suggestion some thought. Then she said, 'Yes, we'll do that. I think we'll call a staff meeting for tomorrow evening, after prep. Talk things over.' She regarded him earnestly. 'I'm sure they're all convinced that I can't manage this, but I do want to try. For the moment, at least. I haven't made any long-term plans. It's been so sudden.'

He smiled. 'From what I hear, you're doing very well so far.'

'Oh, I do hope so. I don't want to upset anyone. I need the staff's support.' As she looked into his kind grey eyes she felt a sudden need to confide in him further.

'There's also been something of a problem, Mr Tremayne, with Chrissie Morgan.'

The words tumbled out and he listened attentively as she explained. When she had finished she said breathlessly, 'I still don't know if I've done the right thing. If anything happens to that girl . . .'

He gave her a reassuring smile. 'I don't think there's any other way you could have handled it,' he told her. 'Your father would have had no option but to confine her to school and inform the parents. Bringing in the police would probably have made matters worse.'

She leaned towards him. 'To tell you the truth, Mr Tremayne, I shan't be sorry to see the back of her. Miss Hock thinks she's a bad influence on the other girls and although I hate to think the worst of anyone — I'm sure there's a lot that's good in her — Miss Hock saw Chrissie and Lucy with their heads together at breakfast this morning. I can't help suspecting that there is more trouble ahead. I'd be grateful if you would keep your ears open and let me know if you hear anything. I don't want to bring in the police — she's committed no crime — but if she is getting out of control I don't know how . . .' She broke off, making a helpless gesture with her hands. 'I don't need that kind of trouble at the moment. I have so much to think about.'

He nodded. 'I'll keep my ear to the ground,' he promised. 'But what about your father's funeral? Are you able to go ahead with that?'

'The police are waiting for the post mortem report and then the coroner's verdict. I have spoken to the undertakers and the vicar, and Thursday or Friday are possibilities.' She sighed and leaned back wearily in her chair. 'It's so strange without Father. I find myself about to speak to him; to ask his advice. Sitting here in his chair seems so presumptuous somehow. He'd have hated it, and yet I have to step into his shoes, temporarily at least.'

His expression changed and he looked at her rather strangely. 'I don't know if I should ask this, but do you know what is in your father's will? Did he ever tell you?'

Rose shook her head. 'Not a word.' She picked up a letter opener and twisted it nervously. 'I'll be frank with you, Mr Tremayne. There is someone else in my father's life — someone to whom he might have left a share of Tye Rock House. I can't explain — at least, I'd rather not explain for the moment. So I have no idea what plans he made for the school.'

'If he made any. He wasn't expecting to make plans just yet. What I mean is, his death was untimely. He may have thought there was plenty of time to make that kind of decision. You disagree?'

Rose was shaking her head. 'Papa was very meticulous. Very cautious in all his dealings. I think he would have made *some* plans, but I have yet to speak with the Edgcombes. They are our solicitors and James Edgcombe . . .' She hesitated, longing for Mr Tremayne to know that she had a suitor. 'Mr Edgcombe is a close friend,' she told him. '*Very* close.' She hoped he was wild with jealousy, but dared not look at him.

To her delight he asked, 'How close is very close?'

141

She now risked a glance, but his expression was unreadable. His voice, however, sounded a little tense. *Was* he jealous? 'We've known each other all our lives. I rely on him for advice.'

'I had hoped you would rely on me, Miss Vivian.' He threw up his hands in mock despair. 'I see I am out of luck.'

'Oh no! Quite the contrary, Mr Tremayne.' She didn't want to lose his support. 'I value your help tremendously. Mr Edgcombe has no knowledge of the running of the school; no understanding of the problems of organisation or management of the pupils. I shall be only too willing to ask you for guidance.' That sounded a little too lacking in confidence so she added, 'Even if the final decisions will have to be mine.'

Again that impenetrable expression.

She went on, 'It was not my father's way to leave matters to chance. I'm sure you discovered that for yourself, Mr Tremayne, on your many walks together. He obviously said nothing to you about the future?'

'About the school? Good Lord, no! He didn't choose to take me into his confidence, more's the pity. I'm completely in the dark.'

There was a long silence. He was leaning forward with his elbows on the desk, his hands clasped tightly in front of him. It was a very obvious hint, she thought, that she should take him fully into *her* confidence, but instead of considering this Rose noticed how dark and long his lashes were. He was slim and fair with elegant hands. His face was unlined as yet, and his well-shaped mouth made her wonder what it would be like to be kissed by him. She swallowed, feeling intuitively that he was well aware of the effect his good looks had upon women and might well guess at her thoughts. To distract herself, she found herself comparing him with James Edgcombe who was what Maud would call 'built for comfort'. He was also older. But that was so unfair. She felt horribly disloyal and ashamed of her comparisons. James Edgcombe was not unattractive, he was as honest as the day was long and would make any woman a good husband. Any *other* woman, she corrected herself, and then felt worse. He *loved* her and she was going to disappoint him with her answer.

Seeing that her companion was still waiting, she said quickly, 'I've advertised the post of geography and mathematics teacher. The trouble is, I don't know what salary my father paid — I'll have to check with the bank — or else find his account book of course. Oh dear! You must think me very foolish, but I haven't had time to deal with that yet. There's so much to do. To be perfectly frank, Mr Tremayne, it's a bit of a nightmare.' She was horrified to hear that her voice shook slightly.

'I do understand, Miss Vivian, believe me. I too have my nightmare. I ask myself again and again if I did all I could when —' He drew in a sharp breath. 'I ought to have saved him and I didn't. I dream about it every night and wake up sweating and terrified. And every time I go through it again. I didn't save your father, and you must surely blame me for that.'

'Oh *no!*' cried Rose, shocked out of her own troubles. Impulsively she reached across the desk to put her hand over his and felt an unfamiliar thrill. 'I haven't blamed you for an instant. You must believe me. How could I even think such a thing?'

They were so close. Abruptly she drew back her hand but his eyes did not waver. To save herself she forced her gaze away — to his clasped hands. Slim hands with nice wrists — the latter covered with fine downy hair.

'I'm sorry . . .' she stammered.

He said gently, 'Have I upset you, Miss Vivian?'

'Oh no. Certainly not.'

She was angry with herself. She must not behave like a weak woman — and she most certainly must *not* think about Mark Tremayne. At least, not in his presence. Once she was safely within the confines of her own room she would replay every word that had passed between them. Now, however, to hide her agitation, she swung round in her chair and began to talk very quickly about the changes she was making to the timetable.

When she stopped he said, 'That all sounds very sensible. Shall I tell the others for you?'

'Thank you. Yes.' She avoided his eyes, afraid to see from his expression that he had understood her confusion.

'If you feel you would like a little help with the interviews I'd be very willing to sit in on them,' he offered. 'Not to intervene, of course, but to offer moral support.'

'But the rest of the staff?'

'Need they know?'

She thought about it and liked the idea of the small conspiracy. 'I'll let you know,' she said at last, 'but I appreciate the offer.'

He stood up. 'I'm beginning to feel rather tired now, but I'll be ready tomorrow morning. I hope you'll allow me back into the classroom.'

It would make everything so much easier, she thought. 'Are you sure you're well enough?'

'Try to stop me!' He laughed. 'May I go now?'

'Of course! And thank you — for everything.'

At the door he paused. 'And in spite of everything that's happened — your father's death, I mean — we're still . . . friends?'

'Yes, of course we are!' she assured him.

She wanted to add that she hoped they would eventually be more than friends, but she bit back the impossible words. The door closed behind him and Rose listened to his retreating footsteps.

When she sat down again she was surprised to discover that she was actually smiling.

Although Rose knew that it had to be done, the task of searching through her father's desk seemed at best intrusive. The Headmaster's study had always been forbidden territory to all

145

except Maud, who was allowed to dust and sweep as long as she refrained from moving anything. Rose had never been encouraged to loiter longer than necessary and she vaguely remembered an occasion when her grandmother had been taken to task for removing the curtains for washing without prior permission.

As she turned the key in the lock of the bureau, Rose felt that at any moment her father's hand would fall heavily and deliberately upon her shoulder.

'Don't be ridiculous, Rose!' she muttered.

Behind her the grandfather clock struck eight. The girls had finished their prep, and were now free to enjoy the rest of the evening in suitable ways. The teaching staff were also free now. Only the kitchen staff were still working, washing up the supper things and resetting the tables for tomorrow's breakfast. Had her father still been alive he would have been reading from his Bible, studying the chess board or staring into the fire, deep in thought. Rose would have been busy with her embroidery or practising the following day's hymns on the piano. All that was now gone. Swept away by a moment's carelessness. She found herself wondering about his spirit. It was said that the souls of those who died violent deaths were likely to hover in the vicinity of their homes. She shuddered. If her father's ghost were nearby, she didn't want to even think about it.

Rose shook off the uneasy thoughts and concentrated on the task in hand. She was fairly sure that she could carry out her search without interruption. Pulling up a chair, she stared at the bureau's contents and wondered where to begin. One small drawer contained a pile of invoices, ready to be sent out towards the end of the term. They either requested payment in advance for the next term and for any extras that had been arranged or, couched in stronger language, insisted that overdue fees *must* be paid within one calendar month. She was surprised to see that Lucy Unwin's parents would receive one of the latter, but she skipped through the rest of them and pushed them back into the drawer. On a small pad, she made a note to send them off on the appropriate date. *If* they were still applicable. *If* the school was to continue. There were a great many decisions to be made in the next few weeks.

The next drawer offered a selection of bills from local tradesmen — the butcher, baker, fishmonger, dairy. She frowned. A few were unpaid, and the butcher's bill went back five weeks. Rose swallowed hard. She hoped she wasn't going to discover money problems on top of everything else.

'Please, *no!*' she whispered. Her father had never given the slightest hint that Tye Rock House might have problems of a financial nature. And maybe it wasn't so. Maybe her father had had the money but was a reluctant payer. She would have a quiet word with the cook in the morning and see if she could shed any light on the matter of the tradesmen's bills. Delving further into the bureau's recesses, Rose discovered bank statements, cheque books, and a few letters from parents. The latter had been ticked, so presumably they had been answered. Rose dipped into them at random. There was one from Kenya asking that the daughter be excused tennis during 'those certain times' of the month. Another from an anxious mother who felt that her daughter's letters home were not as well written as they should be. Rose pursed her lips. How on earth had her father dealt with all these queries?

At the end of half an hour Rose realised that the bureau contained only material that was of current interest. Carefully she returned all the papers and closed and locked the bureau. If she was going to find out anything about her mother, she would have to look elsewhere. That probably meant her father's bedroom, and she made her way up the stairs with something akin to dread. If her father's spirit were to be anywhere in the house, it would be there.

The room smelled strongly of mothballs and mildew and she quickly saw the reason for the latter. The small fire grate was devoid of coal or ash and had not housed a fire for many years. There was no coal-scuttle and no tongs. The bedroom must have been a cold, damp place in which to try and sleep. He had denied himself a basic comfort, had possibly put his health at risk

— although she could never recall him being ill.

'Papa!' she murmured. 'Why?'

Had he *chosen* to live such a spartan existence, she wondered uneasily. Was he punishing himself and, if so, what did he imagine he had done that was so frightful?

A glance inside the large wardrobe showed two suits and three pairs of boots stuffed with newspaper. The drawer beneath produced a shoe box which contained a few yellowing papers and a single envelope. The latter she removed and placed on the bed. A quick look in the chest of drawers revealed shirts, collars and underwear in neat piles in the lower drawers. Scarves, gloves and socks were in the top drawer, with a clothes brush and a box containing a pair of cufflinks she had never seen before. A present from her mother, she wondered, fingering them reverently.

She carried the envelope to the bed and sat down, trying to decipher the postmark. It had faded with the years, however, and she gave up, turning instead to the letter inside. Slowly, hardly daring to breathe, Rose read it. Written in a clear hand on cheap notepaper, it was short and unbearably poignant:

My dear George,

You have never answered any of my letters. Maybe you have destroyed them. If so, I pray that you read them first. This is just to wish you a happy birthday from the two of us. I know I have wronged you and do not deserve to be forgiven, but I beg you to reconsider your attitude towards the child. Don't punish the child, George.

If you can find it in your heart to do so, please write to me at this address. Miss Folkes knows my situation and is willing that you should visit me here with little Rose. Please, George.

All my love to my darling little girl. I miss her so much. Tell her I love her.

Your dutiful wife,
Catherine . . .

Shocked, Rose stared at the letter; '. . . my darling little girl'. Her mother had called her 'my darling little girl' and had told her father to pass on a message to her. 'Tell her I love her.'

'Oh God, Mama!' The words burst from her as simultaneously tears burst from her eyes. Her mother *hadn't* stopped loving her. Tears of relief mingled with rage against her father. He had never told her that her mother loved and missed her; had never reassured her in any way. He had allowed her — no, he had *encouraged* her — to believe that her mother had walked away from them without a moment's regret. He had never given Rose a moment's hope, so that she had grown up believing herself unlovable. As the tears streamed down her face she gulped mouthfuls of air and tried to calm herself.

'She *loved* me!' she whispered with incredible

joy. 'My mother *missed* me!'

For a long time she gave herself up to the confused emotions which the letter had provoked, but at last she stopped crying and dried her eyes. Suddenly she was aware of a great lightening of her heart. In a strange way the tears had washed away some of her insecurities. She felt stronger and her new-found freedom seemed less of a threat and more of a promise. She blinked hard and sat up straighter on the bed.

So who was Miss Folkes, she wondered, who understood her mother's situation and was obviously sympathetic? Perhaps Maud knew something. She stared around her father's bedroom which was so much larger than her own and now untenanted. Was there any reason, she wondered, why *she* should not move into it? Would it show disrespect for the dead? Should she care? She was so angry with him. Would her father expect it to remain empty? If so, then she would move into it. With new curtains, a better rug and a good fire it would be wonderfully comfortable and immeasurably preferable to her own small room.

'Tomorrow,' she promised herself, delighted with the idea. It was the least of her worries, but she would begin the alterations as soon as she could find the time. But meanwhile there were things to be done. On impulse, she ran downstairs to her father's study and rang for Maud. Surely Maud, who had listened at so many doors, must know *something* of what had happened all those years ago. Rose, if she had ever known anything of the events, had blotted it almost completely from her memory. Only vague flashes returned to her in dreams, involving fear and grief and a deep sense of loss.

By the time the knock came at the door she had composed herself. Her red eyes would betray her but Maud, she knew, would say nothing.

'Come in and sit down, please,' she said.

Maud sank wearily on to a chair.

Rose looked at her and was startled to see how old she looked. How old *was* she, she wondered, and a moment's panic filled her. Maud, her dearest Dodie, was the last person who had ever been close to her; one of the few people who had shown her affection during those long, lonely years; who had put up with her childish tantrums and comforted her on numerous occasions. Rose couldn't imagine a time when there would be no Dodie. While she was growing up there had been real affection between them but over the years, as she grew older, George Vivian had created what he considered a 'suitable distance' between the two women. Rose was the Headmaster's daughter, he had explained, and Maud was no longer family but a member of the kitchen staff. She was no longer a nanny and Rose must refrain from the little confidences they had once shared. Rose had protested, but her father had obviously discussed this with Maud herself and eventually he

152

had achieved the coolness he desired.

Rose drew a deep breath. No beating about the bush, she told herself. Get straight to the point. 'I believe you were here, Maud, when my mother left?'

Maud's expression changed and Rose could see that this was the last question she had expected. Or wanted.

'Yes, I was.'

'You must understand, Maud, that I know nothing of the reason behind her sudden departure and I have never been able to ask my father. It was a forbidden subject.'

'It was for all of us, Rose.'

The name slipped out and Rose noted it with pleasure. It was as though, with the death of her father, some of the constraints were weakening. 'So now,' she went on. 'I suddenly feel able to discover the truth. Will you tell me all you can remember?'

She smiled. 'Including anything you may have learned which perhaps you were not supposed to know.'

Maud had the grace to colour slightly.

Rose said quickly. 'I'm only teasing.'

Maud nodded, but hesitated. 'I don't know quite where to start.'

'Tell me when you first knew that my mother was leaving. And don't hold anything back, Maud. I can bear anything except lies and half-truths — which is all I've had so far.' For some reason that she didn't fully understand, Rose didn't mention her mother's letter. 'Just tell me in your own way. There's no hurry.'

Maud frowned. 'Well, it was all rather sudden. Took us all by surprise, as you might say. One day everything seemed fine — well, sort of fine. I mean they never did seem a very happy couple, if you don't mind my saying so.' She looked at Rose anxiously. 'I don't want to upset you.'

'That's all right, Maud. I want to know everything.'

'Well, they didn't shout and carry on but they weren't . . . close. That's the word.'

Rose nodded. She wondered how anyone could have been close to her father, who had mastered the art of keeping those he loved at a polite distance.

Maud went on. 'I heard the mistress crying just after breakfast, and the master was shouting, "You want to betray me — after all I've done for you! There's no other way to say it. You'd humiliate me in the eyes of the world and for that man!" ' She looked anxiously at Rose. 'They may not have been his exact words, but —'

'*That man?* Who was she talking about?'

Maud said nothing.

'Which man, Maud?' She waited, but when it became obvious that she was not going to get an answer she sighed. 'Go on, then.'

'Your mama said something I couldn't catch and he shouted, "No! You leave the child with me. Go! Get out of my sight!" ' Maud looked quickly at Rose. 'I couldn't make head nor tail of it, and that's the truth. Then your ma said, "I'm begging you for one more chance," and he said, "And I'm refusing it!" '

'Refusing it?' Rose was aware of a terrible coldness.

'Yes. Then she said something about you — about "my little girl" — and he said, "She's my daughter now." '

'Now?'

Maud shrugged. 'I don't know what he meant.' She stared at her hands which twisted in her lap.

Rose could hardly breathe. 'You mean I was adopted?'

'Oh no! I was there when you were born. In this very house.' She clasped her hands together. 'We was never told, but I think — that is we all suspected — oh dear! I hardly like to say.'

Rose felt her heart thudding. 'Say it, Maud.'

'That there was another man, and the master found out.'

Rose was stunned into silence. Another man? For a moment or two her thoughts swirled chaotically. Her mother and *another man?* Was it possible? Of all the things she might have imagined, this was the only one she had never considered.

Her voice was shaking. 'She ran off with another man? Is that what you're saying? She just . . . left us.'

'Well, not exactly, no. She didn't want to leave *you.* She wanted to take you, but your father

155

wouldn't let her. He called her terrible things. It was awful. Dreadful. Poor thing. When she left for the station she was so white I thought she'd faint. She was —'

Rose could hardly bear the thought of her mother's anguish. 'Maud! Wait! Do you know anything about this other man?'

Maud drew a long breath. 'Are you sure you want to know? It's all in the past —'

'Of course I want to know! I told you, I want the whole truth and no lies. No evasions. Who was he, Maud?'

'He was one of the bank tellers in Helston. He was unmarried, that much I do know. Very attractive. Very charming. *I'd* have fancied him and that's the truth.'

Rose stared. 'You *knew* this man?'

Maud avoided her gaze. 'I went into the bank once, to see for myself. You see, there were rumours in Helston after they left. I wanted to —'

Rose cried, '*They?* You mean they left *together?* My mother and this man from the bank?' She felt her heart race. Somewhere she had a mother and stepfather of sorts. She thought of the letter she had found and the reference to 'the two of us'. She frowned. Had she actually dared to send her father good wishes from the two of them? It didn't sound very likely.

Maud said, 'Well, I don't know about "together" but when your mother left, the bank teller disappeared. On the same day. People put two and two together — you know how it is.'

Rose was speechless, dazed by so many revelations. And all this knowledge had been available to her for all these years, but she had been too in awe of her father to seek it out. Suppose Maud had left — or *died?* Without Maud she might never have known the truth.

Maud drew a deep breath. 'The fact is that your father is a . . . was a very proper man. Difficult to live with, I shouldn't wonder. Not given to showing affection, if you see what I mean, and a wife does need some little sign to say that she's loved. What I'm trying to say is you shouldn't think too harshly of your mother. Although she did wrong, breaking the commandments and suchlike, you couldn't properly blame her. Leastways, you could but . . .'

Rose nodded without speaking.

Maud continued, 'Some men don't understand women. We fall in love, and it sort of sweeps you along. You don't know whether you're coming or going. You're that moithered.'

Rose caught something in her tone. 'Were you ever in love, Maud? Like that, I mean.'

Maud nodded. 'Head over heels, but I was very young. Such a lovely man, but he was married and hardly noticed me. Then he got himself killed. Shot by a gamekeeper. All for the sake of a couple of rabbits.'

'I'm so sorry.' For a moment Rose quite forgot her own circumstances. All these years Maud had been in the background of her life, and she had never known that she had had her own tragedy.

Maud shrugged. 'Love does funny things to people, Rose. You'll maybe learn that for yourself one of these days.'

Rose wondered what Maud would say if she knew that quiet little Rose Vivian was in love with Mr Tremayne.

Maud shook her head. 'Your mother paid a terrible price for loving the man because she lost you. Mind you, she did her very best to see you again. She wrote and wrote, but he never answered. Whenever a letter came your father would be in a rage all day. Nobody dared speak to him. Then I'd find the letter torn into tiny pieces in the waste-paper basket.'

Rose asked, 'Did you ever get the chance to read one of the letters?'

Maud looked indignant. 'Certainly not! Reading folks' letters indeed!'

Rose thought she looked rather uncomfortable and said, 'I want the truth, Maud, remember. I don't care tuppence if you *did* read them. It was so long ago and —'

'Well then, maybe I did read one. Just the one, and that's the solemn truth. Your poor mother was getting quite desperate by the sound of it. It was after *he* came back.'

'He came back to Helston? The man my mother loved?'

'Oh yes. It was less than three months later that the gentleman returned — alone. Of course, he didn't go back to his job in Helston — I doubt they'd have had him back after the scandal and everything. I mean, Tye Rock House being so well known and her being the Headmaster's wife and running off like that — it was *news!* But he did come back to the area — he had a sister, I think — but he couldn't find another job. Well, who'd take him on after what happened? It was in the local paper, and you know how people are.'

'I can imagine,' said Rose, shocked by this new disclosure. Instead of making a new life for herself with the man she loved, her mother had been abandoned. 'So what was in the letter?'

'A plea for forgiveness, Rose. It was so dignified it made me weep, and I'm not ashamed to say so. Not begging to be taken back or asking for money. Nothing like that. Just how sorry she was to have caused such heartache to so many people. No self-pity, although we knew she'd been left all on her own. The letter came and I recognised the handwriting. Your father tucked it under the blotter, but I saw the corner sticking out. He never guessed that I'd read it.' She shook her head sadly. 'If I'd had any money I'd have sent her something — I was that sorry for her — but I didn't. I mean, how could she manage? There *was* a rumour that she had a child, but I doubt that was true. You know how gossip grows. There was no mention of a little'un in the letter.'

Rose thought of Miss Folkes, whoever she was. Had this woman helped her mother? Was she still alive, perhaps? She asked, 'Does the name Folkes sound familiar to you?'

'Folkes? No. Who is he?'

'Never mind, Maud. Do you know the name of the man my mother loved?'

'It was Gibbs. It might have been Colin — or Alan. Something like that.'

Rose nodded distractedly. 'And do you know where this man eventually settled?'

'I don't know. I reckon he took himself off pretty smartly, seeing as how everyone turned against him. They say he went into the Harbour Inn one day and was snubbed for his pains. His poor sister, too, when she went into the baker's.'

Rose sighed and Maud stood up. 'I'd best be getting back.'

Impulsively she held out her arms and Rose stepped forward. As the old arms went round her, it was as though she were a child again.

Rose hugged her in return, then drew back. There were unshed tears in her eyes. 'Do you remember the nightmares, Dodie? You were always there with a cuddle and a night-light.' Rose still had the nightmares, and now she understood what had provoked them.

Maud smiled. 'You were a poor little soul. My heart ached for you, and that's the truth.' She regarded Rose with narrowed eyes. 'You going to look for your ma, Rose? Is that it?'

Rose hesitated. Then she said, 'Yes, Maud. That's exactly it.'

CHAPTER FIVE

On May 2nd, from her seat at the organ Sarah Gibbs watched the pupils, led by Miss Hock, file into the church and take their places. Shivering a little in the gloom, they hunched down into the warmth of their coats. Thank goodness *someone* had turned up. They were wearing their navy-blue uniforms, but one could hardly expect them to come in black. How could any of them have anticipated a funeral? How they stared at the coffin. Sarah rolled her eyes with irritation. What was it about death, she wondered, that held such a fascination for the young. Not that the coffin wasn't worth looking at — a gleaming dark oak with delicately scrolled edges and ornate brass handles. Sarah Gibbs was something of an expert when it came to coffins. They hadn't stinted on the price, that much was certain, and the flowers were exquisite in wonderful shades of yellow and gold. It never ceased to amaze her how so many flowers could be procured so early in the year.

She glanced around the church, impatient to get started. Apart from the girls, the pews were half empty, but then it was no more than she expected. The Headmaster of Tye Rock School had not been particularly popular and there'd been so much gossip at the time — and him such a proud, private man. Still, the years had passed and memories faded. He'd apparently behaved very well towards his daughter and it was fair to say that latterly he'd been well respected. There certainly should have been a few more people in the church to see him off. After all, Tye Rock House was a substantial building and it stood for something in the town; almost a landmark perched up there on the cliffs, impossible to miss except when the fog rolled in from the sea.

Death. It was a strange and awesome thing. A week ago, larger than life, he had been out for a walk along the cliffs with one of his staff. A man to be reckoned with. Now he was stretched out in his coffin in his Sunday suit, silent and still and of no consequence. A terrible transformation. Sarah sighed and tried to concentrate on her playing. She did love to play to a full church, and the funeral pieces were so beautiful. She knew, too, that she looked well in black and it gave her a chance to wear her best coat with the black astrakhan collar. Self-consciously she tucked her black silk scarf closer around her neck.

She turned the page mechanically. She knew the music by heart. Ah! There was Miss Vivian bringing up the rear with a good-looking young man who was limping slightly. Probably the new history master. Tried to save Vivian by all accounts. Bit of an ordeal for him, poor man . . . Tut! Two of the girls were whispering and giggling together. Miss Gibbs shook her head in disapproval. Their own Headmaster was being buried and they could laugh and joke. What were the young people coming to? She caught the eye of one of the girls and frowned, but it made no difference. Girls of that age were so difficult. If Miss Vivian decided to carry on at the school she'd have her work cut out.

Sarah wondered if Catherine Vivian was aware of her husband's death and the manner of his passing. Probably not, since no one seemed to know where she was. Even Alan didn't know. Or was pretending not to know. She sighed. Her brother should have stayed with Catherine. He had helped bring about her fall from grace and then he'd abandoned her. Not that he had ever said a word against Catherine, he never had, but he wouldn't discuss it. When Sarah tried to drag it out of him, they'd had the only row they'd ever had and he'd walked out. They'd been reconciled to a point over the years, but poor Alan had never had a day's luck since. His marriage to Beatrice had been a disaster and her death in childbirth had been a merciful release for both of them. A terribly un-Christian thing to think, but it was true nonetheless. Strange to think how besotted he had been with poor Catherine. Head over heels in love. And then suddenly it was over and he'd refused to talk about it, even to her, his own sister. Men could be so stubborn. Sarah smiled faintly. How wonderful if she were to walk in after all these years. To pay her last respects! What a commotion that would make. And she could. Nothing to stop her. Presumably she was still his wife . . .

Ah! The Edgcombe family were arriving. Nice people, the Edgcombes. Privy to the contents of Vivian's will, no doubt. That would make interesting reading and no mistake . . . She spotted old Doctor Phillips and his wife and daughter. The Headmistress of Daneside School followed and then . . . Sergeant Wylie?

'Good gracious!'

She was so surprised that she fumbled the notes and heads turned towards the organ. She tutted with annoyance. Now she had lost the place! But the police! What on earth was Sergeant Wylie doing here? Had he been a family friend? If so it was news to *her*. If not then he was here in an official capacity, and that was distinctly interesting. George Vivian had died in an accident, surely. It couldn't have been anything else. So what was the sergeant's interest? She tried to read something from his expression, but he caught her eye and she quickly turned her head the other way.

To chase away any lingering suspicions, she took a long, satisfied look at the coffin with its accompanying flowers. There was something so peaceful about flowers. She had told her brother that she wanted as many as he could afford when it was her turn to go. 'A cheap coffin and expensive flowers', had been her exact words. She did so hate to think of all that beautiful polished

164

wood rotting underground.

The vicar approached, black gown flapping. She gave him a warm smile. Poor old boy. He was over eighty, very frail around the knees, and should have given up years ago. There were moves afoot to edge him out, but she would defend him with her last breath. If it hadn't been for his support when the scandal broke, she didn't know what she would have done.

'I think we can start now, Miss Gibbs,' he whispered.

She nodded, reached for another sheet of music and straightened her back. She would play her best — not only for George Vivian but for Catherine, Alan, Beatrice and her baby, and Rose, and all that might have been and should have been . . . and never was.

The congregation stood up as one. In the third row, Chrissie leaned towards Lucy and said, 'I need your help tonight, so don't let me down, will you?'

Lucy looked at her, startled. 'My help? To do what?' Her voice was louder than intended and Chrissie put a warning finger to her lips and pointed to Miss Hock who sat in the row in front.

'To keep a lookout, silly,' Chrissie whispered, 'and to warn me if anyone's around. It's tonight!' She watched with satisfaction as her friend paled. 'I told you he'd come!'

'But how? That is, where will you . . . you know?'

'Where will we make love? Why, over the stables, of course!'

'The stables? Are you mad? Robb sleeps there.'

'Only occasionally — and that won't be tonight.' She smiled broadly. '*I'll* be there instead and so will Jerry, bless him!' She picked up the hymnal and fussed with it. 'All you have to do is keep watch from the dining-room window and whistle —'

'You know I can't whistle!'

'I'll give you a whistle, silly.'

Miss Hock turned round and glared fiercely at them and for a moment they were silent.

Lucy was looking anxious. Really, thought Chrissie impatiently, she was a faint-hearted little thing.

Lucy whispered, 'And what happens if I get caught? Honestly, Chrissie, you've got a nerve!'

'And you're a scared rabbit!' Chrissie bit back a further comment. She was going to have to rely on Lucy so she mustn't offend her. 'I bribed poor old Robb,' she said, with an adroit change of subject. 'It was so easy. I offered him a shilling and he jumped at the chance.'

'A *shilling?* I should think he would! You've got more money than sense, Chrissie Morgan.'

At that moment Miss Hock turned round and hissed, 'Stop talking, you two. This is a funeral!'

Chrissie whispered, 'I didn't think it was a wedding!' and Lucy giggled obligingly.

Chrissie sat back, content. Lucy would moan

but she'd do what she was told. The hymn came to an end and they all sat down and stared expectantly at the vicar. Only Chrissie was smiling as the clergyman's opening words filled the church. But then she was going to see Jerry, she told herself with a shudder of anticipation. She had something to smile about.

Later, in the evening of the same day, Rose waited in the sitting room to greet the Edgcombes. She smiled at James and his father and shook hands with each of them.

Harold said, 'The worst is over, Miss Vivian. I always think the funeral is the turning point after a death.'

He placed a large manila folder on the table and they all sat down. Maud then arrived with a tray of tea and biscuits which she placed on a small side table. She poured tea for three and then withdrew.

James said, 'It all went very well, Miss Vivian. A nice spread. Wonderful ham. You have a good staff here.'

'Thank you.'

For a moment they sipped the tea in silence, then Harold Edgcombe said, 'Perhaps we should make a start,' and Rose said, 'I think so, yes.'

There was a fluttering inside her as the solicitor's fingers tugged at the ribbon which bound the folder. Rose crossed her own fingers although she hardly knew why. Unless whatever was contained within the pages would somehow alter her life, for better or for worse.

Harold Edgcombe gave a little cough and settled his spectacles on his nose. 'It was originally dated four years before your mother left. It was amended the year she left. The following week, to be exact.'

Rose, taken aback, met James's reassuring smile and attempted one of her own.

He began to read, mumbling the less important details for the sake of speed: '. . . and I, George Edmund Vivian, being of sound mind, do hereby execute my last will and testament on this the third day of June, eighteen eighty-two as dated above and at the aforementioned address . . .'

Rose said, 'Meaning Tye Rock House?'

'Yes.' He went on. 'I leave the entire contents of the house and the house itself and any monies I may have to my beloved daughter, Rose, with the exception of a few minor legacies. Whatever the circumstances at the time of my death, my estranged wife, Catherine, is not to receive a penny of this money.'

Rose gasped.

James Edgcombe said, 'He was very bitter, Miss Vivian.'

'Understandably, Miss Vivian,' said his father sternly.

'But *nothing!* He must have hated her.' The idea chilled her and she shivered.

'Your father was publicly humiliated, Miss

Vivian. In his position I might well have felt the same. Most men would.'

Rose glanced at James, who gave her a large wink but said nothing. A little comforted, she said, 'But there's nothing to stop me giving her some of the money.'

Harold Edgcombe hesitated, then he said, 'Nothing at all, if you think that's wise.'

'I think it's *fair!*' Rose said sharply. 'Please read on.'

There followed a detailed list of minor bequests to be made to some of the staff, including 10 guineas for Maud. Her father had also left 20 guineas to his sister Alice.

'She died some years ago,' Rose reminded them.

'And ten pounds to the Harbour Inn for a supper for the poor of the village.'

Rose said, 'Goodness! I am surprised,' and she meant it. It was a fine crack in the armour.

James Edgcombe said, 'No one is all bad, Miss Vivian — not that I meant . . . oh dear!'

His father glared at him but Rose said, 'I know exactly what you meant, Mr Edgcombe. There is no need to apologise.'

Harold Edgcombe said, 'So congratulations are in order, Miss Vivian. You are now the owner of a fine house and a thriving school.'

She made a gesture of helplessness. 'It's all so sudden. And . . .' She hesitated. 'And debts? Are there any of those, do you know? I should see the whole picture, shouldn't I, before I decide what to do?'

'Ah yes . . . the debts . . .' He drummed his fingers on the table top. 'I believe there might be a few minor ones, but nothing that need worry you unduly. We shall need to consult —'

His son broke in quickly. 'I have already arranged with Miss Vivian that *I* will accompany her to the bank manager whenever she wishes.'

'Oh, you have?' Momentarily disconcerted Harold raised his eyebrows briefly, then smiled at Rose. 'Then you will be in good hands, Miss Vivian. My son will look after you splendidly. I have no doubts on that score. Now, are there any questions?'

Rose nodded. 'There is something — nothing to do with the will, but I would like a word of advice. Mr Tremayne, the history master, has offered to help where he can — with the running of the school, that is.'

Father and son exchanged glances.

'Naturally I shall only call on him in an emergency, but he did offer to sit in when I interview for the post my father's death has left vacant. I'm not sure if that would be a wise thing to do, although I don't feel totally confident to deal with it on my own.'

James Edgcombe was looking doubtful but his father had no qualms. 'That might be very helpful, and it would be a sole occasion. It's not as though you have to interview dozens of people for a variety of posts. Always assuming that the rest of your staff stay on, that is. I have to warn you that a death like this might unsettle them, and they'll be wanting reassurance that their jobs will continue. Best to have a word with them on that score.' He stood up, gathering his papers together. 'I'll draw up a new deed — change of ownership for Tye Rock House.'

Rose also stood up. 'I haven't quite decided . . .' she began. 'The school, that is. I don't know that I want to run it. I haven't really —' She broke off.

He was staring in astonishment. 'Not run the school?'

She stammered a little. 'I *may* do, of course, but I may not. The truth is I'd never imagined having a choice. With Father alive, I'd no option but to support him, but sole responsibility is another matter.' For the very first time she was aware of tremendous possibilities opening up for her. A kind of freedom she had never expected. A freedom that was both wonderful and terrifying.

Harold Edgcombe looked totally bemused. 'Well . . .' he said. 'It's your own affair, naturally, Miss Vivian, but I would think very carefully before you toss away such an opportunity.'

James put in quickly. 'You have plenty of time to decide, Miss Vivian. No need to rush into anything.' He turned to his father. 'Miss Vivian may have other plans for the rest of her life. Or she might want to travel a little.' He turned back to Rose. 'But you wouldn't move away, for instance? Not without discussing it with me first.'

James looked horrified by the very idea, she thought, but understood the reason. Obviously his parents didn't know that he intended to propose marriage to her at some time.

'I don't really know what I mean,' she confessed. 'Suddenly inheriting money has come as a shock.' She smiled at James. 'But don't worry. I shan't do anything rash. It's not in my nature, and I shall consult with you first.'

'I do hope so,' he said.

When they had gone, Rose stood at the window watching them leave. Once the trap had bowled away, she turned back to survey the familiar room. As she stared around her, problems closer to home pressed forward and she gave herself a mental shake. 'First things first, Rose Vivian!' she muttered. She had to supervise the girls' 'prep' — the hour set aside for their homework — and then confer with Mrs Cripps about changing the menus for the coming week. These alterations were her own idea for, like the girls, she had become tired of the repetitive nature of the meals.

'Out goes mutton stew!' she murmured. She loathed mutton stew. 'And in comes a good beef pie!'

But only if they could afford it, she reminded herself. Presumably there was a budget for the meals, and she would have to keep within it. There was so much to learn and she was forced to acknowledge herself a complete beginner.

Still, it was an area in which she felt reasonably competent, and Rose was beginning to discover a growing pleasure in a challenge.

Rose sat in front of the class that evening and stared at the menu she was still trying to revise. Friday must always be fish, but the rest of the week could be arranged on a ten-day rota so that the order of the meals was less predictable. Alternatively, she could arrange three six-day menus and run them one after the other. At the moment, apart from Fridays, there was always a meat dish, but Rose wanted to find substitutes on two days. She wrinkled her brow thoughtfully . . .

In front of her the older girls sat at the desks, concentrating on their homework. Talk was not allowed during prep, and the silence was broken only by the scratching of pens across paper and an occasional whisper which Rose pretended not to hear. Most of the girls accepted the hour's work as an inescapable part of school life, but a few of them found it thoroughly irksome and let their feelings be known to whichever teacher was supervising. It was a quarter to seven and the hour was nearly over. Rose was congratulating herself on a trouble-free session when Lavinia Bray held up her hand.

'Please, Miss Vivian, I'm so cold. Could we have some coal on the fire?'

Rose glanced guiltily towards the fireplace, but the fire seemed adequate.

She said, 'It's not worth it now, Lavinia. We'll be finished in ten minutes. If we build the fire we shall simply be warming an empty room.'

'But I'm freezing!'

Rose hesitated. 'Are you wearing your warm underwear?'

'Yes.'

'Then maybe you feel the cold more than most. Tomorrow, wear a warmer cardigan or even a jacket.'

Rose tried not to show sympathy. If she did, it would be construed as a sign of weakness and the other girls would join the protest. She felt quite sure that Miss Hock would have stifled the complaint at birth and without a single qualm. She ignored Lavinia's continued mutterings and tried once more to focus on the job in hand.

Lavinia said, 'But, Miss Vivian, I might have a chill — or a fever. Should I go and see Matron?'

Rose bit her lip. The girl was baiting her, she was sure. A few of the others were grinning and their expressions were knowing. Could she possibly bear this for the rest of her life, Rose wondered. If she took over Tye Rock House she would be committing herself to years of anxiety and the certain knowledge that she was not properly equipped for the job. The prospect depressed her. She could never survive.

She said, 'I think not. You can see her after prep if you wish. Get on with your work, please.'

The girls exchanged meaningful looks.

Rose tried to concentrate. It doesn't matter

what they think of me, she reminded herself. They are trying to take advantage of my inexperience. In a sharper tone she said, 'All of you — get on with your work.'

In a deliberately loud whisper Chrissie Morgan said, 'Quite the tyrant, isn't she!'

Rose's pulse quickened. Ignore it or deal with it? She didn't know. If only the bell would ring, it would be over. She decided to ignore the comment and turned once more to the menus. Maybe a savoury dish like the one her grandmother had often made. Cheese and onion, or something with bacon. Or an egg dish. She had a sudden vision of Mrs Cripps making dozens of omelettes, hysterically rushing to and fro among a dozen frying pans, and began to realise that the arrangement of a school menu was fraught with problems. So many things to consider. What the girls would eat without waste; what could be afforded on the school's budget; what was easy for the kitchen staff to prepare . . .

She glanced up suddenly to see that Lucy was crying.

'Lucy?'

The girl shook her head, fumbling for her handkerchief. Beside her, Chrissie stared stonily ahead.

Rose said, 'What's happened, Lucy?' She stood up to go to the girl but at that moment the bell rang and the rest of the girls, including Chrissie, gathered their belongings and clattered out of the room. Only Lucy remained. She raised a tear-stained face and gulped miserably. 'I'm sorry, Miss Vivian, but — but I can't say anything.' She struggled with her sobs. 'Please don't ask me.'

Rose put an arm round her shoulders. Remembering Chrissie Morgan's face, she asked, 'Is it something Chrissie's said or done? You can tell me, Lucy. I can help, you know, and we may be helping Chrissie.'

The absence of a denial spoke volumes but when Rose tried to elicit further information, Lucy shook her head. 'I *can't* tell you! I've promised!' and sobbed again.

Defeated, Rose waited until she finally recovered and then sent her to her room to await a large mug of cocoa from the kitchen. She would ask the matron to keep a watchful eye on her, she decided. As Lucy walked away, Rose wished once again that Chrissie's grandmother would get in touch so that the wretched girl could be suspended. And the sooner the better, she reflected uneasily. The conviction was growing within her that Chrissie Morgan was more than just a difficult young woman. Rose was beginning to see her as some kind of threat.

Promptly at eight o'clock Mark Tremayne knocked on the door of the Head's room and Rose said, 'Come in.' She motioned him to a chair and asked, 'How are you feeling? If the teaching is too arduous we could perhaps reduce the hours for you.' She had no idea how this could be done, but felt it was the least she could offer in the circumstances.

He shook his head. 'I'm doing splendidly, Miss Vivian. Please consider me the least of your worries.'

'Thank you. Perhaps you'd like to see the doctor tomorrow? He's calling in for his routine checks on the girls.'

He shook his head again. 'I'm fine, Miss Vivian,' he assured her. 'Quite recovered.'

Rose regarded him carefully. 'Do you feel well enough to help me out with the interviews?' she asked. 'You did offer, and I've thought it over and I think I will find it a bit of an ordeal.'

His expression brightened. 'Of course the offer still stands, Miss Vivian,' he told her with disarming eagerness.

'I would want to make the final decision myself, of course,' she told him. 'I would just be grateful for a little moral support.'

'Anything at all I can do to help ensure the smooth running of Tye Rock House School, I'll do with pleasure. Anything to help you, in fact, Miss Vivian. I could ask the odd question just for the sake of appearances, but leave most of it to you. It would be your responsibility ultimately, but if you wished to discuss matters with me privately . . .'

'That would be best. Yes, I think so.' She was impressed by his perceptiveness. They were her feelings exactly, but she had been unsure how to explain without offending him.

He hesitated. 'Do you want this to be known to the other teachers?'

Rose gave a little shrug. 'I'm in two minds,' she confessed. 'I hate to deceive them, but I can see that Miss Hock would take it very badly if I overlooked her in favour of someone so much younger and — dare I say it — less experienced.'

'That's difficult,' he agreed. '*I* certainly wouldn't mention it, but it might come out. If it did it could be very awkward.'

'But if neither of us speaks of it . . .'

He smiled. 'In my experience, secrets have a habit of escaping into the ether, Miss Vivian! The man you appoint might let it slip one day — might refer to the fact that I had been part of the interview. We can hardly bind him to secrecy.'

Rose sighed. 'I have to make a choice, and either way I could get it wrong.'

He smiled. 'The devil and the deep blue sea. Poor Miss Vivian! I wish I could be more help, but I feel very much an outsider. You really need a male deputy, but obviously when your father was alive there was no need.'

He was so kind, she thought. The expression in his eyes was so warm. There was something about him. It was as though he really did care — about *her* as well as about Tye Rock House.

He said, 'I suppose it's too early to decide what you are going to do about the school. Presumably your father left it to you? The only heir to the Vivian millions!' He laughed and seemed to be waiting for an answer but Rose, startled, said

178

nothing. He continued, 'The staff are very concerned, to tell you the truth. Worried that you will close the school down. It must be a temptation.'

She felt an overwhelming impulse to confide in him; to confess all her doubts and insecurities and to share her feelings with someone so sympathetic. She opened her mouth to say something, then hurriedly closed it. It simply would not do. Most improper, she told herself.

'You were going to say something?'

'No! That is . . . it was nothing.' It sounded very lame, she thought. Discovering suddenly that she was physically leaning towards him across the desk, she hurriedly straightened up and sat well back in her chair. She had the feeling that he was studying her and, confused, searched for something to say.

'The funeral went well, I thought,' was the best she could manage.

He didn't answer at once. Finally he said, ' "Beloved father". Is that what you will choose for the headstone, Miss Vivian?'

'The headstone? I . . .' She found herself stammering. 'To be honest I hadn't thought about it, but I dare say —' Beloved father? Yes, she would have to say something along those lines — but not 'Beloved husband of . . .' For a moment she stared at him.

He said softly, 'Forgive me. That was an unforgivable intrusion, Miss Vivian. I'm afraid I was allowing your kindness to me to colour my judgement.'

Rose felt almost breathless. 'I don't think —'
she began. She took a deep breath. 'I don't think
I understood the question, Mr Tremayne.'

It was his turn to sit back in the chair. He
pursed his lips and shook his head slightly.

'Please, Mr Tremayne,' she insisted.

He gave an almost imperceptible shrug. 'I simply meant — I *thought* . . .' His expression startled her. 'I thought, from my limited knowledge
of your father, that perhaps he had not been a
very warm-hearted man. My own father was very
cold. I'm ashamed to say that I hated him, but he
deserved nothing else. I know what it is to crave
affection, Miss Vivian, and I felt for you. But I
had no right to mention it. No right even to think
about it, and I apologise.'

From a long distance she heard herself say,
'It's of no importance, Mr Tremayne.' But, in
fact, she was filled with astonishment that this
man, hardly even a friend, could have recognised a need in her that she hardly acknowledged
herself. Was he right? Had she craved affection
all these years? The answer, an undoubted 'Yes',
shocked her. Tears filled her eyes suddenly and
with a small, despairing sound she bent her head
so that he should not see her face.

'Miss Vivian! Oh, what have I said? Forgive
me, please!'

She heard the scrape of chair legs and then he
had moved to stand beside her and she felt the
warmth of his hand as he laid it gently on her
arm in a gesture of sympathy.

He said, 'Please don't cry' and that made her cry more. A large white handkerchief was thrust into her hand and she used it gratefully but still the tears flowed. She became aware that Mark Tremayne had put his arms around her and was holding her close.

'I'm sorry!' she told him. 'I don't know why —'

'You've had a bereavement,' he said. 'That alone entitles you to cry if you want to. Whatever sort of man your father was, he *was* your father. Now he's gone.'

She drew a deep breath and reluctantly pulled away from him, embarrassed by the situation. She had wept all over a very junior teacher, allowing him to see her weakness. If he should tell the other members of staff . . .

'This is a private matter,' he told her, as though reading her thoughts. 'Not a word about it goes out of this room. You can be assured of that.'

'Thank you.' Without thinking, she tucked the handkerchief into the pocket of her jacket. The need to explain her feelings was unbearably strong. He alone, she thought, would understand, for his own father had been a cold man.

He returned to his chair and she tidied her hair self-consciously.

She said slowly, 'My father *did* find it difficult to show his feelings.'

'Did he have any?'

The reply, given sharply and without thought, startled her. 'I suppose he must have had feelings,' she said, a trifle defensively. 'But without my mother . . .' She stopped. Enough said about that, she thought. If she found her mother and brought her to Tye Rock, Rose might regret the confidence.

He was very pale. 'I watched my mother die slowly year by year — of a broken heart.'

Rose gasped. 'Oh, how dreadful for you! And for her, of course.'

'A vale of tears!' he said and swallowed hard.

She nodded. She wanted to ask more but had no wish to pry.

He leaned forward and for a moment Rose was almost frightened by the intensity of his expression. His face was taut, his eyes narrowed. 'All she wanted was forgiveness, and it was denied her.'

'Forgiveness? What had she done?' The question passed her lips before she could stop it. Too late then for regrets. There was no unsaying it. 'I'm sorry,' she stammered.

He appeared not to hear her. 'It was cruel and unnecessary . . . but that's the sort of man he was.' He seemed to remember her existence and looked at her directly. 'I watched him die and I was glad. That's the kind of son I am.'

Shaken, Rose tried to say something appropriate. 'I'm sure you were justified,' she suggested. 'He didn't deserve your pity.'

'He didn't deserve to live, Miss Vivian!'

'No, I — I suppose not.'

Hunched in his chair, he was breathing

heavily, and she watched with growing compassion. It must have been terrible for him, she thought, to watch his father being cruel to his mother.

'What a sad childhood,' she said gently. 'I do understand, Mr Tremayne. I, too, have few happy memories to look back on. At least your mother is at peace now. No one can touch her.' It sounded trite, but she was at a loss to know how to comfort him. 'We have a lot in common,' she said.

He didn't reply but gradually he was relaxing. She saw his expression change, and the stiffness left his shoulders. 'I'm so sorry to burden you with all that!' he told her. 'Whatever must you think of me? Please — say that we can forget this conversation.'

'Of course.'

Suddenly, with an effort, he seemed to shake off the mood. He smiled and stood up.

'Miss Vivian, I suggest you have an early night.'

His cheerfulness was forced, she knew, but she admired his attempt at recovery. He went on, 'You've had a hard day, and sleep is a wonderful restorative.'

She said, 'We could both do with some of that.'

'My mother was a firm believer in old-fashioned "bed rest".' He laughed at the memory. 'I used to be put to bed on the flimsiest excuse. Not that I minded. The bedtime stories were happy times. Doctor Tremayne heartily recommends an early night for you.' His smile widened. 'Seriously, Miss Vivian, sadly I can't offer to read you a bedtime story but I do think you need to rest.'

Rose felt her own face break into a relieved smile. There was something so appealing about his vulnerability. Something so brave. Somehow he had survived a difficult and unhappy childhood to become a very charming young man.

'Then I'll take your advice, Doctor!' She stood up and held out her hand. 'Thank you for everything, Mr Tremayne.'

He said 'Goodnight' and left her to ponder his remark about the bedtime story. In a sudden rush of longing, Rose found herself wishing she could call him Mark.

'Mark Tremayne,' she whispered. 'We have so much in common. We could be very good for each other.'

That night Rose lay awake, thinking about her conversation with Mark Tremayne. Much of what he said made sense, she could see that. Particularly the remark about a male deputy head. Perhaps that was what she should be advertising for although . . . might it not lead to difficulties? She would have her own ideas and the deputy might disagree. What would happen then? A powerful male figure on the staff would have advantages and disadvantages. Unless she were *married* to him! The idea popped into her head uninvited and refused to go away. If only she were married, she could entrust the school to her husband and maybe — she felt herself blushing — maybe have a family before it was too late.

She sighed, watching the moonlight creep across the ceiling. She thought about Mark Tremayne's kindness and wondered what had prompted him to speak so openly.

She would certainly be glad of his presence at her side during the interview . . . She closed her eyes sleepily but his image remained. What had he said? *Bed* rest. She rolled her eyes humorously. And he had said he was sorry he couldn't read her a bedtime story! She smiled. He really was a very nice young man. A little forward, perhaps, but he was a very modern young man and she herself might be considered old-fashioned. Feeling rather wicked, she allowed herself to imagine him kissing her. This was purely in her imagination because she had never been kissed by a man. Her father's attitude and the restraints of her position had ruled out any chance of romance. Their social life had been almost non-existent. Quite simply, she had never met any young men.

Her eyes snapped open suddenly. The word romance had reminded her that she had intended to have a talk with Lucy Unwin about Chrissie Morgan. She sat up, wide awake now. Lucy's problem might well stem from Chrissie Morgan, in which case Matron should be keeping both of them under discreet observation. But even Matron couldn't stay awake and watchful all night. She was probably asleep but Rose was wide awake. Without further thought she slipped her feet into slippers and pulled on her dressing gown.

Once again she padded silently along the corridors until she reached the room which Lucy and Chrissie shared. As her hand touched the door handle she paused, arrested by a terrible thought. Suppose the man was *in the room!* It seemed a possibility. Chrissie would do whatever she wished — she was in so much trouble already that she might well think that nothing could make matters worse. This might be what Lucy had been crying about earlier. Momentarily disconcerted, Rose wondered what she would do if there *was* a man in the room. What would her father have done, she wondered, and wished desperately that it was not her problem. She straightened her shoulders. She would have to challenge him — and then call for the police. Or call for the police *first*.

'Please God!' she whispered and carefully turned the handle. Slowly she pushed open the door and stared into the darkness. It took her a moment to realise that *neither* of the girls was in the room. It was empty. Relief turned to apprehension. So where were they? Remembering what had happened the last time, Rose turned and ran — back along the corridor, down the stairs and along to the dining room. Just as she expected, she discovered Lucy waiting by the window, huddled miserably on a chair. The girl turned at Rose's approach, gave a little scream and immediately burst into tears.

'I couldn't tell you —' she said between sobs. 'She's threatened to do terrible things to me if I tell! She said they would send me to Coventry and I'd never, ever have a friend again. I didn't want to — I *told* her it was a mad thing to do . . . Oh Miss Vivian, I *begged* her to leave me out of it —' She burst into a renewed fit of weeping.

Distraught, Rose shook her. 'Just tell me where she is, Lucy. Nobody is blaming you for what's happened. But I must know where she is!'

At first the terrified girl refused to reveal her friend's whereabouts, and Rose was conscious of the minutes ticking away. Allowing God knows what to happen! She would have to frighten the information out of her, she decided reluctantly.

'Lucy, if you *don't* tell me what you know you will *both* be expelled!' Rose told her.

When Lucy turned her tearful face towards her, Rose was filled with pity. But she had to know. '*Tell* me!' she demanded as sternly as she could.

Lucy closed her eyes despairingly. 'She'll punish me! I know she will!'

'We won't let her hurt you, Lucy. Now tell me where she is — and *who* she's with!'

Lucy drew a long shuddering breath. 'She's in the stables — in Robb's place.'

'With?'

'With Jerry.' She looked up at Rose wide-eyed.

187

'And you promise you won't let her do anything to me?'

'I promise!' said Rose, but her mind was on other matters. She now knew the worst and was going to have to deal with it. She would call on Mark Tremayne's help, but in the meantime she would have to act alone. She had no one she could send for the police and, even if she had, it would all take so much time.

She said, 'Run to Matron, Lucy, and ask her to send Mr Tremayne to the stables *immediately*.' She didn't feel able to deal with this man if he turned nasty. 'Then she must telephone the police. Go on, Lucy! Hurry! I'm going down to the stables now alone.'

Without waiting to listen to Lucy's protests, Rose began to run back along the corridor to the door. She was still in her nightwear but dared not risk further delays while she returned to her bedroom to find more suitable clothes. Once outside she shivered in the cool air. Wretched girl! she thought furiously. The stables at this time of year! Even if nothing worse happened to her, she might well have caught a chill. Chrissie Morgan would have to leave, and it couldn't happen soon enough.

As she rounded the side of the house the stables came in sight. There was no light showing. So whatever they were doing, they were doing it in the dark. She ran through Robb's vegetable garden, aware of the night scents — damp leaves, soil, a hint of woodsmoke from the dying embers of a recent bonfire. She ran on down the path to the stables, slowing as she approached. She didn't want to give them prior warning of her arrival. The door stood wide open and she recognised the familiar smell of horse and heard Clipper and the roan, Sandman, moving restlessly in their stalls.

Moving quietly she went inside and stood a moment listening and allowing her eyes to become accustomed to the gloom. From the loft above she heard the sound of giggling and a man's voice, low and urgent.

Chrissie said, 'No, Jerry! You mustn't. Not that!'

The man replied, 'Why not? What d'you think I come traipsing out here for in the middle of the night? I've got blisters on my hands from those blasted oars. Think I'd go through all that just for a kiss and a cuddle? Think again, Chrissie!'

There was a scuffle and Chrissie, her voice rising, cried, '*No*, Jerry! Don't! What are you *doing?* Oh, please don't!'

Rose drew a deep breath and started up the open wood stairs that led into the loft. The fourth stair creaked but went unheeded by the pair above her. As her head drew level with the loft floor, Rose saw them writhing together on Robb's rough bed that was little more than a straw-filled pallet and blankets.

She said, 'Chrissie Morgan! What do you think you're doing?'

Rose's voice trembled but it had the desired effect.

A man's voice said, 'Jesus Christ!'

Chrissie shrieked and sat up, staring at Rose wide-eyed. Her blouse was unbuttoned, revealing her breasts, and her legs were bare. The man Rose knew only as Jerry turned towards her. His trousers were unfastened and his shirt hung loose.

He said, 'Who the ruddy hell are you?'

Chrissie said, 'It's Miss Vivian!' She was struggling to do up the buttons of her blouse and then to push down her skirts.

Rose was pleased to see that for once in her life the girl appeared totally demoralised.

Heart hammering, Rose addressed herself to the man who was now stuffing his shirt back into his trousers and hoisting his braces over his shoulders.

'I demand that you tell me your name, sir, and who gave you permission to enter these premises.' It sounded ridiculous, but she could manage nothing more suitable. 'The police will be here before long and I shall hand you into custody . . .'

'You bloody won't!' he told her. He muttered something to Chrissie which sounded like 'I'm off!' and started to pull on his boots.

Rose persevered. 'If you think that you can get away with this you are very much mistaken. What is your full name and where do you live?'

Chrissie gave a wail and said, 'Oh no, Miss

Vivian. Don't tell them. Please!' To the man she said, 'Don't go, Jerry. Stay with me.'

He said, 'That's right. Tell her my name. Well, I'll deny everything.' He looked around. 'Where's my jacket? I'm getting out of here!'

Chrissie cried, 'Jerry, darling, don't just go. Stay and — and we'll discuss it.' She cast an appealing look at Rose. 'He'll lose his job if the police are called in.'

'That's not my concern,' said Rose, unable to resist a note of triumph. 'He should have thought about that before. Now get yourself back to your room, Chrissie, and —'

'No, I won't!' she cried. 'Not unless you promise me you won't call in the police. Don't you understand, Miss Vivian? Jerry loves me.'

'Does he?' Rose snapped. 'I wonder?'

Chrissie appealed to Jerry who was now standing indecisively. 'You do, don't you, darling?'

'Of course I don't *love* you, you silly creature!' he told her callously. 'It was just a bit of fun, that's all. I thought you realised that.' He made a move to leave but Rose, still standing on the top step, effectively barred his way. He said, 'Out of my way!' but she stood her ground.

'I don't think so,' she told him. 'I've a few more questions for you when Chrissie has left us.'

She cried, 'I'm staying with Jerry!'

He gave her a scornful look. 'Do what you're told, Chrissie. Push off back to beddiebyes like a good little girl!'

'Jerry!' Tears filled her eyes as she stared at him, white-faced.

'You're nothing but a kid. All those promises and then it's "Oh don't, Jerry!"' His mouth twisted bitterly. 'I've met teasers like you before!' His gaze rested on Rose. 'And prim busybodies like you! Can't get a man of your own and don't want anybody else to get one.'

Rose felt the cruel words like a physical blow, but she was damned if she would let him know that. 'That's enough!' she cried. 'I think you forget that you're in a lot of trouble.'

'So you say!'

'I demand that you tell me your name,' she said. 'The police will want to talk to you.'

'My name's my business. And don't think you can frighten me because you can't. I came here because I was *invited*.' His smile was triumphant. 'Ask Chrissie. If you want to make me out to be some kind of monster you'll be unlucky. She was just as keen as I was, if not keener. She loved it!' He shrugged his contempt. 'So what do they charge me with — trespass? Wasting hay? I haven't done anything if that's what's worrying you, so they've got nothing to charge me with. Now I'm going!'

He took a step forward and before Rose realised what he was doing, he reached out and grabbed her round the waist. He lifted her bodily from the step and hurled her out of his way. His strength astonished her and as she sprawled in the hay, winded and furious, she realised just how helpless Chrissie would have been. Her struggles would have been pointless and he would certainly have taken her against her will.

As she struggled upright she caught a last glimpse of the top of his head as he disappeared down the ladder. At the same moment she heard running footsteps and Mark Tremayne called out, 'Where are you, Miss Vivian?'

She shouted, 'Catch him! He's getting away!'

Even as she urged him to action, she realised that Mark Tremayne would have no chance against a taller, stronger adversary — and especially since he was still recovering from his ordeal on the cliffs with her father.

Chrissie was still sitting in the hay, her face hidden in her hands. Rose left her and climbed back down the ladder. Through the window she could just make out two dark shapes struggling together. The two horses were whinnying anxiously as Rose dashed past them and out into the yard. Before she could decide what to do, the two men were on the ground and then Jerry was up again. He gave Mark Tremayne a violent kick for good measure before racing away to be quickly lost among the dark trees.

Rose hurried forward and knelt beside the fallen man who was groaning and holding his side.

'It's nothing serious,' he assured her as she helped him to his feet. 'Just an unlucky blow. I'll be all right.'

'The man's a savage!' cried Rose and her voice

shook with a mixture of shock and anger. Her hands trembled as she reached down to help him to his feet. 'I'll see him in court if it's the last thing I do. Poor Mr Tremayne, are you *sure* you're not hurt?'

'My pride's hurt!' he told her with a laugh. 'But what about you? If he as much as laid a finger on you I'll go after the swine.'

Rose was touched by his vehemence. 'He pushed me backwards on to the hay. Nothing at all, really. Except, as you say, a matter of pride. But he nearly — well —' She was glad of the darkness. 'He almost had his way with Chrissie Morgan. That wretched girl! I'll be so glad to see the back of her.'

He reached down and felt his left knee. Rose heard him wince.

'Mr Tremayne, you're *not* all right!'

'He caught my knee when he lashed out with that damned boot of his.'

'Lean on me if it helps,' she suggested, 'and we'll get you back to the house. Matron can try out her first aid on you!'

To her surprise he took her at her word and put an arm around her shoulders. At that moment a dishevelled Chrissie stepped out of the stables.

She said, 'How very touching!' and flounced past them in the direction of the house.

Furiously, Rose called, 'Christina Morgan!' but, ignoring her, the girl ran on and out of sight.

Together Rose and Mark Tremayne made

194

their way back to the house, discussing what should be done. Once safely inside, Rose discovered that Matron had been unable to reach the police as the operator reported that the line was engaged. Rose decided that, since they had lost Jerry, they might as well leave it until the morning.

She left Chrissie in Matron's good hands and twenty minutes later they had all returned to their beds.

Rose, remembering the warmth of Mark Tremayne's arm against her shoulder, began to feel a little more cheerful in spite of all her troubles. She also thought she was beginning to understand the needs which had led Chrissie to behave so wantonly. For the first time in her life Rose saw 'love' less as a romantic fantasy and more as a powerful, sometimes dangerous emotion. Recalling Jerry's cruel words to the girl, Rose was filled with a grudging compassion. After her romantic notions and expectations, the subsequent disillusion must have been very bitter for a girl like Chrissie.

But then, not all men were as heartless. Mark Tremayne had shown himself to be gentle and concerned, warm and supportive. Rose was put in mind of the well-known phrase — 'a man and a maid'. Strangely it had acquired a most appealing ring.

Chapter Six

Thoughtfully, Sergeant Wylie pressed the blunt end of his pencil into his chin and then wrote 'Mon 3rd May' lines in his precise handwriting. He was in no hurry to get away. There was not much happening in the area and the tea and biscuits were very welcome. He glanced up at Rose Vivian.

'So you don't know this man's surname?'

'No. Only that he's a groom somewhere — presumably nearby because he apparently walked here — although he did say something about blisters on his hands from the oars.'

'Oars? He's never rowed along the coast in the dark!' He whistled. 'Now that requires a bit of neck, that does. Or a man who's desperate for a bit of —' He broke off hastily, covering the slip with a cough. He glanced at Rose Vivian but if she was offended she didn't show it. He went on quickly. 'Not that they don't go out after dark — Lord knows how they'd smuggle if they didn't — but . . .' He stopped again, as a new thought struck him.

She said, 'I'm sure he said "oars" . . . and Jerry is probably Gerald.'

'Or did he mean the Loe Pool?'

196

Her eyes widened. 'The Loe Pool? But isn't that haunted? I mean, they say it must be. All those drownings. Nobody in their right mind would row across that stretch of water.'

He shrugged. 'I'm not saying that *I'd* go rowing on it, but if a man's that determined he might risk it. You know what they say. "You pays your money and you takes your chance!"' He tried to write but the pencil stub was flat and scratchy. Tutting, he returned it to his tunic pocket and found another with a marginally better point. The room was quiet for a moment or two as he committed his recent thoughts to paper. Never write too much, that was his motto. Because in the end you would have to write it all again in a fair hand. Or worse still, *type* it up on one of those dratted machines they were threatened with. It would come. Progress it was called. Sergeant Wylie sometimes wondered what the police force was coming to.

He sighed heavily. 'So, the girl must know but she won't tell. That it?'

'Exactly. She's being very difficult. She's a thoroughly bad influence, Sergeant, and I am waiting for a letter from her grandmother who is responsible for her while her parents are abroad.' Rose Vivian smiled wanly. 'She's a thorn in my side, to be honest. I've so many other problems just now that I could do without Chrissie Morgan and her escapades.'

He watched her, faintly surprised by what he saw. Her expression was lively and her eyes held

197

a faint but distinct sparkle. He had never thought of her as a pretty woman but there was something in her face. Considering her father had recently died — or was that it? Maybe her father had been a bit of a weight around her neck, keeping her in check. If so she was now free of it. Might be coming to life, so to speak. He smiled.

'You're doing very well so far, Miss Vivian,' he told her and saw her smile deepen.

'Thank you, Sergeant Wylie.'

Probably didn't get too many compliments, poor soul, he thought. Still, best get on with the job in hand.

'There's a young groom at the Hatcher place,' he told her. 'That's less than a mile away. Handsome young devil it must be said, in all fairness. Summers, I think his name is. Or Stanners. Tallish. Well set. Dark hair. He could be a Jerry. Would that be him, d'you think?'

'It *was* dark, Sergeant, though he was tallish and very strong.'

'Not that Summers or whatever has done anything wrong. Not so far. Not to my *knowledge,* that is. But he does spring to mind. Fits the bill. Every rogue has to start some time.'

She was looking very unhappy. 'I wouldn't like to accuse the wrong man, Sergeant. That would be dreadful.'

'Should I speak to your young lady? Might scare the truth out of her.' He didn't fancy the idea, though. Bullying young women was never pleasant. They did cry so easily.

Fortunately Rose Vivian was shaking her head. 'She won't tell you anything. She's taking a perverse delight in keeping her secret. Not that the wretch was worth her loyalty. He was quite rude to her before he left. He called her a tease and made fun of her. He really humiliated her.'

'Hmm. Is it likely she was?'

She hesitated. 'A tease, you mean? I have to say it's a possibility. She's very mature in some ways — or maybe the word's "forward". Grown-up in some ways and yet naive in others. I think she was very ill prepared for what might have happened.'

The sergeant hid a smile. Most well-brought-up ladies *were* ill prepared for sex in his experience. Not that he'd had much of the latter. He'd married the postman's daughter when he was eighteen. A harum-scarum sort of girl, but she'd settled down a treat. He tried to imagine Rose Vivian married and failed. On the shelf, poor soul. Not the marrying kind, perhaps.

He frowned at his notes. 'And you say this Jerry had a local accent?'

'Yes, he did. A rough accent — and he swore several times.'

'Good job he ran off when he did. Might have turned into a nasty incident.' He closed his notebook and tugged the elastic band into place around it.

Miss Vivian rolled her eyes. 'I was under the impression it *was* a nasty incident!' she said. 'He fought Mr Tremayne and kicked him quite severely.'

He wrote 'Rough local accent' and wondered if he had forgotten anything. He said, 'This gardener of yours. Bad lot, is he?'

'Who — Robb?' She was startled. 'I don't think so, Sergeant. I don't know much about him to tell you the truth — except that he's good at his job.'

'So you don't know how long this sort of thing's been going on? The girls bribing him to take messages and suchlike? Not a good idea at all. Not the sort of thing you'd want the parents to find out about.'

'Of course not, but until now I hadn't any idea . . . I could ask him.'

She looked unhappy, he thought. Too soft-hearted by far. Probably let folk walk all over her. He said, 'Take my advice, Miss Vivian, and get rid of him. One less thing to worry about then. With staff, you've got to be firm. Ask yourself this now — would your father have kept him on? You see what I'm driving at? Plenty more gardeners around. You'd soon replace him.'

'Oh dear! I dare say my father would have dismissed him but —' She shrugged.

Nice shoulders, he thought appreciatively. She'd have made someone a good wife if she'd had the chance.

She said, 'Sergeant, do you *really* think it's necessary? Couldn't he have one more chance? I think he was just being rather stupid. He's not —

well, to put it bluntly, Robb's very trusting and it *was* the first time he'd accepted any money. Chrissie can be very persuasive.'

Sergeant Wylie shook his head. 'Ah, but it doesn't work like that, Miss Vivian. If he's been "persuaded" by a pretty face — well, all the more reason to suspect it might happen again. All the pretty young ladies you've got in the school! He'll likely forget all about this and do it again!'

Poor soul. She looked very straight.

'But, Sergeant,' she protested, 'Robb's been with us . . .'

Sergeant Wylie was disappointed by her persistence. He was giving her good advice and she was trying to ignore it. He continued firmly, '*And* Robb might miss the odd sixpence or whatever they gave him. In my opinion, you're lucky it wasn't worse *this* time. These affairs get out of hand so easily.' He sighed. The sergeant was not a passionate man himself but he could imagine how it might be. 'Before you know it you have a murder on your hands. Oh yes, Miss Vivian. It's not a very safe world, I'm sorry to say.'

Her expression said it all, he thought, but she needed to be convinced. He was doing her a favour, if she did not know it.

She said, 'Well, then, I will. And thank you for your advice.'

She forced a smile — to show there were no hard feelings, he thought. And a very nice smile

201

it was, too. He popped the last of his biscuit into his mouth. 'We'll get the cheeky beggar,' he told her. 'Don't you worry on that score. It might take a day or two but we'll get him.'

As soon as dinner was over, Rose retired to the Head's room and began to sort through the second post. More bills. She *must* get into Helston to see the bank manager. There was a letter from Kenya from parents of twin girls asking if they could attend Tye Rock House as day girls at the start of the September term. The aunt who would act as their guardian lived in Helston. Rose sighed. Would there *be* a school in September, she wondered, and put the letter aside for consideration later. The last letter caused her deep dismay:

Dear Miss Vivian,
   I am the next door Neighbour to poor Mrs Bretton who is the grandmother to Christina Morgan, the old lady was taken queer two days ago and found by me on the floor of her Kitchen and is in the Hospital up the road and is very poorly and couldn't come and collect Christina nor could she look after herself let alone her granddaughter, I am feeding her cat and doing a bit of washing for her poor woman, I will pass on the letter when she is well enough to read it, yours faithfully

Mary Reed (Mrs) . . .

'Damn!' cried Rose. Chrissie Morgan would have to stay at Tye Rock House after all. The knowledge depressed her and she sat back, trying desperately to come to terms with the extended sentence that fate had imposed on her. Guiltily she realised that she was finding it difficult to feel any sympathy for Mrs Bretton who had fallen ill at such an inconvenient time.

'Damn and double damn!'

There was a knock on the door and Maud put her head round it. 'Robb's here, Miss Vivian. You did say you wanted to have a word with him.'

'Yes, I do, Maud. Ask him to come in, please.' She was going to dismiss him — a task she dreaded.

Maud hesitated. 'He probably didn't understand what he was doing. He's not that bright. Nor dim, neither but . . . sort of stolid. A slow thinker but he gets there in the end.'

Rose's expression was grim. 'It might have ended in disaster, Maud. You must understand that, surely? Christina Morgan might have ended up . . .' She baulked at the word 'pregnant' and lowered her voice. 'She might have had a *child,* for heaven's sake. Worse still, he could have *murdered* her!'

Maud, obviously chastened by this extreme view of the situation, nevertheless continued her defence of the gardener. 'But he wouldn't have meant any harm, Rose, that's what I'm saying. Not Robb. Honest as the day is —'

Rose remembered the sergeant's words. Be firm with the staff. 'Robb will have to go, Maud. I'm sorry, I can't risk keeping him here. If you had been there last night — well, it was a dreadful scene. Sergeant Wylie is going to find the man and question him. The sergeant was right. I can't hide the facts from Miss Morgan's parents, and what are they going to think if Robb is still here?'

'How will they know?'

Rose recognised the mulish tone and said wearily, 'Don't argue, Maud. Just send him in.'

Rose stood up. Robb came in, his cap in his hand and stood awkwardly on the carpet, staring round him. She wondered if he had ever been in the room before. Possibly not, because the wages were paid out in the kitchen by Mrs Cripps. Rose frowned at him and did not tell him to sit down.

Before she could speak he said, 'Maud says I'm in trouble. Real trouble.' His voice was slow and deep and Rose remembered Maud's attempt to help him.

Rose sat down and looked up at him severely. 'You certainly are, Robb. It appears that you accepted money from one of our girls. You know what that was, Robb? It was a bribe.'

'No, Miss, it were a shilling.' His large brown eyes gazed anxiously into hers.

'The shilling *was* the bribe, Robb, and a bribe is a bad thing to accept. It's taking money so that something bad can happen. That's what you did, and it was wrong. Very wrong indeed. You must have known that our young ladies shouldn't be sending letters to men in the village. You *did* know, didn't you?'

Slowly the cap turned in his nervous fingers. 'Didn't seem so at the time as I recall,' he said at last.

Rose sharpened her tone. 'Well, it *was* so and you *should* have known. And then you took *another* bribe, telling Miss Morgan that you would be at home that night so they could meet in your loft over the stable.'

He frowned. 'But I *was* at home. I didn't need it, see. She asked me and I told her. Makes no odds to me, I said. Something like that, any road.'

Rose sighed. This was more difficult than she had expected. She had to sack him — but how could she give him a reference? She said, 'It was a very stupid, very bad thing to do. Miss Morgan might have been — might have come to some serious harm. Can't you see that, Robb? A young lady — a schoolgirl — and a young man together in the hay loft *at night?*'

Did he understand, she wondered suddenly. Had Robb ever found a girl willing to lie with him? Had he ever felt the urge? He looked so forlorn. Like a whipped puppy, she thought unhappily. Would he ever get another job without a reference? She was going to ruin his life.

She said, 'I'm sorry, Robb, but you will have to leave us. I will be unable —'

'Hang on, Miss Vivian! I've got something to say. What Poll told me, though darned if I can remember it.' He scratched his head, frowning with concentration. Then he rested his right hand on his heart. 'I won't never do anything bad again. Not ever. And that's the God's truth.'

He looked at her with obvious relief and she groaned inwardly. Then she resisted a smile, amused that Polly should have coached him and wondering why she had done so. Unless there was something going on between them. Robb might be a little slow, but he was good-hearted and a hard worker. If Polly was fond of him she *would* do what she could to help him. Rose felt an unsettling rush of sympathy for them both. What did life hold for the Pollys of this world, she wondered. The most they could hope for was the love of a good man, enough to eat and a roof over their heads.

She felt her determination wavering. 'You say that now, Robb, but will you keep to it?' She imagined the sergeant rolling his eyes at her weakness and wanted desperately to be convinced. 'No more bribes.'

He was nodding his head so fiercely that she wondered his neck didn't ache.

'Oh, Robb!' she murmured.

When she was twelve, nine-year-old Robb — then newly appointed gardener's 'boy' — had brought her a baby bird which had fallen from its nest. The large hands that now fiddled with his cap had cradled the small creature with infinite

206

care. He had given the fledgling to her as a present and when it died two hours later he had comforted her. He dug a tiny grave for it and wrapped it in a cabbage leaf. They stood together while she recited the Lord's Prayer, slowly and with great solemnity, and he glanced nervously around in case the gardener caught him wasting his time. Could she *possibly* turn him adrift in the world without a reference?

Suddenly Rose knew she couldn't do it. The sergeant meant well. He had given her sound advice, but she didn't have to take it.

She told Robb that if he would keep his promise she would give him another chance.

'No more shillings or sixpences from the girls, Robb. *Never* again.'

'Not never!' he agreed. He stared with apparent interest at the inside of his cap, then carefully rolled it up. He pushed it into his pocket, thought better of it and took it out again.

Rose smiled. Hopefully she wouldn't see the sergeant again for some time and by then he might have forgotten all about Robb. He would assume that he was long gone from Tye Rock House and she needn't disillusion him.

Robb gave his thigh a slap with the rolled-up cap. 'Onions are coming on a treat.'

'Onions?' She stared at him.

'Yep. And carrots. Coming on a treat, they are.'

'Oh, I see. Good.'

She hoped she had done the right thing. She

said, 'Stick to gardening, Robb, will you? You're very good at that.'

He beamed.

She nodded. 'Off you go.'

Just after one o'clock Rose settled herself in a chair opposite James Edgcombe and smiled at the waiter as he handed her a menu. She had invited the young solicitor to a meal at Tye Rock House, but instead he had insisted on taking her out to a restaurant. Such events had been non-existent while her father was alive and Rose was determined to enjoy herself. She had, however, a purpose in the meeting and that was her need for help.

She chose lamb cutlets and her companion said, 'Make that for two, please.'

Rose looked around, impressed by the pale decor and elegant furniture. The cream linen tablecloth was spotless and the glasses shone. A trifle self-consciously, she rearranged the linen napkin which the waiter had carefully placed over her skirt. After the austerity of Tye Rock House she felt supremely cosseted. 'This is a rare treat, Mr Edgcombe,' she told her companion, 'and very generous.'

A smile lit up his round face and the brown eyes behind the spectacles glowed with satisfaction. 'It's my *pleasure* entirely,' he told her. 'But! I forgot to tell you that there is a price to pay!'

'A price?'

'Yes. I would like to suggest that since we virtually grew up together, in a manner of speaking, and since you *did* once invite me to your birthday party, we should feel entitled to be on Christian-name terms.

She was amused. 'Christian names?'

'Yes. The way I see it is this. I *should* have come to your birthday party and then you would have been invited to mine. We would soon have been friends. So we can pretend that I did accept that deckle-edged invitation and proceed from there.'

She was amused by his tone and the look on his face. For some reason she longed to accept. She had never had a close friend; no one with whom to exchange confidences. They could have become friends . . . but today? It was rather unconventional.

'Is it appropriate, do you think?' she asked.

'Totally and utterly appropriate.' He said this with great conviction, but his mouth twitched.

Rose laughed. This man was fun to be with, she decided. 'Then I have to say "Yes"!' she told him.

He poured her a glass of water and said, 'Good. Now — you said you need my help. How, Rose, can I be of assistance?'

She caught his eye and smiled at the very slight emphasis he had put on her name.

'Well, *James*,' she replied, 'I have found out more about my mother and —'

'So have I!' he told her.

'You *have?* Tell me, please.' She leaned forward, listening intently. Any information about her mother was tremendously important. Each snippet was another piece of the jigsaw.

He said, 'It was while we were at your father's funeral. I caught sight of the lady playing the organ, a Miss Gibbs. At the time your mother left the village, the man also disappeared, and he was a teller at the bank in Helston.'

Rose gasped. 'Don't tell me he's still in the area?'

James looked confused. 'You mean he ran away with her, then left her?'

'Yes. Maud told me that she was in love with someone from the bank and they left at the same time. After some time, she was left alone, possibly with a child.'

James gasped. 'You mean *his* child? That means he left his child and your mother and came back here? That's terrible!'

Rose shrugged. The waiter returned with two bowls of creamy vegetable soup and a plate of thinly sliced brown bread. The excitement of James's news had almost robbed Rose of her appetite, but she made a great show of enjoying the soup. In between mouthfuls she told him about Maud's revelations and the reference, in the letter, to Miss Folkes.

'So you see,' she told him, 'I have to find this mystery woman who was obviously kind to my mother. I was going to ask you to come with me — if you can spare the time.'

'I'll *make* time,' he assured her, 'but we might

get some help from Miss Gibbs. She must know where her brother is.'

'I could speak to her; explain why I need the information. I could get her address from the vicar, couldn't I?'

James smiled broadly. 'I've already done that!' he told her and took a slip of paper from his jacket pocket.

Rose took it with trembling fingers. This was the real first step towards her mother. She read the hurried scrawl.

'. . . Sarah Gibbs, Moor Cottage, Porthleven.'

'That's the other end of the village,' she said. 'I could go there! I could write and ask —'

He reached across the table and touched her hand. 'I've done it already. When we've finished our meal I'm going to drive you across to see her!'

'*Today?* Oh, how wonderful! Mr — sorry — *James!* You're an angel!'

'I've always thought so!'

He looked like the cat that got the cream, thought Rose, and was immensely touched by his kindness.

He said, 'But you have to do something for me in return.'

'Anything!' she told him.

His eyes flickered for an instant and then he said, 'Come to lunch with us, Rose. This coming Sunday at one o'clock. Mother thinks you need a break from Tye Rock House. I think she sees you rather like Rapunzel, trapped in splendid isolation at the top of a tower, unable to escape!'

She laughed. 'And you're the handsome prince sent to ride in and rescue me!'

'That's about it!'

'So where's the white charger?' She rolled her eyes.

'Outside in the stable. My lackeys are plaiting the snow-white mane and polishing the golden bells on the harness. Another one is brushing the long silver tail.' He looked at her in mock dismay. 'What? Don't you believe me?'

'I believe you, Mr Edgcombe!' She clapped a hand to her mouth. 'Oh! I've done it again! I keep forgetting.'

'You'll get used to "James" in time.'

'But you don't forget to call me Rose.'

His expression changed almost imperceptibly. His smile hadn't faltered, but there was something in his eyes that she did not recognise. 'I've been practising all my life!' he told her.

Rose was thankful for the waiter's reappearance, which meant that she didn't have to answer. She would have been at a loss to know what to say.

They pulled up outside Moor Cottage at exactly a minute to three. Rose looked at the gaunt, grey stone building. The front of the cottage was separated from the road by a thin strip of grass; the front door was a no-nonsense brown and the windows were heavily curtained. She turned to her companion. 'Are we both going in?' she asked, suddenly nervous.

'No. I think she's more likely to confide in you if you're alone. I have a call to make, but I'll come back for you in an hour's time.'

He hurried round to help her down.

'I'm terrified!' she whispered.

'You'll be all right, Rose. Remember that you have done nothing wrong and the scandal was a long time ago. The passing years will have softened the impact.' He gave her arm a friendly squeeze. 'Go on. Ring the bell. Miss Gibbs won't bite you!'

She watched him climb back on to the trap and urge the horse forward. As they rattled away along the track she felt very alone. But she had come here with a purpose and there was no point in delaying. She reached for the bell-pull and tugged twice.

Sarah Gibbs stood in the doorway, a frail figure with her greying hair twisted into a bun on the top of her head. Rose thought she must be in her late forties, possibly even older. Her face was lined and the downward curve of her mouth suggested a disappointment with life.

'You'd better come in,' she said as though this was actually the last thing she wanted.

Reluctantly, Rose stepped inside, The house smelled of an odd mixture — vinegar, soapsuds and moth-balls.

Rose said, 'You're very kind to spare me some of your time.'

The woman didn't answer but led the way into her front parlour. This was unheated but neat as a pin. The small window was almost hidden by a heavy net curtain which blocked out much of the thin sunlight. There was a large straw cross on the wall as well as a series of illustrated texts from the Bible.

'Sit yourself down,' she told Rose, indicating the only fireside chair. 'I suppose you'll be wanting a cup of tea.'

'No, thank you.'

'It won't poison you!'

'I'm truly not thirsty. Miss Gibbs, Mr Edgcombe has told you why —'

Miss Gibbs sat down on a high-backed chair. 'He wouldn't take no for an answer. Determined, he was, but I liked the man. His heart's in the right place. I can tell a man's nature just by listening to his voice.' She nodded. 'A good man, James Edgcombe. A friend of yours, obviously.'

Rose wondered what James had told her. 'He's our solicitor,' she said, then immediately realised her mistake.

Sarah's expression hardened. 'A *solicitor!* I don't want any trouble with solicitors. I've nothing to say to them. Not then. Not now. As for my brother — you'd best ask him.'

Rose searched for a delicate way to express herself. 'I understand that your brother and my

214

mother were . . . close friends. That they —'

'Close friends? So that's what they call it these days. My brother and your mother *eloped* together. That's how close they were.' Her small fists tightened in agitation. 'Not that they went *together*, thank the Lord, but they met soon after. And lived in sin together.' She glared at Rose. 'Broke the commandments — and me a church organist.'

Rose said quickly, 'I thought you played very well for my father's funeral.'

'You did, did you?' She appeared slightly mollified by the compliment.

Rose swallowed, telling herself to ignore the chilly reception and concentrate on the purpose of her visit.

She said, 'I wonder if they hoped to marry?'

Miss Gibbs raised her eyebrows. 'Divorce, you mean?' Her mouth tightened and she lifted her chin. 'Miss Vivian, I hardly need to tell you that in your father's position a divorce would have spelled the end of his career. The end of his school. How could they hope for a divorce? It would have ruined your father, who was entirely blameless in the affair.'

'I see.' The silence lengthened and Rose tried again. 'Do you know why your brother left my mother? Had they quarrelled?'

'I didn't ask and I never shall. Alan had a respectable job with prospects and he threw it all away to go haring across the country with another man's wife. He shamed us all. It broke my mother's heart and my father never forgave him. They were selfish, Miss Vivian, the pair of them. You came here for the truth and you've got it.'

'Perhaps he didn't really love her.'

It was another mistake. Sarah Gibbs' eyes flashed. 'Love? What has love to do with anything? It was *adultery*, Miss Vivian. They broke a lot of hearts by their actions. And what about you? How did you feel when your mother ran away and left you behind?'

Rose shivered at the depths of the woman's barely suppressed anger. She said, 'I was very young. Later I didn't think she had gone for good. I kept thinking she would come back. I prayed every night for that to happen. But she didn't come back, and at last I accepted that she never would. Not while my father was alive.' She was surprised to hear a tell-tale tremor in her voice. Much later her father had assured her that he would never allow his wife to set foot in the house again. 'She made her choice' he said on the few occasions when she dared ask. He flatly refused to discuss the 'whys and wherefores' that Rose longed for.

Rose said, 'I happen to know that she asked about me in several of her letters and wanted to see me again. I think she did love me.'

Miss Gibbs gave her a pitying look. 'She loved you so much that she left you. She chose her lover over her child.'

'There must have been a *reason*.' An idea was forming in Rose's mind. 'Do you think she was expecting your brother's child?'

Miss Gibbs' eyes widened. 'Certainly not! That's a dreadful thing to say!'

'Do you know that for certain?'

'I asked him and he rejected the idea. When he came back he had nowhere to go, and he stayed with me for a couple of months. I didn't want him here — there was so much gossip — but he's kin and he had nowhere else. He wouldn't lie to me, that I *do* know. "I suppose you've put her in the family way," I said. "You wouldn't understand," he told me. That was all I could get out of him. But this I do know, Miss Vivian. If your mother had had his child he would never have left her. He always wanted a family. He loved children. Poor Alan. He married eventually, of course, but lost his wife and the child in childbirth.'

'Died? Oh, how terribly sad!' Rose's depression was growing. She had come to Moor Cottage full of hope but this unfortunate woman was making her feel worse about her past, not better.

'Sad? Huh!' Sarah Gibbs tossed her head. 'He rejected the sacred teachings of his faith and he reaped the rewards. He got no more than he deserved. They both did.'

'But what about the forgiveness of sins?'

'What about it? You have to show true repentance, and Alan showed nothing of the kind. He insisted that he still loved the woman, even after he left her! Like a lovesick calf, he was. I lost my patience with him in the end. We had a falling out. I told him he'd outstayed his welcome and off he went. He's somewhere in Falmouth now, but he won't thank you for raking it all up again. Best let sleeping dogs lie, Miss Vivian, if you want my advice.'

Rose sighed deeply, overcome with a sense of hopelessness. As a last attempt she asked, 'You don't know anything about a Miss Folkes, do you? She was mentioned . . .'

'Ida Folkes? Yes, I've heard of her.' She frowned. 'The writer woman from London.'

Rose sat up, her hopes reviving instantly. 'You know her?'

'I know *of* her,' she corrected. 'Wrote novels, I believe. Wrote something anyway. She wrote to Alan from Redruth while he was still with me and I opened the letter. She was begging him to return to Catherine. Said she was prostrate with grief. I tore the letter up before Alan saw it. He'd had enough trouble.' She ignored Rose's horrified look. 'I think your mother was the Folkes woman's housekeeper, or her companion. I'm not sure.'

'You don't have her address, by any chance?' Rose crossed her fingers.

'Her address? That woman? Certainly not!'

Rose stood up. 'That woman is a friend of my mother, Miss Gibbs, and I want to find her. She might know where my mother is.'

'Wild goose chase,' she muttered.

'Not to me.' Rose controlled her voice with an

effort. 'I want to find my mother. Wherever she is and whatever she's done, I love her.'

Sarah Gibbs rose also. 'You can't love someone you don't even know!'

Rose met her gaze steadily. 'I can and I do!'

'Then you're a bigger fool than I took you for!'

On this acrimonious note, Rose decided that her meeting with Sarah Gibbs had run out of time.

On the doorstep she turned. 'I'm sorry, Miss Gibbs, that we haven't seen eye to eye,' she said, 'but I thank you for talking to me.'

Sarah Gibbs stared at her with obvious dislike. 'You stay away from my brother, Miss Vivian. D'you hear me? I may not have a good word to say for him, but he's my flesh and blood and I do know he's suffered quite enough.'

Rose said, 'I'm sorry. I can't promise anything, Miss Gibbs. I'll do whatever is necessary to find my mother.'

The door slammed in her face and she was left with an unsettling picture of Sarah Gibbs' furious face. Rose turned in the direction James had taken, struggling with mixed emotions. She felt just a little closer to her mother, but she had expected more sympathy from someone who had been close to the tragedy.

'I'm *going* to find her!' she muttered defiantly, and began to walk quickly along the lane to meet James.

Charlie Robb sat in front of the small kitchen

range, hunched forward, his arms crossed defensively across his stomach which was full of stew. He was talking to his older brother, Tom, about his spot of bother at Tye Rock House. Getting it off his chest. Behind him, his mother was pretending to wash up the supper plates, but Robb knew she was listening to their conversation.

Tom shook his head. 'A bad business,' he agreed. 'I reckon that chap was Summers from the Hatchers' place. Sort of thing he would get up to, randy bugger.'

His mother said, 'Watch your language, Tommy Robb!'

'Sorry, Ma,' said Tom, 'but it's the truth. They say it was him put Sally Noakes up the spout, but he wouldn't have it. No way.'

Robb said, 'Big chap, is he?'

'Big enough!'

A smile spread slowly across Robb's face. 'Mr Tremayne had a go at him, by all accounts.'

Tom grinned. 'Make mincemeat of him, Summers would!'

His mother turned, reaching for the cloth. 'How would you know, Tom?'

' 'Cos I've met him, that's how. Walking on the beach with Vivian. Always give me the time of day, they do. *Did,* I should say. Won't be giving no one the time of day now, poor old lad.'

Robb said, 'Mincemeat, eh? Serve him right then.'

His mother moved nearer, rubbing furiously at a plate. 'What you got against the man, Charlie? What's he done to you?'

Robb frowned. 'What's who done?'

Tom said, 'Tremayne. What's he done?'

'Ah!' His face darkened. 'It's Poll. She thinks the sun shines out of his —' He stopped guiltily.

'Charlie!' his mother warned. She stowed the three clean plates in a cupboard and tossed the knives and forks into the dresser drawer. 'Where did I go wrong with you two?' she asked.

Tom winked at Robb and made a brief yapping sign with his hand.

Robb shook his head gloomily. 'Proper smitten, she is. "Mr Tremayne this" and "Mr Tremayne that"! Makes me sick!'

His brother stared at him with amusement. 'Taken a bit of a shine to her then, have you — this Polly?'

Robb was aware that his mother and brother were regarding him with keen interest. 'Why shouldn't I?' he asked. He had to be careful with Tom. His brother would pull his leg if he got half a chance.

His mother smiled. 'About time, Charlie. Every man needs a wife. Pretty, is she?'

'She's all right.'

She turned to Tom. 'So this Mr Tremayne — what's he like?'

Tom shrugged. 'So-so. Bit of a pretty boy.'

'Pansy,' Robb suggested. 'You could knock him down with a feather!'

'Well, he's a teacher,' said Tom. 'History. What can you expect? Mind you, he was pretty pally with old Vivian. Not that they were all that matey last time I saw him. Day of the accident, it was. Bit of an argument, they was having. "You calling me a liar?" says Tremayne. "Yes, I am!" he says. "I might have known!" says Tremayne. On and on. They didn't see me.'

'Nice hair,' said Robb.

'Who — Tremayne?'

'Poll. Nice and shiny.' He sighed.

His mother said, 'Pity they don't buy their fish from us instead of that Helston fishmonger. Put a bit of cash your way, Tom, you being a local man.'

Tom shook his head. 'Oh, not that again, Ma, please! I've told you before, it wouldn't do. That's a bit order, that is, and regular. What if I didn't get enough? Like yesterday. Half a dozen mackerel and a few plaice. There's near on thirty people in Tye Rock House. I'd be letting them down, wouldn't I? Just wouldn't do.'

'But you've had bigger catches, Tom. Much bigger!'

That was true, thought Robb. Much bigger catches. One day it had taken them the best part of an hour to get the fish out of the net. They'd all three had to go round the houses with baskets of fish, and they still had herrings left over for Ma to pickle.

'But not *regular!*' he repeated. 'Not every Friday!'

Robb said, 'Arguing, was they?'

They both stared at him.

His mother said, 'Arguing or not, Vivian's dead so leave him be. Never speak ill of the dead. That's what they say. Just thank your lucky stars you've still got a job, Charlie. I reckon Miss Vivian's been very decent after what happened in the stables.'

Tom said, 'Old Vivian would have sacked you for sure! Ma's right, Charlie. You was lucky it was the daughter. She's a decent sort, by all accounts. You just keep out of trouble in future.'

Robb nodded. 'And a nice laugh!' He always had to laugh when Poll laughed. Just hearing her laugh cheered him up. Now he smiled at the memory. Maybe next year he'd send her one of those cards with the heart on it and all the flowers and such, but it had to be the right day. A special day for sending cards. And Pansy Tremayne had best keep away from her. Suppose *he* sent her a card. His smile faded. He'd best keep away from her — or else.

His mother said, 'Who's got a nice laugh? Miss Vivian?'

'Or else!' he said firmly.

Sometimes he thought his mother was a bit slow.

CHAPTER SEVEN

While Robb was with his family, the teachers at Tye Rock House had gathered in the staff room for a meeting, called by Rose to discuss the school's future and to deal with current emergencies. On this occasion they were seated round the large table. Miss Hock, at the far end, faced Rose along the table's length. On Rose's right were the Matron and Mr Tremayne. On her left, Adèle Dubois and Arnold Rivers. There was, thought Rose, a palpable air of apprehension and she was conscious that the meeting might not go as smoothly as she hoped. It was obvious that since her father's death they would all have been considering their own futures. They would hardly wish to stay on if they doubted her ability to run the school in a competent way.

She started promptly by thanking everyone for giving up their evening. 'You all have many calls on your time,' she continued, 'but it would be unfair if I didn't keep you up to date with what is happening and what might happen.'

Mark Tremayne gave her an encouraging smile but no one spoke.

'I've drawn up a rough agenda so that we don't waste too much time. Briefly that is Christina

Morgan, the part-time teacher, and the future of Tye Rock House.'

Matron interrupted, 'About Chrissie Morgan —'

'One moment, please. I want to say that I welcome any ideas which you may have to contribute. I don't know how my father used to manage staff meetings, but I certainly don't intend to do all the talking.'

Miss Hock muttered something to Arnold Rivers and Rose tensed. She had hoped that Miss Hock would be supportive. She was a strong character and could influence the rest of them.

Mark Tremayne asked, 'Has Chrissie been suspended or expelled?'

Matron said, 'That girl is becoming a serious liability! Her rudeness is unforgivable.'

'She is being suspended,' Rose explained. Surely, she thought, they would approve this particular move on her part. 'She was to have gone home but unfortunately I have just heard through a third party that her grandmother is seriously ill in hospital and —'

Matron said, 'Oh no! Don't tell me that we have to keep her here! I've been counting the days — no, the *hours!* — until she left.'

Surprised, Rose looked at her. The tone of her comment had hinted at something akin to desperation. 'Last time you put in a good word for her,' she said.

Matron fiddled with a button on her blouse.

'It's true I do try to see some good in all the girls but to be frank, Miss Vivian, I don't think I can face the responsibility much longer. Schoolgirls, yes, but Chrissie is hardly that. She's a wilful young woman, and I for one don't know how to deal with her.'

Before Rose could answer her, Miss Hock said, 'You're paid to deal with girls like that. It is part of a matron's responsibility. If you . . .'

Her unfinished sentence was damning and the other teachers exchanged embarrassed glances. None of them looked at Rose.

Matron stammered, 'But Chrissie Morgan — well, she isn't —'

Miss Hock snapped, 'If you can't manage growing girls, you shouldn't have taken the job in the first place!'

Feeling her face colour with anger, Rose said, '*Please!* Miss Hock! I think you're being rather harsh. We all find Christina an exceptionally difficult pupil.'

Miss Hock glared at her. 'I can deal with her. If I had charge of her for a few weeks I'd soon knock some sense into her!'

'Bully her, you mean!' said Matron, braving further scorn.

Mark Tremayne held up a hand. 'Let's just agree that Chrissie is a problem.'

Miss Hock turned to him. 'Who asked you to interfere?'

He shrugged. 'I'm not interfering, Miss Hock.' He kept his voice level but Rose saw that he was furious. 'I'm giving my opinion,' he went on. 'I'm entitled to do that without inviting a caustic comment from you or anyone else.'

Rose was aware of a growing panic. Adèle Dubois was biting her lip; Matron was pale. Arnold Rivers was looking helpless. If she lost control of this meeting she might as well give up. She said, 'Whatever we think about Chrissie, we shall have to put up with her presence a little longer. The girl is wild, I agree, but there must be some good in her if only we could find it.'

Adèle Dubois nodded. 'She was a nice child when she first came. When she was thirteen.'

Arnold Rivers agreed. 'She's talented, too. Good at art — a good eye and a nice feel for composition — but *so* lazy. A great shame.'

Matron said, 'I do feel it must do something to a child to be separated from her parents. Knowing that they are so far away. Children react in different ways. Some become timid and withdrawn. Others put on a bold front as a means of self-defence. Maybe Chrissie —'

Miss Hock snorted. 'Trust you to make excuses for them. If they've anything about them, being left among strangers develops character and independence. I spent years at boarding school and it didn't do me any harm.'

Rose almost laughed as the rest of the staff struggled to hide their feelings. Rose wanted to say, 'It didn't do you any good, either!' but she let the unkind thought remain unspoken.

Mr Tremayne raised his eyebrows. 'That's a

matter of opinion. We can't see ourselves as others see us.'

There was a shocked silence while Miss Hock inhaled sharply, but Rose intervened before a further argument could develop.

'I am going to give Chrissie her own room,' she told them. 'Not for her sake, but because I can't discipline her so easily if she's sharing. I shall move Lucy and put her in with Kate and Jane in room seven. It's big enough for three. That will mean that poor Lucy no longer becomes drawn into Chrissie's escapades. I shall require Chrissie to report to you, Matron, before breakfast, and to me after the midday meal and again after prep. I want her to feel that she is under constant supervision.'

To Rose's surprise, Matron was looking at her unhappily. 'I really don't think . . .' she began. 'I must confess I was thinking of . . .' She faltered. 'I am seriously thinking of leaving at half-term.'

Rose almost groaned.

Arnold Rivers said, 'But the term's only just started. You have to give a term's notice, minimum.'

'I know, but —'

Adèle Dubois wagged a finger at her. 'But you must not do this thing. It is madness to leave because of this girl. Think of your old age.'

Matron looked at Rose.

Dismayed by the idea of losing her, Rose stammered, 'Leaving? Oh dear! Are you sure about this?'

Matron looked close to tears. 'I don't want to, of course, but I can't sleep at night, worrying about what that girl is up to. I blame myself for the other night.'

Miss Hock gave a short laugh. 'That's right, Matron! Give in! Chrissie will be delighted to know she's won!'

Rose swung round to face her. 'That's just about enough from you, Miss Hock.' Her temper was rising. 'You cannot think that your attitude is in any way helpful.' She turned to Matron. 'You must come and talk to me privately. Will you do that? Maybe tomorrow morning?'

'Yes, I will. I'm sorry. I know it's weak and foolish of me but I can't explain — it's like a huge cloud over my head.'

Her eyes filled with tears and Rose reached out to take hold of her hand. 'Don't worry,' she said. 'I understand. It's been a very difficult week for all of us.' She made a pretence of consulting her notes, crossing her fingers that Miss Hock would let the matter go.

Fortunately, disgusted by Matron's apparent weakness, Miss Hock moved on to another subject. 'So this replacement teacher? Who is he? Or is it a she?'

Rose ignored her for a moment, long enough to let her know that she had overstepped the mark and that she, Rose, would decide when to move on to a new subject.

For a moment she struggled to bring her own

emotions under control.

Then she said, 'Daneside School are lending us their Mr Jones once a week until we can appoint someone permanently.'

Adèle Dubois said quickly, 'Then Tye Rock House — it *will* continue?'

Rose hesitated. 'I feel it is only fair that you should all know as much as I do. The situation is this — that my father left everything to me except for a few small bequests to the servants. I have to take a good look at the finances, and that is not going to be easy, but I shall take advice. There are three options. I carry on as Head and appoint a deputy. I appoint a Head to manage the school but retain control of the business and the property. Or I sell the school as a going concern.'

Another silence as they all digested the implications.

She said, 'Of course I *could* close the school and simply use Tye Rock House as a private residence, but I doubt if that will happen. It would be much too big for me to live in alone.'

Miss Hock folded her arms over her chest. 'So we could all be thrown out of employment!'

Rose said, 'I've just said that I don't think that will happen.'

'But we have no guarantee that it will not.'

Rose's pulse quickened. This is it, she thought. The situation I dreaded. She knew intuitively that her earlier rebuke had provoked Miss Hock and that this was her way of retaliating.

'Miss Hock, I think you are being a little un-fair,' she said, keeping her tone neutral. 'My father has only been dead for ten days, and it isn't easy to step into his shoes and sort out every-thing immediately. I can assure you I'm doing the best I can under difficult circumstances.' If she hoped to shame the woman she had mis-judged her.

Miss Hock shook her head. 'Not much com-fort to us, though, is it?'

Mark Tremayne leaned forward. 'I don't think Miss Vivian has to justify any decision to us. The situation is not of her choosing. She has to con-sider her own future just as we have to consider ours. Only you, Miss Hock, would delight in making her life more difficult than it already is. I have every faith in Miss Vivian and I think she deserves our full support.'

Rose gave him a quick smile of gratitude but Miss Hock recovered quickly. She leaned across to Arnold Rivers and said, 'Buttering her up like that! It's disgusting!'

Mr Tremayne went white with anger. 'If I had the money, Miss Hock, I would buy Tye Rock House School tomorrow. And the first thing I would do is ask you to leave!'

Rose didn't know whether to be grateful for his loyalty or dismayed by his outspoken com-ments. She closed her eyes briefly, awaiting fur-ther trouble.

Arnold Rivers rushed in. 'So it's all in the melting pot, Miss Vivian?'

'In a way, yes. All I can promise is that I will not do anything without consultation,' she told them. 'You will know my decision as soon as I do.'

Miss Hock rallied quickly. 'Is there any reason why you can't appoint a deputy head from the existing staff?'

Rose heard warning bells. 'None at all, but I should certainly want to advertise the post nationally. Existing members of staff would be eligible to apply, naturally.' But you, Miss Hock, would never be appointed, she thought. The last few minutes had demonstrated the total impossibility of establishing a working relationship between the two of them.

At that moment there was a knock on the door and Maud entered with a note in her hand.

'Yes, Maud. What is it?'

'The constable just called with this from Sergeant Wylie.'

'Thank you.'

Maud left the room and they all watched as Rose opened and read the note. When she had finished she looked up with a smile. 'Some good news at last!' she told them. 'The sergeant has found the man who was with Chrissie in the stables. It was a Gerald Summers, a groom with Brigadier Hatcher at Penns Manor. He's been sacked, apparently.'

Matron frowned. 'Aren't they going to prosecute him?'

'Apparently he hasn't broken any laws. Not

232

with Chrissie anyway. It wasn't against her consent, and that makes a difference.'

'She encouraged him,' Miss Hock declared. 'From all I heard *she* was the one urging him on. He has a note from her to prove it.'

Arnold Rivers said, 'I did hear she was using Robb as a messenger.'

Miss Hock said, 'Hah! Then Robb will have to go — and sharpish!' She gave Rose a challenging look.

Matron looked worried. 'Oh, not Robb! He's such a nice man. Always polite. He showed me round the greenhouse once. He's so proud of everything he grows, and very knowledgeable.'

Rose knew she would have to confess. 'Sergeant Wylie felt he should be dismissed, but I've given him another chance,' she said.

'You'll regret it!' Miss Hock's tone was triumphant.

'I hope not.' Rose glanced at the clock on the wall. The staff meeting had been fairly disastrous, saved only by Mark Tremayne's timely help. The message from the police sergeant had been very welcome, arriving when it did and producing one positive result.

She said hopefully, 'Well, it's getting late. Have we covered everything?' She smiled at Matron. 'We'll talk tomorrow at nine if that suits you.'

Miss Hock said, 'I think you should see this,' and passed a note along to her.

Rose's first thought was that this was about

Chrissie Morgan and her elation faded. As she read it, however, she felt her face flush with embarrassment.

'. . . Miss Vivian is getting too friendly with Mr Tremayne. She had her arm round him . . .'

Rose tried to swallow but her mouth went dry. She stared at the neat handwriting — small, thin letters cramped together. It must be Chrissie's doing, she thought, with a stab of fear. That wretched girl would be her undoing. Intuition prompted her to act quickly while all the eyes were upon her. She said, 'Oh that silly girl!' and smiled at Mark Tremayne. 'Take a look at this.'

She passed the note to him. To the others she said, 'I was helping Mr Tremayne to walk after his fight with the intruder outside the stables. His knee was giving him some trouble. If anyone has any comment to make, now is the time to make it.'

Miss Hock said, 'It speaks for itself!'

'Meaning what exactly?'

Miss Hock shrugged.

Matron said, 'We've all seen it, of course — except Mr Tremayne. It was left on my table, and my first instinct was to throw it away. Miss Hock insisted that you should see it.'

She *would*, thought Rose, but she managed a light smile. 'I'll speak to Chrissie. That girl is not going to get away with anything — not even this nonsense.' To Mark Tremayne she said, 'I'm so sorry about this.'

Mark Tremayne said, 'Don't blame yourself.' To his colleagues he added, 'There's absolutely no truth in it, in case anyone is still unconvinced. My relationship with Miss Vivian is purely professional, and I'm sure it will stay that way. While she remains acting Head of the school, I shall always be a very supportive member of the staff.'

The cool words startled her, but heads nodded. Another hurdle over, Rose thought wearily. The meeting had frayed her nerves and more than anything she longed to be away from them all — with the exception of Mark Tremayne. If she could have thought of a reason to speak alone with him she would have used it, but her mind was an infuriating blank. There was nothing to do, she decided, but retire from the scene, clinging to what little dignity she still retained. The safety of her own room beckoned enticingly.

She smiled briefly and left the room, but as she walked back alone towards her own room she was secretly mortified by Mark Tremayne's denial of their friendship. It was true that, in the cut and thrust of the meeting, he had proved himself a wonderfully loyal ally, but he had assured the rest of the staff most convincingly that he would never be anything more to her than a supportive member of staff. Rose had been allowing herself to imagine something deeper between them. Surely he had hinted as much? She was certainly hoping that she could look upon him as much more than a friend. If she was wrong, she was likely to make an awful fool of herself.

By ten o'clock the following morning, Rose felt as though she had already lived through another day. She had had an exhausting talk with Matron and had finally persuaded her to stay on at least until the summer, when they had agreed to reconsider the matter. She also organised Lucy's transfer to Kate's room and had taken Chrissie to task about the note. Rose had not been surprised when Chrissie denied having written it, but she had been taken aback by the manner of her denial. After only a minute or two, Rose was totally convinced that Chrissie was not the note's author. So who on earth *had* written it? Somebody wishing to cause trouble — that much was certain. She sighed. For a moment she felt full of self-pity, but with a determined effort she thrust the notion from her. She had more important things to concern her now that she had created a breathing space.

Tomorrow, Mr Jones was coming over from Daneside School. On Thursday Matron was taking a day off, at Rose's insistence, to visit an aunt in Helston. Rose thought she needed some time off, and that although she couldn't be spared for longer, a day was better than nothing. On Friday two applicants for the vacant position were coming for interviews — one at ten, the other a little later. Mark Tremayne would help her but in the light of the recent interest in their relationship, Rose felt it necessary to make that fact known. Anything that smacked of collusion would cause resentment amongst the rest of the staff, and she had no wish to arouse further hostility. On Sunday she was lunching with the Edgcombes and staying on for tea.

So today was her only opportunity to visit the bank manager and to call on Alan Gibbs. James had willingly agreed to accompany her and would arrive in the trap around ten thirty. For May, the weather was unusually kind and Rose was looking forward to the trip. One reason was that she herself would escape the confines of Tye Rock House for a few blissful hours. Another was the chance to be with James in whose company she could relax. She was waiting on the steps when at last the sound of hooves signalled his arrival. James jumped down to help her into the dog-cart and within minutes they were on their way.

She said, 'It was very clever of you, James, to track down Alan Gibbs.'

'I told you I'd do anything for you.' He grinned. 'You see before you a devoted slave. The princess's wish is my command! So, tell me what's been happening at Tye Rock House.'

Willingly, holding nothing back, she related the events of the intervening days. His comments, she thought, were sensible. Until she mentioned the note; then he gave her a strange look and fell silent.

'What is it?' she asked, afraid that she had offended him in some way.

'It's nothing.'

'It's *something!*' she insisted.

Without looking at her, he said, 'I didn't realise I had a rival!'

'Mark Tremayne?' She tried her best to sound outraged by the idea, but even to her own ears the denial rang false. 'I told you what he said. That there would never be anything between us. He sounded very sincere.'

'I can't believe that. Any man would be blind if he didn't see what an attractive woman you are. He'd be crazy not to —' He stopped.

'James!' she protested. 'Mark Tremayne is one of my staff. He's — he's younger than me. I hardly *know* the man.'

As soon as she uttered the words she realised with a start that it was true. What *did* she know about his background — except that his parents were both dead? She made a mental note to look in her father's confidential files. An unpleasant thought occurred to her. Mark Tremayne might be betrothed. She felt sick with dismay. Was that why he had been so emphatic about the unlikelihood of any relationship developing between them? Oh God! A worse thought occurred. He might be *married!* She swallowed hard and closed her eyes briefly. Would that have been mentioned at his interview, she wondered? Would it be in his file? Tense with this new anxiety, she tried to concentrate. If Mark Tremayne were married he would hardly have left his wife on her own. He lived in at Tye Rock House, so he *must* be single. Mustn't he?

'But you feel something for him.' James was not going to give up. He gave her a quick, sad glance. 'It's what *you* feel that matters to me.'

Rose could think of nothing to say. The speed with which the conversation had swung confused her. She glanced at him from the corner of her eye, but he was busying himself with the horses.

After a while he said, 'You *do* feel something for him, don't you?'

Her natural honesty conflicted with a desire not to hurt him. 'He's very loyal.'

'Aren't I loyal?'

'Of course you are. James, I . . . I value your friendship immensely. I feel entirely — *comfortable* with you. It's a good feeling.'

'Comfortable?'

'Happy and comfortable.'

After a moment he said, 'He's a good-looking devil, I'll say that for him. Slim, fine features, plenty of hair.'

'You're good-looking, James! Don't do this to yourself. You're a — a very attractive man.'

'Five out of ten, d'you think?'

'You're making fun of me.'

'So are you thinking about marriage now? Is that it?' He glanced at her. 'I would be in your position.'

Rose thought about it. What could she say?

'I've never ruled it out,' she said cautiously.

A glance at his face showed that he was no longer joking.

For no good reason, except perhaps to buy a little time, he cracked the whip over the horses, who flicked their ears crossly and made no effort to increase their speed. He said, 'You know how I feel about you, Rose. I have always loved you.'

'Oh, James!' She looked down at her hands, twisting her fingers unhappily.

James continued, choosing his words carefully, watching her reaction. 'So your father was wrong. You *are* the marrying kind?'

Rose shrugged. 'I daresay that until you fall in love with someone you —' She regretted the words instantly but it was too late.

James seized on them. '*Have* you fallen in love?'

She hesitated.

'You have,' he cried. 'You've fallen in love with Tremayne. *Damn* it!'

'No, I *haven't!*' she said wildly. 'He doesn't even know that — that I'm even the slightest bit interested. He doesn't love *me.*' If only he *did.* If only she knew *how* he felt about her. 'Mr Tremayne was Father's friend, that's all. That brought us a little closer. You mustn't say anything more about it, James. *Please!*'

'Of course not.'

'As to how I feel about marriage. Well, I was certainly never desperate to try it. Resigned, I suppose, to the way things were. Marriage seemed to be for other people — and my parents' marriage was hardly an inspiration. Maybe I felt safer where I was.'

'On the outside, looking in?'

'You could put it like that.'

'But now you wouldn't mind being married.'

Rose laughed. 'I rather think I'd like it.'

'But not with Tremayne.'

'No?' She stiffened defensively.

'Certainly not, Rose. He's a dark horse. A closed book.'

Annoyed, she said, 'You're making him sound quite intriguing.'

'He goes deep. I wouldn't put too much faith in him if I were you.' He glanced at her. 'Seriously, Rose, you must be careful.'

She didn't want to hear this, she thought. 'Could you be just a *little* bit prejudiced, James?'

'Never!' He waved to someone at the roadside and then shouted to the horses to 'Come up!' He said, 'I deserve you, Rose. Remember all those Valentines? You must have guessed it was me.'

He was trying to lighten the atmosphere and she made an effort to speak lightly. 'Of course I did, but it never occurred to me that there might be a genuine emotion behind the cards. I'm so sorry. You must think me peculiarly dense.'

'Rose Vivian *dense*? Certainly not. A little naïve, perhaps, but that's part of your charm.' He had relaxed enough to smile at her.

'You're being very kind, James — considering that my father was so unkind.'

241

He laughed again. 'If only I'd accepted the invitation to come to your party!'

Rose said, 'Well, there you are then! You muffed the catch! You have only yourself to blame.'

Rose breathed a sigh of relief that they had somehow avoided a confrontation and had steered the conversation safely back to a gentle teasing. She *did* value James's friendship, and she had been less than honest with him. She most certainly *did* care deeply for Mark Tremayne, but this was not the right time to say so. It might never be the right time.

They rounded the corner a little too fast and Rose was jolted into the realisation that they were on their way to see Alan Gibbs. She would need all her wits about her, and now put all thoughts of marriage out of her mind. James had offered to go in with her to see the man, but Rose had reluctantly turned down the offer. After her encounter with Sarah Gibbs, she didn't fool herself that this meeting might be any easier. If she was going to be disappointed she would rather deal with it alone. If she was going to hear unflattering or unwelcome remarks about her mother, she didn't want James's pity.

They pulled up at the house and for a moment Rose sat staring at it. It was small and drab and somehow sad looking.

She said slowly, 'The man in this house loved my mother — once. He ruined his career for her. They lived together and then he abandoned her.

I have to know why, and I have to find out where she is now.'

'If he knows, Rose. And if he's willing to tell you. Don't set your expectations too high.'

He climbed down and hurried round to help her alight.

'What will you do while I'm in there?' she asked.

He shrugged. 'I'll do some shopping. Have a cup of tea somewhere. Watch the fishermen at the quayside. I'll be quite happy.'

Rose looked into his eyes. No, she thought, you won't be happy, James. You've waited all these years and now you know that I am not interested in you as a husband. But what can I do to help you? She reached across suddenly and kissed him lightly on the cheek.

'The chaste sisterly kiss!' he said.

Rose wanted to kick herself for her stupidity. Instead she said, 'Wish me luck, won't you?'

He regarded her steadily. 'I wish you all the luck in the world!' he said softly. 'I'll wait until you are safely admitted.'

Rose held up crossed fingers. She hadn't dared to write to Alan Gibbs in case he refused to see her. She was taking a great risk, turning up on his doorstep unannounced. Turning from James, she lifted the knocker and banged twice. The waiting was an agony for her. Suddenly, footsteps, and a tall, thin man stood in the open doorway. He gazed at her with large grey eyes, but if he had once been handsome it was no longer obvious. From the stubble on his chin it was clear that he hadn't shaved for days nor, it seemed, had he combed his hair. The worn cardigan had been wrongly buttoned. One way and another, Rose thought, he looked thoroughly defeated. As he looked at her, his expression changed and she tried to read it but failed.

'Good God!' He stared at her in astonishment.

'Mr Gibbs?' she said, her voice hoarse.

He drew a long breath. 'Yes.'

She said, 'I'm —'

He said, 'Rose Vivian. I can see that for myself!'

She waited. This was the moment she had dreaded. If he sent her away, her chance to discover her mother's whereabouts was lost.

At last he held the door open. 'You'd better come in,' he said.

Rose followed him along a passage and into a large kitchen which obviously served also as a living room. There was a sink, cupboards, a range for cooking and a table and two wheelback chairs. There were no curtains at the window and no pictures on the wall. It was adequate, but nothing more than that.

'Sit down,' he said. 'I expect you'd like a cup of tea. I need something a little stronger.' He pushed the kettle further on to the heat and produced a blue mug with a chipped rim. From a cupboard he produced a half-empty whisky bottle and poured himself a generous measure. Rose saw that his hands were shaking and thought, with surprise, that he was probably as nervous as she was.

He sat down. 'Seeing you standing there was like seeing a ghost.'

'I didn't know,' she told him. 'I've never seen a likeness of my mother.'

'You look just like her when I — when we first . . .' His mouth tightened. 'Did that wretched sister of mine send you?'

'No. She didn't want me to find you, she was very hostile about my mother, but she let slip the fact that you were in the area. Mr Edgcombe, my solicitor, actually traced you. I hope you don't mind me coming.'

'Bit late now to worry about that?' As he found milk and sugar and poured boiling water into the brown teapot, Rose studied him unashamedly. This was the man her mother had loved enough to defy all the conventions; for this man she had abandoned husband and child. He might once have been handsome, but now he looked very ordinary. His curly hair was greying at the temples and he looked too thin for his clothes. Was his sister right, Rose wondered uneasily. Had her mother ruined his life? Did he have a job? Did he have any friends?

He said, 'I suppose I half expected it would happen one day — you turning up, I mean. It's because he's dead, isn't it? I read about the accident in the paper. Well, now you can start to live your own life. Oh, don't bother to protest, Miss Vivian. I know what he was like to live with.

Cathy's life was so narrow.'

Rose remained silent, not wanting to be disloyal and afraid that, once she started, she would say too much. After a pause she said, 'I want to ask you so many things but — I'd love to see a photograph if you have one. Just to look at her.'

He shook his head. 'Haven't got one.' He went on looking at her and the intense look in his eyes began to unnerve her. Then he said, 'Well, just the one.' Almost to himself he added, 'Can't do any harm. I'll fetch it.'

He was gone a few moments and Rose heard his footsteps going up and then coming down the uncarpeted stairs.

'Here you are. Catherine Vivian.' He handed her a photograph in a small silver frame and, for the first time in her life, Rose found herself staring at a likeness of her mother. Almost breathless with emotion, she stared intently at the slim, sweet-faced woman who looked very like Rose. She was standing on the lawn of what was obviously Tye Rock House and she held a croquet mallet in a striking position. Her smile was rather tentative, her body tense. Rose was at once aware of a deep disappointment that she, as a small girl, was not sharing the picture with her mother.

As though reading her thoughts, Alan Gibbs said, 'That was a few months before you were born.'

Rose was lost for words. Her eyes were blurred with tears and her feelings were totally confused, veering from delight to regret. 'I can see a likeness,' she said at last. 'How lovely that I look like her.'

'You *sound* like her, too.' He was watching her, fascinated. 'Her voice was exactly like yours. I suppose you've decided to try to find her?'

'I'm determined to, Mr Gibbs. I don't know quite what I'll do when I find her — it will depend on her circumstances — but I do want to speak to her.'

'And suppose she doesn't want a daughter suddenly arriving on her doorstep?' He poured the tea, avoiding her face as she pondered his question.

'I've thought of that. If she's made a new life for herself, I wouldn't want to be an embarrassment or cause her any unhappiness. Just to *see* her would be wonderful.' Just to be held in her mother's arms would be even more wonderful, thought Rose. A hug and a kiss, perhaps. Was that really asking too much? 'I've dreamed about it for years. I was hoping you would know something.' She looked at him hopefully, but he immediately shook his head.

'Nothing,' he said. 'She sent me away and I stayed away. I don't know where she is or what she is doing. I hope she's happy, but I doubt it.'

Suddenly Rose's heart began to race with pent-up anger. Here was yet another man who had failed her mother. First her father had sent her away, then this man had deserted her. 'You hope she's *happy?*' she said sharply. 'How can you sit there and say such a thing? Nobody understood her. Your sister hated her! You *hope* she's happy?' Her voice was rising, but she could do nothing about it. She was losing control of her temper and no longer cared. 'She'd be a lot happier if the men in her life had treated her better! You all let her down.' She put her head in her hands, struggling for breath.

She was vaguely aware that Alan Gibbs was watching her. When at last she looked up again she could see something in his eyes that she was unable to read.

'I'm afraid it wasn't quite like that. Cathy is no saint. She never will be.'

'That's a horrid thing to say!'

'No. She would be the first to admit it. I loved her in spite of her faults . . . We all did. Do you want to know what really happened? Why my sister was so biased?'

Alarmed by his tone, Rose nodded warily.

He folded both hands around the mug and sighed. 'Your mother was very unhappy with George Vivian. They weren't suited. She was so full of life and he was very quiet. A cautious, restrained man. It was just the way he was. The only thing that brought her happiness was you. Her little Rose was the apple of her eye. She adored you.'

'Did she?' Rose felt her hopes rising. The apple of her mother's eye.

'Oh, yes! You were her sunshine.'

Rose smiled. 'I'm so glad!' Her voice was husky with emotion.

'In fact, in a way, she was too fond of you. George was a little jealous — but he had his reasons. You must understand, Miss Vivian. George adored your mother. No one doubted that for a moment. Cathy did her best to love him in return, but he was a difficult man. It was all wrong from the start, but that's —' He broke off abruptly, avoiding her eyes. 'There are some things I can't talk about. I promised Cathy.'

Rose nodded, resisting the urge to hurry him, and after a moment or two he continued.

'Of course, I loved her too. I saw that she was unhappy and wondered if I should take you both away from George. I thought I could make Cathy happy. At first she wouldn't hear of it, but in the end she agreed. She was very much in love with me and there was . . . Well, forget that.'

Rose said, 'Secrets?'

'I promised.'

Rose let it go. If she tried to prise secrets from him he might resent it. She must be satisfied with what he was prepared to tell her.

He continued. 'We knew we would have to go secretly, and it was all arranged. But at the last minute she couldn't bring herself to just disappear. She thought it was too cruel, and that she at least owed George an explanation. I argued with her because I could foresee trouble. The day before we were going away together she told him she was leaving.'

Even so many years after the event, Rose was aware of a deep sense of foreboding. She could well imagine her father's reaction.

He went on, 'When she told him he went berserk. He refused to listen to her and sent for his trap to take her away.'

'Without me?' Rose's hands were clenched so tightly that her fingernails dug into her flesh.

'Yes. He refused to let her take you. You were asleep in the nursery. They fought, literally. She was trying to get back into the house to take you and he was forcibly restraining her. I don't think Cathy ever quite got over that.'

Rose said suddenly, 'But I *wasn't* asleep! That's my nightmare. I've had it as long as I can remember. It hardly varies.' She stared at him wide-eyed. 'I'm in the nursery and I hear voices. People quarrelling and someone crying!'

He was startled. 'Cathy thought you were sleeping.'

'No. I must have heard it all — or some of it. I can see myself looking out of the window down on to the gig and . . .' She put a hand to her heart and drew several deep breaths. 'Oh God! I *saw* it all. I *saw* her leave!'

'I'm sorry. I shouldn't have told you.'

She picked up her mug with trembling hands and drank a few mouthfuls of the strong, sweet tea.

He said, 'I've wanted you to know the truth for so long, but I've upset you.'

'No! I *have* to know. Please go on.'

He went on, 'When Cathy saw that he would never let her take you, she told him she'd changed her mind, that she would stay to be with you. He refused. He said she'd made her choice and she could get out.'

'Poor Mama!'

He took another mouthful of whisky. 'You can't blame him entirely,' he said slowly. 'George had his reasons. He had behaved very well — in the circumstances.'

'Very well? You can't mean that?'

'I can't explain. When she came to me, Cathy was hysterical and she begged me to reason with him. I knew I was the last person who would sway him, but she was in such a state that I finally agreed. I went up to Tye Rock House to talk to him, but you can imagine what happened. It was the only way he could revenge himself and he took it. He didn't raise his voice once, but his answer was "No." Your mother, he said, had forfeited the right to the child.'

Rose closed her eyes, anguished.

He asked, 'Are you all right? You look very pale.'

'Don't worry about me,' she said. 'Go on with the story.'

He leaned forward, his elbows on the table, the knuckles showing white. 'I found a job as a farm labourer, with a cottage to go with it. It was a sad business right from the start. Cathy was broken-hearted, blaming herself for losing you. She wrote countless letters asking to be allowed to see you, but George never replied. I thought she'd make herself ill. Then one day I found her in floods of tears. She told me she was expecting a baby.'

Rose sat, shocked out of her grief. 'You had a child?' She had a step-brother! In her emotional state the revelation was almost more than she could bear. She had an instant picture of the three of them together and felt almost ill with jealousy.

He shook his head. 'That was the trouble. It wasn't mine; it was George's child.'

Rose frowned. 'How could you tell?' she asked and then immediately regretted the naïve question.

He looked embarrassed. 'Just take my word for it. There are ways of knowing these things.'

Rose shook her head. Nothing was what she had expected, she thought numbly. 'How awful for you,' she said.

'It was, I admit. A strange reversal, but I said we would bring up George's child as ours. I thought it would help Cathy to have another baby to love. I hoped that later on we could have another — I mean, one of our own.' He gave her an odd look, emptied his glass and poured himself another drink.

Rose sat forward in her chair. 'So I have a sister or brother?' The revelation left her speechless. 'Was it a girl or a boy?'

'I have no idea.' His expression darkened. 'Your mother saw it as the perfect chance to go

252

home to you. She thought, wrongly, that if George knew that he had another child — especially if it were a boy — then he would take her back. He desperately wanted a son. Naturally I was deeply hurt, but I knew it was you who was dragging her back. She still loved me but she was torn with indecision and, whatever she did, she knew she would hurt someone. She loved me, but she was yearning for her little girl.' He stopped, clearing his throat.

Rose felt guilty. She was putting this man through a considerable ordeal and he didn't deserve it.

For a while there was silence as they both struggled with their emotions. At last Alan Gibbs said, 'Ready for more tea?' and poured it without waiting for an answer.

Rose was deep in thought, still struggling to come to terms with all the information.

Alan Gibbs went on, 'When George didn't answer her letter, Cathy decided that she'd stand a better chance if she was on her own. The fact that she was living in sin with me was spoiling her chances. Oh, she didn't put it quite like that.' He anticipated her protest. 'You mustn't think badly of her. By that time she was a very unhappy, desperate woman, almost out of her mind with worry. At her insistence I left, but I was full of resentment. I felt that your father was still controlling her — controlling both of us, in fact. We were like puppets, dangling on our strings. I said that if I left her I would never go back. She agreed. She was so sure that George would relent. I assume he never did. After I left there was never a word between us.'

Rose was struggling to keep back tears. 'I had no idea!' she told him. 'No wonder your sister was so bitter.'

He threw back his head as he swallowed the last of the whisky. 'I went on loving her,' he said. 'I married eventually, but it was never a great success. Your mother's ghost was always between us, and then my wife and child died when she was giving birth. A sad story all round, really.' His smile was a little crooked. 'Are you glad you came?'

His tone was defiant but tears glistened in his eyes. If they had stayed together, she thought, she would have known this man as 'Papa'.

'I don't know what to say,' she whispered.

He pulled himself together with a visible effort. 'Well, I think that's all you need to know,' he said. 'It's all I can tell you. I know you won't stop searching until you find them. I wish you happiness when you do.'

He pushed back his chair and she rose also. It was clear that he had suffered in the telling of her mother's story and she had no wish to prolong the meeting.

She hesitated. 'Do you want to know — *if* I find them?'

He looked at her thoughtfully, wrestling with his feelings. 'Just a card from you to let me know. Nothing more. And please don't let her know that you've spoken to me. Better for everyone not to reopen old wounds.'

Rose thought that probably pride was behind this last request. He wouldn't want her mother to know how low he had fallen. She hesitated. 'Do you — I know I shouldn't ask this, but do you still feel anything for her?'

'Have I stopped loving her?' He shrugged. 'The answer to that is a definite "No". But if you are planning a "happy-ever-after" reconciliation, please don't! I don't want you to be hurt. You've suffered like the rest of us over the years. Things are never quite how we imagine or how we hope they will be. We hurt each other, and it was never the same between us. I've never believed that Time was a great healer.'

She said, 'Do you forgive me, for coming between you that way?'

'It wasn't you,' he said. 'Don't go blaming yourself. You were only a child. It was circumstances. I would like it to have ended differently.'

In silence he led the way back along the passage to the front door. Rose was surprised how difficult it was to say 'Goodbye' and leave him. She felt so much nearer to her mother because of what he had told her; perhaps that was it. And nearer to him also. As the moment lengthened awkwardly it seemed to her that he, too, found the parting difficult. Impulsively she reached up and kissed him. Before she could draw back he had put his arms round her in a quick, fierce hug and she felt his lips on her hair.

'Take care of yourself, little Rose,' he said hoarsely.

She tried to speak but her throat was tight with emotion.

He said 'You'd best be on your way,' and gave her a little push.

Rose nodded and turned away. After a few steps she stopped and glanced back at him standing alone in the doorway.

His sad attempt at a smile almost broke her heart.

Chapter Eight

That evening, as the tide rolled out, Sergeant Wylie made his way along the beach below the cliffs, a King Charles spaniel cavorting happily at his heels. Above them clouds were gathering, but experience told him they would come to nothing much. It could change within hours and frequently did so. Weather across The Lizard was notoriously fickle. Now the sea rolled grey and cold and a few gulls swooped overhead, but in the summer . . . Ah! That would be a different story. Trippers would arrive by train and would settle themselves on the beach with rugs and picnic baskets. Children would run in and out of the waves, squealing with excitement, and fathers would paddle with their trousers rolled up. Each to his own, the sergeant thought dourly. He could never see the fascination that water held for people, but fascinate it did.

'Ben! Come here!' The dog was too near the water's edge. If he got wet the wife would grumble. Ever willing to please, the dog returned. 'Good boy!'

The sergeant headed for a little knot of people gathered round a small boat which had run up on to the beach. They waited patiently — two women with shopping bags, an elderly man with a newspaper and two young girls with plaits. All eyes were on Tom Robb as he carefully sorted his small catch, eyeing each fish critically. Not the most upright of citizens, in the sergeant's opinion. A disreputable family, the Robbs, one way and another, although the mother was a tidy soul and did her best with very little. Went to church on Sundays while her sons got up to God knows what! No doubt by now Tom Robb would have heard that his brother had been dismissed by Rose Vivian on the sergeant's advice. That wouldn't have gone down very well, he thought, so his welcome might be a bit on the cool side. Not that Tom would dare too far. The law was the law and Sergeant Wylie was its representative.

One of the girls glanced up and saw his approach. She said something to the others and most of them turned to watch his progress.

Tom said, 'Evening, Sergeant.' He seemed in a surprisingly good mood.

The sergeant nodded to him, but Tom had more to say.

'More trouble at the school seemingly. Young lady putting it about, according to Charlie.'

The sergeant glared. 'He had to go, your brother. He was asking for trouble.'

Tom grinned. 'Oh, but that's just it, Sergeant. He ain't gone. Miss Vivian changed her mind, didn't she! Realised he was too good to lose.' He grinned hugely.

Hadn't been sacked? The sergeant was both shocked and mortified. After all he'd said to Rose Vivian, the foolish woman had let Robb stay on. She'd regret it. He did his best to hide his surprise and said severely, 'Then he was very lucky. Let's hope he's learned his lesson.'

Oblivious, the two girls stooped to pet the dog. 'Ben! Ben! Who's a boofus boy, then?' The dog rolled over on to his back, revelling in the attention.

To signal the end of that particular topic, the sergeant addressed the others in turn. 'Mrs Flite. Mrs Pearce. Mr Wellan.'

Mrs Flite smiled. 'Leg troubling her again, is it? Poor lovey. That's nasty, that is. Thought I hadn't seen her round lately.'

'Afraid so. Doctor's given her some liniment. I can't say it's doing much good and it smells like the very devil, but there you are!'

Tom said, 'Horse liniment, most like!' and the two girls went into fits of giggles.

The sergeant frowned, but undeterred, Tom added, 'When your wife starts galloping round the house you'll know for certain sure!'

They all enjoyed this witticism except Sergeant Wylie, who pretended not to have heard it and turned quickly to the elderly man.

'How's things with you, then, Mr Wellan? Any news of that son of yours? Australia, isn't it? Alice was asking only the other day. "How's Ned Wellan getting on," she said. Seems only yesterday he was in the nativity play at the school!'

The man's expression brightened. 'Why yes, matter of fact we have. A letter not two days ago. Melbourne, that's where our Ned is. Talks about joining the Cavalry. Cavalry! My missus says "Cavalry? He don't know the back end of a horse from the front! What do he be thinking on, darned fool!"'

They all laughed and, seeing that he had their attention, he went on, 'But what a rum do with poor old Vivian! Knocked me for six, that did. "Dead?" I said. "Never!" I said. "What was he about?" I said to the missus. Falling off a cliff at his age?'

Mrs Flite said, 'Terrible way to go, falling like that. I mean, all the way down you know you've got no chance. Poor lovey.'

Tom glanced up from the fish. 'Case closed, is it, then?' he asked.

Sergeant Wylie had no intention of sharing his doubts with anyone but the pathologist. He said, 'Near as dammit,' and wondered at the sly look on Tom Robb's face.

Mrs Pearce said, 'Accidental death. That's what I heard.'

Tom held the sergeant's gaze. 'Oh, yes. That's what the police reckon. Cut and dried to them, it is. They've got their witness and that's enough. If Tremayne says so, they'll take it as gospel. Tremayne's a teacher, so he must be a very proper sort of man.'

The sergeant said, 'Now just a minute! The police act on information received and —'

260

Tom ignored him. 'Only I can't rightly make out how it happened.' They all stared at him, but he was watching the sergeant's face. ' 'Cos the pair of them was walking *down here* when I heard them. *On the beach.* Not up top like that Tremayne's saying.'

In spite of his reservations, Sergeant Wylie felt his heart race. If what this man said was true . . . But he was an unreliable sort. Could be muddying the waters for the hell of it. Not averse to a bit of poaching or smuggling, if he got the chance. Could lie like a trooper and frequently did.

Tom went on, 'Oh yes! Arguing like the devil! "You calling me liar?" Tremayne says. Real heated, it was. Never heard them shouting like that before. They was always real pally. Chatty, you could say.' He gave the sergeant a challenging look.

Mr Wellan said, 'Well, I never!'

Mrs Pearce said, 'I heard they was friendly like.'

Neither of them, the sergeant thought thankfully, had understood the significance of what Tom Robb was saying. So it was possible his intuition was correct and Mark Tremayne did have something to hide. He would make it his job to ferret around. For a moment he allowed himself to consider promotion. Now that *would* please the missus.

Tom Robb, having organised his fish to his satisfaction, turned to the two girls. 'Now then, my loves, let's have your basket.'

They handed it to him and he tossed a large

plaice and four herrings into it. 'Give those to your ma. Won't be seeing many more herrings now 'til next winter, and precious little bass, neither.'

Sergeant Wylie wondered why he made no charge, and his policeman's mind at once made a connection between Tom Robb and the girls' widowed mother. Was there something going on there? He would make it his business to find out.

Tom winked at the girls and, pleased, they thanked him and hurried away. The dog chased after them but was quickly called back to sit at his master's heels.

Mrs Flite asked, 'You giving it away now then, Tom, or you got your eye on their ma?'

Tom grinned, unabashed. 'The widow? Now why didn't I think of that?'

Mrs Flite said, 'Most like you *have*, knowing you.' She examined the cod critically and said, 'Pound, Tom, please, or just under.'

Tom tossed it on to his ancient scales. 'Not much of a size yet but that'll eat tender.' He cut a slice through it. 'There you go!'

She paid Tom and waited for her friend, and then the two women made their way back towards the village.

Mr Wellan said, 'Got any mackerel, Tom?'

Tom shrugged. 'Mackerel? This time of year? Them's winter fish. 'Tis nearly summer.'

'Pity. I do love a bit of soused mackerel. A bay leaf and a drop of vinegar. That's handsome, that is.' He sighed. 'Still, if you haven't got any, that's it.'

'Well, I haven't.' Tom gave him a stern look. 'If it's not in the sea, I can't fish it out! Simple as that. There's cod or pollock. Or what about spur dog? That's nice deep fried, that is.'

'You and your spur dog. That's huss, that is.' He pursed his lips, considering, then nodded. 'I'll have some, whatever 'tis called.'

They struck a deal and at last the old man wandered off.

Alone with the sergeant, some of Tom's bluster deserted him. 'Sorry about your missus,' he said. 'They can be very nasty, legs.'

Sergeant Wylie smiled. 'Oh, they can! Useful for getting around on, though!' He chose his fish and wrapped it in a teacloth which he produced from his pocket. He needed the fisherman's help so decided to flatter him a little. Gazing out across the bay he said, 'Weather breaking, d'you think?'

Tom shook his head. 'It'll hold.'

The sergeant whistled tunelessly — a sure sign, had Tom but known it, that he had something on his mind.

'Vivian and Tremayne . . .' he said at last. 'Arguing, you say?'

'Not half they weren't! Hammer and tongs, it was. They didn't see me.'

'And that's all you heard?'

'Hard to say after more than a week.' Tom thought about it. ' "Taken your time, haven't

263

you?" Vivian said that. Or something like that.'

' "Taken your time?" Hmm?' The sergeant considered it carefully. He whistled for the dog who was now scampering blindly towards the water's edge, barking furiously at seagulls. 'Taken his time over what exactly?'

Tom shrugged. 'Darned if I know. 'Less he was asking for the daughter's hand in marriage!' He laughed loudly at this witticism. 'And old Vivian was saying, "No!" '

The sergeant frowned. 'And you're *certain* they were walking along the beach and not along the cliff path?'

'Course I'm certain. I'd never have heard what they was on about if they'd been up top. Next thing I know, Vivian's dead.'

Sergeant Wylie said, 'So what time was this meeting?'

'In the morning. High tide was at eight so . . . ten or thereabouts.'

The sergeant bent down to fasten the dog's lead. 'Would you be willing to come back with me to the station and make a statement to that effect?' he asked.

Tom frowned. 'What, me? Down the police station? Not likely.' His eyes narrowed. 'I *saw* them, that's all. I never was nearer than fifteen yards or so!' Abruptly his voice rose. 'I never *touched* the man! No one can say I done nothing to him! All I said —'

'Tom! Stop it!' The sergeant patted his arm. 'No need to get yourself in a lather over it.

You're not involved. Nobody's saying you are. It's not *you* I'm interested in; it's *them*. Tremayne said quite definitely that they were walking along the cliff path.' He jerked a thumb in the direction of the cliff-top. 'You say they were on the beach. Something doesn't add up.'

But it was obvious that Tom Robb had taken fright. 'Well, I don't want to get mixed up in no statement or nothing. What's the point? Vivian's dead and buried.' He scowled. 'I'm not over-keen on writing.'

'Ah! I see. Then all you need do is tell it again and *I'll* write it. About the argument and where they were. I'll write it down and then you can sign your name. Bit of a squiggle. Simple as falling off a log.'

'Well, I won't and that's that.' Tom's tone was surly now.

Sergeant Wylie lowered his voice. 'I do suddenly seem to remember a couple of rabbits and the odd pheasant that found their way into your bag, Tom. Not so long ago. I seem to remember that I looked the other way.'

Tom looked around as though in search of rescue but there was none forthcoming. The beach was deserted.

'You owe me a favour, Tom, and it's not much to ask.'

'Darn me, you're a mean sod, Sergeant.' He sighed deeply. 'Tomorrow morning, then?'

Sergeant Wylie was no fool.

'*Now*, Tom!' he said.

High on its cliff-top perch, Tye Rock House awaited the day. The only sign of life was a solitary stooping figure, lost in the vastness of the vegetable gardens. Charlie Robb, hoe in hand, eyes narrowed, was searching among the rows of onions for any sign of weeds. Onions were his favourites. He loved the way they grew as well as the way they tasted. Spotting a weed, he lunged forward with the hoe and gave a grunt of satisfaction as the offending plant was dragged from the soil. His eyes were on his work, but his mind was busy with the news his brother had given him about his hated rival, Mr Pansy Tremayne. According to Tom, the police sergeant thought that something funny had been going on, that last day. Robb frowned as he gathered up the half-dozen weeds he had dislodged and threw them into his bucket which already contained the fruits of half an hour's hoeing. He had started work that morning at eight o'clock — his favourite part of the day when there was no one else about. Early morning was a magical time with the sound of the surf rolling and crashing through the sea mist. Reaching the end of the row, he straightened up. Around him now, however, the garden was losing its mystery, but Robb still smiled with a familiar but unexpressed sense of pleasure.

The smile faded. Damn that Tremayne! He was the fly in his ointment and no mistake. Robb shook his head. What on earth could Poll see in him, he wondered. Give him an hour's honest work and the man would be sweating like a pig! Give him a wheelbarrow to push and he'd faint right off, most likely! Robb emptied the weeds on to the compost heap and turned to stare at the sea which, emerging slowly from the mist, was dotted with fishing boats from Porthleven harbour. Likely Tom was among them. The Robbs knew the coast like the backs of their hands, from Newlyn and Penzance in the west to the Lizard Point to the east. His father, after a few jars of scrumpy, had been fond of saying that the Robbs came from a long line of wreckers, and his mother used to say, 'Hold your tongue, Sam. 'Tis nothing to boast on!' Robb didn't know whether to be pleased or sorry. He brooded for a moment on his brother, Tom, imagining him in the police station at Helston under the eagle eye of Sergeant Wylie. Pity he hadn't kept his mouth shut about seeing them, he reflected. Never a good idea to hobnob with the likes of the sergeant. Still, no doubt it would make a good tale to tell down at the Harbour Inn on a Saturday night.

'Morning, Robb!'

Recognising Polly's voice, he swung round, a smile lighting up his face. 'Morning, Poll.' She wasn't so bad, he thought. At least you could have a bit of a laugh with Poll. She was smart and pretty and he was, some said, a bit slow though he'd never noticed it himself. He laid down the hoe, took the proffered mug of tea and clasped his hands round it eagerly. Not as good as a pint, but at this time of the morning a mug of tea went down a treat.

He said, 'Thanks, Poll. You'm looking handsome this morning.'

She smiled. 'Thank you, kind sir.' She rolled her eyes.

He liked the way she did that. Made him feel sort of warm inside. He took a deep breath. 'That pansy fellow you're so keen on — seems he'm a bit of a puzzle.'

'Mr Tremayne? A puzzle?'

'Seems so.'

'Who says?' Hands on her hips, she eyed him warily.

'Police, that's who says!' He watched her hopefully. She wouldn't like hearing that. Not about *him*.

Polly frowned. 'How come, then?'

'Tom reckons they think he knows more'n he's telling — about Mr Vivian.' He blew on his tea and sipped it cautiously, never taking his eyes from her face. 'They think they was having a set-to, like. Shouting at each other down on the beach. Not up on the cliff like he told.' Now then, he reflected, let her ponder that little lot.

She was staring at him open-mouthed. 'What on earth are you saying, Robb? That can't be right.'

'Can't it? Old sergeant lugs our Tom to Helston yesterday — to the *police station* — and asks him all about it. Our Tom heard him talking to the constable, confidential like "I don't like the sound of this," says the sergeant. "I'm getting worried about our Mr Tremayne." '

'Worried about him . . . ?'

Polly looked the way Robb had hoped she'd look — as though she didn't fancy the man so much now.

He said, 'See, if they wasn't up top on the cliff, how could Mr Vivian fall down it? That be bothering the sergeant.' He nodded meaningfully. 'Sergeant do say that Mr Tremayne —'

Another voice interrupted him suddenly. 'Says what exactly?'

They both turned and Robb jumped guiltily. Mr Tremayne had come down the nearby steps and was watching them. His collar was turned up against the early morning chill and his hands were thrust into the pockets of his jacket. His expression was guarded, but there was a glint in his eye that Robb didn't like. Bother the man, creeping up on them like that. Robb's dislike grew. He was a sight too good-looking, and cocky with it. But how much had he overheard? Robb swallowed hard.

Polly smiled at Tremayne. 'Robb was saying you was a bit of a hero. Risking your own life to save Mr Vivian.' She gave Robb a meaningful glance.

'That be it!' Robb agreed hastily. Good old Poll. She was a quick thinker and no mistake.

Tremayne said, 'When did he say that?'

Robb scratched his head. He glanced at Polly,

who looked none too happy.

Polly folded her arms across her chest. 'Yesterday. Tom was up Helston, talking to the sergeant.' She hesitated. 'Something about . . . about fishing. Some nets gone missing or something. Stole off the harbour wall.'

Robb said, 'Nets gone missing.'

Tremayne gave them both a long look. Then to Polly he said, 'You're a very bad liar, Polly!'

Polly's face flushed, and Robb was aware of a small spurt of rage somewhere within him. He stepped forward.

'Don't you go calling her a liar. Less you want *me* to deal with!' Robb was pleased to see the man step back. Following up his advantage, he raised his fist. 'You watch out, else I might just clobber you one!'

Tremayne flushed angrily. 'Don't you dare touch me, you oaf.'

'Oaf?' Robb stabbed a meaty forefinger into Tremayne's chest. 'You calling me a oaf?'

Tremayne grabbed the offending finger and forced it away. 'You ignorant sod! You'll be damned sorry if you mess me about!'

Polly cried, 'You two — stop it! Please, Mr Tremayne! Robb didn't mean nothing.'

But Robb was too angry. He said, 'Why shouldn't I clobber him? He called me a oaf. He called you a *liar!*'

'It doesn't matter, Robb. *Please!*'

Ignoring her plea, Robb grabbed his rival by the front of his jacket and, disregarding his struggles, shook him hard.

Polly seized his arm and hung on grimly. 'Robb! For heaven's sake! Let him go!'

Reluctantly he released Tremayne who, cursing, immediately swung a punch at him. Robb ducked and retaliated with a deep punch of his own which caught Tremayne a blow in the stomach and knocked him sprawling. For a moment he lay there motionless.

Polly screamed and Robb said, 'Serve him right!'

Flushed with humiliation, Tremayne sat up. Robb, his fists still eager, watched as his rival struggled back on to his feet. That'd knocked the smile off his face.

Polly said, 'He didn't mean it, Mr Tremayne. He — he just . . .'

Tremayne gave Robb a look of such loathing that words failed her. As he brushed himself down, he said slowly, 'That's assault, Robb. D'you know that? I could go into Helston this morning and bring charges against you. Very likely I will.'

Robb hesitated. Charges? That wouldn't please his ma. Oh, sod it! He hesitated.

Tremayne repeated, 'Charges of assault — and we've got a witness. Haven't we, Polly?'

Polly said, 'Take no notice of him, Robb. I'd never say nothing against you. Never.'

'You'd have to in court. Never heard of perjury?' Tremayne gave a short laugh. 'Robb would end up behind bars and you . . . Well, I don't know what the penalty is for lying under oath.'

Robb looked at Tremayne's face. His eyes were cold and hard. Polly looked very pale. He said, 'Poll ain't done nothing. Stop picking on her. 'Twas me as hit you — and I'll do it again if you don't leave her be.'

Polly said, 'He'll apologise — won't you, Robb!' and looked at him imploringly.

'No, I won't!' Robb told her. 'No one calls you a liar.' He was breathing hard, frustrated by her lack of support. At a word from her, he'd knock the living daylights out of Tremayne!

Polly whispered, 'Leave him, Robb. I don't care what he called me. You know how 'tis. Sticks and stones may break your bones . . .' She tossed her head and the look she gave Tremayne wasn't friendly.

Robb felt a little better. She was going off him for sure. He said, 'Sticks and stones?'

Tremayne looked from one to the other, suppressing his anger with an effort. 'So Tom Robb was at the police station in Helston?'

Polly opened her mouth to answer, but Robb stepped in first. 'And don't you go calling our Tom a liar, neither. 'Less you want a smack in the jaw!'

Tremayne said, 'Oh, for God's sake, man! You're behaving like an idiot.' Tremayne looked from one to the other, then suddenly he shrugged. 'Suit yourself,' he said and, turning, walked along the drive towards the gate.

Robb muttered, 'Where's he off to?'

Polly said, 'He goes down the village first thing for a newspaper. Every day. I've seen him.'

'I'll give him newspaper! Tom says the sergeant reckons he's a sly dog. Up to no good, like.' He hesitated. 'Still fancy him, do you, Polly? Over me?'

'Course I don't fancy him, Robb.'

'You *did.*' His heart was racing with excitement. 'You said you did.'

She tucked a stray lock of hair under her cap. 'Well, maybe I did. Maybe I didn't. Maybe I was only kidding you along, like. But now I don't, Robb. Got a mean streak, he has. Calling me a liar and that. You was wonderful, Robb, but you shouldn't have hit him; I didn't want you to hit him. If he gets on to Miss Vivian, saying you hit him — hitting a *teacher,* Robb! You could go to jail like as not for that.'

'He asked for it and he got it!'

They stared at each other for a long moment until Polly grinned suddenly. 'Bend down a bit, Robb.'

Wonderingly, he leaned down. Before he knew it she had taken his face between her hands and kissed him. 'That's for sticking up for me, Robb, with old Pansy Tremayne.' She laughed at the expression on his face. 'Now I must get on. Got all the bread to cut and butter. See you later!'

Giggling, she swung round on her heel and hurried away back to the house. Robb stared after her. Polly had *kissed* him! Was it a joke? He picked up the hoe and examined it, as though somehow it might initiate him into the workings of her mind. Then with a wild whoop of joy he raised it above his head and swung it down in a wide curve. It bit into the soil with a satisfying thud.

Then he said, 'Oh bugger it!'

The leaves of one of his prized onion plants had been neatly severed just above the ground . . .

The same morning, the post arrived and with it a letter which provoked a huge sigh of relief from Rose. It came from a Samuel Morgan, one of Chrissie's uncles:

Dear Miss Vivian,

I understand from my mother, who is in hospital, that my niece Christina, is no longer welcome at Tye Rock House. I have therefore, at considerable inconvenience to myself, agreed to take her into my home until my mother is able to care for her or other arrangements can be made.

I shall collect her at the earliest possible moment but, having many pressing business matters to attend to, may not be able to give you much advance notice. The bulk of Christina's luggage can be sent on by train to my address which is above. I may add that I take a very *poor* view of any school which

274

cannot adequately deal with a well-bred but high-spirited girl . . .

Rose groaned as she refolded the letter. There was probably a large grain of truth in what he said, but how well did he know his 'well-bred but high-spirited' niece? He was probably in for an unpleasant shock.

'But that's *his* concern,' she muttered, thankful that at last one of her major problems would be resolved. Later in the morning the applicants for the geography and mathematics post would arrive for interview, and Mark Tremayne was going to help her. At the thought of him, her face lit up and she smiled. There was something about him, an indefinable quality, which drew her to him; and the more she thought about him, the more she liked him. And she was fairly confident that he returned her affection, although he was being very careful not to overstep the mark. He was, after all, only a junior teacher, and she was in effect the Headmistress. He obviously felt that their relationship, if that's what it was, should be kept from the rest of the staff.

A glance at the clock showed her that prayers would be over and the girls would be settling to their lessons. Rose moved thoughtfully to the window and stared out along the drive. The cottages of Porthleven, clustered round the harbour, were warmed by the sun which was already burning off the sea mist. She felt an urge to walk down to the village and back. A little exercise would do her good and she could think about Mark Tremayne. Tempted, she hesitated. A knock at the door cut short her deliberations.

'Come in!'

She hid her displeasure as Miss Hock came into the room. The teacher wasted no time. 'Miss Vivian, I'm afraid that I have had to speak very sharply to the school this morning. It's the usual grumble.'

Rose said, 'Ah! Of course. Flora Day is almost upon us. I'd quite forgotten.' She glanced at the calendar.

Miss Hock said, 'The eighth of May. Friday. The day after tomorrow.'

'Oh Lord!' Rose frowned. It was one problem after another, she thought, exasperated. No wonder her father had always been so distracted. The Helston festivities to celebrate the spring were famous, and hundreds of people made their way to the town each year to watch the fun. The Hal-on-Tow pageant was an exciting event in which a heroic St George triumphantly killed the evil dragon. Later in the day the Furry Dance led those taking part in and out of houses and shops and through colourful streets decorated with gorse and laurel leaves.

Flora Day, therefore, was always a bone of contention with the girls at Tye Rock House. Every year they argued afresh in the hope that they would be allowed to attend the celebrations, but George Vivian had always rigorously opposed the idea. His main argument was that the safety of their pupils could not be guaranteed amongst the huge crowd of people who would attend the festivities. His other argument was that the festival had arguably pagan beginnings and was simply an excuse for frivolity or worse. To Rose, the festivities always sounded harmless enough but, even as a child when Maud promised the strictest supervision, she had never been allowed to attend. Later on her opinion had never been sought, and the ban was absolute.

Miss Hock said, 'They want to be allowed to go, and they're hoping you'll be more easily persuaded.'

Rose said, 'I do sympathise, but I would need longer to think about it. For this year, at least, my instinct is to refuse. It really would be difficult to keep them together and if anything happened to one of them we'd be responsible. There's also the problem of transport and the cost. It would need a considerable amount of organising to do it properly and with minimum risk.'

'I was hoping you would refuse,' Miss Hock told her. 'I told them it wasn't very likely. Some of the girls are silly enough already without deliberately putting them in the way of temptation.'

She looked pleased, thought Rose, irritated, as she searched her mind for an acceptable compromise.

'It's a pity,' she said. 'We've all been through a

difficult and somewhat depressing time and it would be nice if —' She brightened. 'What about an alternative of some kind? It won't be as good in their eyes but it would be better than nothing.' Before Miss Hock could raise any objections, Rose went on quickly, 'I have it! Sunday will be a special day. Oh no! I won't be here; I'll be at the Edgcombes. Saturday, then. We'll celebrate spring in our own way. A walk to the Loe Pool in the afternoon and —'

'You're not suggesting a picnic in *May!*' Miss Hock's disapproval was swift.

'Not a picnic, no, but a walk in the afternoon followed by a special tea, then a musical evening round the piano in the sitting room. Maybe some games. Charades, perhaps?' She smiled at Miss Hock. 'We could all do with something to cheer us up. I'll talk to Cook about it. Maybe ham and pickles, cakes and a fruit jelly. What d'you think?'

Miss Hock was obviously not pleased with the suggestion. The atmosphere between the two of them had been strained ever since the staff meeting, but now she forced a smile. 'If you think it wise. May I tell them?'

'You may. Oh! And I think you should see this letter. Another piece of good news to pass on to your colleagues.'

She handed her the letter about Chrissie and saw the teacher's lips form a silent whistle of approval.

'So we're losing her at last!' she said. 'What a

relief for us all! I'd be a hypocrite if I pretended otherwise.'

'Well, now she's going. I'll ask Matron to see that most of her things are packed ready — and I'll tell Chrissie, too. Sad, though, that we have to say we failed with her.'

Miss Hock snorted disparagingly. 'If you ask me we ought to be congratulated for keeping her *this* long!'

She departed, surprisingly eager to spread the good news. Rose watched her. Perhaps she *did* have a heart somewhere within that somewhat grim exterior?

She reached for her jacket and was about to embark on her walk into Porthleven when Maud announced a visitor.

'Sergeant Wylie,' she told Rose.

Rose took one look at his face and her good humour faded. He looked uneasy and, as she indicated a chair and he sat down, he appeared to be avoiding her eyes.

'Sergeant! What is it?' she demanded as she sat down behind her desk and clasped her hands.

He cleared his throat, and fumbled in his pocket for a notebook. Then, without even opening it, he looked up at her. 'I'm afraid, Miss Vivian, that we have had some disquieting news.'

She waited, then prompted, 'About what, exactly?'

'About your late father's death. Some unexpected information has come to light which suggests that maybe — I only say *maybe* — his death was not due to a fall as we previously thought.'

'Not . . .' Her thoughts churned. '*Not* a fall? You mean he had something else — a heart attack?'

'Not exactly. No.' He bit his lip. 'The fact is that we now believe that your father was *not* on the cliff-top but walking along the —'

'But Mr Tremayne was *there!*' She stared at him. 'So we know how it happened.'

He ignored the interruption. 'It appears that they were walking along the foreshore below the cliff; they were seen by someone who has just come forward. If they were not on top of the cliff, then your father could not have met his death in a fall. You do see our difficulty, I hope?'

Rose shook her head. 'Sergeant Wylie, we have a first-hand account from Mr Tremayne. He ought to know, he was —'

'I have been talking to the pathologist, Miss Vivian. It appears that the wound which killed your father *could* have been made by a rock . . .'

Her eyes widened. 'A falling rock? But that's impossible, Sergeant. Mr Tremayne would have known if my father was hit by a rock. And they *were* at the top of the cliff; he told me so himself. This other person must have been mistaken.' Her heart was beginning to beat erratically and she felt a distinct shortness of breath.

'Miss Vivian, it is just possible that your father was struck on the head by a rock which was wielded by another person. Do you understand me?'

She fought against a momentary blackness. 'He was on the cliff path and he *fell!*'

He went on as though she hadn't spoken. 'We do have to act on this information, and I have come to ask Mr Tremayne a few more questions. Hopefully we can clear up the —'

She gasped. 'You think *Mr Tremayne* hit my father with a rock? But that's utter nonsense, Sergeant. I can't believe it. I don't mean to be rude, but the idea's preposterous. I know him, and he wouldn't hurt a fly. And why *should* he do such a thing? They were friends, Sergeant.'

They were *friends,* she repeated silently, to herself.

He said, 'Apparently they were quarrelling, Miss Vivian. Quarrelling most violently. Mr Tremayne was shouting at your father, who was calling him a liar —'

Rose was aware of a frisson of fear. 'I don't believe it,' she told him. 'Someone is trying to cause trouble for him. Mr Tremayne could *never* have done such a terrible thing, and I'm sure he will convince you of that fact when you talk to him. Since my father's death he has been wonderfully kind to me, Sergeant, and I won't hear a word against him. The very idea is ridiculous.'

Sergeant Wylie gave her a long look. 'I hope you're right, Miss Vivian, for your sake. Because someone is lying about what happened. If Mr

Tremayne was provoked in some way — if he has a hasty temper —'

Rose almost shouted, 'But he *doesn't!* I know the man, Sergeant.' Her voice shook and she swallowed hard.

'I have to make my inquiries, Miss Vivian.' He shook his head wearily. 'I don't think you appreciate that we are acting in your best interests. I have to ask you what you know about this man. You have references, I imagine, and I would like to see them.'

Rose was steadying her voice with an effort. 'Of course we have references.' Jumping up, she rushed to the cupboard where the files were kept, snatched them from the shelf and began to go through them. Rivers, Hock, Dubois, Matron . . . Where was Tremayne? She went through them again, then returned to the cupboard and searched all the shelves. She was aware that sergeant was watching her every move.

He said, 'No luck?' and she imagined a note of triumph.

'It must be here.'

'Could anyone have removed it — without permission, perhaps?'

'It's very unlikely. First they would have to gain access to this room. All the spare keys are kept on a panel on a wall in the kitchen.' She was beginning to feel distinctly flustered and noted the fact with irritation. 'I'll have to make a more thorough search later. I don't normally see the applicants' references, but I do know that my father would not engage anybody unsuitable. He made all the appointments . . .' She put a hand to her mouth in growing agitation. 'Which reminds me. I have several interviews later this morning, Sergeant — we need to appoint a teacher to replace my father — and Mr Tremayne is to assist me with them.' Clumsily, she pushed the files back into the cupboards. Where on earth was Mark Tremayne's, she wondered desperately. If she couldn't find it, Sergeant Wylie would no doubt think the worst. 'It could take me a while to find the file. Is it vital that you see it just now?'

He hesitated. 'I suppose I could come back this afternoon.'

'That would be a great help.'

'But only on one condition, Miss Vivian — that you don't mention anything which has passed between us. If you were to tell him and he were to — to abscond . . . I needn't tell you it would look very bad.'

She gave him what she hoped was a withering look. 'Of course he won't abscond. Why should he? Mr Tremayne has done nothing wrong. But rest assured, I shan't say a word. You see, I can personally vouch for Mr Tremayne's integrity. If you care to return about — let me see . . .' She turned in her chair to study the timetable. 'He is taking the younger girls at two, but three o'clock would be fine.' She drew a deep breath and forced a smile. 'I don't mean to offend you, Sergeant, but I do know my staff. Believe me, you have made a very serious mistake. The sooner it's cleared up, the better I shall like it.'

Rose rang for Maud to show him out and then sank down in her chair. Poor Mr Tremayne! Whoever had started this absurd rumour deserved to be horsewhipped.

She jumped up and hurried to the cupboard once more. When a more thorough search did not reveal the missing file, she rang impatiently for Maud.

Maud came in looking anxious. 'What is it? What's happened now?'

'Nothing's wrong. At least — I'm wondering about the spare keys. Do you —'

'But the sergeant coming again, I mean.'

'Nothing is wrong, Maud.' So she *hadn't* been listening at the door. 'Do you know if anyone could have borrowed the key to my father's — to the study? From the kitchen panel?'

Maud frowned. 'Not without someone knowing. There's hardly a moment when there isn't someone in the kitchen. Is there a key missing?'

'I'm not sure. Don't worry about it. Oh, Maud, before you go. I'm letting the girls have a little party on Saturday so —'

Maud's face lit up. 'A *party?* They'll love that, Rose.'

Rose returned her smile. Impulsively she said, 'About the future, Maud. You will always have a home with me. Just in case you had wondered . . .'

Maud's right hand crept up to press against her chest. 'Oh! That's so kind. I did get to thinking — you know how it is in the middle of the night.'

'I know!'

'So that's wonderful. I don't know what to say really.'

'I should be thanking *you*. All these years you've devoted to this dreadful family!' She laughed a trifle shakily. 'Anyway — there it is.' Seeing tears gathering in the old woman's eyes, she said hurriedly, 'So ask Mrs Cripps to come and see me some time today about the party.'

When Rose was alone again, she sat down and tried to think. So a file had been mislaid. She would have to find it. It wasn't important, but the sergeant would pretend it was and somehow he would turn it into a black mark against Mr Tremayne.

Maud returned to the kitchen in a thoughtful mood. Cook and Polly turned inquiringly as she entered.

Cook, knife in hand, stopped peeling potatoes. 'What is it now?' she asked. 'Not more trouble?'

'No. She didn't mention the sergeant; just something about the spare keys. Does anybody else ever use them? 'Specially the key to the Head's room?'

Polly, who was polishing the cutlery, started guiltily and then hastily bent her head.

Maud pounced. 'What?' she demanded.

'Nothing!'

Her exaggerated innocence was proof of her guilt, thought Maud. 'Out with it!' she insisted. 'What d'you know that I don't know?'

Polly stammered, 'It's nothing. Only . . .'

Cook said, 'Tell the truth, girl!'

Polly rolled her eyes. 'It was just the once . . . someone borrowed one of the keys.'

Maud said, 'Someone?'

Cook asked, 'Which key?'

Polly twisted her mouth unhappily. 'The Head's study.'

Maud said, 'Oh my Lord! Who was it?'

'I — I don't quite remember.'

Maud advanced towards her with a threatening look on her face. 'You'll remember, my girl, else you'll be marched straight along to Miss Vivian. Now who borrowed that key?'

Polly swallowed. 'I promised not to say. He was —'

'*He?*' Maud thought rapidly. 'Not that groom fellow — Jerry Whatsisname. The one that got caught with Chrissie Morgan? You never let him have the key to —'

Polly's voice grew shrill. ''Course not! 'Twasn't him. What d'you take me for? 'Twas Mr Tremayne. He'd left some books in there. Prep, he said.'

Cook said, 'Prep?'

Maud gave Cook a withering look. 'Prep is homework, preparation for the next day's lessons.'

Polly said, 'He'd left a pile of books he had to

mark. He asked for the key.' She looked at them, dismayed. 'That's all. What's wrong with that?'

Maud relaxed. 'Well, let's hope nothing's wrong or you'll be for it,' she said, then added, 'When was this?'

'A few days ago. Maybe a week. I don't know. He said he'd carried the books in when he went to talk to her and then left them behind. He said no need to bother Miss Vivian.'

'Miss Vivian? Then it was after the master's accident?'

'I suppose so. Does it matter?'

Maud dismissed her doubts. 'No,' she said. 'Forget it and get on with that silver. We haven't got all day.' She turned to Cook. 'And you've to go and see her, please, some time today. The girls are to have a party on Saturday.'

Polly and Cook stared at her.

'A party?' said Polly. 'A party at Tye Rock House!' She laughed. 'Wonders will never cease!'

Maud allowed herself a smile as she headed for the pile of breakfast crockery which still waited to be washed up. 'It's been all gloom and doom,' she said. 'I think the girls deserve a treat.'

The interviews were part way over and Rose was beginning to feel a little more confident as the second applicant entered. They had decided to use the drawing room as the study was so

cramped. Mr Daniel Leen would be the final in-
terviewee.

Rose stood as he came in and so did Mark
Tremayne. After an exchange of handshakes,
they all sat down — Rose opposite the newcomer
across the table, Mark Tremayne alone and
slightly to one side.

Rose said, 'Mr Tremayne is our history master. He has agreed to sit in on the interview.'

Daniel Leen, aged thirty-nine, was already
balding but he was a cheerful-looking man. Rose
asked him a few questions about his present
post; it seemed he was a deputy headmaster in a
school for boys in south London.

Rose said, 'Young ladies are a far cry from
boys, Mr Leen. They can be very awkward —
and I speak from the heart!' They all laughed.
'Do you think you would find the change difficult?'

'Not at all. I have three sisters, all younger
than me. I don't find young women daunting.'

She regarded him carefully. He seemed rela-
tively comfortable under the scrutiny, which was
reassuring. 'We are also, of course, a very small
and somewhat select school. Most of our girls
have parents in the far-flung corners of the em-
pire. A few of them have to spend some of their
holidays here, which is partly why we prefer to
keep the number of pupils very manageable.'
She thought guiltily of all the problems they had
been experiencing, but there was no point in la-
bouring the negative aspects of the post. She

continued briskly, 'A small school means a very small staff. That, too, can be difficult sometimes. You do need to get along with each other. And the girls are with us twenty-four hours a day, Mr Leen, which can mean a lot of extra hours. This is their home as well as their school, and we have to be more than simply teachers. It isn't easy.'

Mark Tremayne put in, 'But it's always rewarding.'

Rose flashed him a grateful smile.

Daniel Leen said, 'I'm really very eager to see what I can offer to Tye Rock House. I'm also keen to settle my family in the country. We would hope to rent a cottage in Porthleven as soon as possible, since my wife is expecting our first child in July.'

'Oh! How exciting!'

'It certainly is.'

Rose glanced at her history master.

Taking his cue, he asked, 'Does the curriculum differ greatly from that of your previous school? Our teaching caters for the needs of our girls, few of whom will ever go in search of employment.'

'Of course, but only the geography and maths will concern me.'

Rose consulted her notes, hoping that she appeared more efficient than she felt. There was a glowing testimonial from Mr Leen's present Headmaster and another from the Principal of his training college.

Mark Tremayne asked a few more questions and then Rose drew the interview to a close. She smiled at Daniel Leen and shuffled her papers back into the folder.

'We'll let you know our decision very soon,' she told him. 'If we offer you the post, we will take up your references.'

As the door closed behind him, Rose breathed a sigh of relief. The dreaded interview session was over. She looked at Mark Tremayne and smiled.

He returned the smile. 'That wasn't such an ordeal, was it?' he said. 'I think we work well together, don't you?'

'I certainly do, but I'm glad it's over.' She glanced down at the pad where she had scribbled her notes on the interviewees. 'I have to say there is no doubt in my mind about which one I preferred.'

He said, 'Let me guess — Daniel Leen.'

'Yes. He had a . . . a warmer personality than Mr Bridger, I thought, not to mention the highest references from his previous school.'

'And he has eight years' experience compared with five.'

Rose skimmed through the notes she had made earlier. 'And Mr Bridger did seem a rather nervous person. Almost defensive, I thought.'

'Mr Leen seemed totally at ease with his subject. Very confident. I thought I'd trip him with one or two of my questions, but he was up to them.'

'You were very good, Mr Tremayne. I felt so much stronger, having you with me.' Impulsively she reached out her hand. 'Thank you so much for your support.'

He clasped her hand briefly. 'I should be thanking you. All good experience for me when it is *my* turn to be running a school. I do have ambitions in that regard, Miss Vivian, but that's of no significance at present. The question is what do you do next, and the answer is, I presume, write to them both. Good news for Mr Leen and disappointment for the other.'

She nodded and then sat back in the chair. 'I can hardly believe it's over. It's been like a mill-stone round my neck.'

He shook his head. 'It's too much for that slender neck — if you forgive me saying so. You are going to need help, Miss Vivian, if you intend to remain Head of Tye Rock House.'

He looks so earnest, she thought happily. So concerned for her welfare. Was it possible that there was a future for them together at some stage? The question had begun to loom large in her mind over the last few days, and the past hour and a half had increased her certainty that that was what she wanted. He was personable, clever, astute and a loyal ally. And she was so in love with him.

He said, 'I wanted to say something to you about that day in the staff room when I said that there was nothing between us.'

She waited breathlessly.

'I said then that our friendship was purely professional, but I didn't mean that. I thought it necessary at the time but, Miss Vivian, I have hopes that sometime quite soon the situation could alter considerably.'

Rose tried to hide her growing excitement. He was saying everything she wanted to hear, but she must never let him know how much she thought of him. It would seem very forward and unattractive. She said, 'I, too, hope we can be very good friends, Mr Tremayne.'

He grinned suddenly. 'I would like us to be more than very good friends. I think we deserve it. We are both alone in the world. I think I could say we *need* each other.'

'I — I do so agree.' Rose did the unthinkable — she tried to imagine herself with a child. Mark Tremayne's child. Then with a family of three or four children . . . Then sanity returned and she felt her face grow hot. She tilted her head a little to hide her expression from him.

'I was wondering,' he said. 'whether you would consider it appropriate to spend some time with me on Sunday? I thought we might wrap up warmly, take the steam packet from Falmouth and go to Truro. We might even indulge ourselves in a cream tea!'

His smile made her heart leap and she was gripped by a heady excitement. For a moment she was carried away at the prospect, but abruptly her spirits plummeted. She had a prior engagement with the Edgcombes. In an agony of indecision she stared at Mark Tremayne. Could she possibly ask the Edgcombes to excuse her from Sunday lunch? And if so, what reason could she give for her change of plan? And would it be fair to them?

He said, 'Please say "Yes", Miss Vivian. It's a truly wonderful trip, and being together would make it more so — at least, for me it would.'

'And for me.'

His eyes shone. 'Then you'll come?'

Rose hesitated, longing to accept the invitation. A river trip with a young man (particularly *this* young man) was the nearest thing she could think of to heaven. She felt delightfully dizzy that she had been *asked*.

'I'm afraid I can't,' she told him. 'I have already promised to spend the day with the Edgcombes. I'm so dreadfully disappointed.'

'Not as disappointed as I am. James Edgcombe is a lucky man.'

'James? Oh, Mr Tremayne! I don't want to give you the wrong impression about Mr Edgcombe. It was his mother who invited me. The family have been our advisers for many years and James — I mean the young Mr Edgcombe — is helping me with some family matters.'

He smiled. 'That's such a relief to me. I hope you won't mind me saying this, Miss Vivian, but I do feel a certain rapport with you. I've felt it ever since I came here — as though there is something which draws us together. And because of that feeling, I would like you to have this.'

Startled, she saw that he was offering her a small package wrapped in tissue paper. Wonderingly she took it from him.

'For me? Oh, but —' She faltered.

'Please. Open it. It was my mother's.'

With nervous fingers, Rose unwrapped the paper. A small silver brooch in the shape of a daisy was revealed; the centre was a large green stone. Rose said, 'Your mother's? Should you — would she —'

His voice was soft with emotion. 'She would have loved you to have it. Someone should wear it and enjoy it. My father gave it to her as a wedding present.'

'It's wonderful,' said Rose, 'but I couldn't accept such a gift. It looks very expensive.'

'I'm afraid not.'

Even as she spoke she was longing to be persuaded. Such a gift from Mark Tremayne would be something to treasure.

'I'm not convinced,' he told her, 'and I won't take "No" for an answer.' He took the brooch from her. 'May I?' he asked and pinned it to the bodice of her dress just below the left shoulder.

'It's beautiful,' Rose whispered. 'And you are so generous. I don't know how to thank you.'

He smiled again. A rather mysterious smile, she thought. 'Time will show you a way,' he said.

'Now, if you'll excuse me, I'm on duty and it's almost time for the bell.'

Rose stared after him, dazed with happiness. As the door closed behind him, her face was wreathed in a broad smile and she thought she had never been happier in her life.

CHAPTER NINE

The next day, as the train rattled on its way towards Falmouth, Rose stared out of the carriage window. The address James had given her was in her purse. He was taking her to meet Miss Folkes, and this news had almost overshadowed Thursday's excitement.

James leaned forward. 'You mustn't expect too much, Rose. She may not know where your mother is, and I don't want to feel that I have brought you more heartache. Miss Hollis, the companion, says that Miss Folkes is very frail. I didn't see her, as you know, but she assures me she will be up today if her health permits. There are days when she doesn't leave her bed.'

Rose nodded. 'But you don't know any more?'

'Miss Hollis claims to know nothing about them. She said Miss Folkes never talks about them.'

'Never talks about them?' Rose felt a prickle of unease. 'I wonder why?'

He shrugged. 'She didn't say, and I didn't think it my place to press her.'

'Of course not, James. That was foolish of me.' She reached out and touched his hand. 'I can't tell you how grateful I am that you are going to so much trouble on my behalf. I really do appreciate it. And your father, too, for allowing you to spend so much time on these wild goose chases.'

He smiled. 'My father wants only your happiness; we all do. Oh!' He glanced out of the window as the train pulled into the station. 'We're there. Now all you need is a hansom from the station.'

When the train stopped he opened the carriage door, stepped down on to the platform and helped her out. As he did so he noticed the brooch she was wearing. He glanced up at her; then he studied the brooch with greater interest, causing other descending passengers to move round him.

She said, 'It's a gift.'

'A very generous one. That's a very good emerald. Beautiful, in fact.'

'Oh, no! It's not valuable.'

His eyes narrowed. 'Who told you that? I happen to know quite a bit about emeralds. They are my mother's favourite stone. Who gave this to you, Rose?'

'A . . . a friend.'

'Was it Mr Tremayne?'

Rose fought down a desire to lie. 'As a matter of fact, it was.'

'And he told you it was worth very little?'

She felt intuitively that in some way this was dangerous ground. 'Whatever he said was between the two of us,' she said firmly. 'I don't have to explain everything to you, James.'

'Why does the question annoy you?'

'I'm not annoyed!' She glared at him. 'Now can we talk about something else, please?'

After a long moment he said, 'Of course.' By this time passengers were pushing past them in the other direction. 'I'll find you a cab.'

Feeling wretchedly ungrateful, she trailed behind him.

He hailed one and helped her up into it. 'And remember, Rose. I'll be in the waiting room when you return. We'll take the next train back.'

Rose was suddenly nervous. 'But what shall I do if you're *not* here?'

'I *will* be here.' He looked at her earnestly. 'Above anyone else in the world, you can rely on me, Rose. If I say I'll be here, then I will.'

'I'm sorry. I'm just rather frightened. Silly, I know.'

'Rose Vivian, you are *never* silly. You'll be quite all right. And you'll be one step nearer to your mother!'

Ida Folkes sat in an armchair on one side of the fireplace where a generous fire gave out a welcome warmth. It had obviously smoked earlier in the day and a slight haze still hung below the ceiling. There was also a hint of something medicinal — probably liniment, thought Rose. The spacious room was comfortably furnished with books along each wall. Presumably some of these were her own. In front of the window was a huge desk on which stood various books and papers and a brass pen-and-ink stand. So that was where she did her writing, thought Rose. Or had done when she was younger. There were no photographs, so perhaps she had no family. Not even a husband. If so, she had either been a very successful writer or had inherited money. Behind the desk the large window was framed with velvet curtains, and there was a collection of vigorous potted plants along the sill.

The old lady looked at Rose for a long time without speaking. She was, as James had warned, very frail. Her diminutive figure was swamped by a dark green dress that was much too big for her, and a woollen shawl covered her shoulders. Faded blue eyes stared up at Rose from a chalk-white face. Wisps of fine grey hair had escaped from a knitted bonnet and her gnarled hands were clasped round the knob of heavy walking stick. With a sinking heart, Rose came to the conclusion that the old lady was rapidly approaching her last days. By contrast Miss Hollis, her companion, appeared full of life, middle-aged and plump, with currant-brown eyes set in a cheerful face. She bent over to Rose and whispered, 'Remember to speak up. She's getting a bit deaf although she won't have it, bless her.' Her voice held the familiar West Country burr.

Miss Folkes stared at her. 'So you're Rose. You're very like her, my dear.' Her voice was surprisingly clear, Rose thought, relieved. And her accent was refined. From the south-east, Rose guessed. Possibly London. 'The eyes and the forehead. Oh yes, you're her little Rose.'

Immediately undermined, Rose found her eyes prickling with sudden tears and, seeing this, Miss Hollis said quickly, 'Now don't go upsetting yourself, my lovey. Sit yourself down and take it easy.' She indicated the chair opposite and said, 'I'll make a nice pot of tea. Miss Folkes always likes a biscuit around this time.'

'Thank you.' Rose sat down.

Miss Folkes said, 'I read about your father's death. Quite terrible. I'm so sorry. You must miss him.'

Rose nodded, not trusting herself to speak as Ida Folkes stared into the fire, allowing her time to compose herself. Her desire for information warred with the need for the proprieties. 'You have a very beautiful home.' She remembered to speak distinctly.

'Thank you. I have lived here all my life. I was born in the front bedroom. An only child to loving but elderly parents. They encouraged my writing, for which I am eternally grateful. It freed me from the need to marry.'

Rose allowed the remark to pass. Unable to wait any longer she said, 'Forgive me, but I must know. Is my mother living locally?'

'No, my dear, she is not.'

'Oh dear. I was hoping to —'

'My dear, I'm afraid I have to tell you that your mother is no longer alive.'

Rose gasped. 'Oh, *don't* say that!' The terrible words seemed to reverberate in her mind so that she reeled from the sound. 'Oh *no!* I can't bear it!' She felt hot and faint and her stomach churned. There must be some mistake, she thought desperately. But the calm voice went on inexorably.

'I'm so sorry, my dear. I can imagine how much you hoped it would be otherwise, but Catherine Vivian died some years ago.'

Shocked beyond measure, Rose put a hand to her mouth as speechlessly she digested the unwelcome information. She had anticipated problems in tracing her, but she *had* expected eventually to find her mother alive and well. In spite of all James's warnings she had set her heart on a positive outcome to the search, and now she must face up to the knowledge that the longed-for reunion would never take place. Two large tears forced themselves down her cheeks, but she brushed them quickly away. It was hardly fair to this old lady to cause a scene and she had vowed to behave with great restraint. The inevitable tears must wait.

Miss Folkes said gently, 'This must be very disappointing news.'

Rose nodded, not trusting herself to speak. Seeing the pity in the faded eyes of her hostess, she closed her own. *Catherine Vivian is dead.* Even as Rose struggled to stay calm she was aware of more tears rolling down her cheeks. She brushed them away with a shaking hand. It was a long moment before she felt able to continue. 'Will you tell me what you know about her? How she died, when . . .' Her voice faded.

'I can't hear you.'

'I'm sorry.' She repeated her request.

'I'll do my best.' She frowned. 'It started when I advertised for a companion, and Cathy applied.'

Rose couldn't wait. 'I know she had a child.'

'She had a *what*?'

Rose raised her voice. 'A child.'

'Oh yes, she did. A very young child. Such a dear little boy.'

Rose drew in her breath sharply. A dear little boy! So she had a brother. The thought made her marginally happier. So she was not entirely alone in the world.

Miss Folkes went on, 'She called him Albert George — after her own father and her husband. We called him Bertie, of course. Or "Boy". I called him that to tease him. I wasn't too sure about having a young child in the house — such a distraction when one's writing, you see — but your mother's plight was rather severe.'

Miss Hollis bustled in again with a tea tray which she set down on the small table between Rose and Miss Folkes. It was set with teapot, sugar and milk, a plate of biscuits, one cup and saucer and a mug with a spout. She tucked a white table napkin into Miss Folkes' collar and arranged it carefully.

'I'll be having mine in the kitchen,' she told

Rose. 'I've that many sheets to iron and you two can manage without me, I'm sure.' She lowered her voice. 'Perhaps you would pour? Her poor old hands aren't very good, but she can hold the mug. Don't make it too hot for her, and don't fill it no more'n half else it'll spill and she hates that.' She gave her employer an affectionate smile. 'Seventy-three next month, she is. All due to my coddling, she tells me!' She raised her voice slightly and said, 'I coddles you, don't I, my lovey?'

'You *fuss* over me, if that's what you mean.'

Miss Hollis withdrew, still chuckling, and rather self-consciously Rose poured the tea as instructed. She handed the mug to the old lady, who laid down her stick and clasped the mug with both hands. She took a few mouthfuls, then returned it to the tray.

Miss Folkes continued. 'Your mother had left her husband, not knowing that she was with child. I think she must have panicked when she realised. Poor Cathy! As soon as she found out she wanted to go back. She had left him for her lover, a man she truly cared for, but suddenly she was desperate to go home to her husband!'

Rose, reluctant to reveal her ignorance, still had to ask, 'But how could she be sure it was my father's child?'

Miss Folkes smiled. 'Oh, it was. There was no doubt about that. You see, although I call him her lover they'd never been intimate.' Sensing Rose's confusion she said, 'There had never been anything physical between them. Cathy insisted that she couldn't be unfaithful to her husband while she still lived under the same roof. The boy was her husband's flesh and blood, and she wanted him to take them both back. She longed to be with her little girl; she wanted them to be a family again.' She sighed. 'I pitied that poor man in a way — Alan Gibbs, I mean. He'd given up everything to be with Cathy, and she must have broken his heart.'

She reached for the mug.

Rose thought guiltily of Alan Gibbs and concluded she was probably right, yet a fierce loyalty made her say, 'I don't think we should judge her too harshly.'

'Maybe not.'

For a while neither of them spoke. Miss Folkes stared at the mug she held as though she had never seen it before, and Rose struggled with her feelings. For the first time she wondered if it had been wise to pursue the truth. All she had done was raise phantoms from an unhappy past. She sighed. James had been right to warn her about expecting too much. She had allowed herself to hope for a happy ending, and this was not going to happen.

Although crushed, she was struck by a new thought. 'Did she love my father? I never knew her. I can't remember them together.'

For a moment the old lady didn't answer. 'I don't think she did. She loved this Alan Gibbs, but once she'd sent him away he wouldn't come back. You couldn't blame him, could you? She'd ruined his life. Oh dear!' She sighed. 'Your mother was a very beautiful, unpredictable woman, my dear, and that's about the truth of it. The men didn't know where they were with her. You know what they say? "You can't have your cake and eat it, too." In the end poor Cathy hardly knew what she did want.' She drank some more tea and replaced the mug. 'Have I spilled any?'

'No.' Rose forced a smile. She whispered, 'Poor Mama.'

'What's that, dear?'

'I said, "Poor Mama."'

'Poor thing, indeed. She told me once that she should never have married your father — that she did it for the wrong reason, whatever that means. She didn't love him but he was hopelessly in love with her in his own way. I daresay that impressed her. But he couldn't show his affection, or so she said. Alan Gibbs is the man she should have married. "Alan made me laugh," she told me on more than one occasion. As though that was important to her.' She gave a little shrug.

Rose tried to reconcile the Alan Gibbs she had met with a cheerful, humorous man and found it impossible. Had her mother been responsible for the change in him? It was not a comfortable thought.

Rose said, 'My father was never very demonstrative. I think he did love me but . . .'

'I daresay you reminded him of his wife.' She broke off a piece of her biscuit and chewed it thoughtfully. 'He probably worried that you might grow up like your mother. Reading between the lines, I suspect she was a bit . . . how shall I say it . . . ? Somewhat "flighty", if you'll forgive me. Wayward, perhaps. I'm sure your father wanted what was best for you. Even your mother knew that. "He'll look after Rose," she'd say. But she wanted to share you. Poor confused soul.'

Deeply shocked, Rose was finding it impossible to eat or drink. Miss Folkes's reminiscences had profoundly depressed her. If all the things people said about her mother were true, the saintly mother banished from the family home by a wicked husband had existed solely in her imagination. She must now believe that her beautiful but wayward mother had brought about her own downfall by her irresponsible behaviour. This was not what Rose wanted to hear, and she was having trouble accepting it. More than anything she longed to reject Miss Folkes's view of the truth, but deep down she knew that it must be correct. Miss Folkes had shared her home with Rose's mother for many years. She probably knew her better than anyone else. To break the silence she asked, 'How did she die?'

Miss Folkes stared into the fire. 'She developed consumption. The doctor said she should go to a sanatorium for six months and I agreed to pay for her treatment, but she flatly refused to leave Bertie. I begged and then bullied her, but she said she'd abandoned one child and nothing would induce her to make the same mistake again — not even for six months. I made her rest outside whenever the sun shone, and I fed her calves' foot jelly — whenever I could get her to take it.' She smiled wistfully. 'Cathy hated the stuff.'

Rose said eagerly, 'I can't bear it, either.'

'I did what I could for her. She was like the daughter I never had, and when she died it broke my heart.' She looked up at Rose. 'It happened about six years ago, very peacefully. Just slipped away. I was with her and so was the boy, but the last word she uttered was "Rose".'

Rose, immeasurably moved, could think of nothing to say and they sat in silence for what seemed an eternity. Miss Hollis came in and stirred the fire so that it produced a bright rush of sparks. She added some coals, waited while Rose drank her tea, then took the tray and left them.

At last Rose asked, 'And my brother?' She was surprised by the tremor in her voice.

'Ah! Bertie. Now that's a sorry tale.'

'He's not dead *too?*' cried Rose, horrified.

The old lady's mouth tightened. 'He might just as well be dead as far as I'm concerned. No, he's alive. At least, I assume so. He walked out of this house and not a word since. Not a card. After all I did for him.' She shook her head.

'Did he know he had a sister? Did my mother

talk to him about me?'

'Oh yes. Frequently. Too much, I sometimes thought. Always pretending that one day you would all be together again. Very unsettling for the boy, I thought, but it wasn't up to me to say so. It made him dissatisfied.'

Rose digested this new revelation in silence, strangely comforted by the thought of her mother talking to the son about 'little Rose'.

Ida Folkes continued, 'After his mother died the boy wanted to go back to his father and sister. It was almost an obsession with him. So I wrote to your father telling him what had happened. I thought that after all those years he might soften, because then he'd have his son *without* having to take his wife back. I included a letter from Bertie, but he ignored them both.'

Rose was stunned at the extent of her ignorance.

The old lady reached for another biscuit and put half in her mouth. 'I was fond of the boy, so I adopted him. I thought it best. Sadly, it wasn't the wisest thing I could have done.' She put the remainder of the biscuit into her mouth and removed the table napkin. With fumbling fingers she dabbed at her lips, then folded the linen into an untidy square. 'He didn't appreciate it. I gave him my name and paid for him to finish his education at a good school. With the usual extras — whatever he wanted, really. He was determined to play chess because Cathy had told him that his father — *your* father — had been keen on it.'

Rose had a momentary picture of her father and Mark Tremayne, heads bent over the chessboard. 'He took it very seriously,' she said. 'That and walking.'

'Bertie had chess lessons — and violin lessons — to please me, that was. I love the sound of a violin . . . He did actually have quite a talent for the instrument, but he was lazy and I had to nag him. Oh dear! . . . And what thanks did I get? When he was eighteen he upped and left. Just like that, without a word of warning. Not even a "Thank you, Aunt." He used to call me Aunt. Poor little soul, he had so little family of his own and I used to smile, the way he said it. "Aunt Ida." He loved me, when he was little.' She sighed. 'Not later, I can see it now. He made use of me, then took himself off. Took some of my jewellery with him . . . and two first editions of which I was very proud. Sold them, I expect.' Her mouth trembled. 'Unforgivable.'

Rose regarded her with growing consternation. Here was another person whose life had been disrupted by the Vivian family. Ripples on a pond, she thought, and at once a picture of the Loe Pool rose up in her mind. With surprising clarity she saw the broad expanse of dark, flat water and then, as if in slow motion, a large stone fell into the centre of it, sending shock waves across its smooth surface. Shuddering, she banished the image. 'I'm so terribly sorry,' she said lamely.

Miss Folkes gave her a faint smile. 'Nothing to

do with you, my dear, so don't go blaming yourself. He had every chance, but he chose to throw it all away. I have no family of my own and I would have left him everything — but not now. I would rather leave it to a deserving charity.'

Rose had to ask, 'So you don't know where he is?'

The old lady's expression darkened. 'I don't, and to tell you the truth I don't want to know. He changed when his mother died. He had never been an easy boy — he was inclined to be moody; moped about. I made allowances because he'd just lost his mother, but as time went on he got worse instead of better. Seemed to delight in making other people miserable. I tried to talk to him but he was very stubborn. It was almost as though he relished the excuse to be awkward and uncooperative.'

Rose hid her dismay, searching her mind for a way to mitigate her brother's bad behaviour. Knowing that she was never going to meet her mother, she desperately wanted to discover a brother whom she could love.

'I had another companion after your mother died, but she only stayed six months. Poor Mrs Stuckey. She brought her cat Felix with her — a mangy old thing, but she adored it. The boy hated it — I don't know why — and she caught him teasing it one day. Tormenting it, she said; swinging it by its tail. Bertie denied it pointblank. He called Mrs Stuckey a liar and got quite hysterical. I had to punish him, of course. I do abhor cruelty, and there was no reason for her to lie. So I cancelled a little outing we had planned for his birthday.'

She stopped for breath and dabbed her face with her handkerchief as Rose waited apprehensively.

Miss Folkes frowned. 'When I told him, he became almost hysterical with anger. He blamed Mrs Stuckey and threatened to "get even" with her. Some days later the cat disappeared. Mrs Stuckey was quite distraught. We found it a few days later behind the garden shed. Dead. We never did know how it died, although I think it had been strangled. Poor old Felix.'

Chilled by her words, Rose said, 'You're not suggesting — you don't think that . . . that my brother . . .' It was monstrous. She couldn't put it into words.

Miss Folkes leaned forward in an effort to hear better. 'I don't think *what,* dear?'

'That my brother killed her cat?'

The old lady shrugged. 'I don't know. He never admitted it, but I have to say that I harboured grave suspicions. I think it was his way of taking revenge on Mrs Stuckey over the cancelled outing. Poor woman. She thought so too, naturally, and she didn't stay long after that. Said she didn't like being in the house alone with him; he *frightened* her. He had something of a temper, I must admit, but I hoped he would learn to control it. When Mrs Stuckey left he insisted that we didn't need anyone else. I wanted to replace her, but he made such a fuss.' She shook her head at the memory.

'Maybe he was jealous — of your friendship with anyone else.' Rose was trying desperately to justify her brother's behaviour. 'Maybe he wanted to be your closest friend?'

Miss Folkes gave her a cold look. 'It wasn't like that, Rose. I'm not a fool, and I know exactly how it was.'

'I'm sorry.'

'But he had his way and we stayed on our own, with just a daily woman to clean the house.'

'And was that the end of it?'

The silence lengthened ominously. 'No, it wasn't. After a while even *I* was beginning to get a bit nervous in his company. He became sly, and sometimes there was something almost threatening about him.' Seeing Rose's face, she said, 'But then he *could* be charming. He'd say how sorry he was and give me a hug.' Her expression was suddenly wistful. 'Such a nice-looking boy. I've a photograph somewhere. I'll look it out and send it to you. It's of the three of us — your mother and me and the boy . . . Oh dear!' She drew in her breath shakily and sank back in her chair. 'Forgive me, my dear. So many unhappy memories . . . so much I prefer to forget.' She clasped her hands, pressing them against her chest. 'No matter how we try to escape, the past is always with us.'

Rose watched the flames and tried to come to terms with this latest unwelcome news. She had a brother, but apparently he was not a very nice person. But did that mean she didn't want to find him?

As though reading her mind, the old lady said, 'He left here about four years ago. He said he was going to America. I try not to think about him. I hate to imagine him going to the bad, for your mother's sake. She worshipped him.'

Rose felt a pang of jealousy which she quickly stifled.

Miss Folkes went on, 'Still, let's look on the bright side. Maybe he's made his fortune in America — or is busy making it . . . He'd be twenty-three . . . twenty-four, now. Where do the years go to?'

'He might have married.'

'Might have what, dear?'

'Married.' Rose tried to think positively. Perhaps she had a sister-in-law and nieces and nephews? One day, maybe, they'd meet and it would all end happily.

'God help his wife if he has, that's all I can say.' Then, as though regretting her harsh words, she leaned over the table to pat Rose's hand. 'Take my advice and forget about him. Think about your mother instead, and how much she loved you. She'd be so proud of you.' She closed her eyes suddenly and leaned back.

Rose watched her but her eyes remained closed.

'Miss Folkes?'

There was no response and, alarmed, she hurried into the kitchen in search of Miss Hollis who was on her way to the stairs with her arms full of newly ironed linen.

Miss Hollis laughed. 'Closed her eyes, has she? That's nothing to fret about. She falls asleep at the drop of a hat these days. I'm surprised, to tell you the truth, that she's stayed awake so long.'

'I hope I haven't overtired her. I feel rather guilty.'

Miss Hollis shook her head. 'She'll be perfectly all right. Don't you worry your head about her; you just get along. Your cab's waiting, and Lord knows what you'll be owing him.'

Rose smiled. 'Tell her I said "Goodbye", will you? And "Thank you". I'm so grateful.'

Miss Hollis put the sheets down on the second stair and opened the front door.

Rose forced a brave smile. 'I'll come and see her again if I may?' and Miss Hollis said, 'You do that, my lovey. She doesn't get many visitors.'

Rose's offer was made quite sincerely, but the news about her family had taken a much greater emotional toll than she realised. Exhausted, she leaned back against the cushioned seat of the cab, trying to deny her anguish. Frustration and disappointment overwhelmed her and she burst into tears and cried all the way to the station. In a state of near collapse, she almost fell into James's comforting arms. Infinitely kind, he led her into the small waiting room and brought her saffron cakes and hot, sweet tea from a nearby tea room. At last he led her, silent and shaken, on to the train and sat holding her hand tightly in his. Rose, wrapped up in her unhappiness, was already admitting to herself that she could never make that particular pilgrimage again.

Half an hour later Rose found herself sitting beside a large fire in a comfortable armchair sipping sweet cocoa. Mrs Edgcombe and her husband had withdrawn to another room, ostensibly to check the accounts. James sat opposite her, the glow from the fire lighting up his face. In a vain attempt to hide his concern, he was chattering about his boyhood and, although what he was saying mostly failed to register, Rose was soothed by the sound of his voice and comforted by his presence.

'. . . So I was lucky,' he said. 'Never rich but never struggling, either — thanks to the firm.'

Rose smiled, albeit a little shakily. The emotion and grief had exhausted her but gradually she was recovering, clinging to the knowledge that she was not exactly alone; that somewhere she had a brother.

James said, 'I'm sorry, prattling on about myself. How selfish you must think me.'

'You, selfish? No, James. Never selfish. You've been so kind.'

'I can't bear to see you hurt, Rose. It tears me apart. Will you give up your search — please?'

'For my brother, you mean?' She drew a long breath. 'I don't know.'

James leaned forward in his chair, regarding her earnestly. 'I think you should let it go, Rose. For your own sake. He might be half-way across the world, and you will wear yourself out trying. Isn't it time to make a life for yourself? To think about what you want from the rest of it?'

'I wish I knew. I'm in such a muddle.' She took another mouthful of cocoa and shivered involuntarily.

At once James came to her, wrapping the shawl more closely around her shoulders. She was suddenly aware how tense he was, and when he didn't return to his own chair she guessed the reason. Oh no, James! she begged silently, but it was too late.

Kneeling beside her, he said, 'Rose, I want to marry you. I want to take care of you. I don't want you ever to be hurt again.' He took hold of her hand. As she opened her mouth to protest, he said, 'No! Don't say anything until you've heard me out.' His hand tightened over hers as she wondered how best to save *him* from hurt.

She said, 'I can't give you the answer —'

'Rose, you need someone, and I love you. I always have. You know that, don't you?'

She nodded. Dare she tell him the full truth about Mark Tremayne, she wondered. Confessing that she loved another man was the only way she would convince him.

'James, there's something I must tell you if —'

'Wait, Rose!' He sat back on his heels so that he could see her face. 'I'm not the world's most eligible bachelor, but I know I could make you happy. I swear to you that I would care for you — love you — *cherish* you — until my dying day. You can't spend the rest of your life alone, Rose. Forget Tye Rock House with all its problems and become Mrs Edgcombe without a care in the world.' He smiled. 'My father and mother are already fond of you, and I adore you. You'd be part of a family with *us,* Rose. You don't need a brother who may or may not be a nice person.'

'Oh, James! If you'd only listen —'

'We'd find a place of our own — I've already got my eye on something suitable.'

With growing dismay, Rose heard the excitement in his voice. It was no good, she *must* stop him. She heard herself say, 'There's someone else, James. I'm so sorry.' Her voice, tight with tension, sounded unfamiliar.

It took a moment for James to grasp what she had told him. When he did, he almost fell back with shock. The animation left his face and he stared at her, stricken. Then he sat back on the opposite side of the fire.

'Someone else?'

Rose felt a few seconds' panic. Now he would want to know, and she wasn't sure if she wanted to tell him.

'I don't . . .' he began. *'Someone else?'*

'I'm sorry,' she repeated. 'I wasn't going to tell you — I wasn't going to tell *anyone.* Not yet.'

He looked stricken. 'But who is it?'

'I can't say. Later, perhaps.'

His eyes narrowed. 'You're not just saying this? To — to discourage me?' He was trying to read her expression. 'There isn't anyone else, surely?' He seemed to clutch at the notion. 'There isn't, is there? Rose?'

'There is, James. I love him and he . . . recently he hinted very strongly that he loves me.'

'It's not Tremayne!'

'Yes — at least, I hope so. I'm sure he loves me, but he hasn't actually said so. It's so soon after my father's death . . .' Unable to bear his expression, she studied her hands. 'I didn't want to hurt you, James. I've never encouraged you.' And yet he had been so kind. She was filled with guilt. Then another thought occurred, which filled her with alarm. Looking up, she asked, 'Your parents — do they know that . . .' She looked at him in agitation. Sunday lunch loomed large. However would she get through it, she wondered.

'That I was going to propose to you? No, they didn't. I didn't know myself.' He watched her distractedly, a frown creasing his face.

There was a long silence. Stealing a quick glance at him, Rose saw that he was crushed by the news. Because how could he object to Mark Tremayne? He was young, respectable, respected. There were no grounds for argument. She found herself praying that James would give in gracefully. Then their friendship could continue — and she was suddenly aware just how much she needed him as a close friend.

At last he said, 'Mark Tremayne. But you assured me he felt nothing for you?'

'But now I think he does.'

'And you're sure?'

'Yes. I'm sure.'

He swallowed. 'Then when the time comes I'll congratulate you both.'

'I'm truly sorry, James. Will you still be my friend? I couldn't bear to lose you.'

'You could never do that,' he said. 'So the two of you will run Tye Rock House. Is that the plan?'

'We haven't made any plans. I told you, he hasn't actually asked me to marry him but he hinted —'

James's face brightened fractionally. 'Then nothing's settled. I mean, it just might not happen? There's still a chance.'

She must be firm. There was no point in giving him false hopes. 'I *want* it to happen, James. As to the school, I imagine we'll keep it going when — if . . .' Again she fell silent.

'I shall go on hoping, Rose.' He forced a lopsided smile. 'There'll never be anyone else for me. I shall be here, waiting. If anything goes wrong — and I hope for your sake it doesn't — I'll still be waiting. Still in love with you. Still hoping to look after you and make you happy.'

The coals shifted suddenly, making them both jump. She said, 'I don't want you to wait for me, James. I want you to find someone else — to marry and to be happy.'

He shook his head. 'Can't be done!' he said with a shrug. 'Only Rose Vivian can make me happy.'

'You say that now, James, but in time you'll meet another woman —'

He stood up. 'Don't let's argue, Rose. Nothing you say will make any difference. You love the man, and I hope he's worthy of you. I'll wish you every happiness with Tremayne, but if anything happens I'll be here.' He held out his hands and, grasping hers, pulled her to her feet. The shawl slipped from her shoulders but they ignored it. He asked, 'Do you love me at all, Rose?'

'That's not fair!' She felt that to confess the depth of her affection for James would be to betray Mark Tremayne.

He said, 'Fair or not, if there were no Tremayne — if you are wrong — would you consider marrying me?'

She thought about how she could answer. 'I'd consider it, yes.'

His face lit up. 'Then you *do* love me?'

She gave a small nod.

'Enough?'

Rose regarded him intently. Did she love him enough? She didn't want a future in which he didn't figure somewhere. Was that enough? Would love grow? She drew a long breath.

Seeing that she hesitated, James forestalled her. 'I would have enough love for both of us.' He grinned suddenly. 'If you put your mind to it, you'd find me irresistible!'

She laughed. 'Then the answer's "yes".'

'Ah!' His expression was triumphant. 'Then will you promise me this, Rose — that if anything happens and you don't marry Tremayne — you'll marry *me?* Him or me. No traipsing off round the world in search of someone else. *Me,* Rose. Could you go that far?'

'What *could* happen?' she demanded.

'Life isn't always plain sailing, Rose. Your parents' marriage hit a few rocks,' he reminded her gently.

Hit a few rocks? Rose almost smiled at his kindly euphemism. After a series of violent storms, her parents' marriage had foundered totally in very deep water! But her own marriage to Mark Tremayne would take a different route and she could safely make the required promise. 'Yes, I would marry you, James.'

'A solemn promise, mind?' He held up his left hand. 'I, Rose Vivian, do solemnly swear . . .'

She smiled. 'A solemn promise,' she agreed, thinking that he would make someone a wonderful husband.

Later, on the drive back to Tye Rock, they spoke very little and Rose thought about Mark Tremayne and tried to recapture her earlier exhilaration. She failed dismally and when, from the front steps, she watched James drive away into the darkness, she was aware of a deep and unexpected sense of loss.

Later that same night Polly stood outside the

back door of the kitchen, talking to Robb who was preparing to set off home. She shivered in the cold air, her arms folded across her chest for warmth.

'All you've got to remember,' she told him, 'is that you didn't hit him. If Miss Vivian or anyone asks, you remember. Nobody hit him.' She glanced behind her, not wanting to be over-heard, but a reassuring burst of laughter came from the kitchen.

'Then how come he fell down?'

Polly counted to ten. 'I've told you — he *tripped*. He stepped backwards and fell over. That's what I'll say, and you've got to say the same thing.'

She had waited all day in fear and trembling for a summons to the Head's room, but none had come. So had Mr Tremayne given them away, or hadn't he? She was terrified of what might happen if he had.

'We've got to stick together, Robb. You do understand, don't you? We'll both be in trouble if he's told on us — if he *does* go to the police.'

Robb, slumped back against the wall, nodded miserably. 'He shouldn't have said that,' he told her. 'He shouldn't have called you a liar.'

'And you shouldn't have hit him, but you did. So we've got to be careful.'

She wondered, for the hundredth time that day, why Mr Tremayne had *not* reported them to someone. Surely he would want to get even with them? She was certain of that. The look on his face had frightened her.

She said slowly, 'Perhaps we *should* have told Cook or Maud.'

'But then they'd *know* — that I hit him.'

'I know that, but at least they'd have heard our story, see? They'd believe that was how it happened. That Pansy Tremayne *tripped*. That no one hit him. So if the police came sniffing round . . .' She sighed. 'But then I thought — maybe the less people who know anything the better.' She looked at him sharply. Was he listening to her? He'd been in a funny mood all day.

Robb leaned towards her. 'That was a smacking kiss you gave me this morning!'

'Robb!'

'What?'

'You're changing the subject.' Exasperated, she looked at him. Didn't he realise the seriousness of what had happened? 'It's not funny,' she told him. 'And you've got to remember what to say.' Suddenly, she was full of anxiety for him. How would he get on if the police locked him up? 'You just watch out for him, Robb. He'll have it in for you, I know he will.'

Robb nodded. 'But it was smashing. That kiss.'

She smiled in spite of herself. 'Glad you liked it.'

He grinned. 'I keep wishing you'd give me another one.'

She said, 'Why don't you give me one? If you're so keen.'

'Would you mind?'

'Try me.'

Polly sighed. She had wanted this for years, but now it was happening at the wrong time. Still, if it took the morning's trouble to bring Robb to his senses, so be it. Mustn't look a gift horse in the mouth! She turned her face up towards him and he put his arms round her. She leaned against him and his arms tightened.

'You're *cold!*' he whispered, his breath warm against her ear.

'Warm me up then!' she suggested.

She wondered vaguely where this would all end, but didn't care. As his lips met hers, she was aware of a wonderful excitement. She had never been this near to a man — nothing so far but a bit of a tickle from the boys at school. She wondered what Robb knew about courting.

The kiss was disappointingly short-lived. His arms loosened around her and she stepped back and looked up into his face. So was that it? She searched her mind for a way to keep his interest.

'You ever been in love?' she asked him.

'Course I have!' His teeth were white in the moonlight as he grinned.

'I mean, been out with a girl. Courting?'

'Dozens of 'em!'

'You know all about it then?'

'Oh, I know a thing or two.'

She was intrigued. Was he exaggerating? 'Who, then?' she demanded.

'I'm not telling.'

She laughed. 'I bet you haven't. I bet you don't even know how to do it!'

'Poll!' He was shocked. 'Course I know.' He hesitated. 'I done it with this girl at school. She was mad keen on it.'

'So if you done it, why didn't you marry her?'

After a long silence he said, ' 'Cos I went off her, if you must know. Silly little thing. Her mother scared her off me.'

It had the ring of truth and Polly felt horribly jealous. 'Who was it?' She cast her mind back to school, considering the other girls. 'Not Aggie Tyson!' she squealed. Aggie, a well developed fourteen-year-old, had been the talk of the village and the despair of her ma and pa. She was sent away one Easter and never came back. Everyone said she'd had a baby, but no one knew for sure. 'Not Aggie!' she repeated.

'I forget, don't I!'

She didn't believe him. 'I bet it was!' she insisted. But it hardly mattered all these years on; it was water under the bridge. And she should be pleased, she reminded herself. If Robb knew nothing about courting and she knew nothing — how would they get on?

She said, 'Do you have to go home, Robb? You could sleep over the stables.'

Missing the point, he said, 'Bit cold this weather, I reckon.'

Polly swallowed. Her excitement was growing, and she suddenly knew that she didn't want to let him go. She said, 'Kiss me again, why don't you, before you go?'

This time they stayed together longer and Polly discovered that the kisses were awakening in her feelings she had only previously suspected. So this was it! And about time, she told herself. Life in the kitchen at Tye Rock House left much to be desired, and a family of her own was the sum of her ambition. After the morning's encounter with Mr Tremayne, she had felt closer to Robb. He had tried to protect her and now she was trying to do the same for him. They were in it together and that gave her a sense of oneness, a strange feeling of belonging. Her and Robb . . . though she'd have to start calling him by his Christian name if they were going to . . . well, if anything happened. He wasn't a great thinker, but he was handsome and he fancied her. He had a job. They could find a cottage, maybe. Or live with his folks for a bit.

Coming to a sudden decision, she pulled back. 'You wouldn't be cold if I was in that bed with you!' she said. 'Over the stables, I mean. There's blankets, aren't there?'

'Blankets?' He leaned forward, trying to see her expression. 'For the bed, you mean?' He sucked in a huge mouthful of air. 'Oh aye. There's a couple of blankets.' He stared down at her. 'What — you and me?' He put his finger under her chin and tilted her head. 'You mean it? You're not having me on?'

'Why not? Since you've had so many girls!' She grinned at him. 'One more won't make much difference.' She was glad of the darkness, convinced that she must be blushing as she held her breath, waiting. If he refused her offer . . . She swallowed hard. If he turned her down she would never speak to him again.

'Cook'll know you're with me.'

'I'll go in and go up to bed and then sneak down again. I'll get out of the dining-room window. She won't know. No one'll know.'

Now that Polly had said it, it seemed the most natural thing in the world. She closed her eyes as Robb pondered his answer. She was going to do it at last. With Charlie Robb! Please say 'yes'.

The kitchen door opened and they both jumped as Cook put her head out. 'You'll catch your death, Polly!' she grumbled. 'Come in at once.'

Polly said, 'I'm not cold, and we've got things to talk about.'

'Things? What things?'

Polly bit back a sharp reply. She was still under Cook's thumb, so she must be careful. But once she and Robb were married (she crossed her fingers), no one would tell her what to do. She'd be her own mistress.

Cook wagged a finger at her. 'You'll get a chill, and it'll be me what gets the blame.' She glared at Robb. 'You should know better than to keep her out there. What's got into the pair of you?'

Robb said sheepishly, 'I'm just going then.'

Cook said, 'I should think so, too!' and went back inside.

Polly looked at Robb. 'It's now or never!' she told him.

His eyes widened, then he grinned. 'So it's you and me now, is it? Forget old Pansy Tremayne, eh?'

She didn't want to think about Tremayne. 'Yes, forget him,' she agreed.

A broad grin lit up his face. 'So it's me what's right up your street now!'

Polly, watching him, thought what good-looking children she'd have with this man. 'It's you!' she agreed.

He touched her hair gently. 'Right, then,' he said hoarsely. 'I'll be waiting.'

CHAPTER TEN

From the window of his darkened bedroom, Mark watched a young woman run from the side of the house, across the yard and into the stables. He guessed at once who it was. Only Polly had hair that fair. And Robb was already over there. *Bastard!* He raised his eyebrows. So Robb and Polly had something going, did they? Interesting. Not that it should surprise him, after the way the silly little bitch had tried to protect him. He recalled suddenly how Robb had deliberately whipped up the horse on the way back from the doctor's. Robb had made him look a fool, tipping him into the well of the cart that way. What did Polly see in a lout like that, for God's sake? For a moment he watched, but no light appeared in the window of the stable loft. He imagined them together — groping in the darkness, giggling, fumbling, whispering. And maybe laughing — at him. The memory of his earlier humiliation had stayed with him throughout the day, colouring all that he said and did. For once his iron self-control had failed him, and that also irked him. He had grumbled at the girls and snapped at Arnold Rivers. His charm had deserted him and that was dangerous. Now he longed to punish the pair of them, but threatening to call in the police had been a bluff. There was no way he wanted to draw attention to himself. No way he *dare*.

He left the window and sat down abruptly on the bed. He had come this far and he mustn't take any risks, but he couldn't let that pair get away with it. He would never forgive himself if he let a stupid servant girl and slow-witted gardener make a fool of him. He had punished Miss Hock, and he would punish them. For a moment he considered calling attention to their present whereabouts so that they would be reprimanded — maybe even dismissed. There must surely be rules for the kitchen staff which forbade such loose behaviour. If he could make it look accidental . . . they must never be sure that he was responsible. The gardener was an ox of a man and he landed a hefty punch. Mark put a hand to his stomach, which was still tender, and his expression was grim.

He narrowed his eyes, frowning into the darkness. Maybe he could go to Rose's bedroom and tell her that he had seen an intruder . . . someone who might be trying to steal the horses . . . He could say he couldn't sleep since the accident — or that he had woken from a nightmare and couldn't get back to sleep. That was better. More convincing. But would Robb guess that he was responsible? He daren't risk more trouble, not at this stage. By all accounts Robb had a nasty-minded brother who wasn't averse to meddling in other people's affairs.

What *had* Robb been telling Polly about the police? Hearing his own name mentioned had made him nervous. He threw himself on to the bed and lay stretched out, still fully dressed. He wanted to think about Rose and Tye Rock House, but the thought of Robb and Polly intruded. Damn them! Not only had he been humiliated, but he had muddied his jacket and been *physically* hurt. He had banged his left elbow as he went down and it was throbbing painfully. A little swollen, even. He had longed to snatch up the hoe and smash it into Robb's face, but had somehow resisted the temptation. God! He whistled softly in the darkness. He had been so close to losing his temper. *That* close to disaster.

Fortunately he had survived the temptation. He was still in control — still the hero who had tried to save poor Mr Vivian; still the man whom Rose loved and respected. But he was going to punish Polly and Robb, however long it took. He sighed. He knew he would be able to punish them eventually, but it would be so much more satisfying while the anger still burned in him.

He sat up suddenly, for an idea had come to him.

'Oh God, yes!' he whispered as the idea took shape in his mind. It was so simple. In his mind's eye he saw the two of them, half-naked, stumbling out into the courtyard, panic-stricken. He imagined the smoke billowing upwards, and he could almost hear the crackle of the flames. This time he would *not* play the hero but would pretend to sleep through the excitement. Rose would be roused from her bed and would come running to him for help. For a moment or two he wavered. It was rather extreme, but Robb deserved it and the foolish Polly had thrown in her lot with him. So be it. Closing his eyes, he drew a long, steady breath. He felt better already. The painful memories of the morning's shame were fading; his self-esteem was slowly returning.

He would do it.

Now.

In the hayloft, Polly knelt beside Robb. She was wearing her flannelette nightie under her wool dressing-gown. Her heart was beating fast as a shiver of anticipation ran through her. A faint light from the moon lit up the surrounding gloom and she could see the whites of Robb's eyes.

Polly said, 'You're a bit of a devil, you are, Robb,' and hoped he would take the hint.

He said, 'So are you!'

She said, 'I'll have to start calling you Charlie, won't I?'

'Will you? Why's that, then?'

'It's your given name, silly!' She lay down beside him and leaned her head on his shoulder. 'Aren't you going to put your arm round me?' she asked. 'Friendly, like?'

Obediently, he did as she suggested and she snuggled closer. 'Just like Chrissie Morgan and that Summers fellow,' she suggested.

Robb sat up, startled. 'I promised Miss Vivian!' he exclaimed. 'I said I never would — I said . . .' He looked at her anxiously. 'What *did* I say?'

'You said you wouldn't take any more bribes. No more shillings. From the girls. Nothing to do with us, Robb. I'm not a schoolgirl.'

He glanced around, peering into the darkness as though Miss Vivian might be lurking in a corner. 'I *promised!*'

'It's all right, Robb. You're not breaking your promise.'

Reluctantly he knelt beside her on the straw and, greatly daring, she slipped his braces down over his shoulders. Then they were lying down together and his arm was round her. She said, 'Cosy, isn't it? I can hear old Clipper and Sandman snorting. Don't horses sleep?'

'Course they do.'

'What, standing up?'

'I don't know.'

Polly rolled closer to him and threw her left arm casually across his body which was giving off a surprising heat. She laughed softly. 'You're lovely and warm, Robb! Better than a hot-water bottle.'

'Am I?' He thought for a moment, then added, 'So are you.'

It would be nice, she thought wistfully, if he could say something original, but maybe he was out of practice. Or just not very romantic.

She said, 'Like I was saying, Robb — Charlie's

your real name. You call me Poll. If we're going to be . . . well, walking out together . . .' She held her breath, praying that he would let this pass without protest. If she and Robb were walking out together, then Maud and Cook would have to make allowances.

'We'll see, then, won't we.' He murmured something noncommittal as though his thoughts were elsewhere. She said, 'You can kiss me, Robb, if you want.'

He turned towards her, then stopped abruptly. 'What was that?'

She groaned inwardly. 'What? I didn't hear nothing.'

'A noise. Listen! Like a footstep . . . someone's down there!'

She listened but heard nothing. 'Probably one of the horses.'

Below them a horse whinnied.

'Probably Clipper. He's a fidgety devil,' said Robb. 'Maybe something's spooking him.'

'He's all right! Don't fuss!'

'I'd best go and see,' Robb suggested without actually making a move.

'Robb, don't!' Polly hid her frustration as well as she could. 'I expect it's because they know we're here. We disturbed them, that's all.' She slid her fingers round his neck and up behind his ears. His hair was surprisingly silky. 'I thought you wanted to kiss me,' she whispered. 'I want to kiss you. Lie back down again, why don't you?'

He hesitated, still listening. 'I *can* hear someone.'

'If you say that again I'll scream!' Polly shivered. 'I'm lying here freezing, Robb. If you
aren't going to warm me up, I'll have to go back
to —'

'Ssh!' He put a hand over her mouth.

They waited. The whinny came again, and
they heard hooves clatter on the stable floor.
There was a crash. At once Robb was on his
knees, struggling to his feet, hitching up his
braces.

'Robb! Don't go down. It's probably Clipper
having a nightmare. I expect horses dream like
the —'

He ignored her. 'Who's there?' he yelled and
headed for the steps.

Polly was aware of the first tinglings of fear as
Robb muttered, 'I can smell something. *Smoke!*
Jesus O'Riley!'

From below one of the horses screamed with
fright. At the same moment Polly too caught the
smell of burning straw and she screamed, scram-
bling to her feet.

Robb, half-way down, was forced up again by
heat and smoke. 'Some bugger's set a fire!' he
gasped, his voice hoarse. He staggered back,
coughing furiously. There was a strange glow
from below and a sudden crackle which quickly
grew into a sullen roar.

'We've got to get them out!'

Frenzied whinnying was mixed with a barrage

of crashes as the terrified animals tried to break free.

'Get back!' yelled Robb as Polly, hampered by her nightclothes, stumbled towards the steps. 'We'll never get down the ladder, Poll. It's too hot. We'll have to try the window.' He ran across the loft. As he struggled with the window latch, Polly began to scream for help.

Robb cried, 'Come on, for God's sake, Poll! I'll lower you down. Come *on!*'

Polly wanted to say, 'No', but she couldn't see any other way out for them. The loft was filling with smoke and the heat was growing minute by minute. She coughed, half choking, and scrambled towards the window. Biting her lip in terror, she climbed out and allowed Robb to take hold of her hands.

'I'll break my neck!' she cried. 'It's too far!'

'Not this way,' he assured her. ' 'Cos your feet are half-way down already. OK? I'm letting you go.'

She fell awkwardly, twisting her right ankle, but as he had predicted the drop was not as far as she had expected. Nursing her throbbing ankle, she stared back up.

There was a roaring from inside the stable and an unearthly glow lit up the window. 'How will you get down?' she shouted.

'Never mind me. See to the horses!'

Polly hobbled painfully round the side of the building and approached the stable door with mounting trepidation. How was she supposed to deal with frantic horses? She was terrified of them. She pushed the door and it swung open with a blast of heat and smoke. Dimly through the glow she could see the desperate animals kicking and rearing. The thought of approaching those plunging hooves filled her with a cold dread. Panic gripped her.

'I can't, Robb!' she shouted. 'I just can't!'

He didn't answer and Polly stared round in growing desperation.

'I'm coming!'

A voice startled her and she turned to see a slim figure racing towards the stables. It was a young woman, fully dressed, and after a moment's incredulity Polly recognised Chrissie Morgan.

'I can't go in there!' Polly shouted. The fire was gaining a hold, but it was the thought of the horses which frightened her most.

The stable door was open and from inside there was a high-pitched squeal and a crash which sent a flurry of sparks through the open window. At that moment Robb appeared, miraculously unhurt after his escape from the window. To Polly's astonishment, he put up an arm to protect his face and ran straight in through the stable door closely followed by Chrissie Morgan.

Ashamed of her temerity, Polly hovered outside for a moment, wondering what she could do. Water! She must find water. Water and buckets — and she must get help. She must raise the alarm. She made her way painfully slowly to the front door of the main house and banged the knocker as loudly as she could. Then she tugged on the bell and shouted 'Fire! Fire!' at the top of her voice. Almost immediately lights came on at some of the windows and, after what seemed an age, Miss Vivian appeared closely followed by Matron.

Polly gave a garbled account of what had happened and the three of them hurried back to the stable yard. They were just in time to see Chrissie and Robb each struggling to hold on to a frightened horse who was doing his best to escape. Manes and tails were singed and the animals were greatly distressed, but still alive. Polly, keeping her distance, muttered a prayer of thanks and watched as they were led round to the front of the house where they would be out of sight and hearing of the burning building.

Miss Vivian shouted to Polly to find as many buckets as she could and then to fetch Mr Tremayne. There was a spring of fresh water at the rear of the property and they were filling the buckets from this as well as running in and out of the kitchen. The stables were well alight, defeating all their efforts, and as Polly prepared to run inside to waken Mr Tremayne, the roof fell in with a roar, a crash and flurry of sparks. Smoke billowed upwards.

Inside the main building, Polly ran up the stairs and along to Mr Tremayne's bedroom. She hammered on the door and called his name. Miss Hock appeared from the doorway opposite; she was tying the belt of her dressing-gown and her head was covered with curling rags.

'What on earth's going on?' she demanded.

'The stables is on fire,' Polly told her. 'They need help —'

'On fire! Good God!' She looked suitably shocked.

'— to make a bucket chain,' Polly finished.

Miss Hock hesitated. 'Should I get dressed?' she asked.

'There's no time!'

'Have they sent for the fire brigade?'

'It'll be too late!'

She watched Miss Hock's bulky figure disappearing along the corridor, then the door opened and Mr Tremayne appeared. He was rubbing his eyes sleepily and looked surprised to see her.

'Polly!' he said, his tone distinctly chilly. 'How — that is, what's the matter?'

She stared straight at his chest. 'Miss Vivian says to come quick because the stables is on fire.' She hoped it sounded like an order rather than a request.

It seemed to take him a moment to grasp what she was saying. Then he said, 'Good heavens! Tell her I'll come at once.' He turned away, then glanced back at her. 'Is anyone hurt?'

'I am,' said Polly. 'My ankle, but that's all, as far as I know. I can't wait. We're doing a bucket chain.'

She limped back along the corridor to the stairs. A fat lot he cares, miserable pig, she thought, the memory of their early-morning encounter still fresh in her mind. Still, he hadn't reported Robb to Miss Vivian, so he couldn't be all bad.

Outside she found the bucket chain abandoned as useless. A group of dejected people stood in a half-circle, watching the fire burn itself out. The roof was gone, but the stone walls had survived the heat. Once the straw and hay had been consumed by the flames there was little left to burn. From where they stood, they could see the charred remains of the wooden partitions and a mass of twisted framework — all that remained of the gig and the governess cart.

Miss Vivian said, 'We did what we could, but it was hopeless.' She sounded close to tears but who could blame her, thought Polly. Robb was nowhere to be seen, but she guessed he was with the horses. As expected, she found him in the front courtyard, running gentle hands over Clipper. Standing well back, Polly asked, 'Is he all right?'

Robb nodded. 'Bit of a burn on his foreleg, and his mane and tail are singed. Sandman's lost his eyelashes, but other than that — they'll live. But 'twas touch and go for a bit and no mistake. Miss Morgan was terrific.'

Stifling a pang of jealousy, Polly turned to Chrissie and said, 'You turned up just in time. I never could have gone in there. I didn't know you were good with horses.'

Chrissie Morgan smiled as she pushed damp

340

tendrils of hair from her forehead. 'I've ridden since I was a child. I had a Shetland pony when I was five.' She smiled at Robb. 'You were awfully good with them. They obviously trust you.'

Robb was overcome. ' 'Twasn't nothing, really.' He stroked Clipper's neck and murmured, 'Who's a good old lad, then, eh?'

She said, 'Poor old Clipper will be as good as new once his mane and tail have grown again. Lucky for him you spotted the fire.'

Polly was staring at Chrissie's clothes and, seeing this, Chrissie shrugged.

'I was running away,' she confessed with a shaky attempt at a smile. 'Instead I ran into this!'

'Lucky for us,' Robb told her.

Polly stared. 'Running away? But why?'

'It's a long story. Perhaps it's as well I didn't succeed.' She lowered her voice. 'There'll be trouble in the morning,' she said. 'I've committed the unforgivable sin, haven't I? Running away from Tye Rock House!' She mimicked Miss Vivian's voice. 'Whatever will that dreadful girl do next?' Her shoulders sagged wearily. 'I'm not wanted here. I'm not wanted anywhere — except for the wrong reasons.' She drew a long sigh and shrugged defiantly. 'But why should I care? I'm in so much trouble already —' Tears glistened suddenly in her eyes and impulsively Polly stepped forward and put an arm round her shoulders.

Polly said, 'If it makes you feel any better, Miss, Robb and me are in trouble too. We shouldn't have been in the loft.'

There was a silence.

'You two were in the loft?' Chrissie said.

Robb looked embarrassed, his wide eyes white against his soot-begrimed face. 'We were — that is, me and Poll . . .' He stared at his boots.

Polly said, 'We're walking out, aren't we, Robb?'

He nodded.

Polly said, 'It's quite nice up there!'

'It is, rather,' agreed Chrissie and then both girls began to laugh, albeit a trifle hysterically.

Robb warned, 'Here comes Miss Vivian,' as she came round the corner of the house, giving them just enough time to compose themselves.

There was so much to do, huddled beneath the clear night sky, as they tried to bring order out of the chaos. After some consultation about the two horses, Rose decided that Robb should lead them down the hill into the village, wake the farrier and ask if they could be stabled with him for the time being. 'And apologise for disturbing him in the middle of the night,' Rose reminded him.

Robb nodded. 'He knows it all, does Mr Lippett. He'll look after them.'

At this point they were joined by Mr Tremayne. Robb glared at him and Polly fussed with her shoe. Rose greeted him warmly, however, brushing aside his apologies for sleeping through the emergency.

'Please don't reproach yourself, Mr Tremayne,'

she told him. 'There was nothing else you could have done. Nothing any of us could do, really. It was all over so quickly, thanks to Robb and Chrissie. We must just be thankful that no one was seriously hurt. Except Polly, of course; she has hurt her ankle.'

Tremayne looked at her. 'Poor little Polly. Had a fright, did you? I'm so sorry. You really must take more care of yourself.'

Polly, forced to meet his glance, shivered. The eyes were cold and there was something false in his tone which worried her. Was he *glad,* she wondered uneasily. Gloating over her misfortune? How, she wondered, had she ever been attracted to the man? His smooth good looks now appeared to hide a less than pleasant nature.

Miss Vivian went on, 'It could have been so much worse. It had all the makings of a tragedy.'

As they became chilled by the night air, there seemed no sense in remaining outside. The worst of the fire was over. Now it would simply burn itself out and smoulder until morning.

'Good thing there's no wind,' said Polly.

'And fortunate the house isn't thatched!' added Chrissie. 'That would have gone up as well!'

They all withdrew inside the house to complete their conversation in the drawing room. Maud brought in a tray of cocoa which they all drank gratefully. It was agreed that the local vet should be asked to call at the farrier's in the morning. Alternative accommodation for the

343

horses would have to be arranged until the stables at Tye Rock House were restored. Rose said she would also notify Sergeant Wylie. There would have to be a proper inquiry into how the fire had started but that, along with certain other questions, would have to wait until the next day. Injuries needed to be treated, and Matron had brought down the first-aid box. Chrissie was given a soothing syrup for her throat and a cream for her hands. Polly's ankle was bandaged.

Robb's face was scorched and the front of his hair was singed, but he refused any treatment, saying that he would 'do OK'. One shoulder was painful, the result of his desperate efforts to hold on to a panicking horse, but he insisted that it was bearable and could wait until the following day when the doctor would be called in. Polly, watching him, felt a thrill of pride. She was walking out with a hero. No question now her mother could say that a Robb was not good enough for her.

One by one they all returned wearily to their respective beds, except Robb who had to bed down in the sick-room. Polly, one of the last to leave, was astonished to see Mr Tremayne lay a more than friendly arm around the waist of the late Headmaster's daughter. She was even more surprised when, for a brief moment, Miss Vivian allowed her head to rest against his shoulder. She tutted to herself. Some women had no taste, she thought scornfully.

But it was interesting, she thought, as she

made her way upstairs. It was very interesting indeed.

First things first, thought Rose as Chrissie Morgan came into the study. If she didn't find out what lay behind the girl's latest escapade, she would be sadly in breach of the trust put in her by the parents of the school's students. Aware of a strong feeling of resentment that the girl should put her in a position which cast doubt on her capabilities, Rose was now beginning to appreciate George Vivian's firm hand — a firmness she had often misunderstood. He had lived for all these years with an enormous responsibility.

She looked at Chrissie. As it had turned out, the girl's timely arrival and her coolness under pressure had helped to avert a tragedy at the stables. Rose had spoken to the gardener earlier this morning, and Robb had been adamant that without Chrissie's help he would never have been able to rescue both horses. He might even have perished in the attempt. However, this did not alter the fact that the wretched girl had been intending to run away.

'Sit down, please, Chrissie,' she said, trying to sound at once fair but firm. Chrissie, a stubborn look on her beautiful face, sat down. Her hands were lightly bandaged and her face looked drawn, but her manner was as defiant as ever. The high-necked blouse with its white frill gave a misleading softness to her appearance.

Before Rose could start on the short speech she had prepared, Chrissie broke the silence.

'I won't go to them, so it's useless for you to try and make me.' Her voice shook but gradually steadied. 'I can't explain, but I do know they don't want me. At least my aunt doesn't; she hates me.' She swallowed hard. 'If they come for me, they'll have to take me away by force. I thought it only fair to tell you.'

Rose found herself admiring the girl's courage, and was also touched by her vulnerability. Was she as tough as she pretended, she wondered?

After a pause, Rose asked, 'Where were you going?'

'To my grandmother's house. I know the neighbour has a key and I can live there alone until Grandmother comes home from the hospital. Then I can help her.'

'At that time of night? There were no trains or buses. Were you intending to *walk?*'

'Only through the night. I'd have reached Helston by morning and —'

'You were going to *walk* to Helston!' The girl's determination was extraordinary. 'Don't you realise how dangerous that would be? You might meet anybody on the road. Night time is —'

'I was going by way of the Loe Pool. When Jerry came here he rowed himself across. Someone has left a dinghy tied up at the water's edge. No one would have seen me.'

'Can you row a dinghy?'

346

Chrissie raised her chin. 'It can't be that difficult.'

Rose felt a tremor in the pit of her stomach as she imagined the girl out in the middle of the lake, struggling with unfamiliar oars under a cloudy sky which mostly hid the moon. The girl could have drowned. She tried not to think of the Loe Pool's grisly reputation. Biting back angry words of censure, she reminded herself that to take such appalling risks, Chrissie must have been very desperate. Some of her resentment faded.

She said, 'Tell me about your aunt and uncle — in strictest confidence. If I am convinced that they are not suitable guardians for you, I shall consider keeping you on at Tye Rock House until your grandmother is recovered.'

'I won't talk about it.'

Rose closed her eyes briefly to shut out the sight of Chrissie's mulish expression. She counted to ten. Be patient, she counselled herself. 'I'm not giving you any option,' she said. It was a bluff, of course, as she couldn't force the girl to confide in her.

Chrissie's voice faltered. 'I don't — Miss Vivian, I *can't!*'

There was pleading in her voice now, and Rose was puzzled. What on earth could the girl have done to make her aunt hate her? She decided to take a chance.

'Chrissie Morgan!' she snapped with feigned anger. 'You will do as you're told for once!'

To her surprise, tears flooded suddenly into Chrissie's eyes and she fumbled for a handkerchief. A little taken aback, Rose said nothing while Chrissie dabbed at her tears, fighting for the self-control which had almost eluded her. When she eventually started to speak, the words came slowly at first but then tumbled out.

'It happened last time I stayed with them . . . Four years ago when I was not quite fourteen . . .' She twisted her handkerchief, avoiding Rose's eyes. 'They had invited me for two weeks in the summer, and my grandmother was so pleased. So was I — at first. I'm very fond of Grandmother, of course, but she is hardly the most exciting companion and my aunt and uncle have a son about my own age. Edwin. I thought it would be fun but . . .'

Rose made the jump. Trouble with the son, presumably?

She said, 'Don't you and Edwin get along?'

'Edwin wasn't there.' Chrissie's lips tightened. 'It turned out that he'd gone with a friend to Switzerland, skiing. They knew he wouldn't be there, but they didn't mention it. I thought it was a bit odd, but they were both kind to me. Then on the fifth day my aunt had to go into hospital for a minor operation. Something womanly, she called it. She never did explain what it was. She should have been home three days later, but there was an infection and —' She swallowed. 'She was kept in for a week and while she was there . . .' She sighed heavily and

348

looked at Rose earnestly. 'You can guess what happened.'

Rose, naïve and ill-informed about such matters, wondered what to say. She had no idea what had happened but was reluctant to admit her ignorance.

'Just tell it in your own words, Chrissie,' she suggested.

There was a long silence, then Chrissie bent her head and her voice dropped to a whisper. 'My uncle began to — to take liberties. He would touch my hair and my face and put his arm around my shoulders. It wasn't just like an uncle — it was . . . something more than that. I tried to brush him off; tried to pretend not to notice; nothing worked. One day he kissed me on the cheek. I said I didn't like that and he shouldn't be doing it. He just laughed, said I was "a straightlaced little thing" and he hoped I'd grow out of it.'

Rose, disconcerted, hoped she wasn't looking too shocked.

Chrissie went on. 'The following night, while I was brushing my hair, he came into my bedroom with a bottle of champagne and two glasses. I could see he'd been drinking. He said that my aunt would be back the next day and we should drink a toast to her good health. When I protested that I don't like champagne, he ignored my objection. He filled the two glasses and made me drink one; he said that if I didn't, he would have to make me. I was frightened; he seemed to be threatening me. He refilled the glass and then suddenly I knew that I dared not go on drinking. I was very angry, and I threw the champagne into his face. He was furious.'

Rose listened, at once appalled and fascinated by the story. 'Go on,' she said.

'He caught hold of me, threw me on to the bed and tried to unfasten the ribbons of my night-dress. When he couldn't manage it he pulled up my nightdress, but I wriggled and kicked and . . .' She broke off. Raising her head, she pressed two fists against her mouth and Rose could clearly see the shame in her eyes. 'He was stronger than me, and he was very determined. He kept saying that I was almost a woman and I should grow up. His hands were very clumsy — they were *everywhere* and he was kissing me. Ugh!' The disgust showed in her eyes. 'The more I tried to escape, the more excited and angry he became . . . The more *dangerous* . . .'

Rose forced herself to ask the distasteful question. 'Did he rape you, Chrissie?'

'No, he didn't, but he would have done. I couldn't have stopped him. Then, thank God, there was a hammering on the front door and he had to go downstairs. I locked the door as soon as he'd gone. It was a neighbour with an emergency. His wife had been taken ill, and he wanted my uncle to telephone to call out the doctor. It saved me from God knows what.'

Rose said, 'What a shocking ordeal. I'm so sorry, Chrissie.'

The girl shrugged. 'Next day my aunt came home and I told her what had happened. My uncle called me a wicked little liar and said I had got myself drunk on sherry and behaved very badly — throwing myself at him and behaving like a . . . like a *whore!* My aunt believed him, of course. At least she said she did, though she may have had her doubts. She said that if I promised never to do anything like that again she wouldn't tell my grandmother.'

'And you said?'

Chrissie's face darkened. 'What could I say? It was his word against mine.'

'Did you tell your grandmother what had happened?'

'I've never told anyone — except you.'

Rose frowned. 'So why are they willing to have you back now?'

The girl's eyes flashed. 'Maybe my uncle thinks that I'll be more amenable now that I'm eighteen.'

The silence lengthened. Rose was convinced that Chrissie was telling the truth. She tried to imagine her alone in the house with the unscrupulous uncle, and was aware of an unexpected compassion for her. How would such a dreadful experience influence her future, she wondered. Hardly surprising that she was so precocious.

Chrissie swallowed. 'I knew you wouldn't believe me. Nobody ever does.'

Rose drew a long breath. 'You're wrong, Chrissie. I do believe you. Implicitly.'

Chrissie's eyes widened. 'You *do?*'

'Yes. I shall send your aunt and uncle a telegram saying that I have changed my mind, and you will be staying on at Tye Rock House.'

The sad face brightened dramatically. 'Oh, Miss Vivian, thank you.'

Rose smiled. 'And I must thank *you,* Chrissie. You were tremendously brave last night when the stables burned.'

Rose stood and moved round the table as Chrissie also rose to her feet. Impulsively, Rose took the girl's hands in her own.

'I would like you to remember, Chrissie, that I'm here to help you. I may not be as . . . as experienced as my father but, just like him, I have the best interests of you and all the girls at heart.'

For a moment Chrissie didn't answer. Then, obviously lost for words, she bent her head, kissed Rose's hands and ran from the room.

Rose was still staring after her with very mixed feelings when Maud brought in the morning's post.

She asked, 'Is Robb back from the farrier's yet? Do we know how the horses are doing?'

'Not yet. They do say the vet's a bit slow these days, but he's very competent.'

'Well, send Robb up to me as soon as he gets back. And I don't want him doing any heavy work until his shoulder's better.' She smiled. 'I tried to give him a day off, but he was horrified at the idea. Said his mother would find him jobs to do around the house!'

Maud grinned. 'She would, too. Quite a tough old bird, that one. She was a Trewin before her marriage; grandfather was something to do with the church there. They say that, as a girl, she was sometimes allowed to open the Devil's door at christenings.'

'Open the Devil's door?' Rose was hardly listening as she stared at one of the letters. It came from Falmouth, possibly from Ida Folkes, and she longed for Maud to leave so that she could open it.

Maud said, 'To let the evil spirits out.'

Rose reached for the paperknife and Maud, slightly mortified, went out, closing the door a little too loudly.

Inside the envelope were a letter and a photograph. Rose held the latter with trembling fingers and stared at the three people. One was obviously a younger Ida Folkes. One was a small boy who looked vaguely familiar. Her brother? She drew in her breath. Behind the boy there was a beautiful, dark-haired woman who rested slim hands on the boy's shoulders.

'My mother!' The words hung in the air as she stared at the likeness and she addressed the woman, as though meeting her for the first time. 'Mother?' There was a terrible tightness in her throat as she stared at the mother she could not remember and whom she would never see. They had all said she was a beauty, but Rose was still surprised. She dragged her gaze to the boy and fancied she could see a likeness between mother and son: the same fine eyes and slim shoulders. She smiled at them both as her eyes misted with tears. On the back of the photograph, pencilled in, were the words 'Me, Cathy and Boy.'

The letter was short and to the point:

Dear Miss Vivian.

I promised you a photograph and this is the only one I can find. It made me cry to see Bertie so happy. His mother's death changed everything for him. Please try to put all the disappointments behind you and make plans for a happy future. That is what Cathy would have wanted for you.

With affection,
Ida Folkes.

She was still staring at the photograph when there was a knock on the study door.

'Come in.'

Mark Tremayne entered, smiling. 'I've come to apologise for being so little help last night,' he began. 'I don't often sleep so soundly, but —'

Rose held out the photograph. 'My family,' she said with unconscious pride. 'My mother, there . . . that's my younger brother . . . and that's a family friend.'

For a moment she imagined that his hand trembled, but then rejected the idea.

He smiled at her. 'After all this time,' he said. 'You must be very thrilled. Mother and brother. I'm so pleased for you.' He kept his eyes firmly on the picture.

Rose said, 'Sadly, my mother is dead, as I told you, but my brother is somewhere abroad.'

He turned the photograph over. 'Who's "Me"?' he asked.

'That's Ida Folkes. She was very good to my mother. In a way she looked after them both. At least, my mother worked for her but she gave them a home when they were desperate.'

He returned the photograph. 'Does your brother know that your father's dead? I daresay he'll share the inheritance.'

Rose pursued her lips. 'That's the problem at the moment. I can't reach him. As to the inheritance, that's all been left to me. For some reason my father denied that this was his child.'

'Is that fair, do you think?'

She glanced up at him, surprised by the intensity of his voice. 'Of course it's not. I just wish I could trace him and talk things over. He's welcome to a share in the school.' She hesitated, then took a chance. 'Between ourselves, I'm finding my new responsibilities a little overwhelming.' She gave a light laugh. 'Last night didn't help, either. If I could find my brother I could come to some arrangement with him. Not that he'd necessarily want to take over the running of Tye Rock House. He might be a farmer or a doctor or — or *anything*. I simply have no idea.'

'So you wouldn't want to run the school with him?'

'I don't think so.' She looked at him directly. 'If I'm totally honest, I have to say that I'd like to marry and raise a family before it's too late.'

She hoped against hope that this broad hint would provoke a response which might give her some indication as to his plans. Surely she had not misinterpreted the comments he had made on several occasions — comments which suggested that he had a strong affection for her.

He said, 'And if you never find him?'

Rose shrugged. 'I don't know yet. Maybe I'll appoint a Headmaster to run the school. I shall discuss it with James Edgcombe. He has a very wise head on his shoulders.'

With a sigh, she propped the photograph against the inkstand and turned back to him. 'I've quite forgotten why you came to see me.'

'I understand. Discovering your family must mean a lot to you.'

Rose nodded. 'More than I can say.' She looked at him. 'Nobody likes to think they are alone in the world. You've lost your parents, too. You must know how I feel.'

It was his turn to nod. 'But I do have hopes that quite soon I will have somebody to . . . to love.'

Her heart seemed to somersault.

He went on, his expression unreadable. 'An ally, a true friend. Someone who loves me for what I am.' He swallowed, but his gaze held hers almost hypnotically. 'Someone I can *trust,* who loves me in spite of my faults. In spite of *every-*

thing. For better, for worse.'

She waited breathlessly, but his unwavering look didn't falter.

He said hoarsely, 'My mother went on loving me.'

'And your father?' she prompted.

At last his expression changed. 'No, he didn't love me. I was wrong about my father.'

Rose saw a bleakness in his eyes and was filled with sympathy. The conversation had taken a strange turn — not at all what she had expected. She said softly, 'I'm so sorry.'

The silence lengthened and to break it she asked, 'So why did you come to see me?'

He seemed to rouse himself from his thoughts with an effort. 'Oh — that. Yes. It was to apologise about last night — being of so little help. I was sleeping like a log when Polly came banging on my door.'

'We were lucky to get off so lightly, actually. God must have been watching over us. The police are — oh!' She glanced out of the window. 'Here is Sergeant Wylie. You'll have to excuse me.'

He turned to go but paused in the doorway. 'Do you have any idea how it started?'

'Not really,' she confessed, 'but my own feeling is that it was started deliberately, and my money's on Jerry Summers.' Seeing his frown, she added, 'Chrissie Morgan's amorous groom.'

Chapter Eleven

Sergeant Wylie stood with his hands on his hips and surveyed the blackened remains of the previous night's fire.

'What a sad sight!' he muttered, shaking his head. 'Whoever did this did a thorough job, and no mistake.'

Rose, huddled in her coat and scarf, followed his gaze. In the cold light of day the ruined stables were a mute tribute to the fire's ferocity — blackened walls, a tangle of charred roof beams, piled ash blowing in the wind and an acrid smell that lingered in the nostrils. The curled remains of burnt harness still hung on the walls, and towards the rear of the building the traps were little more than burnt-out shells.

He said, 'I hope you were insured, Miss Vivian. Replacing this will cost a great deal.'

'I expect so; I haven't had time yet to investigate. I'll go through my father's papers as soon as I can, but in the meantime I'll have to order a new trap. We must have some transport.' She gave the sergeant a sideways glance. 'So you do think it was started deliberately?'

'I do, yes. But if you *are* insured they'll doubtless send down an expert on arson to take a look.' He stepped forward.

'I should tread carefully!' she warned. 'The ground is still very hot.'

'Hmm.' He stared round at the desolation, wrinkling his nose at the smell of stale smoke and charred wood.

'Sergeant, I may be speaking out of turn but I can't help wondering about that young man — Jerry Summers . . . the groom. Is it possible he might be harbouring a grudge against us? After all, it was because of the business with one of our girls that he was dismissed. It seems a somewhat vicious revenge — if that's what it was — but a rather appropriate one. I can't think of anybody else who might want to harm us, and there's no way it could have started accidentally.'

He gave her a strange look as he considered his reply. 'The truth is, Miss Vivian, that I'm one step ahead of you on this one. As soon as I got your message I sent one of my men over to make inquiries.'

She was startled. 'Then you know where he is?'

'Yes, we do. He's been taken on by a boat-builder in Gweek. Odd-job-man really, working for next to nothing. Still, he's only got himself to blame. Does Saturday work in the local inn. I'm satisfied he couldn't have set the fire.'

'Someone's given him an alibi?'

'You could say that!' His mouth twisted into a grin. 'He was locked up for the night — on His Majesty's pleasure. Poaching three rabbits from the Penrose estate; the gamekeeper caught him red-handed. Our Mr Summers is a bit of a bad lot, I'm afraid. It's a funny family.'

Rose frowned. 'Then if it wasn't him — maybe it *was* an accident.' She tried to think of ways the fire could have started, but it was difficult. 'Or maybe someone had a grudge against Polly or Robb,' she suggested, without much conviction.

'Did anyone know they were in the loft?'

'I doubt it.' Her eyes widened. 'But that would be . . . d'you mean someone meant to frighten them? Oh, that's impossible!'

'I shall speak to the pair of them, in due course and with your permission.'

'Certainly.' She followed him as he slowly patrolled the scene of the disaster. The sergeant stopped suddenly and lowered his voice conspiratorially. 'I know you're not going to like this, Miss Vivian, but I suspect your history master.'

Rose stared at him open-mouthed. 'Mr Tremayne? You can't *mean* that, Sergeant!'

'I did tell you some days ago that we were not happy about him. He's something of a mystery man.' He folded his arms and regarded her unhappily. 'His version of what happened to your father doesn't tally with another account of that last fatal walk. As I told you, our witness alleges that Mr Tremayne and your father were *not* walking along the cliff path but down on the beach. And not talking but *quarrelling*. If that is the case, then Mr Tremayne —'

'I *won't* listen to this!' cried Rose, her heart

thumping with anxiety. 'Mr Tremayne has — has confided in me, Sergeant. My father was very fond of him and I'm certain Mr Tremayne returned the . . . the affection. There's no reason for him to lie about it. There's no *motive!*'

'Nevertheless we think, Miss Vivian, that Mr Tremayne may have been responsible for your father's death.'

Rose took a step back, increasing the distance between them. Her mind was reeling with the enormity of the sergeant's allegation. She stammered, 'Mark Tremayne would never do such a terrible thing. I *know* this man, Sergeant. He and I are — are very good friends, as it happens.' She realised that her voice was rising and, as he bit his lip pensively, she struggled to regain her composure. Part of her confusion was a growing anger. She was so close to a proposal from Mark Tremayne, and now this pompous policeman was trying to rob her of everything she most wanted. A home and family. He was trying to make her doubt the man she most admired; the man she hoped to marry. Even James had been unpleasant about him. Not that that surprised her, for James was jealous. But there seemed to be an unwarranted conspiracy against a very decent man.

He asked, 'Did you ever find that missing file?'

'Actually, no.' She rounded on him fiercely. 'But don't try to read something sinister into a missing file. He would hardly want to read his own file.'

'But he might not want anyone else to read it?'

'That's utter nonsense.' She straightened her back furiously. 'I do not welcome these slurs on members of my staff, Sergeant. No one has ever been offered a position at this school unless my father had complete faith in them. I have never seen any reason to doubt his judgement.'

To her dismay her stout words were like water on a duck's back, and the sergeant said, 'I'd still like to see that file, Miss Vivian. Just to check whether the references were in order. I imagine you would not object to that, since you're convinced of the man's innocence.'

Rose felt cornered. 'I'll have another look straight away, and when I find it I'll send it down to you with the insurance papers.'

Apparently he was still not satisfied. 'And I shall need to talk to your staff,' he told her. 'Someone may have noticed something. A stranger lurking. A familiar face behaving oddly. The smallest detail might prove vital.'

It seemed to Rose that he was challenging her. Did he think she would try to obstruct the course of justice? She bit back an angry retort. 'Would you like me to call all the girls together in the hall, Sergeant?'

'That might be necessary,' he replied. 'I'll let you know all in good time. Meanwhile, I'll finish my examination of what's left of your stables, and then I'll talk to the kitchen staff.'

'By all means, Sergeant. Now, if you'll excuse me, I have to take a singing lesson at eleven and

I've a busy day ahead of me.'

Rose stalked off in the direction of the house, her throat dry with fear. She wanted to feel anger towards the sergeant but was finding it difficult. Full of self-doubt, she now blamed herself for the way in which she had handled the situation. She had taken offence too quickly, flying to Mark Tremayne's defence like that. She had annoyed Sergeant Wylie, and that had not been sensible. No doubt her father would have remained calm and collected. She had betrayed nervous doubts and an obvious prejudice which would give the policeman food for thought. Damn! 'You're such a *fool*,' she told herself. Now, glancing back at the sergeant, she caught him unawares. He was watching her not with the expected hostility but with a look of deep compassion. That frightened her more than anything.

In the kitchen, the subdued staff listened in silence as Sergeant Wylie talked about the previous night's fire.

'It wasn't Jerry Summers,' he told them, 'although he was a natural suspect. His alibi is cast-iron. So it could have been a stranger. There are people — we call them incendiarists — who take a perverted delight in burning things. The problem with these people is that there is no real motive other than that delight. They have no particular animosity towards the owners of the hayricks or the stables. It's just random, which

363

makes it very difficult to discover the culprit.'

He paused, watching their reactions, and thought Polly looked slightly uncomfortable. Maud was shaking her head and Cook, arms folded, was expressing righteous indignation. The gardener, sitting next to the maid, was staring fixedly at his boots.

Sergeant Wylie continued, 'Now I know that there were two people in the loft at the time.' Polly bent her head — as well she might, he thought. He added airily, 'That's no concern of mine — unless they were lighting a fire, which they obviously weren't.'

Maud said, 'They had no right to be there!'

The sergeant sighed. 'But they *were* there.' He turned to Polly. 'Did you or Mr Robb hear anything suspicious?'

Polly said quickly, 'We've already told Miss Vivian that Robb heard something. Like someone moving about. I thought he was hearing things.'

'Hmm! A great pity, but it can't be helped.' He frowned. 'The big question is — did anyone have an axe to grind? Did anyone hate Miss Vivian or the school? Or anyone *in* the school? I do have a theory of my own, but I don't want to jump to the wrong conclusion.'

There was a prolonged silence broken by the cook, who said, 'I haven't the faintest, and that's the truth. I just do my work.'

Maud said, 'I doubt if Miss Vivian has any enemies.'

As Polly looked at Robb, Maud said sharply, 'What? If you've been up to something —'

The sergeant said, 'I'll deal with this, if you don't mind.' He turned back to Polly.

She flushed a deep red and said, 'Someone hates me and Robb, but I don't like to say who it is.'

Maud opened her mouth but closed it as the sergeant wagged a warning finger. He asked, 'Could this person have known that you were in the loft?'

They exchanged glances. Robb said, 'Might have known. If he was spying, like?'

'*He?*' cried Maud. 'Now what are you on about?'

Ignoring the outburst, Sergeant Wylie said, 'We'll continue this line of inquiry in private,' and he, Polly and Robb went out into the back-yard.

Cook glared furiously at Maud. 'Blow you. Maud! If you hadn't poked your nose in, we'd have heard it all! Now we'll know nothing.'

Maud, thinking the same thing and cursing her runaway tongue, for once could think of nothing to say in her own defence.

From the classroom window, Mark saw the sergeant in conference with Robb and Polly.

'Jesus Christ!' he muttered, suddenly sick to his stomach. Were those two idiots going to ruin everything? He swallowed, but his mouth was dry and his heart was racing. He closed his eyes, knowing that he mustn't panic. He could still win through; he could still beat them all. He just needed to think, calmly and sensibly. He drew in a long breath, and another and another. Please God, help me!

He had known almost at once that his sweet revenge would turn sour, but by then it was too late and the flames had taken a hold. He hadn't meant to kill them, only to scare them, but no one would believe him. Still, the police must not be allowed to connect him to the fire. He had acted on impulse — that short temper of his — and with hindsight he had been a fool. There was no way he could turn back the clock, but he must ensure that the blame was not laid at his door.

'Rose!' he said softly. She was the only one who could help him. And she would do so because she was in love with him.

He turned back to the class. The lower-school girls had been slow to settle down this morning, but that was understandable after the fire. 'I shall be gone ten minutes, no more,' he told them. 'While I'm out of the room, I expect you to get on with the notes and then think about your answer to question five on page sixty-six. We'll discuss it when I come back.' He smiled at one of the girls. 'Charmian, I shall leave you in charge. No noise, please.'

'Yes, Mr Tremayne.' The girl returned his smile.

He left the room and hurried to the Head's study. The door was partly open and he could see Rose; she had finished her singing lesson and was rummaging through the cupboard. As she looked up a broad smile lit up her face. She really was very beautiful, he thought, and so like her mother. In any other circumstances he would *want* to marry her.

At her invitation, he sat down.

She said, 'I'm looking for your file which has disappeared. The sergeant wants to check through them all for some reason best known to himself.'

He stifled a moment of panic. 'The file? Oh, Lord! I've probably still got it in my room. Your father brought it along with him one evening. The probationary assessment, I think it was. He left it behind. I'll let you have it back.'

Wondering exactly what the sergeant hoped to discover, he composed his features into an expression of entreaty.

Her smile faded. 'Is anything wrong?' she asked. 'Or should I say — is anything *else* wrong! Life is hardly uneventful at the moment. We seem to be staggering from one crisis to another.'

Her rueful words gave him an opening and he said, 'I'm hoping you can save me from yet another crisis, Miss Vivian.' He saw the alarm in her eyes and hurried on. 'The truth is I'm in the devil of a spot. I don't mind telling you, I'm seriously worried. I didn't know who to turn to but . . . you were kind enough to suggest that I have been of help to you . . .'

'Oh you *have!*' She nodded. 'Of enormous help, Mr Tremayne. I am forever in your debt.'

That was good to hear, he thought. She could not easily withdraw that remark. 'It was a pleasure to be of assistance. You know, I'm sure, how much I want your happiness.'

She nodded again.

Good girl, he thought. A lamb to the slaughter. 'I desperately need your help.'

Her eyes widened. 'Mr Tremayne! You know I'd do anything I can.'

'It's about last night's fire. I have a horrid suspicion that Robb and Polly will try to blame me.'

'Blame *you?* But that's ridiculous. You were fast asleep when it happened.'

'Miss Vivian, please hear me out.' He sighed heavily and noted the sympathy in her eyes. If that expression remained throughout his story, he would be safe. 'Something stupid happened yesterday morning,' he went on. 'I didn't want to report them, but I had a little brush with Polly and Robb.'

'Oh *no!*' she wailed.

He nodded. 'They were in the garden as I was going down to fetch my *Times*. They were laughing and I caught your name. I don't want to repeat what I heard but I — I had a few words to say to them . . . about showing proper respect for you. Robb took umbrage, I'm afraid, and was rude to me. He got the bit between his teeth and before I knew what was happening, he had struck me.'

That hit home, he thought.

Her eyes were wide with shock. 'Robb *struck* you? I don't beli— that is, I can hardly credit it. Robb is so —'

'He struck me,' Mark told her firmly. 'He went for me a second time and I stepped back and tripped. Then he kicked me.'

'*Kicked* you? Oh, Mark!' Her eyes softened dramatically at the very thought of it. 'That's it!' she declared angrily. 'He will have to leave. I gave him a chance, but this is too much!'

She had called him 'Mark' without even realising it. His heartbeat was already slowing. It was going to be all right.

He held up a placatory hand. 'Please, no,' he said. 'I wasn't going to tell you because, like you, I think he was acting out of character. Probably just trying to impress the maid. I gave him the benefit of the doubt, Miss Vivian, and I would rather this never goes any farther than these four walls. But now we come to the difficulty. If the sergeant hears this from Polly and Robb, what is he going to think?'

For a moment she regarded him blankly. Come on, he urged silently. Make the connection.

Then she said, 'Oh! The motive for the fire! But that's absolute nonsense. No one would ever believe such a thing.'

She was so naïve, he thought, with a rush of unwilling affection. 'I'm afraid the police would think exactly that,' he said, his voice sombre. 'It would be so easy. Think about it from their point of view. A motive. The opportunity. A perfect result. Meanwhile I'm in prison with my good name ruined.'

'But you can't — I mean, I couldn't let *that* happen!' She was so distressed. 'There must be something I can do to help.'

He leaned across the desk and ran his fingers lightly across her hand. 'You can give me an alibi,' he said.

'An alibi?' The word was difficult for her. 'But surely you don't need . . .'

'I do, Miss Vivian.' Mentally he took a deep breath. He was taking a great risk, and he knew it. The stupid business with those two idiots had disrupted the plan. Now he had to hurry it, which was never wise. 'The truth is that I have come to throw myself on your mercy — in a manner of speaking.' Seeing her growing alarm he smiled reassuringly. 'It's nothing too terrible, Miss Vivian. I just need you to tell the police that I was with you when the fire was started. We know —'

'Oh, no! I couldn't!' She stared at him, her eyes wide. 'At least . . .'

He went on smoothly, 'We know I wasn't, of course, but then we also know that I didn't start the fire. It's going to be impossible to prove my innocence without your help.'

She seemed to have recovered a little, although she was still regarding him uneasily. 'Is it . . .' She hesitated. 'You'll think me very foolish, but is it *an offence* to tell a lie in these circumstances?'

He managed a natural-sounding chuckle of which he was quite proud. 'Hardly!' he told her. 'It *would* be if we were conspiring to pervert the course of justice — but we aren't.'

'I'm not a very good liar,' she said apologetically. 'Are you sure it's necessary?'

Keep calm, he told himself. Play her like a fish on a line. 'If you want to keep me on your staff.' He made it sound half humorous.

She was still anxious. 'Why can't you just explain about the — the trouble with Polly and Robb? Point out how bad it looks, but that it's simply a dreadful coincidence? I could back you up.'

Oh, come *on!* He felt the beginning of irritation. 'And if it doesn't work? Do you really want me to take that kind of risk?' He leaned forward. 'The fact is that this has all come at the worst possible time, Miss Vivian. I had something to tell you which would delight you, and I was waiting for the right moment to speak to you. Your father's death, coming so unexpectedly, was rather a stumbling block.'

He kept his face straight as hers brightened. He knew exactly what she was thinking. Well, what he had to say would be even more welcome. He had been wondering when to break the news, and now he decided that this was the right time.

'Something to tell me? About what exactly?'

'Miss Vivian, I have definite news of the whereabouts of your brother!'

Emotions raced across her face — surprise, disbelief, *hope.*

'He is not abroad; he is in this country.'

The radiance of her smile almost disarmed him as she asked, 'But where? Are you sure? I mean, how on earth did you find him?'

He let the seconds tick by, then he said carefully, 'You're looking straight at him, *Rose.*'

The poor girl couldn't take it in. She looked totally bewildered as further signs of her inner turmoil surfaced in her pale face. He hid his triumph behind a gentle smile. No, Rose, he thought, you can't marry me. But you can share Tye Rock House with me — and you will.

She stammered, 'My brother? Mr Tremayne, that's . . . But *how?*'

'Call me Mark. Or would you prefer Bertie?' He smiled broadly, knowing he must dispel any regrets she might feel at losing a potential husband. 'I'm sorry it's such a shock,' he said. 'If you have the time, I'd like to explain it all.'

For a moment she simply stared at him as though he were a ghost — which he was, in a way. Mark understood what she was experiencing; he had been through it already when he told his father the truth. He thought he had handled it well, but the reaction had been disappointing and George Vivian had continued to reject him. He had wanted a son and had probably believed what Mark had told him. His problem was his pride. He couldn't admit, after all these years, that he had been wrong.

He waited. Let Rose assimilate what he had already told her. It was imperative now that *she* accepted him.

At last she said, 'I wish you would explain. I do want to believe it.'

He said, 'When my — sorry, *our* mother left George, she didn't know she was expecting a child. She was —'

Rose said eagerly, 'So you remember her quite well. My mother, I mean? You must do. Did she ever talk about me?'

'All the time.' That was true, anyway. He had grown up with her constant regrets about 'little Rose'.

'And she did love me, didn't she?'

'Passionately.' It was more of an obsession, he thought resentfully, but Rose need not know that. 'She was always writing to him, asking if she could go back with me, but he was certain that I was Gibbs's son so he always refused. She was so disappointed when he sent no reply. Sometimes she cried so much that she made herself ill. Nervous exhaustion, Aunt Ida called it. She was a funny woman. At times she could be very sweet, but at other times she could be cold and spiteful. She was a typical spinster.'

How much had she already discovered, he wondered. He must tread carefully.

Rose said, 'I know she spoke my name, but was there anything else? I'm sorry to ask all these questions, but I missed not having her. You can't imagine!'

'Of course I can!' Steady on. Don't snap. 'I had no father, remember. At least your mother *wanted* you.'

He realised, too late, that his bitterness was spilling over into his story, but Rose was now reaching out her hands to him.

'Forgive me. I'm so selfish. We both suffered. And they suffered, too. But how did you end up at Tye Rock House? Was it deliberate?'

'Of course. I gradually came to the conclusion that if only we met, Father would accept me. And I was longing to meet my sister.' That would please her. 'I told Aunt Ida that I was going to America or some such place. I didn't want her to know what I was planning. I went to college — I'm actually very bright!'

Rose said, 'I believe you!' and they both laughed.

He went on, 'I applied here.'

'Under an assumed name?'

'I could hardly come as Bertie Vivian.'

'I suppose not . . . but why Tremayne?'

'Didn't you know? That was the name Ida Folkes used for her novels. Her —'

Rose said, 'I've met her. I liked her very much.'

He stared at her. 'You've *met* her?'

'James Edgcombe found her for me.'

'Ah!' He nodded. 'Well, her *nom de plume* was Tremayne. She adopted me, as you probably know, so I thought I was entitled to use one of her names.' He watched Rose, fascinated. God, she was so like their mother. 'Fate was on my side for once and there was a vacancy. I hoped that Father would come to like me and that —'

'Hence the walks and the chess!'

'Exactly.'

She said, 'I still can't believe that I'm talking to my *brother.*'

'Are you pleased?'

'Oh, yes! Father wasn't the only one who liked your company. I was — I was getting rather fond of you myself.'

She had the decency to blush, he noted, but he would make no comment. She *had* accepted him. One step at a time.

She went on, 'I didn't know you existed for years. I didn't know why Mother had left. Nobody was allowed to speak about it . . .' Her eyes narrowed. 'So you knew all along who I was — that I was your sister?'

'Of course, but I dared not tell you. I wanted to speak to Father first. I wanted to help him run Tye Rock House. The three of us as a family.'

'And he died before you could tell him, in that dreadful accident. How awful for you.'

He shrugged.

She said, 'So can we tell people? About us?'

He shook his head. 'We can, but not just yet. The point is that if Sergeant Wylie discovers that I'm your brother he will think you're biased, and he may not be so convinced by the alibi.'

Her face clouded. 'Oh, yes! The alibi.'

'The way I see it,' he said, 'is that the sooner I can establish my innocence, the sooner Wylie will start looking for the real culprit. Once all this is behind us, we can break the news. It's going to be a bit of a shock and some people may not like it, but —'

'Why not? It's wonderfully exciting!'

What an amazing girl. She *meant* it! So hopelessly unworldly. 'I'm afraid people like Miss Hock are likely to feel they've been deceived, and they're right. No one likes to be made to look a fool. It may not be very easy, but we've got each other.'

'Mr — I mean Mark.' She smiled. 'I would like to tell James Edgcombe. He ought to know —' She stopped abruptly.

'What is it, Rose?'

'It's nothing.'

'Nothing.' He let her understand that he didn't believe her. 'Rose, I must insist. James Edgcombe might tell his father, and *he* might mention it . . .' He snapped his fingers. 'Are you listening, Rose?'

'Of course I am.' She had the grace to blush.

He said, 'I think we should wait until this fire business has blown over. It's not worth the risk.'

'I agree,' she told him. 'Anything you say.'

He moved to her side of the desk and held out his arms. At once Rose stood up and moved into his embrace, leaning happily against him with her head against his shoulder.

She said, 'Oh, Mark! I mean Bertie. You can't imagine what this means. No, of course you can.'

Mark held her close, stroking her back, nuzzling her hair until he felt her relaxing slightly. When he kissed her she responded wholeheartedly. He wondered when he should mention the alibi, but he need not have worried.

Rose drew back and looked at him. The joy in her eyes made him feel almost guilty.

'Of course you shall have your alibi,' she said. 'I shall be only too pleased to help.'

Half an hour later, as the sergeant entered the Head's study, he thought Rose looked remarkably cheerful in the circumstances. He sat down with a heavy heart. She was not going to like what he had to say, he reflected, but there was no point in delaying.

She said, 'A cup of tea, Sergeant? Or something a little stronger?'

'I don't think so, thank you. I woke this morning with a touch of heartburn and I find tea makes it worse.'

Rose Vivian smiled. 'Have you finished your inquiries?'

He nodded.

'I hope the staff were co-operative, Sergeant. Also the girls.'

'I don't think I shall need to talk to the girls — except Miss Morgan. What a lovely girl; she'll be a catch for some young man!' He grinned. 'Wish

I was twenty years younger, as they say. Yes, Miss Morgan was very frank.'

'She's actually a nice girl at heart. I have only just begun to understand her.'

'To come to the point, Miss Vivian, I learned something from Robb and young Polly which has worried me.' He waited for her to fly to their defence, but she said nothing and he went on, 'It seems they had a falling-out with one of your teachers yesterday.'

She groaned. 'Don't tell me. It is always Miss Hock. I'm afraid she has the unfortunate knack —'

'It wasn't Miss Hock. It was Mr Tremayne.'

Rose Vivian raised her eyebrows. 'Now that *does* surprise me, Sergeant. Polly — in fact all the girls — finds him very attractive.'

And so do you, thought the sergeant. Don't think I haven't noticed.

She frowned. 'I certainly knew nothing about a "falling-out". Does this have anything to do with the fire?'

'It might, and again it might not.' He scratched his head. 'The fact is, that according to them they had a bit of a barney with your Mr Tremayne and Robb lost his temper. He knocked him down, Miss Vivian.'

She sat back in her chair, pretending to be shocked. 'Robb *knocked him down?* That's so — so unlikely, Sergeant.'

She certainly looked surprised, Sergeant Wylie pondered. Could it be that he hadn't told her? That was always possible. Tremayne might feel sure that Robb and Polly would say nothing. If he also kept quiet about the incident, his reputation would remain untarnished.

'He admits it, ma'am.'

'Good heavens!'

He tried to read her expression. Her surprise seemed genuine enough, but her fingers were restless. He pursed his mouth. He was better with men; he could read a guilty man at twenty paces. Women, God bless them, were a different kettle of fish.

'So you must see,' he went on, 'that since they parted on —'

'Did Mr Tremayne retaliate?'

'No, he didn't. Not the way they told it.'

'Doesn't that tell you something, Sergeant? That Mr Tremayne is not a violent man?'

Absentmindedly, the sergeant drummed his fingers on the table but let the question pass. 'But you do see that Mr Tremayne might well have a motive for —'

'Have you spoken to him?'

'Not yet, no.'

'Wouldn't it be fair to do so — I mean, before coming to me with this ridiculous allegation?'

He felt his sympathy for her draining away. After all, he did represent the law of the land. He was used to taking arguments from poachers and the like, but not from people in Miss Vivian's social position. He subjected her to a long, cold stare.

'Miss Vivian, I am not in the habit of making ridiculous allegations. Never have been.'

She had the grace to look abashed.

'I'm sorry, Sergeant. You are quite right. But you must see that from my point of view —'

'I shall need to question Mr Tremayne about his whereabouts last night around the time the fire was started.'

The colour fled suddenly from her cheeks. Instinctively she lifted her hands half-way to her face but then returned them to her lap. Willing herself not to react, perhaps? Interesting.

She said, 'I'm sure that will be no problem.'

'It's possible he may have seen someone or something suspicious.'

'Around eleven, you mean, when the fire started.'

'Yes. If he had been into Porthleven, for instance, and was —'

'He wasn't.' Her hands slid together on the desk, fingers tightly entwined. 'Mr Tremayne was with me, Sergeant. Does that help you?'

'It might.' He hoped he had hidden his surprise, not to mention his dismay. This was a most unwelcome piece of news. If it were true, then Tremayne was not his man and he had to start all over again. If she were lying, his troubles were only just beginning.

She said, 'I hope this will go no farther, Sergeant. The fact is that Mr Tremayne and I are more than friends, if you understand me. Last night . . .' With her right hand she fussed with a brooch which she was wearing on the lapel of her jacket. 'Last night we were . . . that is, Mr Tremayne and I — were together. In my room. We were talking about the future. Just talking.'

Were you now? At eleven o'clock at night? That was more than interesting, it was unconventional. Rash. Possibly, if his suspicions were correct, it might even be dangerous. The memory of George Vivian flashed through his mind. He would be turning in his grave. This was exactly the situation her father had tried to ensure would never happen. He had been dead less than a month and already his daughter was swimming in deep waters. Like mother, like daughter, he reflected unhappily.

He said, 'It may be none of my business, but —'

She stiffened. 'You're right, Sergeant. It is nobody's business but my own. It may have been somewhat improper, but I'm sure you are a man of the world. I hope I can trust you to keep that information to yourself.'

He shook his head. 'I can't promise that, Miss Vivian. What you have told me amounts to an alibi for a man who may or may not be charged with an offence.'

'I see. Not very reassuring.'

'I'm afraid not.'

'But surely, since you now know Mr Tremayne's whereabouts he can no longer be on your list of suspects? If he was with me, he couldn't have been out in the yard setting fire to the stables.'

He allowed a silence to develop. Let her wonder if I *am* totally convinced, he thought. His gaze roamed the room and settled on the desk — on a photograph of three people. Seeing his interest, she smiled suddenly and picked it up.

'My mother,' she told him. 'My brother, and a friend.'

He said, 'I was sorry to learn that she is dead. You must have been very disappointed.'

She gave him an odd look. 'I'm hoping to make contact with my brother. That would be something.'

'You're wearing your mother's brooch, I see?'

She was genuinely startled. 'How on earth . . . ?'

He pointed to it in the photograph. 'Your mother is wearing it!'

She followed his finger and then, to his surprise, her expression changed abruptly. Her lips parted soundlessly as she stared at the picture. Then her free hand rose to her face.

'Miss Vivian?' His sympathies returned as her distress deepened. 'What's the matter? What have I said?'

'I don't . . .' Her voice cracked. 'It's nothing, Sergeant. Nothing.' With a sudden movement, she turned the photograph face down on the desk.

He cursed. It was so obviously *not* nothing. He had missed something. Dammit! What was happening?

He said, 'I can see I've upset you. I'm sorry — but I don't understand.'

She stood up quickly almost tipping the chair over. 'I'm not feeling well, Sergeant. I need to lie down. You must excuse me.'

'But can't I help in any —'

'No!' Her voice was shrill and her eyes flashed. 'Go and finish your stupid inquiries. Do what you like! Ask what you like. I don't care. Just leave me in . . .' She bit her lip, choking back the word. 'Just go.'

Her eyes, he noted, were dark with shock and something else. Despair? Grief? Fear?

He said, 'Shall I send someone to you?'

She shook her head. Then without another word, she pushed past him and hurried from the room.

As she passed him, he saw that the beautiful grey eyes were bright with tears.

CHAPTER TWELVE

Alone in her room, Rose walked slowly to the bed and sat down. Sergeant Wylie had drawn her attention to a brooch which he wrongly assumed had belonged to her mother; the brooch Mark had given her which he *said* had belonged to *his* mother. *Their* mother. But in the photograph the brooch was pinned firmly to the lapel of Ida Folkes's dress. How could that be? Ida Folkes's words came back to her: 'Took himself off and took some of my jewellery with him.'

'Damnation!' She whispered the unladylike word. Why was it, she wondered, that whenever life was particularly good, Fate stepped in to spoil everything? Mark was her brother, that much was certain. And she was glad — even though she had been forced to lie to the sergeant to protect him. The thought that she had done so pricked her conscience but, as Mark explained, there was no harm in it since he had nothing to hide. She and Mark were family and she was merely confirming his innocence. Mark — or Bertie — was all she had left, and she had no intention of losing him. Protecting him was the least she could do after the sad life he had lived. Longing to be reconciled with an absent parent was something she fully understood.

The only thing that marred her pleasure in that respect was the fact that her father had never met his son. Or rather, had never accepted that the personable young man he liked so much was his own flesh and blood. The future could have been so different, so fulfilling for all of them. With time, her father might have put aside his pride and acknowledged his son. Sadly, the accident had effectively prevented that from happening.

Her face burned as she recalled the romantic notions she had woven around Mark. She had been foolish, that was all. The attraction she had felt for him was now explained. Deep down she had *recognised* him; in some strange, instinctive way she had been drawn to him. He was lost to her as a husband, but a brother was as good, if not better. She would settle for family.

In a way she wished now that her talk with Ida Folkes had not been quite so far-reaching. The old lady's words about her brother still niggled at the back of her mind. Better to leave well alone. Better off without someone like that. Obsessive. Vengeful. She thought uneasily about Mrs Stuckey's strangled cat . . . But that was all in the past, she told herself firmly. Probably he had been deeply upset by the death of his mother and his father's rejection.

Rose allowed herself a smile. She said, 'Stop worrying!' There was probably a very simple explanation for the brooch. Maybe her mother had given it to Ida Folkes? Her face brightened.

There was a knock at the door. Polly came in. 'Mr Tremayne asked me to bring this.'

She looked very pale, no doubt upset by what had been happening. Rose hardened her heart. The girl had been through quite an ordeal, but it was her own fault. She had been in the wrong place at the wrong time. She had also taken sides against Mark and was causing him a great deal of trouble. According to Mark, she had also been laughing at Rose with Robb behind her back. That thought stung.

Rose took the proffered file. 'Thank you.'

Polly hesitated but Rose was in no mood to help her. She didn't want to hear whatever it was the wretched girl had to say.

'You wasn't in the Head's room, so I thought you might be up here. Mr Tremayne said it was urgent.'

Rose stared at the file. 'Thank you, Polly. You can go,' she said.

Urgent? She debated whether or not to open it. Would she be prying into her brother's affairs? Or preparing herself for any tricks the sergeant might play? Would her brother mind her reading it? Of course not — because he had nothing to hide.

'Open it, Rose!' she muttered and turned the first page.

There seemed nothing out of the ordinary. A report from the principal of St Mark's College.

. . . This student has shown a firm grasp of the principles of education . . . has mixed well with his fellow students and was at one time a member of the Debating Society . . . willing to take on responsibilities . . . no hesitation in recommending him . . .

The letter was written by hand on headed notepaper. So he had been to the college, and there was nothing for the sergeant to complain about there. She riffled through various papers and came to his original application form for the college:

> Name: Mark Elwyn Tremayne
> Mother: Helen Tremayne
> Father: Reginald Arthur Tremayne
> Address: 37, Park Avenue, South London
> Place of birth: Haverhill, Suffolk

Dismay set in. 'All false!' she muttered.

Falsifying documents! But then he had admitted it to her already and she understood his reasons. Or partly understood them. She put a hand to her forehead uneasily. What had Ida Folkes said? That the boy was sly. Devious. But then Ida Folkes saw him from a different angle. She had loved him as a little boy but later she had changed towards him. So had *he* changed? Rose pushed the unwelcome thought to the back of her mind.

'Sly and devious,' she whispered, and sighed.

It was all so frustrating, and she was beginning to wish she hadn't delved into the contents of the file. At the risk of sounding melodramatic, Mark was her long-lost brother and that was wonderful. All she wanted now was to enjoy the newfound relationship, but that was out of the question while she nursed these stupid doubts. Rose bit her lip in frustration. She laid all the problems at the sergeant's door. Damn the man! She would have to give the file to him, and he might well take it to the police station to study it. He might copy various items. What would he do when Mark's true identity became known? Would Mark be accused of an offence — and if so, would she be an accessory?

There was a letter from a headmaster — a Mr Frank Lennard:

> . . . For the short period he has been with us, Mr Tremayne has been a valued member of staff . . . has contributed to the successful running of the school . . . initiated the setting-up of the dramatic society . . . gives of his time unstintingly in the interests of the children . . . shall be sorry to lose him but . . .

Another glowing report! Mark had been — still was — an excellent teacher. She could quite see why her father had been so keen to appoint him. So why, as she closed the file, did she feel so unwell? Why did she have the feeling that the ground was slowly shifting beneath her?

'Stop worrying!' she repeated. By the time the sergeant discovered the deceit it would no longer matter, because by then the real incendiarist would have been found. 'Don't cross your bridges . . .' she told herself, but almost immediately another thought intruded. Mark had told her — had *told* her — not to confide in James Edgcombe. That really annoyed her — partly because she *wanted* to tell James, and partly because she resented her brother's attitude. The assumption was that he could now advise her. Not only advise her, but insist on her taking the advice. Rose frowned. Since her father's death she had made her own decisions and had begun to appreciate the freedom to do so. Perhaps she should tell James anyway. Afterwards she could mention it in passing to Mark. He would realise then that, despite her sex, she was independent and capable of making up her own mind. He wouldn't be happy about it, but at least he would know where he stood.

'Oh, damn, *damn!*' she muttered. It would mean her first clash with her brother. Was it worth it? She threw the file on to the bed and crossed to the window. It wasn't easy. If she crossed Mark there might well be a coolness between them. If she didn't, she was allowing him to dictate to her. If they were going to share a future, here in Tye Rock House, they would have to come to an agreement.

Equal responsibility. She would want to have an equal say in the running of the school. Rose was aware of a frisson of apprehension.

She threw herself face down on to the bed and lay there, unable to summon any energy.

Twenty minutes later she sat up. Standing, she smoothed down her skirt, then crossed to the mirror to tidy her hair. She must hand the file over to Sergeant Wylie and see what happened next. It was pointless to anticipate the worst.

'Take one step at a time, Rose Vivian,' she told her reflection. 'There's no need to worry.'

But the reflection which stared back at her appeared far from convinced.

Promptly at eight o'clock the following morning, Sergeant Wylie knocked on the door of his inspector's office.

'Might I have a word, sir?' he asked.

His superior was a man named Canwyn, a portly gentleman, who was carefully counting the months to his retirement. Blue eyes blinking through round pebble glasses had earned him the nickname 'Babyface'.

'I'm on my way to a meeting,' he replied. 'Can it wait?'

'Afraid not, sir. It's about the —'

'Very well then. Five minutes. Sit down, for heaven's sake. What's that?' He pointed to the folder which Sergeant Wylie was carrying.

'A file, sir. On Tremayne — the history master at Tye Rock.'

Canwyn frowned. 'That Porthleven business? Chap fell off a cliff?'

'Chap is *alleged* to have fallen off a cliff, sir. It was no accident, I'm sure of it. Intuition, sir. The fisherman swears that they were down on the beach, quarrelling. I reckon the young man did him in. Bashed him on the head with a rock, maybe in a moment of temper. Then he concocted the story of the cliff walk which made him some kind of hero.'

'Hmm. It's a bit dubious. I thought we'd sorted it all out. No evidence, no charges.'

'There may be a chance, sir. Some evidence, perhaps. In here. A few names and dates. Things we can check on. I'm even more inclined to go for this man after the fire they had up at Tye Rock the other night. If we can catch him out in even one lie, we might shake the woman who's giving him an alibi. We could frighten her, sir. Misleading the police is a serious offence. She'd break down, sir. I'm sure of it.'

Canwyn pursed his lips. 'I don't know. Best part of the morning wasted if you get nothing. Intuition *can* be wrong, Wylie.'

He held out his hand for the file and opened it, then riffled through the papers without much interest. The sergeant said nothing. He had learned when to stay quiet. Now he watched as the inspector's plump fingers held up one of the letters and then the birth certificate.

Canwyn said, 'You mentioned the stables. What's the connection?'

'Sir, it seems our man had a grudge against the two people who were trapped in the loft. Now if we can prove that was so, and *if* he set the fire, then we know the sort of man he is — the sort who can deliberately put people's lives at risk. If he's that evil, then he might also be capable of murder: George Vivian's murder.'

'I thought he and Vivian were pally. Chess and walks and cosy chats. You never established a motive for that connection.'

'That's because we don't have all the facts, sir. With respect, my feeling is that we're dealing with an unscrupulous villain who, for reasons as yet unknown, killed his Headmaster and pretended it was an accident. He's laughing at us, and I don't like it.' He leaned forward. 'If I'm right, sir, I think the daughter might be in danger.'

'What? Another motiveless murder? That's a bit far-fetched, isn't it, Wylie? What's he going to do — kill off the entire staff? Why should he? It doesn't make any sense.'

'It might do to him.' After a silence, the sergeant continued, 'I don't know the answers, sir. I just know he's a wrong'un; I can smell deceit . . . And I don't want to see Rose Vivian stretched out on a slab in the hospital mortuary. Because if I do, I shall know it was our fault.' Seeing that he had made his superior uneasy he went on, 'Or one of the schoolgirls. We don't want to make the national headlines, sir. That *would* bring down the wrath of the Gods!' He hoped this reference to Canwyn's superiors would alert him to the risks to his retirement pension.

Canwyn closed his eyes and steepled his fingers — a sure sign he was weakening. Sergeant Wylie held his breath.

At last, with a resigned sigh, Canwyn closed the folder. 'So bring him in for questioning.'

'Can't do that, sir. Miss Vivian's given him a watertight alibi.'

Canwyn eyes rolled heavenward. 'A watertight alibi? Then why didn't you say so? Why waste my time with this cock-and-bull —'

'Because I don't believe her.'

'You think Rose Vivian's lying?'

'Well, she says he was with her in her bedroom, but she's not that sort of woman, sir. She wouldn't do that. Quite out of character. I think —'

'Is there something I'm missing here? Is there a romantic link? Is she *in love* with this character?'

'Maybe. She's certainly shielding him, but I don't know why. Either she loves him or he's got some sort of hold over her.'

'You mean she's done something wrong and he's found out? Is that likely? I would have put her down as particularly respectable.'

Sergeant Wylie shook his head. 'To be honest, I can't begin to imagine what's going on, but something is. I'd like permission to ring all the contacts in this folder, sir. Test his story. If you believe all you read here he's whiter than white! If I detect one false note, I'd like to bring him in. Shake him up a bit. Rattle the bugger.'

'You don't like him, do you, Sergeant?'

'No, sir. Don't trust him an inch. So smug when I questioned him. So damned innocent.' He adopted what he thought was an upper-class accent. ' "How can I help you, Sergeant Wylie?" Butter wouldn't melt in his mouth. So confident — but then he knew he'd got an alibi.'

Canwyn said, 'I can't let you have any more men.'

'Don't need them at this stage, sir.'

'Thought you said he was dangerous?'

'Only to Miss Vivian. If he's fooled her into falling for him . . .'

Canwyn shook his head. 'Hmm. If you're bringing him in, I'd like to take a look at him. When d'you reckon?'

'If I can't get hold of him before lunch it'll have to be this evening, sir. I understand they're taking the girls for a walk in the afternoon, weather permitting, to the Loe Pool. All the staff will go with them. In the evening there's to be a bit of party.'

Canwyn raised his eyebrows. 'A *party? Plus ça change!*' he said.

The sergeant ignored his superior's unfortunate lapse into French. 'Apparently it's a bit of a sop because the girls weren't allowed into Helston yesterday for the Furry Dance. Not that they ever are.'

He gave his superior a knowing look. It had been noticed over the years that on Flora Day Canwyn — while professing disinterest — always managed to arrange an official midday lunch in Helston, usually in the Angel Hotel which offered a good view of the street and the various celebrations.

Canwyn, straightfaced, said, 'I should think not. It can get a bit frisky. Folk get over-excited. Not to mention the odd pickpocket and assorted riff-raff. Right —' He stood up. 'Make your telephone calls and see what you get. If you think it's worth it, haul him in. Assisting us with our inquiries . . .'

Sergeant Wylie rose also. He was grinning broadly. 'Fingers crossed, sir,' he said. 'If he's our man we've solved two crimes for the price of one!'

Canwyn reached for his hat. 'Better get on with it then, Sergeant.'

The weather that Saturday was all that could be desired. Windless, with bright sunshine. The girls wore their own clothes — buttoned boots, serge skirts and warm jackets. Most wore gloves, the rest thrust their hands into warm muffs.

Miss Hock lined them up in pairs and, while she waited for Miss Vivian to join them, gave them a little homily on their behaviour.

'You will stay with your partner throughout the walk,' she bellowed, 'both to and from the Loe Pool. Once there, however, you may walk as you please. There will be no rowdiness and no — Kate, are you listening to me?'

'Yes, Miss Hock.'

'Then kindly turn so that I can see your face and not the back of your head. There will be no rowdiness, and you will walk with extreme care along the path where it runs parallel to the cliff-edge. In the light of the school's recent tragedy, it would be foolish to venture too near the edge. Matron and Mr Tremayne will also accompany us.'

Mr Tremayne said, 'I shall have my beady little eyes on you!' and they all laughed dutifully.

Miss Hock went on, 'No pushing, no raucous laughter. Florence Gray, are you deaf? I said "No pushing". You will all remember that you are the daughters of gentlefolk, so behave as they would wish you to behave.'

From somewhere in the middle of the line a voice asked, 'Are we allowed to breathe if we do it quietly?'

The girls found this hilarious. Miss Hock snapped, 'Who was that?'

There was no answer and her mouth tightened. 'Another remark like that, and you will all go straight to your rooms and stay there!'

The laughter faded. Matron, looking flustered, turned hopefully towards the house, but a hansom had just arrived and a man and woman were alighting. Mam'selle turned at once to the history master and whispered, 'Visitors! Now I suppose we'll have to wait!'

He said, 'Maybe it won't take too long.'

'But it gets dark so early.'

Mr Tremayne smiled at the girls and said, 'I'm

sure you will all behave beautifully. That would be the best way to let Miss Vivian know how much you appreciate this little treat. A walk and a special tea and a sing-song. I think she's been very kind.'

Someone said, 'Three cheers for Miss Vivian!' but Miss Hock quickly reasserted her authority.

'I said "No noise" and I meant it. Isobel Cleary, straighten your hat at once. You look like a hoyden. We may be here a few moments before starting out, so who can tell me the legend of the pool?'

There was an outburst of chattering.

'I said "Who can tell *me*",' she protested. 'I didn't say tell each other . . . Emily?'

Fifteen-year-old Emily screwed up her face. 'A ghost was carrying sacks of sand along the coast and . . . and he . . .'

Lucy said, 'He was tripped by a demon and dropped the sand and it formed the Loe Bar.'

'Near enough. Good. And which stones might you find when we get to the Bar?'

All the hands shot up. The impatient girls called out.

'Agates!'

'Garnets!'

'Amethysts!'

'Good.' She turned to Mr Tremayne with a look of deep exasperation. 'What on earth is keeping Miss Vivian?'

He spread his hands in a helpless gesture.

Miss Hock snorted. 'Maybe we should start

without her. She could catch us up.'

Kate said, 'Oh no, Miss Hock, let's wait for her.'

So they waited.

Ten minutes later, slightly flushed but triumphant, Rose saw her visitors into their hansom and watched it driven briskly away down the drive. A moment or two later she joined the girls and all the faces turned towards her.

'I'm sorry to keep you all waiting,' she told them cheerfully. 'Now, let's make a start. A nice brisk pace, girls, to walk off our dinner and give us all an appetite for the wonderful tea Cook is preparing. When I last entered the kitchen I smelled something suspiciously like lemon madeira cake, which I know is a favourite. And so far we've had seven offers for the evening's entertainment. I shall be singing . . .' There was a murmur of excitement. 'And a little bird tells me that a certain history master, who shall be nameless, has a surprise in store for us.' She glanced at him and he laughed. 'Hidden talents,' she added.

Mr Tremayne mimed the playing of a violin and there was further excitement.

Rose said, 'I shall walk in front, Mr Tremayne and Matron can bring up the rear while Miss Hock . . .' She smiled at Miss Hock, who took up her prearranged position half-way along the crocodile, and they finally set off. After a few moments Rose dropped back to draw level with Chrissie Morgan.

'That was your aunt and uncle,' she told her. 'I said we had had a change of heart and you were staying. Your aunt seemed rather pleased but your uncle was very put out. However, they finally accepted it. I offered them some refreshment, but fortunately they refused.'

Chrissie whistled softly with relief. 'I'm glad they didn't want to speak to me, Miss Vivian.'

'Oh, but they did.' She gave the girl a conspiratorial smile. 'I said it wasn't possible. They're on the way back to the station at Helston.'

Chrissie said, 'Thank you, Miss Vivian.'

'It was a pleasure!' Rose told her and moved back to the head of the crocodile.

The walk to the Loe Pool would take them about twenty minutes and the path would lead them a winding route along the cliff-top, never far from the cliff-edge and always within the sound of waves breaking on the shore and the sight of gulls silhouetted against the blue sky. The ragged shore line stretched ahead in the direction of Porth Mellin, Kynance and The Lizard.

Chattering and laughing, the girls made their way along the path. After passing just one house, they reached the Loe Bar. Here they immediately broke ranks, fluttering across the broad expanse of fine shingly sand like a flock of birds. Some began a search for scraps of dried seaweed, carried inshore by the wind. Others stared into the enchanted water, for sight of the large trout which were believed to live within its gloomy depths. Rose, Miss Hock and Mr

Tremayne watched them with amusement.

Rose said, 'You'd think they'd been imprisoned for years!'

Miss Hock said, 'One or two of them *should* be!' but she softened the words with a rueful laugh. She glanced at Mark Tremayne. 'I didn't know you played the violin.'

'There's a lot you don't know about me!' he answered, his tone teasing.

Miss Hock raised her voice suddenly. 'Not too near the water's edge!' She shook her head. 'That wretched Florence. Just look at her!'

The girl in question had lifted her skirts in one hand to make it easier to search amongst the fine, softly rounded shingle which was specific to the Bar. Suddenly she pounced and then ran to Miss Hock.

'Is this an amethyst?' she asked, her face alight with excitement.

Miss Hock thought not. Disappointed, the girl pouted.

'I'll help you,' Miss Hock volunteered and, excited by this brief show of goodwill, a small group of some of the younger girls accompanied her in search of the real thing. Matron and Mam'selle walked together along the water's edge. The area looked deceptively peaceful in the sunlight; the water was brown and calm and very beautiful. The land to their left rose steeply and was covered with trees, most of which were conifers. Immediately across the water, the farmland rolled softly. Seaward, the Bar was almost flat but rose enough to hide the seashore from view although it was less than six hundred yards away. Hard to believe, thought Rose, that the pool — the largest freshwater lake in the West Country — was immeasurably deep and treacherous. Legend had it that the bones of an entire sailing ship lay below — driven in from the sea during a violent storm. She thought of Jerry Summers rowing across and stared around the lake in search of a rowing boat. Sure enough, something that might be a dinghy was just visible beside a small jetty on the eastern bank.

Mark had come up to stand beside her. 'I have to talk to you,' he told her in a low voice. 'Stay behind with me when the others leave.'

'But why?' she asked curiously. 'Why does it have to be here?'

'I'm going to take you rowing,' he told her. 'Romantic, eh?'

'Oh, Mark, I don't think we should.'

'Why not? They'll manage without us, and we won't be that late. You can pretend to twist your ankle and I'll offer to help you back. Oh, come on, Rose! Have some fun for once. You'll be quite safe with me. I'm your brother, remember.'

'But *why?*' She tried to shake off her anxiety without success. 'Can't you tell me?'

'It's a secret. A *test,* if you like.' He grinned. 'For heaven's sake, Rose. You're in charge here. You don't have to ask anyone's permission.'

He took her hand but she snatched it away,

looking to see if anyone had noticed.

He said, 'Rose! You're not committing a crime by holding my hand. You're my *sister*. They'll all know soon enough. You've got to tell them I'm family. Come *on*, Rose. Let's see some spirit. Say you'll come out on the lake with me?'

She hesitated. 'I might if you'll tell me what it's about,' she offered.

For a moment she fancied his eyes darkened, but then he was smiling again. 'That would spoil the surprise,' he said, 'but I'll say this much. I'm going to trust you with a very great secret. I'm going to trust you, Rose, *with my life!*'

She felt the first stirrings of alarm. 'Your *life?* What are you talking about?'

'When you know the secret, you will know all there is to know about me.'

Rose's thoughts reverted to the conversation she had had with Ida Folkes and without thinking she said, 'If it's about the cat — I know that already.'

His expression was blank. 'Cat? What on earth — ?'

'Miss Stuckey's cat. The one you — the one that . . .' She floundered into silence.

His eyes narrowed. 'What about her cat?'

Nervously, Rose searched her mind for a way out of the mess and decided that honesty would serve her best. 'Ida Folkes thought that Miss Stuckey thought . . .'

'That I killed the stupid animal?' He bit his lip for a moment, then he smiled. 'You shouldn't believe all you hear, Rose, especially from those two old biddies. Of course I didn't touch the mangy old creature. No, it's something else.'

Rose, relieved that he hadn't taken offence at her blunder, wondered what else he could have to tell her.

He said, 'I have to be able to trust you, Rose, if we're to go on together — if we're to run the school between us.' His eyes narrowed. 'We *are* going to, aren't we?'

'I suppose we might. We'd have to discuss it . . .' She sucked in her breath. 'The fact is, I haven't made any firm plans. I — I might want to get married, Mark.'

This time there was no mistake. An expression she couldn't read but didn't like crossed his face. He said, 'Plenty of time for that, Rose.'

She said, 'You sound just like Papa!'

'I wonder if that's a compliment.'

'It's your voice. It's so similar.'

'And you're like Mother — more than you know. Poor Mother. She knew what she wanted but not how to get it. I know both.' He was smiling again. 'Now let's give them something to think about, Rose!' Before she could stop him, he had slipped an arm around her waist. As she tried to struggle free he tightened his grip.

'Don't struggle, Rose. I'm stronger than you.' His words were teasing but his tone was not.

She cried, 'But someone might see us!' Although she protested, deep down a little voice whispered that she was not really averse to being seen by the staff in the arms of a presentable young man. No doubt they had written her off as a spinster.

'Let them,' Mark insisted. 'They'll think you love the history master, and you do. You love your brother.'

Rose tried half-heartedly to free herself. 'Are brothers always like this?' she protested.

He said, 'I'll let you go if you promise to come out in the boat with me.'

In spite of herself, she was sorely tempted. It *was* rather wonderful to be needed by this man. Brother or no, Mark was charming and amusing. Unpredictable, certainly, and maybe even a little dangerous — but she *did* love him. The excitement went to her head like champagne. Mark Tremayne, alias Bertie Vivian, was giving her what she wanted — a little sparkle and excitement in a hitherto drab existence. 'Show a little spirit,' he had urged, and she knew that she *was* too cautious. She imagined the two of them alone together in the middle of the lake and the last vestige of doubt faded. Glancing over her shoulder, she saw that Matron was watching them with a look of astonishment. Catching Rose's gaze, she quickly looked away.

'Very well,' Rose told him hurriedly. 'I'll come on the lake and I'll listen to your dark and terrible secret, but on one condition. You agree to me telling James who you really are, in strictest confidence of course, and you allow me to tell the staff in my own time. That must be my decision.'

His grip did not weaken but his expression changed. He looked at her thoughtfully, and with an intensity which began to worry her. Again there was something in his expression that troubled her, and she was on the point of changing her mind when he said, 'I agree!'

His words and his smile reassured her. 'So, *please*, Mark, let me *go!*' she whispered, but when at last he released her she felt an irrational moment of regret.

He said lightly, 'A very wise decision, Miss Vivian. One should never struggle against Fate!'

In the office of Helston police station, Sergeant Wylie said, 'Well, I'm very grateful for all your help. Sorry to have taken up so much of your time.' He hung up the telephone receiver and, for a long moment, sat staring at the notes he had made. Then he jumped to his feet and almost ran into his inspector's office.

Canwyn looked up irritably. 'There's a door there, Sergeant. You're supposed to knock on it.'

'I must talk to you, sir.'

'I've got Edgcombe due at any moment. Make it quick.'

'Sir!' He drew a deep breath. 'Mark Tremayne, sir . . . he isn't.'

'Isn't?'

'Isn't Mark Tremayne. There is no one of that name.'

The older man sat up. 'Go on.'

'Sir, I rang the college. They said they had had a student of that name, so he *did* attend the college. But I checked the address in south London, the one on his application form; the current tenant says his family has lived in the house for more than forty years — *and has never heard of a Mark Tremayne.*'

'Aha!' Canwyn grinned wolfishly.

'It gets better, sir. I checked local records in Kedington — a tiny village near Haverhill in Suffolk — where he was supposed to have been born. Nothing in the local church about a baptism in that name. Vicar doesn't recall a Helen and Reginald Tremayne.'

There was a knock and a young constable put his head round the door. 'Mr Edgcombe's in the office, sir. Seems they've had a burglary while they were out at lunch. All the petty cash gone and —'

'Ask him to wait. I'll be five minutes. Take down some details.' Canwyn frowned at the door as it closed. 'You were saying?'

'The records, sir. No trace of a Mark Tremayne, or his mother or father.'

'Hmm. Another blank, then. This is looking very bad.'

The sergeant raised his eyebrows. 'Or good, sir, depending on how you look at it. I think we should bring him in. Not an arrest, but enough to scare the — to frighten him. Shake his confidence a bit and he might make a mistake. The thing is, sir, that Miss Vivian might be in danger.

We know who he *isn't,* but we don't know who he *is.* If he killed George Vivian, we don't know why. We don't know that she might not be next.'

He waited anxiously. Why was the inspector so damned slow, he thought impatiently. It was like wading through treacle. The sooner the old man retired the better.

Canwyn frowned. 'But there's nothing definite. We might simply alert him to his danger — let him know we're suspicious. He might abscond. We might lose him.'

Sergeant Wylie drew himself up. 'Begging your pardon, sir, but I'm trying to prevent another crime here. Even as we speak, Rose Vivian —'

'I thought you said they were all going for a walk to the Loe Pool. He can hardly do her any harm in full view of the entire school!' He sighed. 'I'm not wildly enthusiastic, but we've got the statement by Tom Robb. We could confront him with that . . .'

'And there's the fire, sir. If we could shake Rose Vivian over that false alibi.'

'Ye-es . . . Maybe we should show her Robb's statement and drop a few hints about hindering the police in the execution of their duties. That might do the trick.'

'She'd break down, sir. I'm sure.'

Canwyn steepled his hands. 'Well, Sergeant, it's a risk either way, but I think this time we'll go with your instincts.'

Sergeant Wylie let out his breath. 'You mean I can —'

'Yes. Pick the blighter up. We'll have a go at him together and see what we get.' He stood up.

'I could take a cab, sir.'

'Do that.'

They walked together into the front office, where they found James Edgcombe leaning on the desk while the constable wrote laboriously in his notebook.

Canwyn greeted the solicitor warmly. 'I don't suppose you feel like a drive out to Porthleven, do you?' he asked and ten minutes later a grim-looking Edgcombe was urging on his horses as he and Sergeant Wylie sped through the countryside in the direction of Tye Rock.

As Rose stepped into the dinghy she felt the first prickle of alarm. The boat rocked beneath her as she settled herself gingerly at one end and watched Mark take up his position in the centre. Beneath her the boat seemed a fragile craft, a frighteningly slim barrier between herself and the water. She watched with some trepidation as he reached for the oars and slotted them into the rowlocks.

'What exactly did you say to Matron?' she asked.

He grinned. 'I told her I wanted to talk privately with you for a few minutes. Something personal. I made it sound as though it might be a proposal of marriage!'

'Mark!' She felt outraged, but rather flattered as she imagined the effect Mark's hint would have on the staff.

He said, 'I asked her to pass on the message to Miss Hock. Gave them something to think about!'

Rose, flustered and uncertain, made no answer but stared instead at the growing space between the boat and the shore and prayed that Mark knew how to handle the dinghy. She had never been on the water before and was distinctly nervous as, with a few unsteady lurches to one side or the other, they moved further from the security of the shoreline. Around her the light was failing as unexpected clouds rolled in from the west. The water, brown and impenetrable, lay smoothly round them except where the dipping oars broke the surface and sent ripples out in ever-widening circles.

'We mustn't be too late,' she said. 'It's getting dark already.'

'It won't take long.'

She watched his face, searching for a clue as to the nature of his secret, but he was giving nothing away. The surrounding land receded steadily until they were about a hundred yards or so from the shore and Rose, awed by their isolation, wished Mark would say something cheerful. Anything to help dispel the nervousness she was trying to hide.

At last he shipped the oars, and the boat steadied. She smiled, with relief.

He said, 'Well now, Rose, I wonder how you are going to take my news. Sensibly, I hope. I wouldn't trouble you with it, but it's rather important that you know the truth.'

She swallowed. 'I thought I did. About the night of the fire, you mean?'

He shook his head. 'It's about Father. I'm afraid I wasn't entirely truthful. Not that I lied, exactly, but I let you assume that I hadn't had a chance to tell him who I was. In fact, Rose, I *did* tell him.'

She stared at him. 'You mean that just before the accident . . .'

He nodded. 'The fact is, Rose, I misled the police because I had to. Your father . . . *our* father —' He closed his eyes briefly. 'The fact is that we weren't walking along the top of the cliff, we were walking along the beach. I —'

'But you told the police that —'

'Forget what I told the police! I plucked up courage to tell Father that I was in fact his son but . . . but he . . .' His mouth tightened. 'The bastard rejected me!'

'Mark!' Rose felt the colour rush from her face. No one had ever used that word in her hearing before.

He folded his arms tightly across his chest. 'After all my hopes, all my scheming. I was so sure . . . But he refused point blank to believe that he was my father. He said my mother had lied, and I was lying, and I must think him a fool if I thought I could trick him after all these years!

410

He said he wasn't surprised because of Mother. He called her a whore and said thank God he'd managed to save you from her clutches.' He ran out of breath and gulped air noisily but before Rose could speak he rushed on, his face furious, his voice a low hiss of suppressed anger. 'He said I'd deceived him, and he could never trust me again. I was to leave Tye Rock House and he'd see that I never got another position in any school. He even threatened to turn me over to the police.'

'Oh, Mark!' Rose was torn between shock at the revelations and sympathy for her brother. She quailed at the image his words created. She could see the two men screaming at each other below the cliff while the incoming waves crashed on relentlessly, breaking repeatedly against the rocks. Poor Mark, she thought tremulously. Somehow, over the years, she would make it all up to him. No wonder he had been unable to tell anyone the truth. But then . . . Her stomach felt suddenly hollow and her chest was tight. If Papa hadn't fallen from the cliff-top . . . ?

As Mark rushed on, his face was white and drawn in the gathering gloom and the intensity of his anger frightened her.

He said, 'He turned to go home and suddenly I knew that he meant to ruin me. All my dreams . . . all my plans for the future . . .' He pressed his fingers against his eyes as though to shut out painful memories.

'Oh, Mark! I'm so dreadfully sorry!' Wanting

to show him that she understood and sympathised, she reached out and touched his knee.

Ignoring the gesture, he went on, but his voice was strangely quiet. 'I grabbed at his arm. I was giving him one last chance. I wanted to make him listen, I wanted to make him believe me. I didn't mean to hurt him, but he slipped on a rock and fell. I held out my hand to help him up and he said, "Don't come near me. Don't touch me. I never want to see you again." '

Rose gasped as Mark opened wild eyes and stared at her. 'He struggled back to his knees without my help.' Suddenly his voice was hoarse. 'I couldn't let him go, Rose. How could I? I knew what he would do to me.'

She stammered, 'But he would have come round, Mark. I would have talked to him. It would have been all right.' The words sounded unconvincing. Would it?

'No, it wouldn't. You know him even better than I do. I had to make a decision, Rose. I snatched up a rock and I hit him on the head with it.'

For a moment Rose could hardly credit what she had heard. Then there was a roaring inside her head and the shock swept through her. Her vision seemed affected and she watched him through a dark mist; the sound of the birds overhead was suddenly stilled; her lungs seemed to have stopped working and she fought for breath.

Mark, apparently unaware of the effect his words had had on her, said quietly, 'I killed Father, Rose. I hit him twice and I knew at once he was dead. I didn't want to kill him but he made it necessary. We could all have been happy.'

Rose clung to the side of the boat. 'You *killed* him?' she repeated dazedly. 'Oh, Mark, don't say that. Don't —'

'You believe me, don't you?'

Rose wished she could say 'No' and mean it. Instead she was forced to nod her head.

'Then we now know where we stand. I had to tell you, Rose, because I want you to be the one person in all the world that I can trust. You have to know the worst about me and still love me.'

Rose fought to hide her growing horror, trying to stop the trembling of her hands.

He rushed on. 'If the police question you, you *must* say that you saw the two of us walking along the cliff-path — from an upstairs window. You can say you've just remembered it. Then it will be your word against Robb's, and they will have to believe you.'

She stammered, 'The police already suspect you, Mark.'

'I know they do, but they can't *prove* anything. They have no motive and they know absolutely nothing.'

'But Robb says —'

'He could be lying.'

'But why should he?'

Above them, the dark clouds sent down the first heavy drops of rain, and she watched them splash into the water around the boat.

He leaned towards her. 'Don't quibble, Rose. What I'm saying is that they can't *prove* that I started the fire either, because —'

She gasped. '*You* started it? Oh, God!'

'— you've given me an alibi. It's very important, Rose, that you understand all this. We mustn't give them the chance to prove it . . .'

She felt as though he had punched her in the stomach. 'Wait, Mark. What are you saying? That *you* started the fire? But you said — I told them —'

'For God's sake, grow up, Rose!' he snapped. In the gathering darkness his eyes were hard, his voice harsh. 'Life's not always how you'd like it to be. Life's what you can make it. The big question is this — are you going to tell the police about Father? That I killed him? If you do, they'll hang me. *They'll hang your brother!* You'll have that on your conscience for the rest of your life. If you don't tell them, you're an accessory to murder, and that's a criminal offence. Not much of a choice, is it?'

She stared, appalled. In her mind's eye she saw her father sprawled helplessly on the ground and Mark reaching for the rock that would kill him. How, she wondered helplessly, had this happened? Where had she gone wrong? What had she done to find herself in this position?

It came to her slowly that she was in great danger. Trapped with a murderer in the middle of the lake — with no way of escape. Turning her head, she searched the shore line but saw no one. She fought down a rising panic, struggling to think. Play for time, Rose. *Think.* One small step at a time. Lie if you have to. First get back on to dry land. Then get back to Tye Rock House. Then talk to James. He would help her.

With an effort she said, 'I don't think I could see you hanged, Mark.' Her voice shook.

'Wise girl,' he told her.

The rain was falling more heavily. She said, 'We shall get drenched,' and then realised how ridiculous that sounded. What were a few rain-drops when their very lives were at stake?

He said, 'So you do understand, Rose. I need your answer.'

If only she could swim, she would make a dash for the land. But she couldn't. Even if she could, she'd be hampered by her clothes. She would have to keep him talking while she thought of a way out.

She asked, 'Why did you start that fire? Did you mean to kill them?'

He hesitated. 'I hoped so. They deserved it, the way they spoke about you.'

Rose said nothing to contradict him. The thought occurred to her that he was mad — either that or a cold-blooded killer. Miss Folkes's account of the cat's death came back to her. Had he, even as a boy, had this terrible destructive urge? He *was* her brother. They had the same mother and father. How could their parents have produced such a monster, she wondered. And if he was mad, then they might not hang

415

him. But they would lock him away for a very long time, which might be worse for him. And suppose he escaped and came after her? She would be forever looking over her shoulder.

He said, 'So now it's time for your decision, Rose. Are you going to stand by me?'

She had to agree. Later she would talk to James. 'Of course I am.'

'What I shall want is your signature on a document that makes Tye Rock House over to me. I shall also want your agreement that you will never marry —'

'Oh, but Mark!' She was startled into the protest, regretting it instantly. 'I — I've already promised James Edgcombe that —'

'You think I could take that risk, Rose? No, no. Don't you see what would happen? You'd confide in him and, being an upright citizen, he'd tell the police and that would be disastrous! No, Rose. If we are going to live together, there'll be no marriage. I will be the legal owner — as I should have been all along. As the male heir I should have inherited.'

He leaned forward and gently took hold of her hand. Rose steeled herself not to flinch as his fingers closed round hers. If she shouted, no one would hear her and Mark would be enraged. Somehow she had to persuade him to row back to the shore.

He said, 'I'm truly sorry about everything, but I can't turn back the clock, Rose. What's done is done. We can either go on together or . . . or I go on alone.' His grip on her hand tightened.

The words had chilled her. The direct threat.

'Alone?' The word burst from her.

'A boating accident . . .'

Vomit rose in her throat as she struggled to remain calm. Anger overrode caution as she said, 'Two accidents? A bit of a coincidence.'

'But no witnesses to the contrary. I brought you out here to propose, and in the ensuing excitement the boat overturned. Remember, no one else knows that you're my sister.'

She shuddered, resisting the urge to snatch her hand from his. 'Let's go on together, Mark.'

'Can I trust you?'

'Yes, you can.' Once she was safely home she would telephone James and ask for help.

'And do you still love me, Rose?'

'I do. Yes, Mark. Of course I do!' She wondered if it was possible to love a murderer? Suppose he had *not* been her brother but *had* killed her father? Suppose she had married him and later, as Mrs Tremayne, had learned of the murder . . . Suppose she had been his *mother* — would her mother have continued to love him? Her thoughts swirled helplessly as the safe world she had always known shifted around her, leaving her lost and utterly confused. She knew in that instant that if she survived the day, her life was changed for ever.

Mark drew a long breath. 'Then let's go home!' he said with lopsided smile. She clenched her hands as he repositioned the oars, thinking that she had never heard a sweeter sound than the creaking of wood against wood as he started to row. Now there was just a chance for her.

They were half-way back when two figures ran into view. One she recognised as James; the other was a policeman.

'Hell and damnation!' cried Mark, and he immediately stopped rowing. 'The bastards have come for me.'

Rose's momentary relief was shortlived. She knew Mark would never give himself up quietly.

James shouted, 'Rose! Are you all right?'

Before she could answer, Mark put a warning finger to his lips. 'Not a word from you,' he threatened, 'or you'll go into the water!' He stood up. 'I've nothing to say to you!' he shouted.

Another voice called, 'Don't try anything, Tremayne,' and Rose recognised Sergeant Wylie's voice.

Terrified, she cried, 'Sit down, for God's sake, Mark. Do you want to drown us both?'

'What a neat idea!' he said. 'It wouldn't take much to turn this little craft over!' To prove his point he began to throw his weight from side to side and Rose screamed as the boat rocked alarmingly.

Please God! she prayed. Help me!

James had thrown off his jacket and was pulling off his boots. Rose froze with terror; he was going to swim out to her. She watched in dismay as she saw him wade into the water until it came up to his waist, then begin to swim.

'Bloody little hero!' muttered Mark and, leaning down, he pulled one of the oars free, stood up again and held it in readiness. He laughed at Rose's expression. 'That's right!' he told her. 'As soon as he gets near enough, I'll give him a clout with this. I told you to forget about marriage, didn't I!'

Rose felt faint with desperation, but still she couldn't quite give up. She wondered if she could tilt the boat suddenly so that he fell into the water — but then she would probably fall in too. It was a terrible risk. If she misjudged it, she would be dead long before James could reach her. Her thoughts spun wildly. Unless she could push Mark into the water using the other oar? But if he saw what she was doing, his oar would doubtless come crashing down upon her own head.

She glanced towards the sergeant, but he was watching helplessly from the shore line.

The pool was full of weed and James was making slow progress. Rose forced herself to think clearly. She could not sit by and watch Mark kill James, but all she had on her side was surprise. Impulsively she braced herself, lunged forward and drove her fists into Mark's thighs. Taken by surprise, he gave a furious shout, wobbled and then fell back on top of her. The boat rocked violently. Rose, sprawled in the bottom, struggled to steady it, but Mark leaned on it and deliberately turned it over. As she went into the water, the last thing she saw was the expression of hate in her brother's eyes.

The water was so cold and dark, and the weed clung to her hands as she fought to bring herself to the surface again. When at last she came up, gasping and spluttering, James was still twenty yards away and Mark was clinging to the over-turned boat and reaching for the lost oar. Rose knew at once that though he was in the water he was still dangerous. As she reached for the boat, he pushed it away from her. Then he began to work his way towards her and she knew what her fate would be if he ever reached her. Her terri-fied scream was cut short once more as the weight of her clothes dragged her down. She heard James shout, 'Rose!' but she went under again. This time it seemed for ever that she sank into the cold depths. At any moment she ex-pected Mark's hands to reach through the cling-ing weed and take her down. She kicked desperately, determined to reach the surface, but when she did she knew he would be waiting for her.

Oh God! She was *so* tired. But suddenly she was moving upward and finally her face was out of the water and she was gulping in air. Mark had retrieved one of the oars and he now used it as a barrier to prevent her from reaching the boat, holding it out like a lance to keep her at a dis-tance while with his free hand he clutched the dinghy. Only his head was visible above the water. Suddenly an idea came to her. It was risky, but her strength was failing and James was still ten yards away. There was no time to think. Somehow she heaved herself forward, seized the end of the oar and with her remaining strength, drove it backwards through the water into his neck. She saw his head go back, but the sudden movement had drawn her under again and she knew that this time was her last. Her hands clutched uselessly at strands of weed and the light was gone for ever. Down into the darkness. Her last thought was for James . . . Poor James . . .

Her lungs were bursting and she was on the point of losing consciousness when strong hands grasped her and miraculously the dark descent was halted. Rose felt herself lifted upwards until together they burst through the surface and she was clinging to James. Coughing and retching, she tried to speak but couldn't.

James said breathlessly, 'Thank God, Rose! You're safe.'

She began to sob. 'Mark . . . I had to do it . . . Oh God!' She looked round fearfully.

James said, 'You're safe now, Rose. He's gone.'

They buried Bertie Vivian on the last day of May and, as the small congregation knelt, only Rose cried for him. As she watched his coffin carried to the altar she tried not to hate him. Remembering that once he had been a 'sweet little boy', she wept for him. She was glad that there had been no arrest and no trial, and that he had not lived to be incarcerated somewhere. He had only been locked up within his own mind.

Rose bowed her head, whispering the Lord's Prayer, and tried to ignore the legacy of pain and horror from their time together on Loe Pool. She was full of regrets for the happy life he could have had, for the happy family they might have been, and for all the dreams which would now never come true. Father, mother and brother — all gone. She had James, of course, who knelt beside her, a dear and comforting presence, but her own family no longer existed.

As they rose to sing, she forced from her the memory of the limp body they had taken from the pool the following day: the lifeless form and grey face, the mouth opened in a last desperate gasp for life. And *she* had killed him! She told herself again and again that she had acted in self-defence, but she was sure the dreadful memory would never leave her. A post mortem had been held, and the subsequent inquest found that the blow from the oar had broken his neck but there was some water in his lungs. James insisted that she had saved him from a worse fate — a slow death by drowning — but she would never be entirely convinced that this was so.

The service was very short. They remained standing while the coffin was carried outside and then followed it. With James's arm around her, she walked out into the sunshine, carrying a single lily. Overhead the sky was a cloudless blue, but her brother would never see it. Neither would her father. Her thoughts hardened. His life had been cut short by his own son. Rose felt a tightness in her chest at the thought of so much cruelty, misery and waste.

They buried Mark Tremayne in a little-used corner of the churchyard. Earth pattered down on to the plain wood coffin and Rose dropped in the solitary tribute. For a moment the pale petals glimmered, and then disappeared beneath the next spadeful of earth. Rose pressed her handkerchief to her eyes as fresh tears gathered. James's arm tightened round her and he bent his head to whisper, 'Not long now, darling.'

'Ashes to ashes, dust to dust . . .'

Rose raised her head and looked for the first time at the other mourners. There were a few familiar faces. James's parents had both come, and so had Miss Hock. With a start, she saw that Alan Gibbs was there. Sergeant Wylie was also present, and she recognised the local reporter from the *Cornish Herald*. Rose could anticipate tomorrow's headline — LOE POOL VICTIM BURIED. Many more people, like Robb and Polly, were notable by their absence. The rest of the small group were strangers. Strangers possibly drawn by a sense of the macabre. It was inevitable.

Rose closed her eyes and leaned wearily against the man she loved — the man who had waited so patiently for her all these years. Soon she would be Mrs James Edgcombe. The thought warmed her heart.

They murmured a final 'Amen' and at last it was over. There would be no funeral breakfast. Slowly the small crowd drifted away and James paused to talk with the vicar.

'Miss Vivian.'

Rose turned to find Alan Gibbs standing beside her. She was pleased to see that he looked less dishevelled than on the last occasion she had seen him. His hair had been cut, the rough beard was gone and he was wearing a dark suit which sat well on his tall frame.

'Mr Gibbs!' She held out her hand. 'It was kind of you to come.' She added, 'You're looking very well.'

'I had to come,' he said simply. 'I wanted a chance to talk to you before my courage failed. I wanted to say what Cathy would have said — that you must put all this behind you. She would have wanted your happiness, Rose.'

'I know. But thank you, anyway.'

'I understand congratulations are in order — you and James Edgcombe. He's a very lucky man.'

'Thank you.' She smiled faintly. 'At least something is going right for me. He's a wonderful man and I'm looking forward to becoming his wife. We're getting married in July.'

'I hear that Tye Rock House is up for sale?'

'Yes, it is. We've had three enquiries already. I'm optimistic that it will continue as a school —

at least for the foreseeable future.'

He smiled. 'You need a fresh start — you deserve it.'

Rose nodded. 'I'm investing some of the proceeds of the sale. Edgcombes are opening a new branch office in Falmouth. James will run it with the help of a junior partner and a clerk. I'll help how and when I can. It will be hard work, but we're looking forward to it. Next week James will —'

She stopped, aware that he was staring at her, that he was no longer listening. She asked, 'What is it, Mr Gibbs?'

He said, 'I want to tell you something — I don't think Cathy would mind now. She made me promise then, but she couldn't have foreseen all this . . .' He sighed, frowning.

She waited. After a moment's indecision he held out his hand and, wonderingly, she allowed herself to be led through the churchyard to George Vivian's grave. Turf had already been laid over it and a small posy of mixed flowers nestled against the headstone.

She looked at her companion. 'Why *here?*'

He said, 'You'll see, Rose.' His voice shook slightly. 'I don't know how to tell you this, but I do it in the hope that it will complete the jigsaw and somehow make you happy. The fact is, Rose, you are *my* daughter. When your mother —'

'*Your* daughter? Oh, but that's —' Shocked and breathless, she could only stare into the grey eyes.

The confession tumbled out. 'When your mother discovered that she was expecting my child, we were both shocked. We were very much in love, but we hadn't married. George was also in love with Cathy. I'm ashamed to say that I let her down, Rose. I panicked and turned away from her. She had a reputation as a breaker of hearts, and I knew my parents would never approve of the match. I had just started in the bank, and had very little money. I told myself that I was just not ready for marriage — not that that's any excuse. Of course, poor Cathy wasn't ready for motherhood, but it happened. I'm not proud of myself, but I've since paid for my sins.'

Without missing a single word, Rose was studying his face, and now she knew why she had been so drawn to him when they last met. She saw the likeness between them: same grey eyes, same cheek-bones.

He went on, 'Poor Cathy was desperate. When her parents also rejected her, she turned to George for help and he agreed at once to marry her. He knew you were not his child, but he was desperately in love with Cathy. It was his only chance and he took it. We all agreed that no one would ever know you weren't his daughter. Afterwards, of course, when I tried to put things right I only made matters worse. When Cathy wanted to leave George, you can understand his bitterness.'

Rose could find no words.

'By then he thought of you as his own daughter. He *deserved* to keep you. He had been so generous earlier. We betrayed him, Rose.'

Rose shook her head helplessly as she stared down at the headstone. Once again she was having to change her perception of someone she had thought she knew. She had misjudged her father. Her lips moved silently. 'Forgive me, Papa.'

The man beside her said softly, 'I'm the one you should blame for all the unhappiness. The man you know as your father had a very generous heart beneath that gruff exterior. Your *real* father is shallow and selfish.'

'Don't say that! We all make mistakes and . . .' Rose searched for something comforting to say. 'And Mother loved you.'

'I think she forgave me, Rose, but can you?'

Rose looked into the eyes which were dark with regret, and thought of all the years he had lived alone. This man was her natural father. So she *did* have family!

He said, 'You needn't tell anyone. We could still be friends.'

Rose considered the suggestion and slowly shook her head. 'Let's not pretend,' she said. 'I don't think I could bear it. No more lies. No more deceits. Just the truth. I can live with that if you can.'

He nodded. 'I don't deserve to be "Papa".'

'Perhaps I could call you Alan?'

His 'Yes' was hoarse with emotion.

Rose reached up and kissed him. 'I'm going to

find my mother's grave,' she said. 'Will you come with me? We could lay some flowers. I think she'd like that.'

He nodded, unable to speak, and Rose searched for a way to help him. 'I shall need someone to give me away,' she told him. 'Will *you* be free on July the eleventh?'

His arms tightened round her in a fierce hug. 'It would be my pleasure!' he whispered.